THE COMPLETE CASEBOOK
OF SGT. BRINKHAUS

Frederick Nebel

FREDERICK NEBEL

THE COMPLETE CASEBOOK OF SGT.
BRINKHAUS

BY
FREDERICK NEBEL

INTRODUCTION
WILL MURRAY

PRIMARY ILLUSTRATOR
JOHN FLEMING GOULD

ALTUS PRESS

BOSTON • 2016

EDITED AND DESIGNED BY
Matthew Moring

SERIES EDITOR
Rob Preston

COVER PAINTED BY
William Reusswig

PUBLISHING HISTORY
"Introduction" appears here for the first time. Copyright 2015 by Will Murray.
"The Mystery at Pier 7" originally appeared in the September, 1931 issue of *Detective Action Stories*.
"The Crooked Spot" originally appeared in the October, 1931 issue of *Detective Action Stories*.
"Whispers of Death" originally appeared in the December, 1931 issue of *Detective Action Stories*.
"The X Circle" originally appeared in the January, 1932 issue of *Detective Action Stories*.
"The Crimson Fist" originally appeared in the March, 1932 issue of *Detective Action Stories*.
"Murder By Ballot" originally appeared in the April, 1932 issue of *Detective Action Stories*.
"Tailormade Clue" originally appeared in the June, 1932 issue of *Dime Detective Magazine*.
"The Devil's Slouch" originally appeared in the December 10, 1932 issue of *Detective Fiction Weekly*.
"The Green Widow" originally appeared in the February 11, 1933 issue of *Detective Fiction Weekly*.
"The Lemon" originally appeared in the May 6, 1933 issue of *Detective Fiction Weekly*.
"Strangle Hold" originally appeared in the July 29, 1933 issue of *Detective Fiction Weekly*.

THANKS TO
John Benson, Joel Frieman, Joel Lyczak and Rick Ollerman

TABLE OF CONTENTS

INTRODUCTION

WILL MURRAY

WHEN AFICIONADOS of Frederick Nebel talk about his work, they focus on his three significant hardboiled series: the MacBride and Kennedy stories which ran in *Black Mask* magazine, a companion series featuring Ben "Tough Dick" Donahue, and the similar Jack Cardigan novelettes written for *Dime Detective Magazine*. All recently reprinted by Altus Press.

Seldom mentioned is a fourth series, the Inspector Larsen and Sergeant Brinkhaus stories, which originated in Popular Publications' *Detective Action Stories* in the late summer of 1931. Nebel produced eleven of these tough-talking gems, yet they have been unfairly overlooked, in part because they sprawled over three different magazines. Set in the seaside city of Portsend—presumably somewhere on the Atlantic coast, and possibly a doublet of Gravesend, New York— the Inspector Larsen series began as just that. Grim Police Inspector Peter Larsen was the star, and creaky-shoed Detective-Sergeant Brinkhaus—familiarly known as "Brinky"—was his right arm and semi-comic foil. Together, they ran Portsend's Detective Bureau. The capable pair were introduced in "The Mystery at Pier 7" which ran in the September, 1931 issue of *Detective Action Stories*. At this point in his career, Nebel's literary star was cometing, owing to a relentless stream of stories running in Joe Shaw's celebrated *Black Mask*. Hardboiled detective fiction was in vogue, thanks to Dashiell Hammett breaking into hardcover books directly from its hard-hitting pages. The literary wave he initiated carried Fred Nebel along with it. Nebel's reliably excellent work inevitably came to the attention of rival pulp editors, who were always hungry for solid copy from a seasoned professional. Especially one who was appearing regularly in the prestigious pages of *Black Mask*. Nebel's name on a magazine cover helped sell copies during the dime-depleted Great Depression.

So Popular Publications publisher and editor Harry Steeger tapped Nebel on the shoulder and invited him into the pages of *Detective Action Stories,* then wrapping up its first year of publication. The first Inspector Larsen story was the result. Two months later, Steeger issued *Dime Detective Magazine,* explicitly aimed at *Black Mask* readers. He offered Nebel a princely four cents a word to climb aboard. Thus began the Jack Cardigan private investigator stories, which ran for several years. *Dime Detective* sales exceeded Steeger's expectations, and *Detective Action Stories* suddenly looked like a poor cousin. The magazine was folded with its April 1932 issue, which included Nebel's "Murder by Ballot," the sixth Inspector Larsen story. Except by that time, it was no longer the Inspector Larsen series. So popular had Brinkhaus become that with the story entitled "The Crimson Fist," Nebel saw fit to disclose Brinky's full name, which was Otto Herman Brinkhaus. Before long, the writer forgot all about the Otto, and the amiable detective-sergeant was simply Herman Brinkhaus after that. He was also promoted to undisputed star of the series with that entry. Much as it happened in the Steve MacBride stories, where irrepressible alcoholic reporter Steve Kennedy slowly rose to prominence, all but eclipsing the flinty, no-nonsense police captain, Brinky captivated readers with his constant character-actor scenery chewing. At the same time, Popular Publications copywriters started spotlighting his name in their blurbs, excluding Inspector Larsen from even a glancing mention. It made sense. Brinkhaus was the one who did most of the legwork. When *Detective Action Stories* folded, a presumed leftover Brinkhaus story entitled "Tailormade Clue" landed in *Dime Detective.* Inasmuch as *DD* was already Jack Cardigan's established turf, after that solitary appearance, no more was seen of the police duo in Popular's pulp pages.

His star still in ascendancy, Nebel took Sergeant Brinkhaus and company over to Munsey's *Detective Fiction Weekly,* and an additional four stories appeared in its respected pages. This was all at the expense of "Tough Dick" Donahue, who dropped out of *Black Mask* after the October, 1931 issue, not returning until the following August. Although highly prolific, Nebel had but ten fingers, and only so many hours in the day to write. It's possible that, due to the close parallelism between agency sleuths Ben Donahue and Jack Cardigan, that the former was obliged to take a vacation. Jealous editors could be that way. Why write a Donahue short story for *Black Mask* at approximately two—or perhaps even three—cents a word, when Popular

Publications would pay four cents for a Cardigan novelette? The Sergeant Brinkhaus stories—for in the final analysis they must be so termed—are solid, tough, hardboiled fare of the type in which Nebel specialized during speakeasy days. During the two years he penned this series, he kept up his *Black Mask* market, while his other regular markets, *Action Stories, North•West Stories* and *Air Stories*—in which Nebel had been steadily producing adventure fiction since 1925—were unsentimentally abandoned. Fred Nebel was one of the emerging hardboiled writers, and the expanding market forced him to capitalize on this historic trend. Larsen and Brinkhaus were not the only participants in this unreservedly obscure series. Police Chief Norman Pentcost and Assistant District Attorney Wells Gatlin made frequent appearances. Other members of the Portsend Detective Squad came and went, some perishing in the line of duty. In that sense, these fine stories were 1930s police procedurals, definite offshoots of Captain MacBride and his tough-nosed crew, and now they have been gathered together in a definite casebook—the last such extended series by Fred Nebel.

Turn the page, start "The Mystery at Pier 7" and follow along as Brinky steals the show. But please don't feel bad for Peter Larsen. Before the series is over, he will be promoted to chief inspector, no longer a star, but at least he got a raise in pay!

THE MYSTERY AT PIER 7

FOR A YEAR THE
D.A. HAD LED THE
FIGHT AGAINST
CORRUPTION AND
GANGDOM. NOW HE HAD
VANISHED SUDDENLY,
MYSTERIOUSLY, UNDER
FIRE FROM THE VERY
CRIME BUREAU HE HAD
ORGANIZED. BUT GRIMLY
PETER LARSEN SWORE
TO FERRET HIM OUT AND
BRING HIM BACK TO
JUSTICE IF IT WAS THE
LAST JOB HE EVER DID.

CHAPTER ONE

THE D.A. DISAPPEARS

WHEN LARSEN was made an inspector and put in charge of the Portsend Detective Bureau, two things were notable. He was the first man to rate that rank at the age of thirty-eight, and the first squarehead to rise that far in the history of a department with a roster of German and Irish names. He landed in the job when Portsend, a city of one hundred and thirty thousand, was howling with crime and reputations were being lost overnight. He landed calmly, coolly, with his yellow hair, his six even feet of well-clothed leanness, and certain set ideas about right and wrong. Wiseacres predicted that he would last six months, because he was honest, square, and couldn't be touched by graft with a six foot pole.

He had things on his mind that summer morning, one year later, and did not hear the birds singing in the venerable elm which a sentimental Chamber of Commerce retained in a street crowded with brick and stone buildings. He worked grimly in a mass of reports, making notes as he went along.

Sergeant Brinkhaus, woolen-suited even in summer, came in sighing and wiping the band of his straw hat.

"Not a thing, boss—not a thing," he said. "Not hair nor hide of him—anywhere."

"Got men covering the Post Road?"

"Butchman, Little and Groves."

Larsen went on writing. "How about the Valley Road, and the summer camps around Lake Windborne?"

"Merkel and Deering called in from Three Corners and Trask just phoned from the lake station. Like I said—ixnay—nothing doing."

"All right. Keep dragging the city and the outlying farms. I want every roadhouse overhauled and every farmhouse that looks as if it might be shut down—barns, everything. Every speakeasy, every hotel and rooming house. That end for the vice squad, too. I want all central office detectives to drag in any suspects, no matter what for, and the precinct men too. And no passing the buck, either. I want a line-up tomorrow morning at nine o'clock and every dick on hand to look them over. I want the telephone exchanges to keep their ears open for any phony conversation and to report any call, origin and destination, if Paddison's name is mentioned. That's all, Brinky."

Brinkhaus sighed. "It's a tough break, boss," he said.

Larsen, writing on, made no comment, and Brinkhaus went out, mopping his red sweaty face.

Maddox, of the missing persons bureau, came in nibbling the end off a fresh cigar. "Brink told you, eh?" he addressed Larsen.

"Hello, Maddox."

Maddox chuckled drily. "So the eminent district attorney's folded his tent and lammed."

"You anything to add to Brinkhaus's valuable information?"

"Don't be sarcastic, Larsen."

She saw a body topple out of the car, strike a fire hydrant, sink to the curbing. The car boomed off.

"Don't you. Blow off when you know for sure that Paddison lammed. If he did, I'll get him, and if he didn't, I'll get him."

Maddox colored. "Hell, I was only kidding."

"Yes, you were. You and a lot of other birds around here would like to see me get a black eye. And you know that if Paddison's lammed I'll get it. Because I indorsed him as a hellion for his job and labeled him as the squarest D.A. this city's ever seen. The crime bureau had nothing against him. They started breaking a lot of judges that deserved to be broken, but they've lost their heads now and are going after everybody."

Maddox smiled at his cigar. "Funny, though, how he goes and fades when he's under fire."

"If he has—" Larsen stared grimly at the desk—"if he has, I'll finish him." He shrugged and rattled papers. "But until it's proved, Maddox, I'd appreciate it if you'd keep your back-biting to yourself."

He rose abruptly, went to a filing cabinet. Maddox tongued his cigar, leered at Larsen's back, then turned and left the office. Ten minutes later Larsen put glass weights on his papers and went out.

LOLA PADDISON looked through the window with eyes red-rimmed from tears, saw Larsen get out of the black sedan, saw him disappear beneath the porte-cochere five stories below. She went into the bedroom, powdered her face, sobbed once or twice. She sat for a moment staring transfixed at her image in the mirror, started at sound of the door bell, and went into the living room.

"Sorry," said Larsen. "I chased those newspaper men."

"Thank God you did! A person can't be alone at a time like this. Why do they?"

She made a limp motion toward a divan and Larsen sat down, dropping his big fair hands to sturdy knees. Lola Paddison sat down with her back to a window, her face in shadow.

"I'm sorry as the devil," Larsen said. "We've got every available man out. I—this is straight, Mrs. Paddison—I don't think he ran out. You and I haven't met much, but you know I was always behind him to the last ditch. I liked his—well, his guts. Isn't there anything you know?"

"I wish I did. This anxiety—"

"I know, I know," he placated. "I came over personally to get what details you have."

She raised her head back, drawing in a stifled breath.

"Well, we had a dinner date. Down at Sciarvi's—you know, in Two Street. I like their ravioli. Dan was at his office when I called him and asked him to meet me there. He liked the place too. Well, I left here at six, in a cab. The date was for seven. Dan said he was staying late at the office, and he was to go to Sciarvi's straight from there.

"I got there at ten to seven and waited. Waited half an hour—an hour. I began to get worried. So I telephoned the office. The operator said no one was there. She found out, though, that the night janitor saw Dan leave at six-fifteen. It would have taken only fifteen minutes or so to walk from City Hall Square to Sciarvi's. Well—there you are. What's happened to him?"

"Did he say anything to you about trouble?"

"No. He wouldn't even speak about this crime bureau business. He laughed at them. They had nothing on him."

"But isn't there something he might have said—some remark about somebody?"

"Not a thing. Dan very seldom brought business into the home, you know. Which is why we've been so happy. God, Mr. Larsen, who could have done anything to him?"

Larsen eyed her thoughtfully. "You're sure you've received no calls for ransom?"

"No—no, of course not. If I had—" She stopped short, sighed. "Well, I'd at least know that he's alive. But this way he may even be— Oh, no, no, I mustn't think that. He couldn't be dead!"

She began crying in her handkerchief.

Larsen got up, fumbling with his hat. "I wouldn't take it so hard, Mrs. Larsen. He may be all right. Though if he is—"

"What—what, if he is?"

"Well, he'll have justified the crime bureau's charges. One way or another, I've got to find him. I can't believe he lammed. He's too much of a fighter."

Still, Larsen had his doubts as he rode toward City Hall Square. So many judges were toppling today. Men he had believed the symbols of honesty were being thrown from the bench, branded with corruption and double-dealing. It was hard to believe it about Paddison. Because Paddison had helped reveal connivance on the part of two judges and a city magistrate. And because he and Paddison had worked together, their friendship doubly cemented by mutual interests and hard teamwork toward an end.

"If he has lammed," Larsen told himself, "I'll go harder on him for it. I'll help break him."

Doane, Paddison's secretary, was filing papers when Larsen walked in on him. Doane was a young man, with a thin white face and large horn-rimmed glasses. He had a voice soft as plush, a scholarly air.

"How late were you here last night?" Larsen said.

"I stayed until six. Mr. Paddison wanted me to go, but there were some reports I wanted cleared up."

"Was he nervous?"

"Well, I don't know, Inspector, whether he was nervous or whether he was annoyed that I stayed on."

"Was he working at anything?"

"Yes. Briefs of some kind?"

"Do you know what they were?"

"No. Something personal, I supposed. The D.A. had a way of being secretive about a lot of things. I imagine, though, it was something in connection with another exposé. He was working furiously when I left and looked strained, darting among his papers in his brief case—"

"Brief case?"

Doane's eyes blinked. He waited half a second, puzzled perhaps by Larsen's tone, then said, "Yes, his brief case."

"Where is it?"

"Well, I suppose he took it with him."

Larsen smacked his knee. "H-m-m. Took it with him. He was working on papers the contents of which you knew nothing about. He took the papers with him when he left. You left here at six. Where did you go?"

"Why, home."

"How?"

"The way I always go. I caught a street car at the safety zone on the north side of the square." Doane spoke slowly now.

"When you went out, did you see anybody hanging around the corridors?"

"No."

"Outside? I mean anybody who might arouse your suspicion."

"No. I—"

"What time did you catch a car and what time did you arrive home?"

Doane swallowed. "I must have caught a car about six-ten. I arrived home at six-thirty."

"All right." Larsen eyed him bluntly. "Now you are certain that the D.A. gave you no hint he was afraid of his life. You're sure he said nothing—nothing whatever, of what he was working on, and who he was on his way to expose."

Doane swallowed twice. "Yes, sir."

LARSEN kept looking at him with a blue level gaze, a gaze that was neither truculent nor curious, but blank—provocatively blank. Doane colored a bit.

"You don't believe me?"

"I believe everybody, young man, until he's proved guilty. Do you know if the D.A. bought any railroad tickets, or if there were indications that he intended going somewhere out of town?"

"Why, you don't think—"

"Never mind what I think."

"No, there were no indications."

"You're not trying to hide your employer."

Doane trembled. "Of course, not. There's nothing to hide. Why, Mr. Paddison—you know Mr. Paddison was fighting for right against wrong."

"I know that." Larsen got up. "And I'm trying to believe he was all on the up and up." He leveled a finger at Doane. "But if he wasn't, I'll break him for life. And anybody who knowingly conceals evidence."

He went back to headquarters and dived into a new batch of bulletins and precinct reports. He tried to get hold of Brinkhaus, to see if anything new had turned up, but Brinkhaus was out. It was warm, and he left his office door open. Half an hour later a familiar creak of shoes came down the hall.

Brinkhaus came in wearing a mournful face. "It ain't good, boss, it ain't good at all."

"What?"

"The D.A."

Larsen crouched, expecting something unpleasant.

"I was over at the bank," Brinky said, "depositin' my monthly ten bucks toward the wife's Christmas fund, which she uses to buy me a present with. Well, I got a notion, so I asked. The D.A. drew out five hundred bucks yesterday afternoon."

Larsen lifted his chin high, as if trying to catch a stray breath of air. His blue eyes became glassy for a moment, staring into Brinkhaus's passionless brown ones. He leaned forward, planting elbows on the desk, covering each ear with broad palms. He stared transfixed at the glass paperweight.

"Brinky, he couldn't have gone back on us. He couldn't have fallen for the graft and played a part all the time, kidding up that he was on the square."

"Lookit my pal Warburgh. Didn't I think he was on the up and up and not crossin' corners with me? Well, lookit. The bum was shakin' down his own father-in-law. I ain't believin' anybody any more, boss."

"Me, Brinky?"

"Shucks, I ain't gonna say you."

Larsen got up and took a turn up and down the room, his face gray and forbidding.

"Do this, Brinky. Find out where Paddison bought his clothes. See if he bought anything within the last few days. Try the Acme Sporting Shop, too. I remember he used to trade there because he O.K.'d a charge account of mine there. They handle luggage and sporting goods. I buy my fishing tackle there. Go on, Brinky."

Brinkhaus went out and Larsen stood looking through the window at the old elm. Sturdy old tree, something faithful about it. If Paddison had broken faith with him— He snorted, so loud he surprised himself. He trembled in all his big-boned leanness. Trembled for fear that Paddison had run out on him. And he had praised Paddison. Their names were linked together all over. And if Paddison were proved a charlatan, might not the spotlight be turned on him too?

"By God!"

Larsen made big knobs of his fists. He and Paddison had been hand in hand in the war on corruption, on gangdom. "Oh, Larsen was hand in hand with him on other things, too," the wiseacres would say. "A lot of shouting about righteousness, but what do they do when they aren't shouting?"

Larsen flung back to his desk, at war with his own thoughts. They had tried before to show that he was not what he appeared to be. Someone, or some gang, had tried to get him into the coils of a notorious night club hostess. He had seen through that. He plunged into his work. He dictated letters. He worked furiously, but in the back of his mind bitter thoughts persisted.

He was on his way to lunch when he ran into Brinkhaus in the central room. Brinkhaus looked guilty.

"Come on, spill it, Brinky."

"There was an order for a blue suit, shoes, three shirts and some underwear, two ties and six handkerchiefs. A week ago. They had his measurements on file. He has a charge account there. He sent a messenger for the clothes night before last. Nothin' at the sport shop, though."

Larsen's appetite left him. "Did you get a description of all the clothes?"

"Yep. They were white Oxford sport shirts and blue bow ties. The shirts had London House on the labels and the blue ties had the shop's own name. The blue suit was kind of a rough wool for knockin' around in, with a kind of belt sewed on the back. The underwear was rayon shirts and white broadcloth shorts, and the socks were wool-lisle—"

"In my office, Brinky." The interruption was soft, low-voiced, yet oddly tense.

Brinkhaus knew that tone. He knew that when Larsen was really and vitally mad his voice got soft, almost casual, and his eyes began to seem dreamy and meditative.

They walked down the corridor together, Larsen whistling a soft melody. But far back in his eyes was the white heat of anger and remorse, and on his left temple a blue vein pulsed.

CHAPTER TWO

PRINTS ON THE GUN

HALF A mile south of City Hall Square is Portsend's waterfront—the fruit docks, the coal piers, the lighterage companies and, along Harbor Alley and India Street, the mercantile houses and ship chandlers. At night the lights of the drawbridges arc across the river, but between the ramp to the bridge and eastward to India Street, the back alleys are dark and deserted.

The girl in the blue one-piece dress and the small tight-fitting hat came west on Mercantile Alley and turned north into India Street.

Her high heels rang smartly on the silent pavements, and her jaw was firm, her eyes keen. It was ten-thirty and small sounds were magnified by the absence of greater ones. Purpose was evident in the girl's pace and the set of her face.

When the headlights of a car swung south into India Street some three blocks beyond, the girl steered for the house fronts, and deeming caution the better part of virtue, paused in the shadow of a recessed store front.

Through the angle of the windows she was able to see that the approaching car hugged the curb and moved slowly. The purr of the motor sounded powerful. The girl shrank farther back into the shadows as the car drew abreast of the store. It passed slowly, and the girl's eyes followed the tail-light.

Suddenly two shots rang out. The girl tried to scream but couldn't. Her mouth sprang open and her eyes riveted on the red tail-light. She saw a body topple out of the car, strike a fire hydrant, sink to the curbing. She heard the ring of metal on pavement, then the blast of exhaust pipes, the snarl of rubber on rough pavement. The car boomed off.

"One... two... one... three... two," murmured the girl.

She saw the red tail-light swing east into Mercantile Alley. She looked up and down India, her hands pressed to her breast. She let out a short choked cry and ran across the street, brought up by the huddled figure on the curbing, its legs sprawled in the gutter, face down. She saw blood dripping from the curb to the gutter.

A police whistle shrilled far away.

"Help! Help!" the girl yelled, and shook her little fists up and down.

Heavy-soled feet came hammering down India Street. Shield and buttons flashed beneath a lone street light.

"Here! Here!" yelled the girl.

A cop puffed up, took one look at the inert form, one look at the girl.

"Who are you?"

"They went down to Mercantile and then turned left without even slowing up."

"Who?"

"The car. He was— I heard the shots. I was—"

"How'd you hear 'em?"

"I was over there"—she pointed—"in that doorway there."

"What was you doing there?"

"Gawd—why don't you look and see if he's dead!"

The cop looked surprised by the thought. He muttered and knelt down, rolled the man over, felt around. He looked up and scowled.

"Sure, he's dead. What's your name, sister? What the hell were you standin' over there for? Come on, own up."

The girl's eyes popped. Her mouth hardened. "Listen here, you smart aleck, cut that baloney! I was on my way to the street line and—" She stopped and looked up the street toward another uniformed figure that raced beneath the street light. A second cop reached the scene.

"Hello, Berk," he said.

"Hello, Weinstein. Guy got it."

"Cold?"

"Cold meat. The jane says he was pitched from a car." Weinstein turned on the girl. "Was he?"

"Sure. I heard two shots—"

"Hey!" Weinstein exclaimed, and took four hard steps, stooped down, hesitated. "A gat, Berk!"

"Easy. Grab it by the muzzle."

A siren moaned down the street. The cops looked toward two headlights and a sweeping spotlight that came down India Street.

People appeared out of alleys, asking questions.

A Packard touring drew nearer, its spotlight steadied and remained on the two cops, the girl and the dead body. The Packard stopped next to the fire hydrant.

Larsen and Brinkhaus got out and Larsen struck a match on the hydrant and lit a cigarette, looking through the glow at the girl, the two cops, and then down at the motionless body.

"Who's the girl?"

"The guy's dead, inspector."

"Got it in a car and was kicked out. Weinstein's got a rod."

Weinstein held the gun by the end of the barrel. "Smith & Wesson 38."

Larsen twisted his head. "Horan, put that spotlight down on the stiff more."

He started to bend down as the spotlight moved. He didn't bend all the way. The cigarette fell from his hand and in a split second he was standing erect, looking vacant-eyed at Sergeant Brinkhaus.

He turned to the girl, his eyes oddly white in the spotlight's glare. His voice was a slow, repressed monotone.

"You saw the car and saw the man thrown out. What kind of a car? Did you get the number?"

"Yes, sir. Twelve, one thirty-two."

"Take that down Brinky."

"It was a black sedan, kind of bulging out in the back—a big one, maybe a Lincoln or something like that."

"See any faces in it?"

"No. It was too dark and they left too fast. Say listen, I ain't around here because I want to be. I'm a telephone operator at Eastern Terminal, and my relief showed up late after a bender. My name's Gladys McIntyre and I live out at 2006 North End Avenue with my old man."

"Got that, Brinky?"

"Yep."

"All right, Miss McIntyre. Hang around and I'll give you a lift to the car line. Berk, shoo that crowd away. Weinstein, find a phone and call the cold-meat wagon over. Call headquarters too and give 'em that license number and have 'em flash all the precincts. Tell 'em to have Louie Baum ready with the flyer in case we get a tip, and see that the Tommy guns are O.K." He spoke slowly, with an effort.

"Uh-huh, yeah. And I should just say a unidentified hood was bumped off—"

"Doane's his name," Larsen said quietly. "Victor Doane. The D.A.'s secretary."

"Oh-oh," grunted Brinkhaus.

"Just that," said Larsen.

"Oh, mister," the girl said. "Listen, mister, I ain't goin' to get in any trouble because I saw this, am I? I couldn't help it. I was hurryin' home from work, and when I seen a car comin'—well, I dunno, I just natcherally ducked in that doorway over there. Like any girl would, in this neighborhood. Because that policeman started slurrin' at me right away for no reason at all because—"

"I must apologize for his bad manners, Miss McIntyre," Larsen said. "You hear that, Berk? Don't think that because you wear a uniform you can get tough."

"Yes, sir, but I didn't—"

"Weinstein, before you go let me have that gun." Larsen drew a silk handkerchief from his breast pocket and spread it on his palm. "Brinky, go out to Doane's house—"

"Geez, boss—"

"Go out, Brinky. But before you tell his wife about it, ask when Doane left the house. Ask if he received a telephone call before leaving. Try to get the exact time he left and also, if there was a phone call, try to get the exact time of that. And of course ask her where he went. Ask that first, in fact."

Brinkhaus swallowed hard, clenched his fists, stared down his bulbous nose.

"I know, I know," muttered Larsen.

Brinkhaus walked away with a firm tread, a dogged look, and a sheen on his eyes. There was a lump in his throat.

THE HEADQUARTERS dispatcher sat at a desk with ear-phones on. He watched a broad array of colored lights on the wall—small bulbs, some lighted, some not, that marked the various police precincts of Portsend. Another bulb flashed on. The dispatcher made a notation on a chart, looking at an electric clock. He spoke into a mouthpiece.

"Third precinct squad car out at ten fifty-five. Fifth precinct car came in at ten-thirty, out again at—" he looked at the clock—"ten fifty-seven. Fourth precinct squad car went to a speakeasy fight at ten twenty in the black belt. Hasn't reported yet, but Adams is broadcasting on the short wave and they should pick it up. That's all for the moment."

Three floors below, Larsen turned from the loudspeaker and walked the length of the room. Sergeant Kilpatrick, of the stolen car bureau, came in carrying a sheet of paper.

"Nah, I thought so, Pete," he said. "There y' are. The plates were swiped a week ago tonight from the parkin' lot back o' the Palace Theatre. From a Buick sedan, a maroon one. If that jane was right about it bein' a Lincoln, hey, how about that Lincoln was bent Wednesday night from the driveway o' the Broom Hotel?"

"How about it?" said Larsen, morose, absent-minded.

"Well, look, cripes, if it was the Lincoln, the guy owns it said the rear bumpers were brand new and the front ones wasn't. And there's a weldin' mark on the arm the tail-light's on. I was just thinkin' maybe, well, if—"

"Good headwork, Kil. Tell the dispatcher that and have him give it to the precincts and on the short wave to the cruising cars."

"Sure. Hey, we got every car out almost, ain't we? If we don't get them guys it ain't our fault."

"Did Marks go right to work on that gun?"

"On it now. Well, be seein' you, Pete." Larsen grunted and remained staring into space. He knew the city by heart. He knew it well at night. In his mind's eye he saw the squad cars and the patrol flivvers cruising the bright main drags and the darker byways. He saw plain-clothesmen, in pairs, on the walk-about, picking up known characters and suspicious ones. He himself had started the ball rolling.

"Why?" Maddox had said, sneering. "You know damn well the D.A. took it on the lam. Why kid yourself and try to kid the papers by starting a front page man-hunt. Paddison took the easiest way out. He had clothes picked up by a messenger. He—"

"On your way, please," Larsen had said.

He felt caged in that room now. Restless. From time to time he heard the dispatcher's voice. Fatigue showed on his lean fair face. His yellow hair was rumpled, and a haunted look burned in his pale worried eyes. This would be a blackball for him. Bureaucratic intrigue would get its tentacles on him. He had been too staunch a supporter of Paddison to go unscathed now.

The door slammed open. Brinkhaus came barging in like a man who had seen a ghost. He flopped to a chair, slumped back in it, rolling his eye's and puffing his mustache.

"Gawd, Pete, don't ever ask me again to break news like that again! Don't ever, I ask you. Geez, the look on her face, and her with a kid t' be born soon, and the nice little house out there and only married two years and makin' baby clothes. Gawd, I felt like bustin' right out o' the house. It was worse than facin' a wild wiper with a couple o' hot rods in his mitts. It was— I ask you, Pete, don't ever! But she did a dive and there was me with her on my hands, so I got a woman over from next door and I left before she comes to."

He sat rubbing hot palms along the arms of the chair, his eyes staring and tortured, and a broken crack in his voice. Larsen went over and laid a hand on his shoulder and smiled wanly.

"It's tough, Brinky, old man. It's a thing like this that makes us want to knock a gunman's brains out every time we get our hands on one. Any news, Brinky?"

"Yeah. She said there was a telephone call at nine o'clock for Doane. He answered it. He seemed surprised. There wasn't much talk. He looked mysterious when he hung up. He went and put on his coat. She asked him where he was going. He said he couldn't tell her. He said, 'I'll be right back.' She said he never looked so queer. So he went out."

"He knew something," Larsen said quietly. "He was shut up for good. Either he knew that some mob bagged Paddison or—"

"Or," said Brinkhaus, "he knew that Paddison lammed and Paddison knew he knew it—and, hell, you can get a guy bumped off in this burg for fifty bucks. Doane might have been with the D.A. on a racket and maybe the D.A. had a notion Doane 'd go copper-heart and pull a squeal."

"Paddison would have to be out of his mind to do that."

"Yeah. Then maybe he's out of his mind." Brinkhaus got up. "Well, I gotta grab some chow. Take only a half an hour. I'll be at Nick's if you want me, boss."

"Go with you, Brinky. I'll probably be here all night, and I need some Scotch to take away the blues."

When he returned at a little past midnight he was surprised to find Maddox sitting in his office. Maddox was enjoying a fresh cigar. He rose and bowed with a glittering smile.

"Waiting for you, Inspector."

Larsen smelled trouble. He went past Maddox without looking at him and sat down at his desk, spreading a newspaper.

"Yes?" he said.

Maddox rocked importantly on his feet, blew smoke through his nostrils with relish.

"Well—well!" Larsen muttered, scowling at the newspaper, turning the pages without seeing them.

"You remember," Maddox said, "that last year the chief of police got the bright idea of having all of us, that is all city employees, fingerprinted, in case of accident. You had yours done, didn't you?"

"Years ago. Why?"

Maddox grinned broadly, licked his lips.

"Why, damn it, why?" Larsen said.

"Well—" Maddox, a heavy man, made mincing steps toward the desk and laid the tips of eight fingers on its shiny surface— "I have a surprise for you!" he exclaimed in a hissing whisper, his grin fixed.

Larsen smiled dreamily, murmured behind his teeth. "Why don't you go on the stage, Maddox? I hear there's an opening at the Lennox for a man who can impersonate a jackass. Except your ears are a trifle long."

Maddox showed most of his horse teeth in that fixed grin. "I was right, Larsen! I was right, you poor fool of a squarehead! Paddison lammed! Paddison killed Doane!"

Larsen's eyes seemed to shake once, violently, in their sockets. But his face remained deathly calm, provocatively vague.

"Yes, Maddox?"

"Yes! By God, yes! Why don't you say something? Killed him! Marks came up to tell you about the prints on the gun. I was here. He said I should tell you. I am. The prints on the gun that killed Doane are Paddison's. Laugh that off! Ha! Ha-ha!"

"Ha," said Larsen, in mimicry, not in laughter. "Thanks, Maddox. The door's right back of you."

"Ha! Kind of hits you where you live, eh? Maybe there are some more guys'll get hooked with Paddison, guys who think they're high and mighty now."

"Please go."

Larsen rose, a slab of yellow hair falling over his forehead, a misty look in his eyes, his knuckles white.

"Sure. Ha! Think I'm afraid o' you? Me? Ha, that's a laugh!"

But he made the last step to the door quickly, squeezed out with unbecoming haste.

Larsen collapsed in his chair, jammed his face into palms clammy cold.

"I'll get you, Dan Paddison!" he croaked, brokenly.

CHAPTER THREE

PIER 7

"LOUIE THE NOSE" was a free man by the grace of God and Inspector Larsen. God expected no tangible returns, but Larsen was a mortal, and a policeman—and did. And Louie knew he did and acted accordingly.

The noon rush was over. Stevedores and laborers had gone back to the docks and the coal yards. Louie nibbled on a toothpick and scanned the newspaper and from time to time arched his rooster neck and looked up Front Street. The lunch wagon was empty and Louie was nervous.

Larsen came at last, a tall personable figure in a lightweight blue serge suit, a snap-brim gray fedora, a wedge of silk protruding from his breast pocket. Louie watched him cross the cobbles of Front Street.

"Geez," said Louie, "the inspector looks the ritz."

Larsen opened the screen door. "Hello, Louie," he said.

"How's it, boss?"

"Not so swell." Larsen sat down on a stool, leaned on his elbows. "Why the phone call, Louie?"

Louie went into a huddle. "That dick Magalloway was nosin' around here this mornin'. He asked me if I seen a Lincoln around here around ten-thirty last night. He says he was askin' around and he finds after the Lincoln left that kill in India Street it got down here on Front Street and a watchman over to the Four Street Stores seen a car like that bustin' this way. Well, boss, I heard a car bust past here about ten-forty. There wasn't anybody in here, so I sticks my knob out and watches the car tear away. Boss, I seen the car turned right at Watkin's Slip and disappear."

"Why didn't you call me up?"

"Geez, did I know anything was wrong? I didn't think any more about it. Lots o' cars bust past here late at night, and if I ain't doin' anything I just kinda look out natcherally. Well, seein' it turn in at Watkin's Slip, I figured it 'd stopped there and maybe there was booze runnin'. You told me I shouldn't bother booze traffic."

"Go ahead, Louie."

"Well, before that—say about nine-thirty—'Butch' Bachmann come in here and set around. He read all the papers and ate some ham and eggs and I didn't think of it then, but now— Well, I remember Butch was lookin' at the clock a lot. At ten the phone rings and it's somebody for Butch. All Butch says on the phone is, 'Yeah, I getcha. O.K.' He hangs up and goes out.

"Now this mornin' I hear all about the kill, and begin to think back, and I remember Butch's steam lighter, the *Annie Moore*, lots o' times ties up at Watkin's Slip. Goin' off duty at midnight, I walks past

Watkin's Slip, like I always do, and there ain't no steam lighter there, and no car."

Larsen looked at Louie a long time, vacantly.

Louie got fidgety. "Geez, boss, God's honest truth!"

Larsen laughed, came out of his thoughts. "Good kid, Louie."

"But don't tell anybody I told you, boss. I don't want no cross on me. And I ain't told this to Magalloway either. I figgered it was a hot tip for you."

"Red hot, Louie."

The first clue worth a damn! Larsen left the lunch wagon and walked along the river wall past warehouses and docks. He reached Watkin's Slip, one time a ferry terminal, now condemned for loading purposes but still used by independent river boats.

He walked around with his hands in his pockets, his eyes on the cobbles, then on the slip. He saw tire marks to the very edge of the slip. He bent down to study them closely. He recognized the tread marks of a popular and expensive brand of tire. His lips twisted back and forth reflectively. He left the slip casually, but with a steady glow in his eyes.

He took a cab to headquarters. Maddox, of the missing persons bureau, was working overtime with a vengeance. He had every available man on the hunt for the missing district attorney. It would be a feather in his cap if he got him. He shot his tracers in the bordering states, as far as New York, Pittsburgh, Boston and Montreal. He was certain that Paddison had lammed out of the state.

Larsen concentrated on the city. He walked in on Brinkhaus and sat down.

"All right, Brinky. Get word to all the patrol cars and all the patrolmen along the waterfront. I want to know where the steam lighter *Annie Moore* is. I don't want anyone to go on board. I want a report of where she is."

Brinkhaus went out. Larsen dived into an accumulation of mail, bulletins and homicide squad reports. He skipped lunch and at one-thirty Brinkhaus came in.

"That boat's tied up at Pier 7, in the harbor, boss."

Larsen went to the wall, studied a map. He reached for his hat. "Come on, Brinky. We're going to make a pinch."

A steam lighter is a combination tugboat and cargo barge, the engine-room, pilot house and funnel well aft, the midships and foredeck given over to space for cargo.

Larsen and Brinkhaus got out of the Packard official in front of the Fruit Line Pier and left Horan at the wheel. They walked along the river, saw the *Annie Moore* alongside Pier 7. They walked out on the pier. Larsen jumped down into the bows and was walking aft when a big man in an undershirt thrust his head out of the pilot house.

"You Bachmann?" Larsen said.

"Yeah."

"Come down here a minute."

The man stared, then disappeared from the window and came down to the deck.

Brinkhaus came squeaky-shoed from the bows, and police department was written all over him. It was Brinkhaus, not Larsen, that made Bachmann tighten his plowshare jaw.

"We're from headquarters," Larsen was saying. "You were tied up at Watkin's Slip last night, weren't you?"

"Huh? Oh, yeah—sure. I tie up there a lot."

"What time did you leave there?"

"About eleven, I guess."

"Where did you go from there?"

"Here. I come here."

"What time did you arrive here?"

"Twelve. Good time, too."

"Excellent. Any cargo?"

Bachmann jerked his thumb. "See them ingots, don't you? I'm waitin' for the stevedores. They was gonna unload last night, but the tide was too low."

Even now the dock was on a level with Larsen's head. Bachmann looked bored.

"Did you see a car at Watkin's Slip between ten-thirty and eleven last night?"

"Huh? Oh, yeah. Sure. I seen a car there. Just before I was leavin'. Geez, I thought it was goin' clean over, but they had good brakes."

"How long did it stay there?"

"Dunno. Was there when I left. They doused the lights, so I figgered maybe there was some neckin'."

Larsen nibbled on his lip and looked about the deck. The copper ingots were piled from the base of the pilot house to a line about forty feet from the bow. The space between the bow and the ingots was empty.

"Anybody here when you arrived, Bachmann?"

"Yeah. The night watchman was sittin' up there smokin'."

"H'm," Larsen said absent-mindedly and walked aft. He entered a room fitted up with two bunks, a cupboard, a stove and a couple of chairs. A bottle of Scotch stood on the table. Larsen sat down as Bachmann and Brinkhaus came in. He pulled the cork out of the bottle, smelled its contents, put the cork back and turned the bottle around in his hands.

LARSEN got up and went to a cupboard, opened a door and saw four similar bottles, seals unbroken. He closed the cupboard, turned and looked quizzically around the room, ignoring Bachmann. He pried into a cabinet and looked under the bunks.

Bachmann watched him with squinted eyes. Larsen passed within a foot of him, ignored him, whistled to himself and probed all corners. He tapped the bulkhead with his knuckles. He put his ear to a broad panel. He looked up and saw a coat hanging from a hook at the top of the panel. He looked for a knob, or a lock but found none. He reached up, grabbed the hook and pulled. There was a click and the panel came outward and downward, hinged at the bottom.

Larsen drew out a sub-machine gun, five twenty-shot magazines and three eighteen-shot magazines. He threw them down and took out a 410 gauge sawed-off shotgun, an eight-shot Colt automatic and a heavy Colt revolver.

"Going in the business, Bachmann?"

He stood with a gun lying in either palm, smiling.

Bachmann wore a fixed grin. "I wouldn't take them guns serious, copper."

"You wouldn't," Larsen said.

Bachmann gaped apparently unconcerned, but back in his eyes were watchful, steady lights.

"You own this boat?" Larsen said.

"Yeah. Sure I own it."

"These guns, I suppose, are just keepsakes."

"Look at them yourself. They ain't ever been used. I got 'em figurin' to run some booze in. You wouldn't pinch a guy because he has some guns on board, would you, copper? In times like this? Hell, the river ain't safe for no man. A guy's gotta carry guns."

"Frisk him, Brinky," Larsen said, offhand.

Bachmann held his arms out and Brinkhaus went over him.

"Nah, nothin'," Brinkhaus said. "Bracelets?"

"Yeah," Larsen said, looking at the guns.

"Looka here, you guys!" Bachmann bellowed. "Now looka here!"

"We'll let you talk at headquarters," Larsen said.

Bachmann started to struggle. Brinkhaus caught his arm seemingly without effort. "Use your knob, fathead!" he said dully, and clicked a bracelet on Bachmann's left wrist, linked it to his own.

"I'll carry the arsenal," Larsen said quietly.

"Geez, now looka here, guys. Now looka here, lemme—"

But Brinkhaus hustled him outside and toward the bow.

"See, Brinky," said Larsen, pointing to the cleared space on deck. "See, Bachmann?"

"What?" Bachmann growled.

"You didn't say you lost an automobile between Watkin's Slip and here last night."

"A—what?"

"Treads, my boy, on your dusty deck." Larsen chuckled softly and motioned Brinkhaus to continue. Bachmann gulped and stared hard into space, the red draining from his cheeks, his jaw going slack. They swung up to the pier and started down.

Suddenly there was the vicious sound of an automatic stripping.

Bachmann reared up, screamed hoarsely, and slammed down to the pier, hurling Brinkhaus with him. As he fell, Brinkhaus dragged at his gun.

Larsen dropped everything but the Tommy gun and fell flat behind a big iron cleat. His nape bristled. The echoes of that stripping automatic still rattled, and he couldn't place its source.

Bachmann roared with pain, tossed mightily.

Brinkhaus reached around and unlocked the cuffs.

"Behind them crates on Pier 5, boss," he muttered.

Horan came on the run from the Packard hefting his revolver.

"Stay back!" yelled Larsen. "Stay back!"

Laborers on a barge stood stock still, watching.

Larsen saw a man darting behind the crates—another. He rose to one knee, cut loose with the Tommy gun. A Tommy gun can fire one hundred aimed shots semi-automatically a minute. Larsen emptied the clip of twenty in twelve seconds and cut one man down with five hits.

He jumped up and started down toward the base of the pier. The laborers were yelling. There came the scream of a siren. Horan spun around and cried out. Larsen sped past him and shoved in another magazine. When he reached the front of the Fruit Line Pier he saw the Packard speeding away.

He raised the Tommy gun, but held his fire, cursing. A truck was between himself and the Packard. The siren was clearing the way. The Packard swung up a side street and disappeared.

"That's a sweet one!" Larsen said.

"Should I telephone?"

"Yes. He'll ditch that car but telephone anyhow."

Brinkhaus came puffing up. "Bachmann's dead. He took seven shots in him."

Larsen swung away and went down on Pier 5, elbowing through a crowd that was gathering. Brinkhaus came at his heels. They found a man huddled against one of the crates. He was bloody and quite dead.

"Know him, Brinky?"

"No. You, boss?"

"No."

"Hell," said Brinkhaus. "Looks like somebody's been importin' hoods. They killed Bachmann so he wouldn't talk."

"This is a horse on us. Go call the morgue."

Larsen strode out on Pier 7, took a look at Bachmann, and jumped down to the steam lighter. He came back carrying a bottle of Scotch.

"What you got, boss?" Brinkhaus said.

"I've still got ideas, anyhow," Larsen said.

WHEN the taxi bearing Larsen and Brinkhaus arrived in front of headquarters, the inspector stepped out and set his jaw.

"Now don't let them get your goat, boss," Brinkhaus said.

Larsen went up the stone steps and through the wide glass doors. A group of detectives were standing near the desk. They turned and one of them started to say something when a door opened and Maddox barged out.

"Well, well!" Maddox said, in a tone that forebode no good. "Come here, Inspector. I've got something for you." He bowed and crooked a finger.

"Now cut out the comedy," Larsen said. "I'm busy."

"You can take a long rest," Maddox laughed. "Come, see what papa has."

Maddox retraced his steps to the door from which he had issued, opened it, stood bowing and leering and extending a hand toward the room beyond.

Larsen went toward the door suspiciously, a scowl bending his yellow eyebrows. He stopped short at the threshold.

Paddison sat in a chair, his collar torn and a red bruise on his cheek. He sat sullenly, his dark eyes mutinous, a curl of derision on his wide, nimble lips. His breath pumped through his nostrils. He said nothing.

Larsen said nothing. For a moment he felt light-headed. He had not expected this. The jolt corkscrewed cruelly to the depths of him, and alternate waves of cold and warmth lapped down his spine.

In a daze he took note of things—a blue suit of heavy material, a blue bow tie dangling, new shoes. Then he heard Maddox chuckling at his elbow. He stiffened, but still he could say nothing.

"Well," rapped Paddison vindictively, his eyes blazing, "get it out, Pete! Call me a two-timer! Get it off your chest!" His hands clawed his knees, and his breath grated hoarsely between words.

Larsen moved into the room, and Maddox followed and closed the door.

"What do you think of the missing persons bureau, Pete?" he said airily.

"The missing persons bureau!" snarled Paddison contemptuously. "I always said that head of yours was merely a knot to keep the rest of your miserable carcass from falling apart."

"Really!" mocked Maddox.

The black, penetrating eyes of Paddison jumped to Larsen.

"I'm glad Maddox made the pinch, Dan," Larsen said slowly.

"Maddox!" exclaimed Paddison. "That half-wit never made a pinch in his life."

"Cut it out, Paddison!" Maddox snapped. "Remember you're not the D.A. to me any more. You always did razz me. But it doesn't go now. Shut up or I'll take a pass at you."

Larsen felt oddly inarticulate. Face to face with the man with whom he had worked, he couldn't believe that Paddison was a prisoner.

"Say something, Pete!" Paddison laughed on a note of hysteria. "Call me a double-crosser. Maddox did. It doesn't matter. Go ahead, say it."

"Oh, shut up," Larsen said. He turned to Maddox. "How did it happen?"

"One of my men, Lewis, saw a fight at Bridge and Locust Streets. He ran up and saw Paddison fighting with a taxi driver. Paddison had gone up to the cab and he gave an address. The driver had been leaning against the mudguard, reading a paper with Paddison's picture. He looked up, dropped the paper, and flung his arms around Paddison."

"What he did," Paddison said, "was to say, 'Just a minute, sir,' and then reach in front. The next thing I knew I was stopping a wrench with my face. I'll let no taxi driver do that to me. So I swung at him and was showing him his place when two cops came up. Naturally, the cops hit both of us, so I hit one of the cops, and the other cop hit me and I woke up right here."

"Anyhow," drawled Maddox, "the little details don't matter. Here you are, Mr. Paddison, in the suit you bought to lam in, and we have the gun you killed Doane with."

"That's the richest of all, Maddox," Paddison said, sneering. "You can't hang a thing like that on me. I'm still the district attorney, and I'll beat every charge you've got against me. You're just very little tomatoes, Maddox—a bad smell in the department."

"You can't beat your own fingerprints," Maddox said.

"Don't try to kid me. My fingerprints aren't on any gun."

"Yes, they are," Larsen said flatly. "They're on the gun Doane was shot with in India Street."

Paddison stood up, his eyes widening. "You're a liar, Pete!"

"I wouldn't lie to you, Dan. Those clothes you have on were never delivered at your home. You had a messenger call for them. You drew five hundred out of your bank."

"I never ordered these clothes."

"Ha-ha!" said Maddox. "A little birdie brought them."

"Moron, yes! And what if I did draw five hundred?"

"To lam on," Maddox laughed.

"To lam on my eye! I loaned it to young Doane."

"Yeah," leered Maddox. "And Doane ain't here to prove it."

Paddison tightened his lips, thinned his fiery dark eyes. "To hell with you, Maddox. I'm not doing business with you. I want to see the chief—and the mayor."

"You forgot me," Larsen said ominously. His eyes had that dreamy, dangerous look. "Get out a minute, Maddox."

"Sure, Pete."

When Maddox had gone Larsen sat on the desk. "Sit down in that chair, Dan," he said. "Keep your head and don't wisecrack with me."

"All right, you big Swede," Paddison laughed.

"I want the truth, Dan."

"What good will the truth do? You believe already that I'm a two-timer."

"I want the truth."

"It's the shortest story ever told. I had a date with my wife. I left the office and walked to Sciarvi's. I never got there. In Cross Street a fellow jabbed a gun in my back. A sedan pulled up and I was hustled in. As soon as I stepped in I was knocked out. I came to in a room, a dirty little room. I was bound, and it was dark. The room smelled. Then somebody came in. I started asking questions, and then I was doped. I remember coming partly to, but as soon as I talked somebody doped me again. Reality is mixed with nightmare. I don't know whether I was really on a boat or whether I dreamed it. I remember men, but only as shapes, and voices only as toneless mutterings. I came to an hour ago—a free man."

"Where?"

"In Civic Park, sitting on a bench. I looked for my clothes. These aren't my clothes. I got up and walked for a taxi, to go home and see Lola and get things straight. Then the fight."

Larsen eyed him vacantly. "That's a pretty vague story," he said. "As a lawyer, you ought to realize that."

"But, damn it all, Pete, you don't believe I'm—"

"Could you identify any of the men?"

"No. I was held up from behind, told not to look around. As I shoved my head into the sedan I was cracked. From then on until I woke up in the park everything was a nightmare. I was kept drugged all the time."

He looked slantwise at Larsen, as if trying to calculate the impression he made. But Larsen had that blank look that defied penetration.

Then Larsen was saying, "You're asking me to believe a lot, Dan. I'm not going to be a fool for friendship. God, man, they have your fingerprint record. I found out that you'd ordered the clothes you have on. Brinkhaus found out you drew five hundred from the bank. Doane said you looked fretful that evening before you left. What happened to your brief case?"

"Gone—gone."

"What was in it?"

"A lot of junk. I had a list of names of men I hoped to expose, and a lot of detailed data. Suppose I was fretful? I was nervous from overwork, I wanted to be alone, and Doane insisted on puttering around. Tell me, why the hell should I kill Doane?"

Larsen shrugged. "Why did you loan him five hundred?"

"His wife was having a kid. He'd lost what little he'd saved in the market and didn't want his wife to know. And what do you mean when you say I bought these clothes?"

Larsen told him.

"Absurd," Paddison said. "I never ordered these clothes."

"They're on your bill. They were called for by a messenger."

Paddison looked up and walked around the room, running his hands through his hair. He stopped short, extended his hands palmwise.

"The thing is, Pete—do you believe me or don't you?"

"I'll believe you, Dan, when I find reason to. This fantastic tale you've handed me doesn't hang together at all."

Paddison's lips curled. "All right. You have nothing more to say?" His dark eyes flashed. "Believe what you want. It makes no difference to me. I'll beat this—beat it and come out on top smiling."

"You'll never beat this, Dan," Larsen said flatly, "while I'm in the department."

He turned and went out.

Brinkhaus joined him and they went up to Larsen's office. Brinkhaus set the bottle of Scotch on the desk and regarded it longingly.

"The Packard was left in Davis Street," Brinkhaus said. "All the shootin's over. It looks too bad for Paddison."

Larsen stared. "Only the shooting's not over, Brinky. Call Mrs. Doane's house, ask where her husband used to bank, see if he deposited five hundred dollars the day Paddison disappeared."

CHAPTER FOUR

THE MURDER PLANT

LARSEN WENT around to Nick Batanzio's spaghetti and red-ink joint with the bottle of Scotch under his arm.

"Back here, Nick," Larsen said, walking through the restaurant.

They entered a private room and Larsen sat down at a table. Nick took a chair opposite and beamed.

"What you drink, boss?"

"Nothing today, Nick. Take a look at this Scotch. Good stuff?"

Nick drew the bottle across, looked at the label, ran his fingers up and down the neck.

"Good stuff," he said. "The label don't mean nothin', boss. Lots o' imitations o' that label. But this is the real stuff."

"How do you know?"

"By the bottle. The good stuff— Well, you run your hand up and down the neck and you feel two kinda waves in the glass. That's the secret. This stuff I'd have to get eight bucks a bottle for. I can't handle it. The imitation, same label and all, I handle here and get four a bottle, and I know it's cut twice. This stuff ain't cut at all. It's on'y sold in high-tone joints like the Alamo Club and the Venetia and places like that, and by the case to guys can pay for it. It's only sold in case lots to the clubs and the clubs charge a buck a drink and don't sell it out by the bottle."

"It's the real stuff, eh?"

"Yeah. If you want, of course, I might be able to get you some, or you could go right to Mike Mulvaney. Mike 'd give you a case. It's run in from the fishin' boats that come down from Canada. Mike's the only guy handles it wholesale."

"Thanks, Nick. I thought it was good stuff but I wanted to be sure."

"Hell, it's the best money can buy in this city!"

Larsen went back to headquarters.

"No, Doane didn't make any deposit," Brinkhaus said.

"No? Well, go out to Mrs. Doane's and tell her to look around in the house for it. You help her."

"What the hell, boss?"

"On your way, Brinky."

Brinky shrugged and went out and Larsen called the switchboard. "Holt, this is Larsen.… Michael Mulvaney lives at 29 Laurel Drive, in the Astor Apartments. Use your influence with the telephone exchange that handles that district. Have a record of all calls made, to or from that address, and a transcription of the messages.… Yes, that's all."

He hung up, took his hat and went out. Outside, he hailed a taxi and climbed in. He sat back and lit a cigarette. He sighed heavily, and weary creases appeared between his brows. Maddox was razzing him now. The whole department was razzing him. In the last analysis, Larsen was stubborn—a die-hard. Paddison's story was fantastic, to say the least. If Paddison had lammed, there must have been a reason. Was his apprehension an accident, or was Paddison telling the truth? If he was crooked, he must have had connections with the underworld.

"I'll break him," Larson told himself, "or make him. One way or another, I'm not satisfied yet. I'll bring out all the dirt against him—or all that's good in him."

Number 29 Laurel Drive was a ten-story apartment house, with green window boxes all along the second floor. Larsen entered the lobby and got Mulvaney's apartment number from the elevator boy, backing up the request with his badge.

On the fifth floor he walked down a green-carpeted corridor and knocked on a door that had 515 in brass on it.

A big handsome man in a black silk dressing gown opened the door and smiled.

"Well, Inspector, this is a surprise!"

"Hello, Mike, how are you these days?"

"Just fine. Come in."

Larsen went in, threw his hat on a divan and dropped down beside it. Mulvaney kept smiling like the genial host. He was about forty, had a thin red mustache and slicked-down red hair.

"What's the honor, inspector?"

Larsen leaned back and smiled. "Oh, I just happened to be out this way, and I hear you handle the best Scotch in town."

"You wouldn't hold that against me," Mulvaney grinned.

"Not at all. I'm going to throw a little party and I thought—"

"Of course, of course, Inspector. I'll send you out a case."

"Swell of you, Mike."

"You know me for a regular guy. How's tricks otherwise?"

"Rotten. We've got the D.A. back, and it looks bad for him. And I ran into trouble down at Pier 7. I was poking around to kill time and picked up a guy for toting a gun. Some other guy took a pot-shot at him. Feud, I guess."

"You don't say!"

Mulvaney sat down and showed genuine interest, his eyes wide and bland on Larsen's face.

"You've kept pretty clean, haven't you, Mike?"

"It's a religion with me."

"Looked bad for you a year ago. I mean about that police patrol boat that was rammed and sunk by a runner—and two cops left to drown."

"I got out of that, though."

Mulvaney laughed and got up and poured two drinks. Larsen drank and talked on and on, about everything: old times, bum liquor, good liquor, the past elections. He showed no intention of leaving. Mulvaney's smile left him, he kept looking at his wrist-watch.

Presently the telephone across the room rang. Larsen picked up a magazine and Mulvaney crossed the room.

"Hello.... Yes.... I'll call you back.... No, I'll call you back."

He hung up, turned. "Well, I'll send that stuff around, Pete, then."

"Thanks, Mike." Larsen got up. "You're a swell guy."

"How about another drink, Mike?"

"Sure."

Larsen killed ten minutes over the drink. "Well, I've got to be going. Mind if I use your phone?"

He called headquarters. "Larsen, Holt. Anything new?... Sure, go ahead.... Uh-huh, I get you.... Yeah, go on.... I see. All right, thanks." He hung up, turned. "Nothing new, Mike. A cop's life is hell."

"Good old Pete!"

They shook hands at the door.

Larsen made a record trip to the lobby and flashed his badge at the switchboard operator. "Number 515 made a call yet?"

"No, sir."

"If he tries to, don't connect him. Say the line's busy. For ten minutes at least. Disobey that and you'll get in trouble."

He strode out of the lobby and hailed a cab. As he climbed in and sat down, he saw Mulvaney at a window on the fifth floor.

"Price and Larrimore Streets, and step on it."

The taxi covered the distance in five minutes. It was a deserted intersection on the edge of Little Italy. Larsen walked down Larrimore looking at house numbers. Number 410 was a two-story red stone with an areaway paralleling the sidewalk. Just above the areaway door was a white light, burning even in daytime. Larsen gave it the once-over, walked on, saw a parked sedan, climbed into the sedan and sat down, drawing the rear curtain halfway down.

He waited fifteen minutes. A black roadster with red trimming came around Price into Larrimore and parked near the corner. Mulvaney climbed out and walked ten yards and then ducked down into the areaway.

Larsen heard the door bang shut. He got out of the sedan and walked to the areaway. He opened his coat. He stood there for two minutes, then descended into the areaway, pushed open a door and strode down a corridor where one light burned. He pushed open another door and entered a bar. No windows were here. Lights were burning.

The bar was empty. A barkeeper was absent-mindedly throwing poker dice for his own amusement. He looked up—and remained that way.

Larsen looked into a side room. It was empty. He said nothing to the barkeeper, paid no attention to him. He spotted a telephone booth. It was empty. At the end of the bar was another door, a swing door with a frosted glass panel. He went toward that, walking on his toes.

Larsen knocked the swing door in with a slap of his left palm.

Mulvaney stood with a handful of money, counting. A wiry youth with sideburns and dark skin spun around. Larsen recognized him as the one who had escaped from the pier and gone off in the Packard official. The youth snarled and tore a gun from his armpit.

Mulvaney dropped the money and grabbed for the gun. The gun went off and crashed through a mirror back of Larsen's head. Larsen fired and the youth yelled and spun back against a wash basin.

"Stop it," Larsen said.

"For God's sake, Mike, get him!" the youth screamed, then sank down.

Mulvaney didn't draw, but he whipped up a hard blow that caught Larsen on the side of the jaw and floored him.

"Finish him, Mike!" the kid mumbled.

Mulvaney turned and bolted out.

Larsen reached the bar as the front door slammed shut. He went down the corridor. He reached the areaway and saw Mulvaney starting into the roadster.

"Stop it, Mike!"

Mulvaney fired and the bullet smashed the little white light over the door. He saw he couldn't make it in the car, so he sped across the street. He paused on the corner, aiming. Larsen flopped behind a fire-hydrant and heard the bullet snap past. He fired and got Mulvaney in the left leg.

Mulvaney ran up Price. Larsen turned the corner and Mulvaney dived for an iron-railed stoop as Larsen fired. Mulvaney fell down, rolled over and fired from his back, blindly. Larsen felt a jolt in his right arm and his gun fell to the pavement. As he bent, another bullet whined over his head.

Mulvaney toiled to his feet and started half running, half limping, reloading. Larsen picked up the gun with his left hand because his right was bloody. Mulvaney swung his gun around. "No, Mike," Larsen said to himself, and put a bullet in the small of Mulvaney's back.

AT TEN that night Maddox sat on a tipped-back chair, thinking. Brinkhaus and two other detectives were seated around a desk playing penny ante.

At five past ten the door opened slowly and Larsen leaned there, his yellow hair disheveled, his left arm in a sling.

"Mulvaney died," he said. "He couldn't help it. I had to give him that last shot to save myself. I broke his spine." He tapped his chest. "But he talked."

Maddox got up and walked to a window.

"He talked," Larsen said. "He imported two torpedoes from St. Louis to do this job. Doane was on his payroll—that nice-faced scholarly double-crosser. Doane told Mulvaney that Paddison was getting up data to collar him for that patrol boat sinking. Doane telephoned Mulvaney that Paddison was going to Sciarvi's that night. The two torpedoes waylaid him. He had the papers with him.

"Doane borrowed the money because Mulvaney told him to. He figured we'd look up the bank. We would get the impression, as we did, that Paddison drew it to lam on. They kept Paddison doped up, unconscious most of the time. They telephone Doane. They killed Doane. It was done while Paddison was unconscious in the sedan. One of the guys wore gloves and pressed the gun in Paddison's hand, hence the fingerprints. They tossed Doane out. It was a murder plant on Paddison.

"Mulvaney figured that Paddison wouldn't have a show. Mulvaney was the one telephoned for the clothes in Paddison's name. Building up evidence against Paddison, you see. He planned to and finally did, let Paddison go, figuring that with the evidence against Paddison the state would put him away. Paddison, being unconscious all the time he was in their hands, would naturally give a fantastic story that no one would believe. They killed Doane because Mulvaney was getting worried about him, and they killed him in a way that threw suspicion on Paddison and gave the impression that Doane and Paddison had been in cahoots and that Paddison killed him to be sure of his silence.

"I've got Mulvaney's confession here. They ran the car on that steam lighter, dumped it in the river, and a motorboat met them and took them off before they got to Pier 7. The two torpedoes killed Bachmann to silence him. I got one of them on the dock—the other in that speakeasy, as Mulvaney was paying him off."

"The five hundred was locked in a desk drawer in Doane's house," Brinkhaus said.

"I am going to apologize to Dan now," Larsen said, looking at Maddox's back. "And so are you, Maddox."

Maddox turned around. "Sure, sure," he said in a creaky voice. "Sure I will. That's me all over. You think I wouldn't? Ain't I glad Dan's proved on the square?"

Brinkhaus and the two detectives burst into laughter.

Maddox reddened. "Yah, go ahead, laugh! I'm always willing to own up when I'm wrong. Think I'm afraid? Ha-ha!"

"Ha," said Larsen, in mimicry, not in laughter.

THE CROOKED SPOT

A GANGSTER HAD SHOT
A COP! SIRENS WAILED,
SQUAD CARS PURRED BY—
THE LAW'S GREAT NET
WAS SPREAD. BUT ALONE
THROUGH DESERTED
ALLEYS AN UNKNOWN MAN
WAS FOLLOWING A BLOOD
TRAIL STRAIGHT TO THE
CITY'S MYSTERY SPOT.

THE DOOR whipped open and Detective-Sergeant Brinkhaus barged in. His brown fedora was in his hand, and beads of sweat gleamed on his broad, honest face. He puffed to a stop, shut the door with a jolt of his hip and stood mopping his face and making awkward gestures with his hat.

"I'm sorry, boss, I wasn't around. I—I—"

"Sit down, Brinky," Larsen said abstractedly.

The yellow-haired inspector's eyes were glazed with thought, and a cigarette was so motionless in his fingers that the smoke rose in a straight, thin column agitated slightly by the draft of Brinky's arrival.

Woolen-suited even in summer, his face looking like a boiled lobster, Brinky ran his stubby forefinger around the inside of his collar and spoke apologetically.

"Y' see, boss," he said, "me wife, Emma, was took to the horsepittle last night—we're hopin' it's gonna be a boy—and I just kinda up and ran over there this afternoon, not knowin' you'd maybe want me." He planted his broad hands on his broad knees and got out a breath that had been stifling him. He blinked his bland brown eyes. "What's up?"

Larsen made an uncomfortable grimace, moved his right hand in the sling in which it rested—memento of the late and not lamented Mike Mulvaney, shot down to death in a gun duel with the yellow-haired inspector.

"Huh?" muttered Brinkhaus leaning forward.

"I—"

A rap sounded on the door.

"Come in," said Larsen.

The door opened and Lieutenant Maddox looked in. "Hasn't Brink—" he stopped short at sight of the Irishman. "Oh, there you are, Sergeant. It's about time. The chief's been looking high and low for you since three o'clock."

Brinky swallowed. "I'm sorry, Lieutenant. Y' see, me wife Emma was took—"

"You've told him, Inspector?" Maddox shot at Larsen.

Larsen rose, shoved his left hand in his pocket, strolled to the window. "You tell him."

Maddox, formerly head of the missing-persons bureau, now advisor to Norman Pentcost, the new chief of police, closed the door and bowed. He was a big fat man, with gray shiny eyes that always seemed to gloat and a small waxed mustache that was never out of trim.

"Brinkhaus," he said, "the chief wants Nick Paoli. He's detailed you and Sullivan to get him. The chief issued an ultimation to Paoli demanding him to clear out of town in twenty-four hours. That was yesterday. Paoli called up this morning and told the chief to go to hell and try putting him out."

"What's he want Paoli for?" Brinky asked.

"We're putting him out of town. He comes from St. Louis. He was in the dairy racket out there and he's come here with a notorious reputation and an idea that he's going to go far in a big way. We have information through informers that he's starting to muscle in on the fruit and vegetable trade. The chief wants him thrown out before he gets a foothold."

"Listen, Maddox." Larsen came halfway across the floor, his lean face serious. "This is your idea, not the chief's. For God's sake, man, use your head and call it off. Don't go nuts because you're Pentcost's right-hand man. You can't kick Paoli out of this city. He hasn't done a thing you can hang on him. All right, suppose he has a record out West. There are at least ten guys right in this man's town that should be picked up before Paoli. Why the hell do you single put Paoli?"

Maddox rocked on his heels, hooked white thumbs in his vest, beamed all over his fat face. "Inspector, I am only the mouthpiece of Chief Pentcost. The chief is all steamed up. Paoli had the insolence to give an interview to a wise-cracking newspaper reporter. The paper printed it. Paoli called the police a lot of boy scouts and the chief a loud-mouthed scoutmaster—"

Red flame burst from the
stern of the life boat.

"You'll see," cut in Larsen. "We can't hold Paoli and I'm damned
if we can throw him out of town. We've nothing on him. That muscling
in—that's just rumor. It's probably true, but we haven't the evidence.
We have a lot more evidence against other guys: 'High-Collar' Gold,
Sammie Baum—guys like that. Why the hell—I ask you, Maddox—
why the hell pick out Paoli?"

"I didn't come in here, Inspector, to answer a lot of questions. The
chief wants Paoli. Brinkhaus and Sullivan have been detailed to get
him—"

"Two of my best men!" Larsen barked. "You know what a laughing
stock a pinch like that will make of the department! Damn it, Maddox,
you've been throwing wrenches into my business since I made a jackass
of you on that Mulvaney case." He came closer, jaw muscles standing
out. "You watch your step, Maddox. I stand just so much from you or
the chief of police or anybody."

Maddox smirked. "Technically, you are my superior, Inspector." He made a mock bow. "Pardon me if I leave."

Bland-eyed Brinkhaus watched him go out with mincing steps, watched the door close. Brinky raised his hand, looked at the palm, ground the palm on his knee, looked at Larsen.

"I wouldn't let that wildflower git you all stormed up, boss. Him and Pentcost are runnin' this here department like a merry-go-round, but I wouldn't get all stormed up, boss. You ain't lookin' well, and with that bum arm— Hell, you should be home."

Larsen dropped to his swivel chair. "The thing is, Brinky, that personally Pentcost is an honest, sincere man. They appointed him chief of police because of that. But he doesn't know police work. And Maddox—well, Pentcost thinks Maddox is real ripe red tomatoes. Maddox!" Larsen growled with contempt.

Brinkhaus sighed. "I'm gonna feel like a jackass, havin' to collar Paoli."

"The orders are," said Larsen quietly, "that you're to just say the chief wants an interview with him."

"There's somethin' about this I can't understand. A lot of fireworks over a St. Louis wiper that wasn't nobody practically till the chief started declarin' himself. Well"—he slapped his knee—"orders is orders, I s'pose, and jackasses ain't horses. Where's Sull?"

"Playing penny ante with the reserves." Larsen leaned forward suddenly. "Brinky, be careful. I've got a feeling, I don't know why, that there might be more to taking Paoli than just taking him."

"I'll be sociable with him," Brinky said. "I ain't goin' around playin' Fourth o' July, with Emma in the horspittle the way she is."

"And watch Sull. You know he's a wild young devil."

Brinky stopped at the door. "I broke Sull in, boss. There ain't no harm gonna come to Sull, can I help it."

THE ALVARADO RESTAURANT is in Maria Street, south of Union Circle, two blocks east of South Broad Street and on the fringe of Little Italy. It specializes in spaghetti, ravioli and Dago ink. It contains twenty tables.

Upstairs, Nick Paoli walked up and down carrying a glass of iced ginger ale. He was tall, young, dark, wasp-waisted, with black eyes like the jab of a rapier.

"Yeah, imagine," he said. "Imagine them guys landin' on me for no reason at all!"

"Yeah," said "Joe the Rock," his nose in a glass of Scotch.

"Yeah," said Tony Gorio.

Paoli waved his glass of ginger ale. "They can't land on me like that. I ain't done a thing in this lousy burg."

"Yet," said Joe the Rock, lifting his nose out of his glass.

"I should get out of Portsend? Not in these pants. I'll show that louse of a punk-faced Pentcost if he can put me out. You know what I'm gonna do?" He came to the table and set down his glass. "I'm gonna call on that wisenheimer tomorrer. I'm gonna call on him!"

Joe the Rock looked pained. "For cryin' out loud, Nick, don't be a horse's neck. Let him rave. G' on, let him rave."

"Listen, Nick," put in Tony Gorio. "Once I paid a call on a police station. I was wise, see. It was out in Akron. I ain't done nothin', see, only I hear a couple of flatfoots is pokin' around for me. So I walk in intendin' to ask why, and I walk into a shamus and he says, 'Hello, Tony,' and hands me one on the kisser—"

"Whaja do then?" asked Joe the Rock.

"Passed out. And, cripes, if when I come to they didn't charge me with assault and battery!"

Paoli took a long drink. "Well, anyhow, and to hell with that bedtime story, these cops ain't got no right to land on me. I'm strictly kosher so far here, and I'm gonna call on that guy Pentcost—"

The door opened. Pantone, the owner of the Alvarado, came in with his eyes wide and his lips shaking. He closed the door softly and came quickly to the table, staring at Paoli.

"Just got a tip, Nick. You're on the spot."

Paoli's face didn't change. "Yeah?"

"On the phone. Some guy called up, he didn't give his name."

"What heel's putting me on the spot?"

Pantone leaned forward. "The cops!" he hissed.

Paoli chuckled. "Don't you know the difference between a pinch and the spot?"

"Yes," Pantone nodded slowly.

Paoli's mouth tightened. "What the hell do you mean?"

"What I said. The guy calls up and says I should get word to you that the cops 've put you on the spot. It ain't a pinch. Brinkhaus and Sullivan is out to get you."

Joe the Rock stood up. "Maybe because you went and back-talked to the chief, Nick," he muttered.

"You better lam, Nick," Pantone said.

"Yeah?" said Paoli.

He seemed to grow cooler, taller and darker—not suddenly, but gradually.

"Beat it, Pantone," he said, quietly.

"But look, Nick, I don't want any trouble around here if I can help it."

"Beat it."

Pantone made nervous, fluttering motions with his hands and went out. Tony Gorio got up and went to the window, looked down into Maria Street. Joe the Rock picked up his glass, drained it and turned the glass round and round in his hand, staring at it.

"Brinkhaus, eh?" he muttered. "I heard a lot o' Brinkhaus. He don't look it, but I heard he's some shakes with a rod. But I ain't ever heard he'd put a guy on the spot." He looked up. "Gonna lam, Nick?"

Paoli smiled thinly. "Give me a year and I'll have every racket in this burg sewed up. I've got the fruit markets now, damn near. I'll get the dyers and cleaners and the builders. I'll take a pinch—they can't hold me over twelve hours and they can't chuck me out of town. But I'll be damned if any flatfoot's gonna put the cross on me for nothin'!"

"Take it on the lam, Nick," Joe the Rock rumbled slowly. "Only for a while. Ain't no use hangin' around if the cops put you on the spot."

"You know damned well that if I left this racket here I'd be through! Lam? Ixnay, Joe! Not this baby." He went to the window, took a quick look down, came back his eyes beady. "I'm gonna show these punks," he snarled. "I'm gonna stay in this burg and I'm gonna do what I started out to do. High-Collar's soft and I'm gonna muscle him right out of everything. Now I'm gonna call on my lawyer Julius Silverstein and I'm gonna make him make Pentcost file charges against me. And for what can he file charges? Nothin'. That 'undesirables' don't go when I got a mouthpiece like Julius Silverstein."

Joe the Rock grabbed his arm. "Think it over, Nick. Don't get snotty too much with the cops. Let them get fresh. You lay low and play dumb. It's the only out in this racket. Don't push 'em too far."

"I got to get off this spot, don't I? Silverstein will fix that, and I ain't gonna walk around no streets with a couple of dicks primed to fog me." He struck his chest. "I'm gettin' to be a big fella, Joe! I'm gonna run this town in another year. That's what I came here for. I ain't gonna lam. Not me!"

Joe the Rock swore. "All right, Nick, all right. Don't yell the roof off this dump."

Tony Gorio left the window, poured a drink at the table and flung it down. "It's gettin' pretty terrible," he said, "when honest racketeers can't be let alone a-tall. Why don't they go after High-Collar? He's in the big dough—"

"He won't be!" Paoli snapped. "I'm gonna muscle his joints from right under his Kike's nose and make him like it!"

BRINKHAUS and Sullivan crossed Union Circle and headed south. Sullivan was young, lean, hard, and had a spring to his step. Brinky struck his heels hard on the pavement.

"And let me do the talkin'," Brinky said.

"Oh, I suppose maybe I don't speak good enough United States for the Dago, huh?"

"Well it ain't that, Sull, but you got a habit o' usin' a lot o' exclamation points. You let me handle this. It's a lot o' foolishness, anyhow, collarin' this Paoli, so there's no sense gettin' serious about it. The chief'll haul off and do a lot o' preachin' to Paoli and he'll put him on a train. Maybe he'll send me with him. But Paoli 'll come right back again."

"O.K., papa. You do the talkin', then." They swung left off South Broad into Henry Street, walked east through a tatterdemalion neighborhood and turned south into Maria. Brinkhaus perspired freely.

"I got to call the horsepittle again too," he said. "Between callin' the horsepittle and runnin' over there and havin' Maddox crack wise— There's the Alvarado. He ought to be there, and if he ain't Pantone 'll know where he is. Now remember, Sull, be nice and—"

"I'll remember, papa."

Brinkhaus pushed open the screen door of the Alvarado and Pantone looked up with a start from behind the cash register on the cigar case. Brinkhaus helped himself to a cigar from a box on top of the glass case.

"Hello, Pantone, how are you these days?"

"Fine, Sergeant."

Sullivan strolled to a nearby table, took a breadstick from a glass vase and came back crackling it between his teeth.

"I'm lookin' for Nick Paoli," Brinkhaus said. "Just a little friendly call."

Pantone swallowed. "He ain't here, Sarge."

"He lives upstairs," Brinkhaus said.

Pantone shrugged. "Sure, I know, Sarge. But—but he ain't here now. You want to leave a message, I'll tell him."

Brinkhaus took a few experimental drags on the cigar. "I got to see him personally, Pantone. It ain't serious. I just got to talk him, friendly like, see. Me and Sull here just took a pleasant walk down from headquarters. This ain't a bad cigar, Pantone."

Pantone said, "Take half a dozen, Sarge. But Nick ain't here now."

Brinkhaus looked at his watch. "Well, we'll wait. Hey, Sull, you stay here while I phone the horsepittle. Where's a booth, Pantone? O.K., I see it."

Brinkhaus crossed to a telephone booth, entered it and pulled shut the door.

Sullivan leaned on the cigar counter munching breadsticks. He chuckled.

"Brinky worries more about his missus than two other guys put together, Pantone."

"Yes—yes," Pantone said nervously.

Sullivan slanted a glance at him. "You're sweatin'."

" 's hot."

"Under that fan, eh?" Sullivan laughed. "You don't lie good at all, Pantone. What are you shakin' about? Hell, you'd be a good guy to have at a cocktail party."

"Y-yes," stuttered Pantone. "Have some cigars, Sull."

"No, thanks. Gimme a couple packs o' Luckies."

Pantone, dripping perspiration, handed out two packs. Sullivan shoved them in his pocket, smiled drily at Pantone. Pantone lowered his eyes. Sullivan leaned with both elbows on the cigar case.

"You ain't shaky—no, not at all. You just got that way when you were young—from bein' shaken in a baby carriage all day. Come on, Pantone, go tell Paoli we want to get on a social basis with him."

"I tell, you, Sull, s' help me, honest to Gawd, I don't—" He stopped short and his eyes bulged.

Paoli and Tony Gorio and Joe the Rock came walking through the restaurant. They walked rapidly, in single file, down an aisle between two rows of tables. Paoli saw Sullivan leaning against the counter, so did Tony Gorio, so did Joe the Rock. But they kept on walking, Paoli fingering the left lapel of his coat, leading the way.

Paoli's face was a sleek dark mask. His lids were narrowed, so much so that his eyes were seen as mere glints of dark fire. His lips were tightly compressed, a vein in his throat pulsed.

Pantone knelt down behind the cigar case.

Sullivan, after one look at Pantone, twisted his head and looked over his left shoulder. He saw the three men coming. He smiled to himself. He took one arm off the cigar case, thrust his hand into his coat pocket, rummaged for a toothpick.

Paoli and his men saw only Sullivan. They expected Brinkhaus, did not see him. Paoli's dark eyes darted fiercely around the restaurant.

Brinkhaus, in the telephone booth, did not see them. He hung up, sighed contentedly and pushed, open the door.

Paoli cursed. "There he is!"

Sullivan started. He saw Paoli looking toward the booth, then go for his gun. He saw the look on Paoli's face. Sullivan whipped out his gun.

"Paoli!"

Paoli made a sound like an enraged cat. He swung toward Sullivan and his gun belched. It was a .45, and the slug drove Sullivan back against the cigar counter. His elbow went through the glass. He slid off and crashed to the floor.

Paoli dived over him. Joe the Rock smashed the window in the door of the telephone booth with a fast shot, and Brinkhaus, dragging at his gun, got a shower of glass in the face. He staggered a step backward, spat glass splinters from his lip.

The few people in the restaurant had ducked beneath tables. A woman was screaming.

Brinkhaus moaned, but not because he was hurt. He was thinking of Sullivan. He flung a chair out of his way and barged to the showcase. He took one look at Sullivan. He lunged for the door, his gun raised, and reached the sidewalk. He saw no one. The neighborhood was infested with alleys.

He pivoted and went back inside, dropped to his knees.

"Sull—Sull!"

"Get 'em, Brinky! Get 'em!"

"Sull, where'd they nail you, boy?"

"I dunno. Side or somethin'—or guts."

"Oh, Geez, Sull." Brinkhaus stood up and saw a uniformed cop loom in the doorway. "Come in here, Casey."

"God, Sarge—did Sull get it?"

"Grab Pantone."

The cop caught Pantone in two bounds.

Brinkhaus ran heavily to the telephone booth called for a police ambulance. He dialed over to Larsen.

"Geez, boss, they got Sull.... Oh, hell, it happened so fast.... Well, see, I was phonin' the horsepittle in the booth.... Yeah, here in the Alvarado. Well, when I hang up, I push open the door, not expectin' nothin', and I hear Sull yell, 'Paoli!' just like that, see. Them guys drew first, boss.... Yeah, I called the ambulance.... Two was with him. Joe the Rock and I didn't git time to pike the other bird.... Paoli had on a light gray suit, a Panama, and brown shoes. Joe the Rock...."

LARSEN hung up, his face white, his left hand trembling. With that left hand he had scrawled notes. He opened the transmitter to the dispatcher's office on the top of the building.

"Larsen.... John Sullivan, Central Office, wounded at Alvarado Restaurant, 358 Maria Street. By Nick Paoli, Joe the Rock Mandano, and an unidentified man; at 5:10 p.m. this evening. Broadcast to all precincts, patrol cars, signal booths. Paoli—five feet eleven, dark, clean-shaven, light gray suit, no vest, brown shoes, Panama hat with a dark blue band. I've heard he has a short scar across the knuckles of the left hand. Joe the Rock Mandano—six feet, about one-ninety, blue suit, gray fedora; he's pigeon-toed and has a gold left eye-tooth. He fired once at Sergeant Brinkhaus, missed. Sullivan was just taken to the City Hospital. Serious, but chance of recovery. All precincts should block outgoing roads in their territory, railroad stations, bus terminals. All patrol cars out, and all flyers. More later."

He signed off as the door opened and Sergeant Mahoney came in and saluted briefly.

"How is Sull, Inspector?"

"He lost a chunk of his right side but he'll stand a chance, I hear. Brinky's bringing Pantone over. Take your flying squad, Jim, and the big Packard. Swing out the machine guns and go to it. Scour Little Italy."

"O.K., Inspector."

Mahoney went out on the double. Larsen got up, took a turn up and down the room, holding his clenched left hand above his head. He had feared this. He could not have explained why, but he had feared just such a casualty.

He went out and headed for the central room downstairs. He ran into Chief Pentcost at the head of the stairway. Pentcost gestured with his black-ribboned pince-nez.

"I knew that Paoli was a bad one!" he said, vehemently.

Maddox came out of the chief's office.

"How is Sullivan?" he asked.

"A hell of a lot you care," Larsen snapped.

"Now, now," Pentcost said. "None of this."

"Maybe you'll admit now," Maddox said stiffly, "that Paoli is a dangerous criminal, that I was right in wanting him hauled in. Maybe you'll admit now—"

"Now, now—yes now!" Larsen clenched his left hand. "Now we've a reason to get Paoli. Don't talk to me yet, Maddox. I want to hear Brinkhaus out. There's something funny about this case and I'll get to it if I have to break another arm."

"My dear man," complained Pentcost. "The attitude you take is insufferable, to say the least. You have done nothing but ridicule Lieutenant Maddox."

Maddox forced an indulgent smile. "It's quite all right, Chief. The inspector has a case of nerves due no doubt to his wounded hand."

Larsen swallowed hot words that rose to his lips. He set his jaw and went down the broad staircase. He saw Brinkhaus coming in the front door with Pantone. Brinkhaus looked a little wild. His brown hat was out of shape and perched way back on his head, a slab of hair had fallen down across his forehead. His collar was sweaty and wilted and his tie was out of place.

"Take this guy, boss," he said in a rusty voice, "and let me git started after Paoli."

"Come up to my office, Brinky."

In Larsen's office, Brinkhaus slammed Pantone into a chair, crossed to a water cooler and drank three glasses of water. Sweat streaked his face like skeins of shiny silk, and his big hands shook, his voice was clogged when he spoke.

Pentcost came in with his chin in the air and his eyes glaring down along his thin, autocratic nose. Maddox followed with his short, mincing steps, and patted his cheeks tenderly with a handkerchief. He looked slightly nervous, slightly ill at ease.

Pantone crouched in the chair his hands gripping the sides.

Brinkhaus stood with his arms dangling, his thick shoulders droop-ing. "I can't explain it, I can't. I had a talk with Sull. He didn't go first for his gun at all. Six people in the restaurant swore to that. He was leanin' on the cigar case.

"Paoli and these other two eggs come walkin' through the restau-rant. I'm told this. I didn't see it. I was callin' the horsepittle about Emma. Paoli sees me open the telephone booth and drags his rod. Sull calls his name and he turns on Sull and lets him have it and Joe the Rock tries a shot at me and misses and the three o' them lam."

"Who is this man?" Pentcost asked, pointing at Pantone.

"Pantone," Brinkhaus said thickly. "He owns the Alvarado. He said Paoli wasn't there. I went and asked him in a nice way and he said Paoli was out. So I figgered me and Sull'd wait a while. Boss," he said to Larsen, "call up the horsepittle and see what chance Sull stands."

"They'll call here," Larsen said, "as soon as they can make certain."

Brinkhaus wagged his head and ran his hand through his matted hair. "I shouldn't ha' gone in that booth. I shouldn't ha' let Sull out there alone—"

"Indeed you shouldn't have," declared Pentcost. "It indicates a lack of training or a total disregard of—"

"Now wait a minute, Chief," broke in Larsen. "Let me do a little talking. Pantone, why the hell did you lie to Sergeant Brinkhaus?"

"Please, Inspector, I didn't want no trouble around my place. It's bad for business—"

"There would have been no trouble. Sergeant Brinkhaus told you that, didn't he?"

"Yes, but—"

"Do you realize that you have attempted to thwart justice and have abetted a crime?"

Pantone squirmed. "I was just tryin' to play square by all hands, please, Inspector, and everything she goes wrong."

"You must have thought that trouble would occur. You must have had reason to think that a meeting between Sergeant Brinkhaus and Paoli would result in trouble, despite the fact that Sergeant Brinkhaus was on a comparatively quiet errand. You must have known that Paoli would resent arrest because he had some reason to. Now didn't you?"

Pantone made gasping motions with his mouth and clawed at his collar. He almost wept. "Geez, boss, I'm all mixed up. I didn't do nothin'. Paoli's have two rooms upstairs, that's all I know."

"Why," insisted Larsen, "did you think that a meeting between Paoli and Sergeant Brinkhaus would cause trouble? You did think that, Pantone. And by God, you'll tell!"

Larsen took three long strides and stood over him. He took Pantone's hair and jerked back Pantone's head, staring down into the man's terror-stricken face.

"You understand, Pantone, we mean business. A cop has been seriously wounded. You know what happens to any man who lays a hand on a cop. Answer me!"

Pantone choked. "Please—look—some guy call me up and say, 'Tell Paoli Brinkhaus and Sullivan put him on the spot and gonna fog him out on sight.' That's all. The guy hang up and I go tell Paoli."

"Who was the guy?"

"Holy mackerel, boss, I don't know!"

Larsen released him slowly. Pantone slumped in the chair and began to weep.

"That's funny," Larsen said slowly. He went to his desk and lit a cigarette. "That's funny," he said again.

"Well!" Pentcost exclaimed.

Larsen looked at him. "Beg pardon?"

"Now who could have telephoned this man and told him that?"

Brinkhaus croaked brokenly. "Listen, boss," he said to Larsen. "If the horsepittle calls up about Emma take the message. If there's anything to be done, boss, do it, please. Them guys are hidin' out in Little Italy, I'll bet my hat. I'm gonna get them."

"Another case of locking the door after the cow has been stolen, Sergeant Brinkhaus," Pentcost said testily. "It seems to me that you certainly bungled this case miserably."

"Maybe I did," Brinkhaus said. "I dunno. There's always something a man can't foresee. I dunno. I'm sorry about Sull. I would ha' laid down my life for that boy, but I didn't have the chance. He drew the fire to save me and, by God Almighty, I'm gonna get Paoli!"

"Brinky," said Larsen, and went around and grabbed Brinkhaus's arm. "Just a minute, Brinky. The flying squad is down in Little Italy now. Just a minute, old-timer."

"But, boss, I got to—"

"Orders, Brinky. Stay here."

Brinkhaus made a weary, hopeless gesture.

Larsen turned on Pantone. "When did you receive that telephone call, Pantone?"

"Was about four-thirty."

"You're sure of that?"

"Yes. Luis, one of my waiters, always comes on work four-thirty. He come in just while I was talkin'."

Larsen gushed smoke through his nostrils. "Brinky, take Pantone downstairs and lock him up. Then come back here. All the squad cars, patrols and flyers are out, Chief. Outgoing arteries are watched at the city limits, also bus and rail terminals. I'll report any new developments."

Pentcost adjusted his pince-nez. "I hope you will be able to report more successful results than you have been able to so far, Inspector."

"Remember, Chief, you forced this job on me against my advice. You took the advice of Lieutenant Maddox, who, if you want my frank opinion—"

"I don't care for your frank opinion," Pentcost said. "I want results. I've had enough of this bickering, enough of this casting slurs hither and yon—"

"If you'll think back, Chief," Larsen interrupted quietly, "you'll find that my slurs haven't been cast hither and yon, but in one direction." He nodded toward Maddox.

Maddox licked his lower lip. "Yes—yes." His big white hands opened and closed fitfully. "And I've had just about enough of it, Larsen. Just about enough of it." His face was white like dough, his nostrils quivered. "I'm not going to stand it for much longer."

Larsen chuckled sardonically, dropped to his swivel chair, and reached for the telephone.

"Do something about it, then," he said with lazy contempt.

Maddox patted his cheek with his handkerchief. "You-you think I'm afraid. You-you— Oh, what's the use talking to a squarehead, anyhow! You're crazy, just crazy."

"Yeah," nodded Larsen. "Like a fox. Get out of my office, Maddox, before I throw this telephone at you, you big milk-fed bum!"

"Inspector Larsen!" exclaimed Pentcost.

"No, little girl," Larsen said into the telephone, "I didn't call you a bum. Get me the City Hospital."

BRINKHAUS turned Pantone over to Sergeant Glass, in charge of cell blocks in the basement of headquarters. Instead of returning to the central room, however, he left headquarters by way of the big garage where the police cars were stored. This brought him to Exeter Street, in the dusk of evening.

He paused for a moment gnawing at his lips, his eyes were troubled. Larsen had commanded him to return to the office. Brinkhaus hadn't. It was the first time he had ever disobeyed his immediate superior.

There was a light growing in Brinky's eyes, it burned there with a latent fierceness. He cut back of City Hall Square and turned south into India Street, past state and federal buildings. His brown fedora was tilted over his shaggy brows, his thick substantial heels thumped the pavement solidly. Outwardly, there was nothing outstanding about this man—his face, his clothes were plain. He walked with a slight roll, due to his broad, thick bulk. He would have attracted no attention in a crowd. He hadn't even the air of a detective.

Down India Street he walked—down where the tall buildings petered out, where old brownstones grew instead, and then past the brownstones to the frame flats and stores, where he caught a faint smell of the salt marshes from the harbor. Then west—southwest down Platt Street, past houses with little front yards, on across Cherry Square, with the old watering troughs in the middle, and on down West Platt and into the heart of Little Italy, as the first street lights began to glow.

He heard a police siren. He stepped into a doorway and saw a big black squad car cruise by. Bach at the wheel, the second precinct squad car. Heads popped out of windows, women chattered from window to window. Brinky went on, his eyes peering keenly from under the shadow of his hat.

He looked up his stoolies. He spoke briefly with them. One worked in a hat-cleaning store, another worked in a restaurant, another in a speakeasy. And there were others, sprinkled throughout Little Italy.

"I want Paoli," Brinky said. "Keep your smeller to the grapevine. Git any news to me right off the bat."

They were his friends, these stoolies, partly through fear and partly because at some time or another Brinky had withheld the hand of the law for a minor offense. No policeman can work without them. They are his stock in trade, the antennae through which he picks up information from the underworld.

Tirelessly Brinkhaus made the rounds. He shoved his hard old head into dangerous territory. He poked into flop houses, into speakeasies, into cheap rooming houses. From time to time he heard the wail of a police siren. He saw patrol flivvers roll down the dark street. He saw squad cars purr past. He called the City Hospital and found that Sullivan had a better chance to live. He called the Brooks Hospital and found that his wife was resting comfortably. And by way of celebration he had a glass of beer at the bar from which he had telephoned.

Going out, he paused in the areaway as he saw a man step from the curb at the corner toward a sedan that had just stopped. There was something vaguely familiar about the man's back and the set of his head, but for the life of him Brinkhaus could not associate the man with a name.

The sedan started off. It was a dark and deserted section of the city, and there had been something furtive about the man as he climbed into the sedan. Brinkhaus reared up out of the areaway and walked rapidly to the corner, prompted by nothing more than a cop's hunch.

He peered after the rolling car, automatically memorized the license number as he started after it on the run hugging the shadows of the house walls. The car rolled down Brewer and Brinky saw it swing left into Front Street the street along the river. But when he reached Front Street the car was no longer in sight. He slowed to a walk and went on half-heartedly. He crossed the cobbles and then proceeding along the river's edge, past warehouses, docks and moored barges.

He spotted a car parked near a dock. It had no lights on it but Brinky made out the form of a man walking up and down leisurely beside it and smoking a cigarette. He heard, too, the sound of a motorboat somewhere on the dark water. He began whistling to himself and strolled toward the parked car. The man there stopped walking, and the red end of his cigarette arced from his mouth down to his side, where it remained motionless.

Brinky recognized the sedan, affected light-heartedness with his whistle and strolled nearer. He came up close to the man and peered good-naturedly at him.

"Oh, hello, 'Snifter,'" he said.

The man took a drag at his cigarette. "Oh, hello, Sarge. I didn't know you was on the river."

"I get around, Snifter. What you doin' here?"

"Parkin'."

"Lemme see. You drive for High-Collar these days, don't you, Snifter?"

"Yeah."

"What you waitin' for?"

"I got a date with a night operator in one o' the terminal buildin's. The boss let me have the car."

"You wouldn't lie to me, Snifter, would you?"

"Why should I lie?"

"Because maybe High-Collar wouldn't like I should know he went out on his yacht."

Snifter took quick pulls at his cigarette, snapped the butt away. "You're actin' funny, Sarge."

Brinky's thick right arm shot out and grabbed Snifter by the throat. "Who the hell did you pick up at Brewer and Argus Street?"

"I didn't—"

"There's nine chances that I'm wrong, Snifter, and one that I'm right—about who I think it is. Maybe my eyesight's wrong. But I'm takin' the chance. My pal Sullivan got himself smacked with a slug."

"Who says High-Collar was in on that?"

"Paoli did it. We know that. I seen it. But High-Collar's been the big fella shakin' down the fruit and vegetable markets, and I been hearin' Paoli's been musclin' in on him. Some guy told Paoli we had him on the spot. I'm beginnin' to guess—and damn you, Snifter—who did you pick up at Brewer and Argus before?"

"You're cracked, Sarge. I'm waitin' for a broad. Leggo me neck, for cripes sake!"

"Come clean, Snifter."

Grimly Brinkhaus tightened his hand on Shifter's throat, until Snifter began to sag. He choked, stuck his tongue out. He became a dead weight in Brinky's hand, and Brinky cursed and let him fall. Then he lifted him up, manacled him to the door of the car and let him sit on the foot board.

He reset his hat, brushed his hands together and went to the end of the little dock. He stared across the dark water, saw a faint pin point of light moving away and heard the sound of a far-distant motorboat.

He left the dock and walked past a few covered piers. He saw a lighted door and went toward it, entered a small watchman's office and showed his badge.

"C'n I git a boat or somethin' around here?" he asked.

"There ain't nothin' right around here except a rowboat I use sometimes to fish in."

"You any idea where the yacht *Success* anchors?"

"Yeah. Right across the river from here off them salt marshes. Come out and maybe I can show you."

Brinkhaus went out to the pier with the watchman and the watchman pointed. "See that light that blinks on and off slow? Well, that's Duck Reef. You head for that, then go to the right of it. The *Success* always anchors about a hundred yards back o' that reef."

"C'n I borry that rowboat?"

"Sure."

BRINKHAUS set alone in the old flat-bottomed boat. He could use oars fairly well, since he had fished a lot off Oak Point. Rubber guards in the oarlocks dulled a lot of sound, but Brinky did not care much about the noise he made. He rowed steadily, looking over his shoulder occasionally to get a bearing on the Duck Reef light. A tug with a tow of three barges strutted past, and the swell rocked the rowboat.

He passed to the right of the blinking light, kept on for a few minutes, and then turned to look at the few lighted ports and the mooring lights of a boat. He took up his oars and pulled on, and when he looked again he could make out the shape of a small white yacht and saw a small boat moored alongside it.

As he bumped against the motorboat, he let the oars clatter in and almost fell overboard on his way from the rowboat to the motorboat. Feet thumped on the yacht's deck and a dark figure appeared at the rail.

"Who's there?" a voice growled. Brinkhaus made his way to the accommodation ladder and started up, gripping the rope railing.

"Hey, you can't come up here! This is a private yacht!"

Brinkhaus climbed on, saying nothing, and a man faced him at the head of the ladder.

"Just be calm," said Brinkhaus. "I'm only Brinkhaus from headquarters and I come out for the air."

Other footsteps sounded on the dark, quiet deck, and a tall, loose-limbed man came hurrying.

"What's the matter, Gus?" he rapped out.

"Hello, High-Collar. It's only me, Brinkhaus."

High-Collar Gold didn't stop or even slow down until he reached the head of the accommodation ladder.

"What's the honor, Brinky?" he snapped.

"I just want to look your new yacht over. I been hearin' a lot about it."

"I ain't got time right now," High-Collar said. "Come out some other time and I'll be glad to show you around. I'm busy."

"That's all right, High-Collar. You don't have to show me around. I c'n look around myself."

High-Collar scowled. "Come on, Brinky, what's on your mind? What the hell are you doin' out here?"

Brinkhaus pushed his hat back on his head and looked up into High-Collar's angry eyes. "You wouldn't be tryin' to get fresh, High-Collar, would you?" He started past High-Collar.

High-Collar side-stepped, stopping him, "I ain't gettin' fresh, Brinky, but I'm tellin' you you can't look my yacht over unless you got a warrant."

Brinky moved his arms with a deceptive awkwardness, and a gun appeared in his hand as he stepped back and covered High-Collar and the other man.

"Once I git started on somethin'," Brinky said, "I don't have time to bother about warrants. Keep the hands up, you eggs. Back up to that rail, the two o' you, and go down in that motorboat. Keep 'em up, High-Collar," he warned again as he took a gun from High-Collar's armpit. "You go down first, High-Collar."

"You can't pull this, Brinky!"

"I'm pullin' it, ain't I? Hey, you, keep 'em up." He took a gun from the other man. "Go on, now—go on down. And clear out."

He waited in the shadows, grasping a gun in either hand. He made no reply to the threats and oaths of High-Collar. The motorboat started off and Brinkhaus turned and went down the deck, sticking close to the wall, ducking under the ports.

He reached an open door and looked into a comfortably furnished saloon. It was empty. In the center of the room was a table with three glasses on it. He entered the saloon holding his guns level. He paused and listened.

He heard light footsteps on the deck above. He crossed the saloon and went out the opposite door, stopped on the deck and looked fore and aft. Then he went forward noiselessly, reached a ladder and climbed it. He paused at the top, looked past the pilot house toward the funnel and the ventilators.

Again he heard the footsteps. He rose and lunged to the shadow of the pilot house. He waited there. In a few minutes he saw a man start from behind the funnel toward one of the life boats.

"Hey!" Brinkhaus barked. "I got you covered!"

The man dived for the shadow of the life boat. Brinkhaus fired. The echoes bounced across the dark water. Red flame burst from the stern of the life boat. Lead shattered a pilot-house window and glass rained down on Brinky. He flung back, went around the pilot house, heaved over behind a ventilator and fired across a skylight.

He heard a loud moan and the thump of a falling body. He ran to the funnel, crept around it, flung back with his breath in his throat and escaped a shot that chipped paint from the funnel. Quickly he circled the funnel in the opposite direction.

Stopping, he heard hoarse breathing. "Better stop it," he said grimly. He peered around the funnel, his gun raised. The dark shape of the man jerked. He was on his knees. Brinkhaus fired, the muzzle flame tearing through the darkness.

The man fell over backward. His gun flew from his hand, clattered away on the deck. He rolled over and over, clawing toward the edge of the deck—toward the water. "Oh, no," said Brinkhaus. "Not that." He ran heavily across the deck and stopped the man. He dropped to one knee.

The man fought with him, cursing, clawing futilely. Gradually he weakened, sobbed, and lay inert.

"I had to give it to you, Maddox," Brinky muttered. "I had to give it to you."

He heard a siren wail across the water. He stood up and looked past the funnel, saw a bright searchlight creeping across the river—police boat. He dragged Maddox to the pilot house, found a blue light inside and set it off, holding it above his head.

The searchlight swung around.

"They're comin' all right," Brinky said.

"Brinky, give me a break. Let me jump—the river...."

Brinky knelt down, his face grave. "I'd like to, Maddox. Not because I got a hankerin' to do you a favor, but because if I did it might save a lot of scandal. But I can't do it, Maddox. Because High-Collar would know, and because a watchman knew I came out here. You gotta take it, Maddox, on the button."

"It wasn't my fault, Brinky, so help me God! High-Collar thought he would be smart. I didn't want any killing. That's why I talked High-Collar out of taking his mob and wiping Paoli's out. He wanted to do that. But I promised him that I'd find a way to get Paoli out of town without a shooting. I did, didn't I? I talked the chief into it—into putting pressure on Paoli. The chief knew nothing else. But High-Collar had to have blood and he made that telephone call to Pantone."

"You don't have to tell me all that," Brinkhaus said. "I'm only the sarge on the case. You tell that to Chief Pentcost."

"God, I can't face him!"

The searchlight swung across the bow, settled on Brinkhaus kneeling beside Maddox.

Maddox buried his face in his arms.

CHIEF PENTCOST stood by the window of his office looking down into the street, where clear summer sunshine shone.

The door opened quietly and Larsen came in, carrying a sheaf of papers.

Pentcost turned, flexed his lips. "Good morning, Inspector."

"Good morning, Chief."

"How is Sullivan?"

"He'll recover."

"Good."

Pentcost crossed to his desk, sat down.

Larsen sat down facing him, shuffled the sheaf of papers. "Maddox died at four this morning. I was with him at the end. Casey and the flying squad fought it out with Paoli and his men on Ocean Pike, killing Paoli, Joe the Rock and Tony Gorio. High-Collar Gold, of course, was picked up by the patrol boat."

"And about Maddox," Pentcost prompted.

Larsen bit his lip. "High-Collar has been paying him five hundred a month for the past two years."

Pentcost shook his head. "Such double-dealing!"

"High-Collar wasn't satisfied with Maddox's plan to get rid of Paoli, so High-Collar had one of his men make that anonymous call informing Paoli that Brinkhaus and Sullivan were out to kill him in cold blood. High-Collar knew that Maddox wouldn't dare spring anything. Maddox, however, got in touch with him late yesterday afternoon and they went out to High-Collar's yacht to have a long talk. Brinkhaus saw Maddox enter High-Collar's car and followed, boarding the yacht alone in the face of great danger."

"But why did High-Collar make that phone call?"

"He knew that if Paoli or one of his gang killed a cop, or even wounded him, it would bring the whole force down on Paoli and wipe him right off the map. Paoli was grabbing off a lot of High-Collar's rackets."

Pentcost cleared his throat. "I've been a fool, Larsen. I must apologize. I put faith in Maddox and depended on his judgment. You can't realize how this miserable double-dealing of his has shaken me up. I thought that the antagonism between you two was merely one of those departmental grudges."

Larsen stood up. "Here are my full reports." He turned and went to the door, turned around to say, "I have no doubt you meant well, Chief. If I can be of any assistance at any time—" He made a palm-upward gesture.

Pentcost smiled. "You're white, Larsen, damned white. By the way, send in Sergeant Brinkhaus, will you?"

Larsen went out and closed the door quietly. He started down the corridor toward his office and almost reached it when Brinky heaved out and came barging toward him, his hat yanked over one ear and his coat-tails flying.

Larsen reached out his hand. "Brinky, I—" He caught hold of Brinky's arm and dragged him to a stop. "Hold on, Brinky. The chief wants to—"

"Nix on the chief or the mayor or anybody, boss."

"He wants to shake your hand—"

"Nix, boss. Leggo me arm. Look, I was just talkin' to the horsepittle and me wife Emma. It's a boy, boss, and so help me I'm gonna make Housman drive me over in the squad car!"

He wrenched free, reeled against the wall, then straightened out and went barging on down the hall like a bat out of hell, his coat-tails in the air and his hard substantial heels ringing on the floor. Connolly, the gun expert, opened a door. "Who's making all the racket, Inspector?"

Larsen chuckled. "Brinky—on a hospital case."

WHISPERS OF DEATH

A CHILD HAD BEEN
MURDERED. PUBLIC
FEELING WAS AT HIGH
PITCH. YET THOSE IN
THE KNOW WOULD NOT
SPEAK, FOR AN ICY
HAND HAD STRETCHED
OUT FROM DEATH'S
THRESHOLD TO RAISE
A WALL OF SILENCE.
A SILENCE WHICH
INSPECTOR LARSEN
REALIZED COULD BE
BROKEN ONLY ONE WAY—
THE ROUTE OF THE GUN.

CHAPTER ONE

FINGER OF SILENCE

DEMETRIO CAPPILLARI'S florist shop was the finest on the South Side. Cappillari himself was a fat man with sparkling dark eyes, fine olive skin and a jovial manner. The kids in the neighborhood raved about him, and he liked kids and sang for them sometimes and always gave them flowers.

Little Sophia Simioni had peeked in that warm August afternoon and Cappillari had whisked her in and let her choose a flower. She chose a poppy and then she stood by the pool in the shop and stared at the dark cool water.

Cappillari, leaving her behind the potted palms, went to the front of the shop to continue with a bouquet he had started before Sophia's arrival.

The front door was wide to the summer sun, and three men in neat suits entered. One waved his hand and went toward Cappillari with a friendly, good-natured grin. He wore a wide-brimmed Panama with a thin black band. His two companions paused to sniff flowers and one of them sighed ecstatically. Then they looked at each other and smiled.

The man in the Panama said, "How's every little thing, Cappy, these days and nights?"

Cappillari frowned quizzically.

"What you want?"

The man in the Panama began to wear a pained expression.

"I dunno, Cappy, I guess I been a dope. I'm sorry for all those things, and—well—" he shrugged—"if it's O.K. by you it's O.K. by me. I'm sorry, Cappy. I just come around."

"It's O.K. by me," Cappillari said, still puzzled.

"Jake. Then's O.K. by me. I guess I was off my nut. I guess it's better for everybody all around. A guy gets all steamed up sometimes and he says things. Like you."

"Yeah," said Cappillari.

"Sure. You didn't mean that. You was just steamed up when you said it. The same as me. I was all steamed up."

One of the other two men sauntered to the door, leaned there and began whistling.

"You must come around some night," the man in the Panama said. "Sort of get-together-again party. Let bygones be bygones, Cappy."

"Sure."

"Say Wednesday night, huh?"

"Sure."

"Jake. Well, I'll be seein' you then. Give my best to the folks. G'-by, Cap."

He tried to heave away. The man in the Panama grinned. His gun blazed.

He thrust out his hand. Cappillari took it. The man in the Panama grinned, held on. His left hand went in beneath his lapel. He held on with his right. His left hand came out with a gun. Cappillari tried to heave away. The man in the Panama grinned. His gun blazed three times and he let Cappillari go and the florist tumbled backward and took a potted palm down with him to the tiles. The three men walked out briskly.

Joe Cappillari came bounding through the store.

"Pop!"

"Mother o' God, Joe!"

"Pop!"

Young Joe Cappillari was on his knees, cradling his father in his arms. "I just—seen—them—pop! I'll—"

"Joe!" Cappillari gripped his son's wrist. "You didn't see nobody. You hear me, Joe! Remember mama—and little Adamo—and Rosa—Joe, remember—you didn't see nobody! Nobody, Joe!"

"Pop, them guys—I seen them—"

"Holy Mother, Joe, you got to promise me! Keep your mouth shut! I'm done for, Joe—and there wouldn't be no use. Only they'd get back at you—or mama—or— Joe, you hear me! Be a good boy, Joey— Papa asks you."

Joe said, "Pop, wait here. I'll get a doctor."

"I'll wait—" Cappillari said, with a twisted smile.

Joe, bounding to the door, ran into Patrolman Quagliano.

"Git back! Git back!" snarled Quagliano, hefting his gun.

"My father—" Joe pointed.

"Yeah?"

"Please, I got to get a doctor!"

"Whatsa matter with the phone, goof?"

Joe looked surprised. "Gee, that's right." He hopped to the cash desk.

Patrolman Baumberg poked his head in the door and clipped, "Is this the joint?"

"Hello, Gus," Quagliano said.

"Is this the joint, Mike?"

"Nah, I'm buyin' posies for me mother-in-law."

"Ain't that nice," said Baumberg, marching in. "Hello, Cappy. What's the matter with Cappy, Mike?"

Quagliano, kneeling, looked up. "Pipe down a minute." He bent over Cappillari. "Who did it, Cappy?"

"Holy Mother—"

"O.K., but who did it? Listen, Cappy." He began speaking in Italian, gesturing.

JOE WAS stammering into the telephone. Baumberg stood twirling his nightstick and snapping gum with his tongue and teeth. Joe hung up, ran his hands through his hair and hurried back to his father. He dropped to his knees. He kept looking anxiously from his father to Quagliano, who went on speaking in Italian rapidly.

Cappillari's eyes were dark and shiny like lacquer. He raised a limp hand. The hand fell to his face. It fell in such a manner that the forefinger touched his lips, and the hand remained there while Cappillari died.

Quagliano sat back on his heels, took off his cap, ran a handkerchief around the sweatband. Looking at the dead face, he said to Joe, "Tough, kid. Tough."

Joe stared. Joe was young—only nineteen—and had never looked at death before. He was a clean-looking lad. He had a good jaw. Good clear eyes. But his eyes were dimmed a bit now. He heard the babble of the crowd that was beginning to mill on the sidewalk. But he heard it only faintly. Echoes of words pounded in his brain. Mama. Little Adamo. Rosa. His father's words.

He almost went to pieces—but didn't. He got hold of himself, squaring his jaw, tightening his mouth. A hand prodded his shoulder.

"Get up, kid."

Joe rose, white-faced, his hands clenched at his sides. Quagliano looked at him. Quagliano was hard as nails and a good cop and he had eyes that cut like a poniard. Joe looked away, around at all the beautiful flowers. His father loved flowers.

Baumberg came over smelling a rose he spun between thumb and forefinger.

"Who did it, kid?" he said, slyly.

Joe said, "I—don't—know."

"Listen, you!" Quagliano gripped his arm. Joe looked at him. It was hard to meet Quagliano's dark, suspicious eyes. Baumberg shoved his jaw closer. "Ixnay on that baloney, kid."

Joe looked at Baumberg.

"I said—ixnay," Baumberg drawled, patting air down with his palms.

Joe gritted, "I—don't—know."

Quagliano started. His eyes narrowed wickedly. He stepped past Joe quickly, over Cappillari. He bent down and swung aside the big potted palm that had been knocked over.

Sophia Simioni lay there. Shot through the head. Dead.

PORTSEND was no paradise wherein every man did unto others as he would have others do unto him. It was a pretty sophisticated city where crime was no novelty and where an ordinary killing hardly rated a stick on the front page. Men may come and men may go—and even women—by the route of the gun, without much stirring the mechanical precision of a police department. But a child, age six, is another matter.

Yellow-haired Inspector Peter Larsen said, "Brinky, this hits me where I live."

"It's lousy, boss."

Larsen spoke into the boxlike transmitter beside his desk.

"Yes, Walters, every road. Every piece of rolling stock the department owns—out on the roads. Patrol flivvers, squad cars, flyers. And get in touch with all the outlying booths. A dark gray Cadillac phaeton—that's what an insurance agent saw roll through Cherry Street a minute after he heard the shots. Had a black top and a chrome stone screen on front and glass wings on the windshield. I want every road covered, and reports every half hour.... No, he didn't get the pad numbers. It wouldn't matter anyhow. And get out a dozen men to look in every public garage in the city."

He switched off. Brinkhaus nodded.

"Now if the kill wasn't done in a Dago neighborhood we might stand a chance. I'll bet six or eight guys saw them birds walk out o' Cappillari's. But try to get 'em to say so. Yeah, try!"

"We've got to get them, Brinky. Got to. This code of silence may be an old Italian custom but we've got to break it down. We've got to get the rats that bumped off Cappillari and that little girl."

Brinkhaus, woollen-suited even in summer, shrugged.

"Every Dago is goin' to forget how to speak English. And when the Italian Squad bears down on 'em, hell, they're even goin' to forget how to speak Wop."

"Quagliano said he's certain that just before Cappillari died he looked at his son Joe and put his finger to his lips. Joe saw those birds. Joe knew them, probably."

"Which don't mean a thing when Joe plays dummy."

Larsen stood up, lean and well-groomed and clean-cut as his reputation, the youngest inspector in the history of the department, the first squarehead to be in charge of the detective bureau.

"Brinky," he said, "I'm going to break this silence."

He went down to Cherry Street in the Packard official. Business went on the same as ever. The peanut vendor sold peanuts at Cherry Square, the vegetable stores were open, people walked in the streets. But at sight of the police car men and women who were idling in front of doorways retreated out of sight.

The air of tension was there. And the air of silence. Even for blocks. The unspoken warning had percolated throughout the district. The late afternoon sun was warm in Cherry Street, but children were not playing and the hurdygurdy at Cherry and Sisson was silent.

The florist shop was closed, locked. Larsen got out of the car, let cigarette smoke dribble upward from his nostrils. Father Bonomino came out of the hall door beside the store, saw Larsen, made a gentle motion with his hand. He was a large, fat man with cheeks like red apples.

"Inspector Larsen," he said, extending his hand.

"Hello, Father."

Father Bonomino lifted his eyes aloft, sighed.

"It is terrible, Inspector. Demetrio, and the little girl. He was beloved of the neighborhood."

"Cappillari's family all upstairs?"

"Yes. And I was just down to see Sophia's mother. There is not much one can do, Inspector. You are on the case?"

"The whole department is, Father." He went upstairs.

Mrs. Cappillari lay on a couch with an ice-bag covering her forehead and eyes. Adamo, aged eight, sat beside her and held her hand. Rosa, who was eighteen, looked at Larsen with eyes red-rimmed from crying and Joe stood with his back to a window, his face in shadow.

Larsen made a slight bow with his head.

"I dislike intruding at a time like this, but I find it necessary." He spoke slowly, with an effort, finding it difficult to choose words, for he was a man of sentiment and feeling.

Rosa said, "Won't you—sit down, Inspector?"

"Thank you," he said, but did not sit down.

Mrs. Cappillari was hardly aware of his presence. She kept moaning and muttering incoherently and little Adamo kept patting her hand.

Larsen said, "You must know, you must have an idea who was responsible for this murder of your father and little Sophia Simioni. We need your help. Joe, you were in the store."

"I was in the back," Joe said. "I came running in when I heard the shots."

Larsen went on in a quiet voice.

"Patrolman Quagliano said that when your father died he looked at you and placed his finger to his lips. That would indicate he knew you knew who did it."

"His hand just fell on his face like," Joe said.

"Please, inspector," Rosa murmured, "at a time like this—"

"I realize," Larsen said. "But it's vitally important that we strike while the iron is hot. I want to be fair with you, and I assure you that I'm much gentler than the men who'll come here later on the general investigation. You know, Joe. You know who did it. You put us up against a stone wall by acting the way you are. You—all of you people around here—forestall justice because of a barbaric tradition. I want to know, Joe."

Mrs. Cappillari moaned on the couch. Adamo patted her hand. Rosa kept rubbing her palms together and biting her lips. She was lovely. Dark and supple and rather tall with gleaming dark hair worn casquelike.

Joe's voice was muffled when he said, "I don't know, sir."

Because his face was in shadow Larsen did not see the beads of sweat on Joe's forehead.

"Remember," Larsen said, "it is not only your father who's dead. It's that little girl too. She was killed by one of the shots that went right through your father. It's your duty, Joe, to tell what you know."

Mrs. Cappillari moaned louder and started crying Joe's name over and over. Adamo began crying. Rosa shuddered and beat her hands against her temples.

"Please, Inspector, please!" she cried.

Larsen felt awkward. He felt like a brute. It was distasteful work. He looked at his strap-watch.

"Joe," he said, "I want you to be at my office at five-thirty—in an hour and a half."

CHAPTER TWO

BUM STEER

YOU MUST understand and believe that Joe Cappillari was a good boy. He was accomplished on the violin and he had a flare for pathos and melancholy in his music. Also, he loved flowers, like his late father. And you must believe that up until the moment he died Demetrio Cappillari was, like the majority of Italians, a good father and a good husband.

Larsen liked Joe. He had seen the boy grow out of short pants and once he had heard him play at the Cherry Square Italian Business Men's Club. Larsen had an ear for music and a sense of appreciation for fine things acquired in his effort to strike a balance against the meanness and sordidness of his cop's life and the crime in which he dealt. True, he was a layman, but a good one, and in certain rough, tough and nasty quarters he was called the "Swell Swede." But courage he had—and hardness when hardness was needed.

Joe came into his office at a little before five-thirty. Larsen indicated a chair facing his own across the neat, flat-topped desk. Brinkhaus turned from regarding a venerable elm through the front window.

"Hello, Joe," Brinkhaus said.

"Hello, Sergeant," Joe said, sitting down.

Joe was nervous. Nervous but unafraid. He sat straight in the oak-veneered chair, his straw hat resting on his knees, his hands resting palms down on the hat.

Larsen was drawing reflectively on a cigarette, one eye squinted against a column of smoke that rose steadily.

The windows were closed. The hum of traffic in City Hall Square was muffled and distant. It accentuated the silence of the office.

Brinkhaus stood on his thick, substantial heels, his square-built bulk in silhouette against a window pane, his hands clasped behind his back, his big, ruddy face a blank.

Larsen was relaxed in his swivel-chair, his right elbow on the arm, his forearm vertical and its fingers holding the cigarette. He wore a dreamy, meditative look. He smoked his cigarette well down, then rubbed it out in a tray, crossed his arms on the desk.

"I didn't want to cause a lot of hysterics in your home, Joe," he said. "But now—I want the truth."

Joe inhaled deeply, spoke quietly.

"Honest, Inspector, I—I don't know. I was in the back of the store. I heard the shots and I—"

"I know all that," Larsen said. "I don't want to know about that. You heard the extras on the street already? Joe, this is bad. Murder's bad enough. I knew and liked your father. That's murder. But the little girl— Joe, you've got to open up. You've got to give us a steer. We've got to get the man who did this double kill. We've got to, Joe. You're young. You've got a certain amount of common sense. You're good— square. I'm all for you, Joe. But we've got to work fast. We've got to get the man who actually did this—and his confederates. All of them. Believe me, Joe; I'll protect you, your family, if I have to use the whole police department."

Joe shook his head, whispered hoarsely, "I—I don't know, Inspector. I don't know."

Brinkhaus thumped his heels to the desk, leaned on big fists. Joe crouched back a bit, looked up at Brinkhaus. Suddenly one of Brinkhaus's fists unfolded; a broad forefinger pointed at Joe.

"Looka here, Joe. Now looka here. You know, see? You know all about it. You saw the guy, Joe! Are you goin' to double-cross us by keepin' your jaw shut? Are you goin' to let the mug that bumped off your pop and that little kid get away? Are you?"

Joe gulped. "Honest, Sergeant—"

"Honest my eye! I can tell by the look in your eyes that you ain't tellin' the truth. You ain't on the up and up, Joe. You're double-crossin' us, and you're fixin' so's the wiper 'll get away. You ain't helpin' justice, Joe. We're good guys here. We liked your old man. He was the squarest spaghetti bender that ever planked his pants down in Portsend. But he was old-time Wop, and he was borned and brung up with the idea that silence is gold or somethin'. Which is a lot o' liverwurst. And you know it. For cryin' out loud, son, do the bright thing and spring what you know."

Joe took his hands off his hat, gripped the hard smooth arms of the oak-veneered chair. He looked into the big, hard eyes of Brinkhaus—brown eyes, round and staring, that seemed to cover him all over. He knew Brinkhaus. He liked Brinkhaus—old "Sergeant Brinky."

HE COULDN'T look any longer. He shifted his eyes and looked at Larsen. Blue eyes there, cool and oddly dreamy and infinitely wise. Kind eyes—but steady, too. Steady and strangely penetrating for all their mildness. Suddenly they moved nearer across the desk.

"You know, Joe, I know you know. I pledge myself to protect you and your mother and brother and sister. You know my reputation, Joe. I wouldn't let you down. Give us a break. Forget this damned tradition of silence. It's barbaric. You know it is."

Joe shook his head.

"I told you, Inspector—"

Brinkhaus grabbed his arm.

"You didn't tell us the truth! You're lyin', Joe! We want the truth. We want to know who you saw run out of the store."

"You've got to tell us," Larsen said. "I'm not going to let this tradition come between a pinch. I'm going to make a pinch and you're going to help me."

"Spring it, Joe!" Brinkhaus said, shaking him.

"For God's sake, I don't know!"

Larsen pointed at him. "You do, Joe! Do you realize that you're impeding justice? That you're abetting a criminal? That whatever personal motives you may have the law won't recognize them? Do you?"

"God, Inspector—"

"And this," Brinkhaus rumbled. "We'll hold you, Joe. We'll hold you because you saw the killer."

"I'll hold you, Joe," Larsen said. "I'll lock you up. I won't book you. I'll lock you up until you come across."

"You wouldn't do that!"

"I would. I will. I intend to. Unless you tell me—right now—who you saw leave the store. Remember, Joe, I can be almighty hard. I like you but I won't let that stop me from making you come across. It's my job to get the killer. I can suspect you of being in cahoots with the killer! I can make you tell, Joe, and I will!"

Joe hardened his jaw, shook his head.

"No you won't."

It was the first challenge. And it was by way of being an admission that he knew.

"You won't tell?" Larsen said.

"I won't tell."

Brinkhaus shook him, lifted him out of the chair. Larsen got up and came around, grabbing his other arm.

"You're going to tell," Larsen said with a quiet deadliness. "You're going to tell me here, Joe, or you're going downstairs to a cell-block. You're going to tell me or I'm going to have you grilled all night and all day and all of another night. I'll break you down, Joe. I've broken stronger men than you—and I'll break you if I have to. Now what is it, Joe?"

Joe could not move because Larsen and Brinkhaus held him in grips of iron. Their faces were very near, very grim and determined and relentless. He felt a little giddy, and all color had drained from his face. He felt a little hysterical, too.

"You can't do it. You can't do it! You can't hold me! I haven't done anything! I haven't done a thing!"

"You're doing everything to let the killer escape," Larsen flung back at him. "And I can do a lot of things. I'll do them. I'll break this case, Joe. I'll break it and make a collar if I have to frame you!"

They tightened up on him.

Larsen said, "What will it be, Joe? Are you going to give me a steer—"

"No! No! No!" Joe screamed. "You can't make me tell! I won't!" He struggled with a new frenzy. He kicked and cried out and his eyes blazed dark and turbulent, and in the chaos of his emotion he saw Larsen and Brinkhaus as mortal enemies, as ogres, fiends.

Brinkhaus said, "Leggo, boss."

Larsen let go and Brinkhaus, an old cop, tied Joe up suddenly and twisted him back into the chair.

"Take him down, Brinky," Larsen said. "Put Girolamo and Spinozi on him for a while."

When Brinkhaus returned to the office Larsen was pacing up and down. Larsen stopped, made a vague gesture with both hands, grimaced.

"I hate to do this, Brinky," he said with emotion. "I hate like the very hell to do it! I like that kid. He's fine. But I've got to get a steer. I've got to break him—for his own good! I'm sick as hell of this no spikka English, this old Italian custom. He saw that killer. He knows him! But a jumbled tradition and perhaps a dying promise extracted by the old man is keeping his mouth closed. No faith in law, no faith in its protection. They take the easiest route of silence. Even though their flesh and blood has been snuffed out. All of them! Even the little girl's father and mother. Dumb. No hear, no see, no speak."

"You got any idea, boss, why Cappy was smoked out?"

"No. None. As far as I know he was in on no racket. He was a clean, honest Dago."

Brinkhaus scratched the back of his neck.

"Yeah. Maybe that was the trouble. Me, I can't figure Dagoes. They clan together, settle in one neighborhood, and then suddenly they bust out like a rash and start mobbin' out each other."

Down in City Hall Square the newsboys were yelling, "Extra! Extra! Double killin'! Get y' extra here!"

IT SPREAD to every nook and cranny of Little Italy. Though a man and a child had been shot to death, though the man was beloved of the neighborhood, the child little more than an infant, the custom of silence spread. Mothers held their infants closer, fathers admonished youngsters sagely. They prayed for the souls of the dead, hurried to console the two stricken families, for they were a sympathetic, emotional people; but the silence remained, grew tighter, knotted up.

Surely someone in that street—at least half a dozen—had seen that gray Cadillac phaeton roll through Cherry Street. But in the face of the police they were pious, wide-eyed, innocent. The Italian Squad threshed the district. Its men spoke in Italian, pleaded, wheedled, browbeat, stormed. They collared every man with a police record. Sometimes they were rough. They ransacked every garage, public and private, dusted through houses, cellars, flats, speakeasies, window-tapping joints. They were an earnest, grim and hard-boiled body of men and they turned Little Italy upside down, shook it, dumped it back on its feet again and left it—in silence.

While at headquarters Joe Capillari cringed beneath a barrage of rapid-fire questions. Larsen had ordered that no blows be laid on him. But Girolamo and Spinozi gave Joe no rest. One, then the other, whipped questions, threats; or both at the same time, one on either side of Joe.

Larsen took a hand, talked himself blue in the face, until his collar wilted and his yellow hair fell in gobs across his sweaty forehead. He had no doubt that Joe knew his father's murderer. He was stretching his authority to the limit, beyond the limit, but he was sincere and he was making a mighty effort to tear down the barriers of a vicious tradition. Against a boy he liked, a boy he knew was innately good.

Back in his office, he combed his hair and straightened his tie, took a jolt of Scotch, listened to the drone of the dispatcher's voice coming through the loud-speaker. The personnel of the force had been thrown into action fifteen minutes after the crime. Yet nothing tangible was in hand. Eight Cadillacs were held up. Owners got indignant, ranted over telephones. It developed that only one of the eight was a gray phaeton, and that was owned by an Episcopalian minister in the fashionable West End. Headquarters and all the station houses were filled with suspects. Bondsmen remained close by their telephones. Amateur criminologists kept telephoning and offering ideas. In the late editions newspapers tacked up rewards.

Brinkhaus rolled in, his usual calm knocked into a cocked hat.

"If only that gazabo would open up. If only we could get a steer and start after some guy. Any guy. Just so long as we could start after him."

"They couldn't have lammed out of town," Larsen said. "We had all the roads blocked within half an hour, all the suburban trolleys and busses watched for suspicious characters, and the railroad station. This job was done by a guy I'll bet we've met before. A real hood. And an important one. Else Joe would not be taking a sweat now."

The telephone rang. Larsen answered it. He frowned, bit his lip, said, "All right, send her up," and put the phone down.

"His sister," he said. "Rosa Cappillari."

Brinkhaus reached for his hat.

"I ain't goin' to hang around any hysterical jane. Be seein' you."

"Leave the door open, Brinky."

Rosa came in grave-faced and Larsen, standing, made a slight bow, a palm-upward gesture toward a chair. She sat down and Larsen sat down facing her and leaned back, creaking his swivel chair. She looked at him steadily with her lovely dark eyes.

"Why can't Joe come home?" she said tonelessly.

"Because I decided to hold him for questioning."

"Why?"

"He was in the store when your father and Sophia Simioni were killed. He's holding back the name of the man who did the crime."

"How do you know he is?"

"He as much as admitted it."

Her voice kept toneless and low and her eyes were steady, but Larsen knew that her emotion was knotted up inside her and that the flat glibness with which she spoke was merely another form of emotion.

"Is that a crime?" she asked.

"I am trying to believe that it's as much a crime as if two gangsters killed a man and the one refused to give the name of the one that got away. Joe knows. I hate to hold him, but on the other hand I want to get the man who killed your father."

She said, "How long will you hold him?"

"Until he talks."

"But maybe he won't talk."

LARSEN leaned forward, spoke softly. "I'll hold him and keep on holding him. I'll grill him hour after hour, as he's being grilled now. No rest. No sleep."

She touched her breast.

"He won't talk—because he knows if he does—he knows that vengeance will come back at us. Mama and little Adamo and me. That's why he won't talk. Joe is no criminal. Joe is a good boy. He loves us."

"I know," said Larsen, nodding. "I know Joe is a fine boy. But the murderer must not be allowed to get away if we can help it. And Joe can help it. He must be made to realize that we can protect him and his family."

She looked around the room.

"I want to see him."

"You can't. I'm sorry."

Her eyes whipped back to Larsen, became suddenly alive.

"I know!" she cried. "You—they've been beating him!"

"They haven't laid a hand on him."

"They have! You can't do that to Joe!"

"He's being grilled. Just grilled. My orders. And he'll be grilled all night, if he lasts that long, and then grilled again as soon as we can wake him up."

She fell back in the chair, wilted, put her hands to her eyes.

"Oh Joe," she whimpered brokenly.

Larsen grimaced. He got up slowly, sighed, walked slowly to a window and looked down into the street. Looked up at the early stars. He was not a cold-blooded man. He knew he had taken the bull by the horns. And he knew that he had to steel himself against letting down.

Rosa was saying, "You will kill Joe. He is not strong."

"He will have to talk."

He heard the chair scrape. He turned around. Rosa was standing, trembling, her nails digging into her palms. Dark red color flooded the tawny-brown of her smooth, oval face. Her breath came hoarsely in uneven explosive outbursts, her breast convulsed spasmodically.

"What—what kind of protection?" she cried.

Larsen squinted. "What do you mean?"

"For us."

"Anything and everything within my power. Special undercover men to watch you at all times until the murderer and anyone connected with him is in our hands."

She felt her throat. "But—Joe would have to identify!"

Larsen nodded. Rosa covered her eyes with her hands, shook her head, sobbed. Larsen crossed the office, cupped a hand under her elbow, looked down gravely at her dark shiny hair.

"Maybe you know," he said.

She looked up suddenly at him, biting her lip. Tears dropped from her eyes. Her jaw hardened, and her nostrils dilated.

"I was not there. I have only a suspicion."

"Tell me."

Horror welled in her eyes. She drove it back with a visible effort. Larsen steadied her with his hands gripping her arms gently but firmly.

"I don't know," she said, breathless. "I may be all wrong. It is hard to say. Papa—a week ago papa had an argument with Niccolo Luigi. In the store. I was in the back. They didn't know I was there. Nick and I—Nick had been taking me out. I met him several months ago at the street festival in Napoli Lane. He was tall and handsome and very agreeable.

"My father saw us once after that and scolded me. He said I should never see Nick again. I asked him why. He wouldn't tell but he was very shaken up. But Nick met me after that and we went around places. Then I told him I couldn't see him any more. He began to make me uneasy. He was so nice and had such a nice smile all the time—it began to be sinister. I can't explain why—but it was.

"Then he came to the store that day, when I was in the back, and I heard him ask papa if he said I shouldn't meet him. Papa said yes, and they got in an argument. Papa got very excited and finally he said, 'Nick, I tell you, stay away from Rosa. You don't stay away from Rosa and I will tell the cops about that business last June.' Then there was silence, and then Nick walked out, without saying anything."

She wiped her eyes with her handkerchief. Little sobs kept breaking from her throat.

"It—it may be nothing," she said. "But the way Nick walked out—without saying anything. And when I saw my father he was angry and shaking and then he put his arms around me and held me tight."

Larsen patted her shoulder.

"There may be nothing in this," he said. "We'll see. You're a very brave girl, Rosa. I'm going to let Joe go home with you. I want you to impress on him we're his friends. Keep him home unless you hear from me. Try to convince him that his best course is to tell us the truth and that—"

The door whipped open. Brinkhaus growled.

"Joe got away!"

Rosa cried out. Larsen said nothing. His lips tightened, his hand tightened on the girl.

Brinkhaus said, "Girolamo and Spinozi left him in a room with old Keller. They thought he was passed out. He socked Keller on the dome with a desk lamp, took Keller's gun and beat it. There was no one in the halls. He went out through the gym past the gun range—covered Merrick there—and lit out through the garage. I'll go after him with some boys—"

"No," Larsen clipped. "Not a bit of it, Brinky. He's steamed up and he's got a gun. I don't want"—he moved a knotted fist up and down grimly—"I don't want that boy to make a killing."

"But, cripes, boss—"

"You heard me, Brinky. He'll cool off. Let him beat it." He turned to Rosa. "You go home now. When Joe comes home you take him in hand. I'm depending on you. Get that gun away from him. Return it to me."

"You—you won't harm him—for this?"

"Quick. Home, Rosa. I won't harm him. For your sake. But you've got to help me. Will you?"

"I promise," she choked. "Yes, yes, I promise. Oh, I thank you so."

"Your place will be guarded, at any rate. You won't know the men who are guarding it, because that's safer. Now—go. Take a taxi. I'd send Sergeant Brinkhaus with you but it'll be best if you're not seen on the streets with a policeman."

HE TOOK her to the door, opened it and took her downstairs to a side entrance, where she went out. He went briskly through the central room, where half a dozen detectives were waiting. He shook his head, his hands.

"I'm letting Cappillari go."

He went on down a corridor, entered an office. Sergeant Pozzo looked up. "Hello, Inspector," he said.

"Lou, two of your best undercover men to watch Cappillari's place. On regular shifts. But send two now. Have 'em disguised. Night and day. And I'll put a cop on peg post in Cherry Street, too. On the double, Lou."

"Oke."

Larsen, his yellow hair flying, hurried downstairs and into a room where old Keller sat in a chair looking woe-begone. Girolamo and Spinozi were rubbing his head with ice.

"Hurt much?" Larsen asked.

"No—but, b' cripes, I never expected it," Keller groaned.

"When I lay my paws on that baby—" Girolamo snarled.

"We're not tailing him," Larsen said.

"Not tail—"

"Exactly. I'm giving the lad a break. And if I find out that you boys laid a hand on him I'll attend to you personally. Do you remember the number of your gun, Keller?"

"No, sir."

"Spinozi, look it up."

Larsen went upstairs, taking steps three at a time. He strode purposefully into his office, stuck a cigarette in his mouth, got a light from Brinky's cigar.

"Now, get this, Brinky. We may have a bum steer, but we'll find out. I don't want a general alarm on this little job, but I want you and three picked men—you can pick them—to work with me. Locate Nick Luigi. Get your stoolies working. Locate him and find the strength of his mob. Get every man of his mob located. When you do that, draw on more men and set a man out to watch each one of Luigi's, to follow and know at all times where each of Luigi's men is."

Brinky grinned.

"Been gettin' on the inside track?"

"I don't know yet. And understand this, and make your men understand it. I don't want a pinch yet. I want Luigi located and every man in his mob. But no pinch. Until I say so. Is that clear, Brinky?"

"Clear as clear, boss."

"Then sail."

Brinkhaus went out whistling and Larsen took a few turns up and down his office, rubbing the hair at his temples back with the heels of his hands, staring hard at the floor. Then he rang for a civil clerk.

"Down to the record room, Martin, and lug up the records of unsolved crimes during June of last year."

In ten minutes he was wading through sheafs of typewritten reports. He studied, weighed, discarded. Most of the crimes were petty ones: assault and battery, petty larceny, two knifings in the Black Belt and one cake-slashing—assault and mayhem. A bombing in the Greek quarter—no deaths. Robbery and murder at the Blue Spruce Inn on the night of June 14, 1930. There had been a big Saturday night crowd at the inn on Ocean Pike. Five men, masked, armed, walked in, raided the till, robbed eighty guests and shot down and killed a man who had offered resistance.

In jewelry and cash—a loot of approximately ten thousand dollars. And a clean getaway. Detective-Sergeant Hyams had handled the case; died of the flu the following winter. A stolen car had been found abandoned near a florist's hothouse, two miles down the road from the inn.

"Well!" said Larsen out loud.

Another car had been waiting there.

"H'm!"

The caretaker at the hot-house, a man named Sebastiano, had heard a car out front but hadn't looked. This was among the minor details. As, also, was the notation that the hot-house was owned by Demetrio Cappillari, wholesale and retail florist.

CHAPTER THREE

HEARTS AND FLOWERS

B **RINKHAUS AND** his men dived into the city, bored down into its nether world. They went quietly, with precision and dispatch. No fanfare, no display or ceremony. Each went his secret way, each tapped fonts of underworld knowledge, spoke quietly but to the point with those shadow men who stand precariously between the law and the lawless.

Here and there information was secured, bit by bit; and bit by bit it was built up. Clues are not pulled out of thin air. Nor is the breath of a clue coaxed to life by one man. The system does it, the moving organization of a modern police system and the welding together of stray bits of information.

Toward this end Brinkhaus was relentless, painstaking, and he made his men into a similar mold. No mastermind, but a plain cop who had the knack of asking the right questions and remembering the answers. No executive, no leader, but a hard-headed, honest and thorough sergeant.

At ten that night he tramped into Larsen's office. Larsen, who had not left the building since early evening, was eating hamburgers and drinking hot coffee, his coat off and his collar open. Brinkhaus had his hands full of scrawled envelopes and odd pieces of paper. He sat down and tipped back his hat.

"Me notes," he said, frowning importantly. "I picked Butchman, Little and Groves, and we fanned the town. Got their notes too. Nick Luigi's got dough. Me, I got him placed, me personal. He's got an apartment in the Trevelyan Towers and goes Spanish there under the name of Nicolas Cordova. He must have seen a movie once. He's puttin' up a frail there but I ain't got her name."

"Where's that place?"

"Seaview Terrace. You know, overlookin' the bay. Then he's got another layout in Fallon Street—a two-story frame house rented by his right-hand man Ignatz Mojecki, a Polack. Nick hangs out at the Big Italy Restaurant, the Casonova Club, a speak at 19 Waters and another at 206 Linden. His mob pals at them joints too.

"Then there's Tony Cario, who lives at the Merit Hotel with a hood named 'Creeper' Pazzi—you know 'The Creep,' who makes knives out of files. Guido Mattanzio and 'Berries' Dvinak live at the layout in Fallon Street, and 'Jo-jo' Michaels, a young punk, hangs his hat on the hook of a Portuguese dame in Slow Street, number 62.

"As Little says—you know Art—he says they're general sort of practitioners. He got it straight from a stool o' his that they got their mitts in dope, the lottery racket, the old badger game—which is still payin' good—and plenty stick-ups."

"And that's the whole mob?"

"Me and the boys checked up on the dope we got and it all figures that that's the mob. They don't play with beer or alky. They're workin' a few call-houses for the badger game, but they're off vice in a big way."

Larsen drained his coffee cup.

"Great work, Brinky. Now get Butchman, Little and Groves on the job. Keep those addresses covered constantly. You'll need more men. I want an eye on every one of those heels at all times."

Brinkhaus shuffled his notes together.

"It's done, boss. I hauled out Jonson, Metz and Zimmermann and sent 'em with Butchman, Little and Groves to keep the tail hot and tight."

"Brinky," said Larsen admiringly, "I guess I could take a vacation any time and leave you in full charge here."

"Shucks," said Brinkhaus, grinning.

Larsen pointed.

"Like a good scout, Brinky, look up Cappy's telephone number. I want to speak to the girl."

Brinkhaus picked up the telephone directory as the phone rang. Larsen answered it. He stopped a cigarette halfway to his mouth and stared hard at the desk.

"Yes, this is Inspector Larsen.... He hasn't! Well, why didn't you call me?... I see. I know, but you should have let.... But be steady now. Has he telephoned?... Yes, I heard you.... Now listen. Stay there.

If he calls, let me know right away. And try to be calm. But stay there until you hear from me…. Yes, your place is covered. You're perfectly safe."

He hung up slowly, leaving his hands on the instrument, staring into space with his eyes suddenly vague and dreamy. Brinkhaus knew that queer look. It meant that Larsen was stirred up, that an obstacle had arisen suddenly against him and cornered him.

And then his voice, soft and far-away. "Joe never showed up at home, Brinky."

Brinkhaus frowned.

"Gosh!"

"He's loose in the city—with Keller's gun."

"Gosh!"

Larsen took his hands off the telephone, looked at them. The palms had become sweaty suddenly.

Brinkhaus, staring round-eyed at him, gulped. "We should have busted out right after him. We should have—when he lammed like that—we should—"

"I wanted to give him a break. He's a good lad. When he lammed out of here he was all worked up—blind, unreasonable. A boy—even a good boy—in a condition like that, with a gun, is dangerous. We might have had to shoot him. One or more of our men might have got shot. I did what I thought was best."

"I know, boss, I know," Brinkhaus muttered, his brown eyes stirring. "We got to get that kid, boss."

"He's scared—just scared. We must have scared the wits out of him. Yes, we've got to get him. There'd be no use hauling in Nick and his mob unless we had Joe to identify the killer. But"—he ground his palms together—"we've got to be careful, Brinky. I promised his sister. Joe with that gun is a dangerous boy to have loose. And I'm"—he stood up, taking a breath—"in no bed of roses right now."

"General alarm—"

Larsen snorted.

"Anything but! The papers don't know we had Joe here. Nobody knows but you and our men. It's got to stay that way until we get Joe. Meantime, a close watch on Nick's mob. I stand a swell chance of getting the razzberry and facing a police trial if this case goes haywire. Take Girolamo and Spinozi and fan the flophouses."

He knotted his tie, put on his coat, took out a holster and gun, clipped the holster to his pants belt.

"Where you goin', boss?" Brinkhaus said.

"On my lonesome."

JOE WAS DRUNK. Joe, who had never before taken a drink, was drunk. He had walked the streets for hours and then he had gone into a speakeasy and taken Scotch. He had gone to other speakeasies.

He was in one now, leaning against the bar, still drinking Scotch. The bar was crowded and Joe stood against it like a man, his straw hat tipped down over his eyes, his eyes narrowed and his mouth a tight, grim line. The conversation of men made only a vague hum and drone in his ears. He emptied his drink and went out into a dark street.

He walked with his chest out, the back of his neck straight, his chin down. He felt old and grim and the liquor made a faint singing noise in his ears. Sometimes the street lights danced. He passed a cop on the corner, but he wasn't afraid. He chuckled in his throat and went on.

The gun was warm in his pocket because he never took his hand off it. His step felt light and springy. He had a feeling that he was strong and dangerous and that he could lick anybody. He stopped in a dark, deserted alley, squared off, muttered threats at an imaginary enemy, whipped out the gun, laughed, put it back in his pocket again and went on. His chest swelled. He felt mighty. He didn't know that the faint singing in his ears indicated a heart that was not as strong as it might have been.

He sloped down into an areaway speak, slapped a half dollar on the bar.

"Gimme Scotch, guy—straight."

There were not many people in the bar. The bartender poured a pony of Scotch, gave Joe a blank stare, slid across the glass. Joe downed it.

"Again, guy."

The bartender smirked.

"Lookin'-glass drunk, eh?"

"Cut out the wisecracks, bimbo."

"O.K., O.K.," the bartender said with uneasy cheerfulness.

Joe drank three and pushed out into the street. He took in a reef on his belt, looked truculently up and down the street. He took a punch at a pole.

"Right now," he muttered, "I can lick any six guys."

He headed for Union Circle, crossed it and went down Union Avenue past a row of noisy radio shops. The fumes of the liquor began to smoke through his head. His feet lagged a bit. But he set his jaw harder. The streets got quieter, darker. He turned into Fallon and went down the hill. Half-way down he crossed the street, pushed open a rusty iron gate and climbed wooden steps to a small porch. He pressed a button, stood swaying on his feet.

His gun was in his hand, the butt close to his side. When the door opened he snapped, "Stick 'em up!"

He was facing a red-headed girl. She gasped, stepped back, raising her hands. Joe sagged in, kicked the door shut with his heel.

"Where's Nick Luigi?" he said.

"He—ain't—here."

"Back up."

She backed up and they went into a large living room where a blonde was lighting a cigarette.

"Stick 'em up!" Joe rasped.

The blonde left the cigarette between her lips and raised her hands. The two girls looked at him fixedly.

"Where's he?" Joe snapped.

"I told you he ain't here," the red-head said.

"Who's he lookin' for?" the blonde asked.

"Nick."

"Nick ain't here," the blonde said. "For God's sake, honey, don't fool around with that gun."

"I ain't foolin'," Joe said.

The red-head tried a winning smile.

"Gee, boy friend, you're just about the toughest guy I ever seen."

"Yeah?" said Joe, swaying.

"I wouldn't kid you."

Joe felt hot. Heat waves lapped up his body. The floor heaved like the deck of a boat and the girls looked funny and vague, their faces blurred. He ground his teeth together.

"Where hell's Nick?" His voice was thick. "Y' got' tell me where's Nick!"

He staggered, struck a table. The electric lamp on it tipped, but didn't fall over. Joe's feet scuffled on the carpet, the muzzle of his gun swung around. He tried to plant his feet against the heave of the floor.

The red-head came up close to him, said lovingly, "Gee, boy, you're sick. You ain't feelin' well. Sit down a minute. You wouldn't hurt a woman, would you?"

Joe fell into an arm-chair. The red-head sat on the arm of it, put her arm around him, pressed her cheek against his. Joe closed his eyes. Her cheek felt cool and she smelled nice. He could feel sweat rolling down his chest. His head spun. He let the last thin, taut string of resistance go and was swept into a vast darkness.

Cautiously the red-head took his gun, stood up, said, "Whew!" and wagged her head.

"Gosh, Mabel," the blonde said, "who is this kid?"

"Ask me another, sweetheart. I don't know him from Eve's weakness. But he's gunning for Nick. I'm jumpy. Whew! To think of this heel wobbling in here with this gat."

The blonde said, "Listen, Mabel. I'm leaving this scatter. Come on. This is no place for two nice young things like I and you. Me for the wide open spaces. This John is headed for more than a bust in the mouth and I don't want to answer pointed questions at headquarters. You heard Jo-jo say the gang was coming here. Take his gun and we'll ditch it somewhere."

The doorbell rang.

Mabel said, "Oh-oh."

The blonde said, "Well, here's hearts and flowers for somebody, darling."

The red-head set her jaw. "Quick. Take his legs. In that closet with him."

"For cryin' out loud—"

"Quick! I'm not going to be party to no murder!"

They lifted Joe, lugged him across the room, piled him into a large clothes closet. The red-head closed the door, ran to the table, shoved the gun into her pocketbook.

"Get the door," she clipped. "And act like we been smoking Murads."

The blonde took a long breath, exhaled, then sauntered out into the hall trying out a dizzy smile. She opened the front door and some men came in.

"We thought you'd never come, Nick," she said.

"Come on, baby, you and Mabel take the air," he said, striding past her and swinging into the living-room. "Hello, Mabel. Go places. Take a trot down to the Casonova. The girls are there and we'll try to join you later."

"Why the run-around, good-looking?"

Nick Luigi, black-haired, handsome, said, "Come on, you heard me. We got to talk business here."

The others drifted in. Broken-nosed Iggie Mojecki. Little, fat-faced Guido Mattanzio. Creeper Pazzi, of the sliding eyes. Rock-built "Berries" Dvinak, who used cigars for chewing-tobacco. Tony Cario, humming, executing fancy steps. Jo-jo Michaels, with a cast in one eye and part of one ear gone—Jo-jo the Punk.

The red-head said, "Well, come on, beautiful," to the blonde. "Maybe we can find soma gigolos at the Casonova."

The blonde hurried, grinning dizzily.

"Listen," said Mojecki, "has this dame been hittin' up the giggle-water again?"

"Farewell, fish-face," the red-head gave him as she pushed the blonde into the hall.

CHAPTER FOUR

FRAME

LARSEN walked down Fallon alone and Brinkhaus stepped out of a shadow. "Hey, boss," he said softly.

"Hello, Brinky. What are you doing down here?"

"I just run into Butchman at Fallon and Casey. The boys are down the street further. Nick and his gang are all together and they just went in his dump down the street."

"Any sight of Joe?"

"No."

Larsen said, "I got a tip in a speak over on the east side. Joe's drunk and he's been making the rounds. He's been in several places but I've lost the tail. I'll never lay me down to sleep until I find Joe. Where's the rest of the boys?"

"Down further."

Larsen and Brinkhaus moved down the street.

"Who was watching the house?" Larsen asked.

"George Metz."

Butchman and Groves stepped from a doorway. Butchman said, "Listen, inspector. I was just speakin' to Metz. There's another guy in that mob. We got the seven accounted for, but Metz says a guy went in the house about twenty minutes ago. That'd make eight."

"Before the others?"

"Yeah."

"Was he let in or did he have a key?"

"He was let in. Metz says two janes went in a couple of hours ago. I guess the janes let him in. Metz says he thinks the guy was tight."

They moved on down the street and joined Metz and the others.

"Yeah," Metz said, to Larsen's question, "he was tight. He crossed the street when he reached that lamp-post. A young kid. I guess a punk."

Larsen's revolving thoughts stopped and one leaped out and shimmered in his brain. Half a block farther on was the house. Metz pointed it out. Larsen looked at it.

Butchman muttered, "Somebody comin' out."

The plainclothesmen moved back into the shadows.

"The two janes," Metz whispered.

The two girls came up the hill, their high heels rapping the sidewalk.

Larsen said, "You boys stay here."

He left them, sauntered across the street and reached the sidewalk opposite as the girls slowed down. Larsen stopped in front of them. The girls stopped.

"Well?" snapped the red-head.

"Where are you girls going?"

"No place that 'd interest you," said the red-head.

"On the contrary—"

"Nix on the ritzy line, big boy."

Larsen said, "Larsen's the name. Headquarters."

The girls looked at each other, startled. Larsen was tranquil.

"I just thought you might tell me who went in that house down the street before the crowd came."

The red-head looked at the blonde.

"Gee, honey, did you let anybody in?"

"Oh, no, I didn't let nobody in. Did you?"

"You know I didn't."

They turned surprised looks on Larsen. Larsen smiled with faint irony. "I wouldn't try that sort of stuff if I were you."

"Honest, Mr. Larsen!"

"So help me, Mr. Larsen!"

Larsen said, chuckling softly, "No go, little girls. The place has been watched. We saw the man go in. Now be good and you can go on about your business. Try to take me for a two-year-old and you'll be sorry."

"If a guy went in," the red-head snapped indignantly, "then he sneaked in! Come on, honey." She gripped the blonde's arm and tried to start past.

Larsen grabbed at her. She flung up her hand and he caught hold of her large purse, ripped it free. Both girls kicked him. His fingers felt a familiar shape through the purse's cloth. He whistled. Brinkhaus, Little and Groves came over and took hold of the girls. Larsen opened the purse, took out a gun. "Big—for a little girl," he mocked quietly.

He went to a house-wall, struck a match, looked at the gun. One eyelid lowered. His lips set. The match went out. He turned to Brinkhaus.

"It's Keller's," he muttered. "Same number."

Brinkhaus stared. Larsen crowded the girls. "What happened to the kid that went in that house? No lip, now—and no lies!"

"Well," the red-head panted, "he was drunk. Plastered. He come in jabbin' the gun in my face. He couldn't hardly stand up. Finally he fell in a chair and passed out and I took it away from him."

"And you left him there for those seven mugs that just went in, didn't you?"

"No. I was scared. I didn't want to be mixed up in no trouble. So we hid him—I and my girl friend here. Didn't we, honey? In the living room closet we hid him."

"Sure we did. And he's still there."

"We hid him and I put the gun in my purse like you found it. Then—the guys came. We hid him because we heard the guys comin'. And they chased us. Honest, we didn't want no trouble. The kid was nuts—pure meshuga. He was wantin' to kill Nick. He was all steamed up about somethin'."

Larsen moistened his lips.

"Butchman, handcuff these two, grab a taxi up the street and take 'em to headquarters. Don't say anything or book 'em. Just keep them there. I'll probably let them go. But take 'em."

When Butchman had gone Larsen got his men together. Brinkhaus, Little and Groves, Jonson, Metz and Zimmermann. They went into a huddle in a dark areaway. Larsen spoke under his breath. "It's Joe, all right, in that house. There's no telling how long he'll stay under—in that closet. If they find him it will be just too bad. The kid got loaded on hooch and I guess decided that he'd wipe the slate clean. We've got to get that kid without a scratch on him. Right now nothing else matters. Get that. Nothing else matters but getting that kid out of a jam. That clear?"

His men nodded and Larsen gave brief instructions.

THEY moved down the street. Larsen and Brinkhaus walked ahead rapidly. The others split up. Some took up posts directly across the street from the house. Others crept within a dozen feet of the house and buried themselves in shadows.

Larsen and Brinkhaus climbed the steps to the porch and Larsen rang the bell. A light went on in the hall. The lock clicked and the door opened on a crack.

"Larsen and Brinkhaus," Larsen said. "I want to have a talk with Nick Luigi."

He shoved the door open and Iggie Mojecki stumbled backward. Brinkhaus followed, closed the door, put his hand behind his back and set the catch on the snap-lock so that it wouldn't snap shut. A head looked out of the living room door.

"Hello, Nick," said Larsen, walking down the hall.

"Oh—hello. This is a surprise, Inspector."

"Thought it might be."

Larsen stood in the doorway, ran his calm blue eyes over the men seated around the table.

"Just a little family gathering, I suppose."

"Yeah. Just," Nick said, grinning.

Larsen located the closet door. He said, "We're cleaning out some houses in this neighborhood, Nick. You and the boys will have to put your coats on and take the air."

Nick looked puzzled. "What?"

"Do I have to say that all over?"

"But what's the idea?"

"I'm closing it up, Nick. I don't want any arguments. Just take the air."

Nick looked at him, bit his lip, shrugged. "O.K. I don't get this at all but— O.K. Come on, boys. The inspector has a brain-wave all of a sudden."

Nick put on his coat, buttoned up his vest. The others rose and did likewise, taking their time. Larsen stepped into the living room and Brinkhaus followed.

Suddenly there was a thumping sound. Larsen's heart missed a beat. Nick and his mob tensed.

The closet door whipped open and Joe reeled out. He fell against Nick, gripped him for support, stared at him with glazed eyes. At first he didn't know it was Nick. But through the haze he realized.

He screamed. "You—murderer! You—killed—papa!"

Jo-jo Michaels snarled, "A frame!" and went for his gun.

Brinkhaus fired and the shot shook the room. Jo-jo leaped backward with a piercing scream and went through one of the front windows with his head and shoulders. Glass shattered.

Nick ripped out an oath, hurled Joe from him. Weak-kneed, Joe toppled back into the closet.

Tony Cario, agile as a rabbit, bounded to the door. Guido Mattanzio bounded at the same, was just as agile. They crashed together and Berries Dvinak tried to wade through both of them.

Nick pivoted as his gun leaped into his hand. Larsen was looking at him with a fixed dreamy expression. He shook his head ever so slightly.

Flame burst from his revolver and Nick turned around, staring, and caught hold of the back of a chair, grimacing. Larsen took a long leap, slammed shut the closet door, hid Joe.

Little and Groves came running down the hall, followed by Metz and Zimmermann. Berries Dvinak, having forced his way between Tony Cario and Guido Mattanzio, rose and opened his mouth in shock and terror. His big super-automatic came up. Little fired twice and Dvinak put his head on one shoulder, wore a stupid glass-eyed stare and began backing down the hall on slow feet. Suddenly he crumpled.

Tony Cario, rising, took Groves' blackjack between the eyes. Cario flung backward, careened off Brinkhaus and took a bullet in the back that Creeper Pazzi had meant for Brinkhaus. It broke his spine and he fell against the chair on which Nick was leaning; knocked it over. Nick swore hysterically, ran to one of the front windows. He heard a shot whang past his ear, saw it tear away the window-sash. He spun into the nearest corner, fired blindly.

Zimmermann, leaping through the door, was turned half around by the bullet.

Larsen let fly with a shot that pinned Nick in the corner and Nick made a sour face and slid down the wall. Little and Groves clubbed Iggie Mojecki to the floor and Brinkhaus, gnawing on his under lip, knocked one of Creeper Pazzi's legs from under him with a low shot and Metz got Pazzi from behind with a blackjack.

The echoes of the guns petered out. The plainclothesmen stood around the room, breathing thickly, still holding their guns tightly. Bits of plaster fell from the ceiling and walls. The room was a shambles of broken chairs, broken glass, and prostrate men.

THE PLAINCLOTHESMEN began looking at one another. They were motionless, sweat standing out on their faces.

Brinkhaus broke the silence.

"Is it over?" he wanted to know.

Larsen moved.

"I guess it is. Get the ambulance, Brinky. Also the morgue wagon."

Brinkhaus moved to a telephone.

Larsen turned and opened the closet door. Joe huddled there, his knees up to his chin, his eyes wide. He wasn't so drunk now. The sound of guns is apt to sober any man.

"Get up, Joe," Larsen said.

Joe got up. He didn't say anything. He stood in the room looking around with startled eyes, his face white.

Larsen said, "So it was Nick."

Joe gulped. "I guess—you—heard me—before."

"You fool, what were you trying to do?"

"I—I don't know," Joe said. "I got drunk. I never had a drink before in my life. I got drunk. And I felt I could do anything. I was afraid to go home. I was afraid you'd find me. I heard liquor would steady a man. So I drank it. And then—I don't know—I went sort of out of my head. I wanted to get the man who'd killed papa. Oh, God, what have I done!"

"Steady, Joe," Larsen muttered. "Sit down and pull yourself to-gether."

Larsen crossed the room to Nick Luigi.

"What a sweet frame!" Nick choked.

"No frame," Larsen said. "I knew the kid was in here and I tried to get him out without a fight. But you birds had to go for your guns right away. You might just as well go this way, Nick, because we would have got you anyhow. For this job and for that Blue Spruce Inn job a year ago. Going this way will save the State a lot of expense. You can't bump off babies, Nick—and get away with it."

"How the hell did I know that kid was back there?"

"And you can't bump off good men like Cappillari. Even though he knew about that Blue Spruce Inn job. He was square by you, Nick. He never peeped."

"He was—goin'—to."

"Yes, if you tried to monkey around his daughter."

"It wuss him and de dames alla time—him and de dames," yam-mered Iggie Mojecki through split lips. "I tol' him it wuss no good. But he wuss always afraid from what Cappy knew, and he gets him de bright idea of gettin' de dame to run away wit' him and marry him, figgerin' like he wuss dat Cappy would never pull a snitch on his son-in-law. Yah!"

"O.K., O.K.," said Nick. "Rub it in, Polack. But I'm passin' out here, Iggie—and you're startin' on a long trip to the hot seat."

Iggie gulped, lay back and groaned.

Larsen went out into the hall, where Zimmermann was sitting up, chalk-faced.

"I'm all right," Zimmermann said, smiling up at Larsen.

An ambulance bell clanged outside.

Larsen turned back into the room.

Brinkhaus said, "The cold-meat wagon for Nick."

Larsen bit his lip, crossed the room, laid his hand on Joe's shoulder.

"I'm sending you home to your folks, Joe. They're worried about you. I'm sending you home before the reporters get here. Keep your mouth shut. I'll handle this. I'm giving you a break. We've got every last man of Nick's gang."

"Gee, you're swell, Inspector."

Larsen beckoned to Brinkhaus.

"Take Joe home in a taxi, Brinky."

Joe rose, gripped Larsen's hand. Tears were in Joe's dark eyes.

"Gee, Inspector—"

Larsen nodded to Brinkhaus and Brinkhaus hustled Joe out. The stretcher-bearers came in.

"What the hell started this?" the ambulance doctor said.

Larsen said, "Just an old Italian custom."

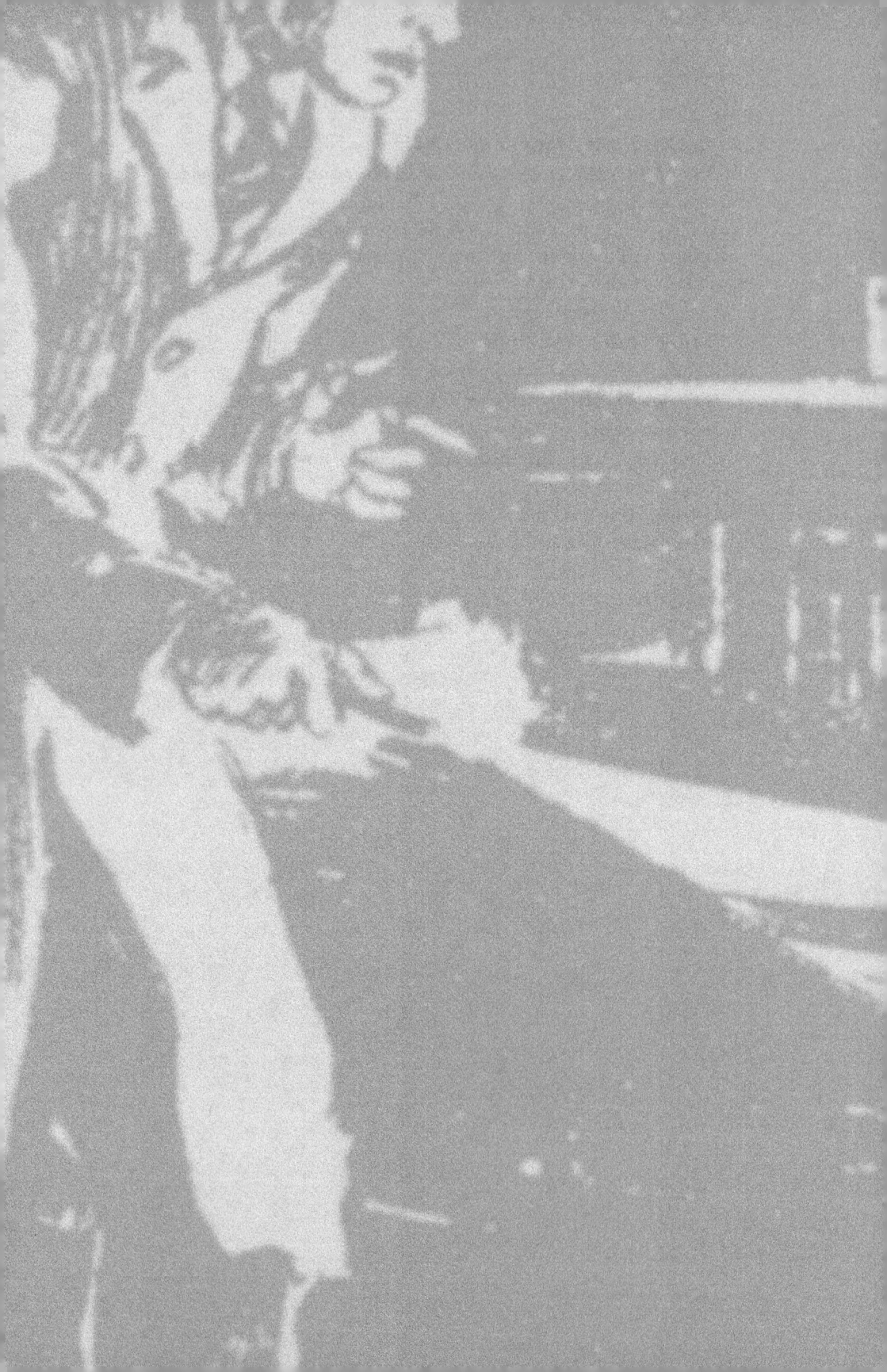

THE X CIRCLE

AN EMPTY ROWBOAT—A
FOOTPRINT IN THE
SAND—THESE WERE THE
ONLY CLUES TO THE
WATERFRONT KILLING.
BUT INSPECTOR LARSEN
FOLLOWED THEM GRIMLY,
SEEKING A MYSTERY GIRL
WHO HAD DISAPPEARED
DOWN A KILLER'S TRAIL.

CHAPTER ONE

MYSTERY WOMAN

HALF A mile south of police headquarters is the waterfront, and the Portsend River, which east from the end of India Street becomes Portsend Harbor. Front Street is the bulwark between city and the river, straggling its battered cobbles from the drawbridge near the freight yards clean around eastward to the Breakwater and Bayside Park, where it becomes Ocean Pike and graduates to smooth cement, swanky apartment houses and impressive lamp posts.

But Front Street is the real waterfront: a mile of cobbles, piers, warehouses, ship chandlers. Here the trucks come up like thunder; here ships go down to the sea. The lamp posts are few and far between, and they aren't impressive. The nights are dark, the smell of the river pungent. The cops travel in pairs and carry their nightsticks in their hands.

Kilkenny's Wharf lies at the foot of Merchant Alley. Kilkenny was a man who made a lot of money in the wholesale junk business, got himself elected to an aldermanic post and in the course of time got himself bumped off for trying to play both ends against the middle.

It was eleven o'clock of an early autumn night when the girl came up the ladder from the river, clawed her way to the wharf and lay flat, breathing hoarsely. Some sheer green material clung wetly to her body. Her bobbed hair stood in wet curls. The wharf was dark, deserted, and back of her the river was a black desert sprinkled with lights of the farther shore and lights that moved. Below her the water made slapping, gurgling sounds among the piles.

In a few minutes she sat up. She ran fingers through her wet curls. She arched her neck. She looked over her shoulder at the dark river. She put up her hands to her ears, as if to shut out the memory of some sound. She stood up, shoeless. She went along the wharf, wincing at touch of the rough boards. She reached the harsher cobbles of Front Street and stopped, listening, peering up and down. River water trickled from the hem of her skirt.

She turned left and crept along in the shadow of a vast, silent warehouse. Once or twice a choked sound issued from her lips. She walked gingerly. The cobbles were rough against her feet. She passed the warehouse and crept along a wooden railing at the river's edge, hastening toward the shadows of another warehouse beyond.

Suddenly she stopped. There was a tiny red glow at the corner of the next building. The point of light arced downward. A few sparks showered. The point of light arced upward, remained motionless— brightened, then dimmed, then brightened again.

The girl crouched against the rail. She was halfway between the two warehouses. She took a step backward, her eyes fastened on the tiny red glow in the shadows beyond. She took another step backward.

One hand rose to her breast. The other remained at her side; knotted, it pressed hard against her thigh. Far off, a tug's whistle snorted, the echoes throbbing across the black water. Nearer, a channel buoy tolled.

The girl shivered. As much from the autumn chill as the touch of fear. She backed up another step. Still that red point of light dimmed, brightened, over and over again. Then suddenly it shot outward, struck the cobbles. Sparks spurted.

Shoes struck the cobbles. The tall figure of a man came out of the shadows, hands in topcoat pockets. The man did not hurry. He almost sauntered, but he came toward the girl.

She turned and ran. She covered perhaps a dozen yards when a stone or a cinder jabbed into her foot. Her left leg buckled. She lost her balance and went down with a little cry. She tried to struggle up but stopped, cringing when she saw the man only a few feet away.

"Well," the man said.

"Let me go!" she cried.

"I haven't touched you yet." His voice was slow, a little amused. "What's all this hocus-pocus?"

Her teeth chattered. "L-let me g-go!"

A flashlight the size of a large fountain pen sprang to life in his hand. The meager beam was strong enough to reveal her dripping dress, her white water-beaded face, her shoeless feet.

"Well!" he said.

"Put that light out!" she said in a low whisper.

"Put that light out!" she
said in a low whisper.

He didn't put it out. "You're scared. Don't be. I'm Inspector Larsen.
I just walked down from headquarters to get the air."

He could see her shivering, heard her teeth chattering. He took
off his topcoat and moved nearer. She shrank away.

"Don't be an idiot," he said.

He draped the coat around her shoulders. Gratefully she drew it
closer.

"I'll get a cab for you," he said. "Come on."

He took her arm and led her toward the shadows of the warehouse
she had attempted before. On the other side was a small watchman's
office. The watchman wasn't there. Larsen stopped in the doorway
and looked down at her. Her hair was black as jet, full of wet little
curls that clung close to her head. She was young, pretty in a wild,
frightened way. Her eyes were round, wide open, dark like her hair.

He said nothing. He crossed the little office to a wall telephone, took a small notebook from his vest pocket, thumbed the pages. He repeated a number half aloud, then took down the receiver, spoke to the operator. Waiting, he turned and leaned against the wall.

He started. The girl was gone from the doorway. He let the receiver hang and sprang to the doorway, looked out—up and down the dark street. She was not in sight. He wheeled back into the office, hung up the receiver, went outside with long strides. He came to a dead stop, his finely chiseled nose in the air, his keen eyes probing the darkness on all sides, first one ear and then the other lifting in quest of stray sounds.

He thought he heard a sound farther along. He started off, a lean soldierly figure of a man dressed in well-cut, conservative clothes. He reached a pier-shed, stopped, listened. He went on a few yards, stopped. A truck slammed past, empty milk pails clanging and banging. He turned and retreated his steps. The sounds of the milk truck petered out. Larsen stopped in front of the watchman's office, put his hands on his hips.

"I'm damned," he muttered.

He went on toward the shadows from which the girl had first come. He stopped at the foot of Kilkenny's Wharf, walked out to the end of it. It was deserted. He heard a thumping sound and looked over the edge. A rowboat was moored to the square float below. The boat was empty.

Larsen went back to the cobbles. He felt annoyed, a little angry, a little foolish. He walked on past the darkened warehouses. He cursed. His gun was in his topcoat pocket. The girl had his topcoat. He felt like a halfwit. He, Inspector Peter Larsen, in charge of the detective bureau—

Bang! Bang!

Brittle echoes of gunfire crackled along Front Street. But they came from the north, from those ragtag alleys, that honeycomb of crooked streets, blind alleys—

Bang!

His topcoat—his gun—

LARSEN broke into a run. His head rode uneasily on his broad shoulders. He was a man of imagination—not your knock-down-and-drag-out cop. A slightly sentimental man. He had come down to the river to smoke and meditate in silence. He liked the mystery of the river flowing through the dark night. He—

Far distant the shrill blast of a police whistle. Larsen reached the opposite side of Front Street, stopped, listened, moved north on Oakum Street, which had only one sidewalk, on the left, and that wide enough for only one pedestrian. The rest was cobbled. The buildings were brick. There was a smell of mould, damp decay. No street lights.

He groped through it to Harbor Alley. He stopped at the next corner and listened again. There was a lull in the sound. The honeycomb was confusing. The lone street light on the corner yellowed the shadows.

He turned north. His ears ached to catch a sound. Only once had a police whistle been blown. Three shots. Now the silence was complete and final. This was no residential section. Only warehouses, provision stores, ice houses.

He turned another corner, his head full of misgivings, his nerves tingling. Ahead a solitary street light glowed. He saw a shape motionless on the cracked sidewalk, behind a fire hydrant. He broke into a run.

He kicked something. Saw it bounce into the street. Caught a glimpse of a shiny visor, the flash of a shield. He bent over the motionless shape. Clutched in one hand was a revolver, in the other a police whistle. Blue coat. Bright buttons. Gray hair.

Larsen dropped to his knees. He shook the broad uniformed shoulders. Then he stopped shaking them. The eyes were wide open, staring, the jaw slack. The shield on the chest was punctured.

Patrolman Charlie Storrs, aged fifty-five, a veteran beloved of the force, who had been slated for retirement a month hence. No pulse. No heartbeat. Well, the eyes, the slack jaw, told the story. And the punctured shield. Dying, Charlie Storrs had blown his whistle for the last time.

Larsen pried the service revolver from the dead fingers, smelled the muzzle, examined the cylinder. Two bullets had been fired. He heard footsteps coming rapidly up the street. He looked up and saw a figure coming toward him. He caught a flash of metal.

"Hey, you—don't move, you!" a hard voice barked.

Larsen did not move. A cop came heavy-footed into the radius of light, his gun leveled. Larsen looked up at him.

"Oh, it's you, Inspector! Excuse me, I didn't—"

Larsen said, "Charlie Storrs got it."

"What! You don't—"The cop's nightstick clattered as he dropped down beside the body. "If it ain't!" he muttered. "Poor old Charlie. Cripes, Inspector. I been bustin' around these lousy alleys ever since I heard the whistle. Alleys like this is enough to drive a guy nuts— Poor old Charlie!"

He was young, the cop—young and emotional. "B'jeeze, it was old Charlie broke me in last year, in this same neighborhood." He straightened from the knees up, stretching his lean corded neck, peering bitterly up and down the street. "Who the hell would ha' wanted to fog out Charlie!"

Larsen said in a quiet, restrained voice, "Telephone headquarters. Dougherty's your name, isn't it? Report this." He looked at his strap watch. "Shots heard at about 11:10. Body found in Blueberry Street at 11:20—approximately—by you and me. Take this down, Dougherty. That's better. To be notified: the morgue, the medical examiner's office, the district attorney's office, and—according to the new rule—the new bureau of fingerprint and photography. They'll want a flashlight picture of him—position and all.

"And this: Assailant unknown, but broadcast on the short wave to all precincts, police booths, and patrols, description of a woman, age about twenty-five, hair black, short, curly; eyes dark; height about five-feet-three and weight about one-twenty. Was last seen in the vicinity of the murder wearing a green one-piece dress, beige stockings of silk mesh; no shoes; a man's gray topcoat, light in color and weight, with raglan sleeves and patch pockets, and label on the inside pocket with the word Porter, the tailor. Also, in the right pocket of the coat, a .38 Smith & Wesson revolver—blued, swing-out, checkered walnut stock. The coat and the gun are the property of Inspector Larsen—"

"Huh!" gaped Dougherty.

"That's all."

"But, hell, Inspector—look, can't you keep that mum till—till we find out somethin'? A bust like that 'll raise hell and the district attorney's office 'll go crazy with joy!"

"Find a telephone. Quick, now, Dougherty. Storrs has been murdered—and it's my duty to— Go on, now. Beat it. I'll wait here."

Dougherty took a few gulps, backed up a few steps. Suddenly he turned and went off on the run.

Larsen remained on one knee looking vacantly at the dead man's face.

CHAPTER TWO

THE SMOKE TAB

ASSISTANT DISTRICT ATTORNEY Wells Gatlin was a lean, wiry man with a dark, tight-featured face, intense brown eyes and a big, predatory nose. He had a trick of firing questions with the rapidity of a machine gun, then stopping suddenly, putting his right ear toward the person questioned and staring fiercely from the corners of his eyes.

"O.K. then—O.K. You were down on Front Street, near Kilkenny's Wharf, taking the air and getting sentimental about the river. The dame came out of the shadows of the shed. She was wet and you got big-hearted and put your coat around her. Then you walked her to the watchman's office at Pier 26, started to telephone for a taxi. You looked around and the dame was gone. You shadow-boxed up and down the street and then heard three shots."

Larsen moved in his swivel chair, stuffing tobacco into his pipe. "That's about it, Gatlin."

"And you—the chief of detectives—the brass hat of this so-called efficient branch of law and order—you leave your gun in the pocket of the coat the dame runs off with!"

Larsen said, "She was shivering with the cold. And wet. My first thought was to keep her warm. She was frightened and evidently had come from the river. I admit I did a foolish thing by leaving the gun in the coat. I thought of it while phoning, intended to take it out when I'd finished."

"My God!" groaned Gatlin.

He strode up and down the office, his hair disheveled, a cigar rocking from one side of his mouth to the other. He looked fierce, intense.

"Listen," he flung out suddenly. "Why the hell did you go down to the river anyhow?"

"I told you. For the air and—" Larsen shrugged—"for the walk. I do it sometimes."

Gatlin's voice grated with sarcasm. "And then a nice pretty piece of fluff pops out of nowhere, wet from the river, and right away you pull a Sir Walter Raleigh or something! She gets your coat and gun—and a little later a cop is bumped off. When you saw her that way, scared and shaking, why the hell didn't you grab her and shake some information out of her? No. Oh, no! 'Mademoiselle may have my coat. Come, I shall telephone a cab!' I would have given her my coat. Yes, I would! I'd have—"

"I know what you would have done," Larsen interrupted. His voice was quiet, yet it carried an edge. "But I preach courtesy to the men under me. I've never stood for a cop of mine acting like a gorilla. And I practice what I preach. And another thing, Gatlin." His voice took on a keener edge; he pointed his pipe stem at the A.D.A. "I'm head of this detective bureau. I could have kept this break inside the police lines. I didn't have to report that a woman had walked off with my gun and coat. But I saw it as my duty. I thought she might still be roaming the streets and that if a description of her got out quickly she might be picked up. Understand, you've got no right to come in here and act like an A.D.A. to me. I won't stand for it. Your office will get a copy of my full report in the morning. Now take the air."

Gatlin snorted, jumped to the desk, smacked down the palms of his hands, leaned halfway over, his predatory nose wrinkling. "Says you, Larsen! I represent the district attorney's office, homicides, and I've got an inalienable right to question anybody from the mayor right down the line. I've heard goofy stories in my time, but you hand me a lulu. How the hell do I know you weren't with a dame? Or how the hell do I know there was any dame at all?"

Larsen began to wear a dreamy smile.

"You don't, Gatlin. That is, you have no concrete evidence. But I'm telling you. And I told you once to take the air. Now take it."

Gatlin slapped his hat, dark with anger.

"You're a cool Swede, Larsen. And pretty contented with yourself. Well, maybe you won't be. Maybe—"

The door opened and Detective-Sergeant Brinkhaus came in looking glumly at a newspaper.

"Cloudy with showers," he said. "I dunno, either we get too much rain or we don't get enough— Hello, Mr. Gatlin."

Gatlin stamped across the office, ignored Brinky's greeting, yanked open the door. "Good-by, Inspector!" he rasped vindictively and slammed out.

"When he was young," Brinkhaus said glumly, "his old woman must've dropped him on his head. Um. Gosh, boss, this is a bad one. Why'd you go and spill that about your coat and gun?"

"Had to, Brinky. Now let's forget it. Any news?"

"Nope. Like you said, I got in touch with all the taxicab companies, gave 'em a description of the gal and asked 'em to ask the drivers when they check in if they carried her between eleven and twelve. I did the same with the street car company. I shot out Butchman, Little and Groves to fan the speaks in that neighborhood. There's a squad car out of here and squad cars out of the first, second and fourth precincts. I went right down the river, went over the ground and didn't find nothin'. The rowboat you mentioned is still there, tied up, and I put Gus Kempf on the dock there. The boat's white, clinker-built, but ain't got no name on it. I looked for the maker's name but it ain't there. And there's no number on it. There was some sand in the bottom of it and a footprint in the sand, heel and all. The print was eleven inches long, and the sole must have been rubber. There was six ridges across, a circle and an X across the circle. Here, I drew a picture of it."

"Good job, Brinky!" murmured Larsen.

"I found the watchman at Pier 26, and I asked him if a boat was usually tied up there. He said no, and he said there wasn't no boat there at six in the evenin' on his way to work. You ask me, boss, I think that boat stands for somethin'."

Larsen stared at Brinky's rough sketch of the footprint. "Someone was after that woman, Brinky. When I saw her—she looked frightened as hell. A bundle of nerves. 'Put that light out!' she said—like that— when I turned a flash on her. And then she knew I'd ask her things— things she wouldn't want to answer. So she lammed on me. She came from the river. Did she come on that boat?"

"Um," mumbled Brinkhaus.

"She was wet. Soaked. She might have been in the river, then in the boat. But if she was in the boat, someone must have been with her—the one left that print. There were no other prints?"

"Nope."

"Then she must have come right out of the river. Maybe the boat was following her. But where did she swim from?"

"Um," mumbled Brinkhaus.

"And where did the boat come from?"

"Well, look," said Brinkhaus lugubriously. "There was sand in the boat. It probably got there over a long period, from people climbin' in it all the time with sand on their feet. There ain't no sand on this shore. There's sand up past the breakwater, but that's three miles away. The nearest sand to Kilkenny's Wharf is over to White Island, half a mile away."

"White Island," repeated Larsen thoughtfully and nodded. Then he looked at Brinky, leaned forward. "Brinky, you believe things happened the way I said, don't you?"

"Huh? Sure. Why shouldn't I?"

"She didn't look like a bad woman, Brinky. She didn't look like a moll. There was something—something about her—I don't know what—that made me want to help her right away."

"Well, lookit me pal, Ogglecarp. Once he found a jane cryin' in Civic Park. She said she was starvin'. So he took her in a restaurant and bought her a feed. B'jeepers if she didn't frisk him of his watch and fourteen dollars! Janes—well, there's janes and janes. I mind Ogglecarp said her eyes was like stars, but then he's another guy that got dropped on his head when he was very young."

"If she killed Charlie," Larsen said. "If she killed him, she'll burn—as sure as I'm sitting here!" He stood up. "I'll stay here tonight. I'll grab some sleep downstairs. Be on tap at seven sharp, Brinky, will you?"

"Seven—sharp."

THE MORNING papers had something to talk about. Larsen read them while snatching breakfast in a one-arm restaurant near police headquarters. Once or twice red color rose to his face. "Inspector Larsen Duped By Mystery Woman." And a picture of him. "Larsen, champion of courtesy to the public, plays gallant to pretty woman, his coat and revolver stolen." "Aged Policeman Shot to Death." The sheets with a salacious leaning were very salacious. They liked to write about "mystery women." Assistant District Attorney Wells Gatlin was seen leaving police headquarters "in a high state of anger, but would make no statement."

It was the dark hour for Larsen. His position was a bit ridiculous. The gibes hurt him, even though he would not have admitted it publicly. Because he tried to give his position some dignity, because he handed out reprimands for discourtesy on the part of his men and was dead against manhandling of first offenders, the smart Alecks never lost an opportunity to razz him.

"To hell with them," he muttered. But he was a sensitive man, and the gibes rankled.

He spent ten minutes in a barber shop, went back to headquarters looking keen, refreshed. He ran into Brinkhaus in the central room. Brinky always looked the same. You never knew whether he had things on his mind or not. He was always an anchor to windward.

"Look," said Brinkhaus. "I went down to the Excelsior Shoe Emporium the minute the joint opened. I took along the diagram I made of the print. It's a Hull Make shoe—and the model is dark brown, with no tip, and the place where you lace it up is lighter brown. It bein' eleven inches long, the shoe size is seven, worn ordinary by a man of medium height. The price of the shoe is fourteen dollars, more'n twice what I pay for mine. The guy wore it must ha' had jack. Twelve stores in the city handle it, and two department stores."

"Keep the diagram. What else?"

"I had the rowboat towed to the police dock. I called up all the boat hirin' places at White Island to see had they been rentin' boats out for longer'n a day. There was eight places. They didn't. Was any swiped? Nope. So that's that, boss—and it ain't so la-de-da."

"Good enough. If the boat came from White Island—and wasn't stolen—that means it was owned by someone there. Send two men— send Merkel and Trask—to White Island and have them search the beaches for a pair of lady's pumps. Have them ask around if anybody heard any screams last night—or shots, or any kind of disturbance."

He went upstairs to his office, was seated only a few minutes when Sergeant Connolly, the ballistics expert, came in. Small, dark, spectacled, he looked like a professor.

"Here it is, Peter." He dropped a slug on the desk. "A .38 long Colt, adapted to Colt and Smith and Wesson revolvers. Weight 150 grains; muzzle velocity 772 feet per second; energy of 190 pounds. Gatlin was just down and looked at it. He asked what kind of bullet you usually used. I said I didn't know."

"I use a long Colt."

"Yes, I know," Connolly said drily.

"Ten to one it's a slug out of my gun. But thanks, Henry."

Connolly went to the door. "I wouldn't let Gatlin disturb me too much, if I were you, Peter. Once he must have read a book somewhere called 'Dynamic Demeanor'—or the like. It must have been put in his hands when he was very young."

Through the dispatcher Larsen punched all the precincts, hoping for news. He had to clear up routine work. He dictated reports for an hour. At nine-thirty he was summoned to Chief Pentcost's office. Pentcost, with his black-ribboned pince-nez, had an ambassadorial look. Appointed to his post from civil life, he was a well-meaning man—but unsteady, a bit too oratorical, and influenced a great deal by public opinion. He gave Larsen a dressing down rich in metaphor. Larsen took it quietly, his shoulders squared, his mane of yellow hair in the air.

"—and, my dear Inspector, the district attorney's office, represented by Mr. Wells Gatlin, is not satisfied. As a matter of concentrated fact, Mr. Wells Gatlin—"

"To hell with Mr. Wells Gatlin," said Larsen finally.

Pentcost looked shocked.

Larsen said quietly, "Are you going to pander to the whims of an assistant district attorney or are you going to stand by your department? Gatlin's a stormy petrel, steamed up over his own importance. My record's clean. I tried to help a woman in distress—and the unexpected happened. I admit I was dumb according to Gatlin's way of thinking. But to me Gatlin is just one of those bad smells we have to endure. I'll clean this case up, Chief—before the week is out."

"You had better. Else popular opinion—prejudice—mockery—will necessitate your being removed as head of the detective bureau. Possibly demoted to captain and placed in some outlying precinct. Good morning, Inspector."

Larsen went out. He could feel the hair on his nape bristling. His face was white, the cheekbones looked higher. There was a queer radiating brilliance in his eyes.

There was a large-jawed young man sitting in his office. "A guy sez I should park here."

"Yes? And who are you?"

"O'Brien's de name. I check in dis mornin' at eight an' de boss asks me a lotta questions. About a dame in a guy's overcoat an' no shoes on. So he sez I should bust right over here and see a gink by de name o' Larsen."

"Taxi driver?"

"Me? Yeah. Metro. C'n I spit in dat spittoon? T'anks. See, it was like dis. At a eleven-t'irty—about dat, anyhow—I was night-hawkin' up India Street. A gink flags me, an' I pull up. He turns an' gives de high sign t' a broad an' de broad comes outa de shadders an' dey climb in. I figger it funny de broad's wearin' a man's coat an' den I figger, hell, de guy lent it her. But den I use my bean an'—ha!—de guy have a coat on. And de skirt ain't got no shoes on! Well, I'm a broad-minded guy, and I t'ink what de hell, it's none o' my business. He's got her right by de arm, an' he looks mean. De jane looks sorta dazed like."

"Would you recognize the man if you saw him again?"

"Sure. I t'ink I would. Tall as you. Tan overcoat. He had a gray tweed suit on an' a tweed cap like it. Say a guy about thirty. He had a little blonde mustache. He looked like a hard guy too. You know, one o' dese smooth hard guys. No gorilla."

"Where'd you take them?"

"Dey got off at Central Boulevard an' Ocean Pike, right by da park. Dey took one o' de sidewalks t'rough de park, de jane walkin' like her feet hurt. I looked in de back, like I always do after a fare. But dere was nothin'—only dis."

He tossed an empty cigarette box on the desk. English Sun Flakes. A little oval tab had been pasted on the box. It said: The Clevedon Smoke Shop. That was in the Clevedon Hotel.

"Thanks, O'Brien. Leave me your address and telephone number."

"Oke."

Larsen picked up a phone. "Locate Brinkhaus. Send him up." He hung up. "Mind coming with me, O'Brien?" he said, pulling a .32 revolver from his desk.

CHAPTER THREE

NO. A-505

THE CLEVEDON HOTEL was on the west side of Bayside Park. It overlooked the park and—beyond the park—the harbor. It was a beautiful white building of ten stories with a marquee adding to the elaborate façade.

Larsen and Brinkhaus got out of the Packard official, and O'Brien followed. They entered the ornate lobby through revolving doors. Brinkhaus and O'Brien sat down in a massive leather divan, and Larsen crossed the lobby to the cigar counter. The attendant was a young man wearing a black alpaca coat.

Larsen introduced himself and laid the empty cigarette box on the counter. "Is that a popular brand?"

"No sir. We just carry them as a courtesy to the house guests. Usually we have to order them specially."

"How many regular customers have you?"

"Three. Sometimes, of course, we sell an odd one."

"The three regulars live here?"

"Yes, sir."

"You know their names?"

"One is Mr. Abel, the furrier. Then there's Mr. Parmly, the English novelist. And a Mr. Rounds."

"Describe them."

The clerk did and Larsen listened intently, said, "Thanks," and turned away.

He went into Vic Groom's office. Groom was the house officer, and a stout, dandified man—cherubic, good-humored.

"The Swell Swede himself, eh? Sort of ladling a lot of the old razzberry in your back yard, aren't they Pete?"

"I may raise some hell here, Vic. What do you know about R.B. Rounds, in A-505?"

"Nothing. Should I?"

"It depends. Want to come up with me and see him?"

"What's it—rod work?"

Larsen shrugged. "I don't know. I've got Brinkhaus out there and a guy who might do some identifying. I don't want the guy to be seen though."

"The management would hate like hell to have blood spilled here, Pete."

"So would I."

The two men looked at each other. Then Groom put a gun in his pocket and said, "Wait here till I look at the books."

He went out and reappeared a couple of minutes later. "He's still on the books. It's on the residential side, through the arcade. We lease those suites by the month. No leases on the transient side."

"You better give me the key, Vic."

"No, that's my job. Get Brinkhaus. What about the other guy, Pete?"

"Leave him in the office here."

Groom sighed. "I've got a funny feeling," he said and began whistling.

They got Brinkhaus, put O'Brien in the office, and went across the lobby, through the arcade flanked by small, exclusive shops, windows lighted. It was a rich, luxury hotel. The elevator boys wore white spats.

Groom got out first at the fifth floor. He was still whistling uneasily, but he stopped when the elevator doors closed. He nodded down the wide corridor. Larsen poked him.

"Give me the key, Vic."

"Be your age."

"I am, damn it! I'm not going to have you shoving your face into trouble on my account."

"I'm not going to use the key, Pete. The management would fire me. I have to knock. If nobody answers in a reasonable length of time, then I use the key. See?" He grinned with his apple-cheeked face. "This is a swell hotel, not a flop house."

"All right, all right, go ahead."

Larsen put his hand in his pocket, gripped the gun there, released the safety.

Brinky's broad, honest face began to wear an expression that was half curious, half grim. He planted his broad substantial heels in the resilient carpet, watching his boss sidewise as they moved down the corridor.

Groom stopped his bobbing walk, turned and raised his eyebrows, lowered them, flashed his cherubic smile. Raised his hand, struck lightly on the door of A-505. He listened, making a whistling mouth, but not whistling. He knocked again, this time sharply. Then he winked at Larsen, held up the key, bent to insert it.

Larsen took it from him quickly, shoved him aside, inserted the key and turned it quickly. He spun the knob, whipped open the door. Brinkhaus battened him aside and reared in the open doorway, his gun gripped in his big, hard hand, his broad face brown and somber.

But the room was empty. The somberness passed from Brinky's face. He looked curious again. He stepped aside.

"O.K., boss."

"Damn you, Brinky!" Larsen muttered, red spots on his fair face. Brinkhaus looked innocent.

Groom said, "I never saw such guys. I never saw guys so anxious to get in the way of trouble."

Larsen said nothing, and Brinkhaus suddenly crossed the oblong living room to a bedroom, his revolver cocked. Larsen looked in the bathroom. It was empty. Brinkhaus turned, let the hammer down.

"O.K., boss," he said.

"Close that door, Vic," Larsen said. "Take the bedroom, Brinky. Leave everything as you find it—unless you find something. Do you mind, Vic?"

"What's the use?" Groom chuckled and sat down.

Larsen lit into a clothes closet, called out, "Say, Vic, I suppose you could get hold of the man or men who were on elevator duty last night?"

"Sure."

"This guy had a woman with him."

"So. There's a way up from the basement garage, though. A special elevator. You operate it yourself."

"Hell," said Larsen.

In a couple of minutes Larsen came out of the closet, went to a low secretary, rifled the drawers, the shelves back of the glass-paneled doors.

"There's a trunk in here, locked," Brinkhaus called.

Larsen went to the bedroom door and looked in. The room was in perfect order.

"Did you search everything else?"

"Yup."

"Break it open."

With the aid of a heavy jack-knife Brinkhaus forced the lock. It was a wardrobe trunk, stood on end. There was nothing in it but a dark gray topcoat.

"There's your benny, boss," Brinkhaus said, holding it.

Larsen took the coat, held it by the neck, ran his hand into the pockets. His gun wasn't there.

"Look at this," he said, shaking the sleeve.

"Slug went in here—out here. Brinky, Charlie Storrs wounded the girl."

"My, my!" exclaimed Groom softly.

"Say, Vic," Larsen said. "You're sure this bird Rounds has this apartment alone?"

"Say the books. But on this side of the hotel you can't stop a man from having a woman in an apartment—naturally."

Larsen draped the coat over his arm. "Oh, she was in here all right! No call for a doctor?"

"I would have been told."

"Look in the hamper in the bathroom, Brinky."

Brinky looked and reported. "Nope. Two soiled towels in the hamper, one clean, one on the rack. One soiled bath towel on the floor and one on the rack."

"There should be four hand towels," Groom said.

"Then one was used to wash the wound and carried away. All right, we want this guy. It's a pinch we want. Will you go downstairs, Groom, and tell O'Brien he can breeze?"

Groom nodded, but remained, staring absently at the topcoat. The three men remained silent for a long minute, each with his own thoughts. Then Groom, saying nothing, turned and walked quietly across the living room. He pulled open the door and found a man bending over. The man had been on the point of inserting a key.

GROOM stopped short, his face expressionless. The man was stocky, dark, well-dressed. Groom said nothing, but his hand jerked to his coat pocket. The dark man's fist came up in a short, hard blow. Groom took four reeling steps backward, struck an end table, bounced into a divan.

"Pete!" he called.

Larsen came out of the bedroom.

"Quick, Pete." He pointed. "Stocky—five-feet eight—dark—light brown suit—dark brown hat—"

Larsen flung at Brinkhaus. "Cover this room!"

Groom gasped, "Stairway around the L—to the right. Go left here and then right."

Larsen was in the corridor. He heaved the topcoat back into the room, ran down the corridor. There had been no sound of elevator doors. He ran past them. Turned right at the L. He reached the stairs and went down in bounding jumps. He heard muffled footsteps below hurrying. He reached the lobby and saw a man running. His gun came up, but Larsen shook his head, dared not fire because too many people were there. The revolving doors spun. The man in the brown suit was outside.

Larsen went through the revolving doors, past a gaping doorman. The man in the brown suit was across the street, heading for the park. Motor cars hummed by. Larsen darted through the traffic, reached the other side of the street and saw the man running down one of the park lanes. People who had been walking stopped. Some remained motionless. Others darted out of the way. The running man passed between them, and they still stared stupidly.

A small girl came pedaling a bicycle blissfully out of an intersecting lane. She tried to avoid hitting the running man. She failed. Girl, bicycle, man went down. The man scrambled to one knee, raised his gun. Larsen flung himself behind a cement lamp post. A shot rang out. Wild. The lanternlike structure encasing the light-bulb crashed. The glass was heavy and hit the sidewalk with a sound like metal.

Larsen raised his gun, but the little girl was in the way. He couldn't fire. The man in the brown suit took to his heels again and Larsen followed. The little girl was screaming. The bicycle wheels were still spinning. There were many people standing around, petrified. Time and time again Larsen started to use his gun but people were in the way, always in the way. He was a good man with a gun, but not loose with one. Ahead were Ocean Pike and the Breakwater.

The running man reached the edge of the park. He looked around. He fired. The bullet missed a dozen people between the gunman and Larsen. It missed Larsen by a hair. He heard the "snick." That meant it was very close. It rang in a green refuse drum. Still Larsen dared not fire. His fair face was read with anger, a sheen was on his eyes. His mouth, usually mobile and friendly, was now a tight line, bulging his jaw muscles.

Then something fast happened. The man in the brown suit was darting to make a break through the motor traffic on Ocean Pike. Rubber screeched as tires skidded. The front wheel of a red police motorcycle yanked at right angles to the frame. The machine skidded wildly. The cop got a foot on the ground, swung the other up and let the machine wheel from beneath him. He did it like a showman. But impetus flung him against the man in the brown suit and the two went down. The cop hit the cement first, on his head, his legginged legs flying upward. The man in the brown suit struck with his gun. It rang against the cop's head. The man in the brown suit scrambled up, his eyes blazing, his teeth bared. Pedestrians shrank back.

Larsen came leaping from behind. The other almost got around, but not quite. Larsen's gun-barrel came down hard. The man's knees buckled. His gun went off, and the bullet slammed into the pavement. Larsen struck again, harder, and the man went down violently, his gun clattered away across the sidewalk.

The motorcycle cop sat up and said, "Whew!"

"Good work, Baggot," Larsen said.

CHAPTER FOUR

FLOATING DEATH

THE YELLOW-HAIRED inspector stood in his office, looking down at the venerable elm which a sentimental chamber of commerce retained in a street of cold masonry. Men and women hurried on their way to lunch. A light rain had begun to fall.

Merkel and Trask came in, and Trask began undoing a package. He dropped a pair of ladies' pumps on the desk, shrugged and said, "How's that?"

Larsen came slowly to the desk, picked up one of the pumps. "Where'd you find them?"

"At Logan's Point, White Island. Way out the end o' the point. Way out. I mean, it looked like the jane ran like hell—maybe in the dark—and then came to the end and decided to swim. Because she left footprints. Then she must have flung the shoes away. They were layin' in some bushes. There were other footprints."

Larsen looked up, squinting.

"Wasn't there?" Trask asked Merkel.

"Uh-huh. A guy's. Like the kind Brinky saw in the boat. Yeah."

"But he didn't chuck 'em away," Trask hurried on eagerly. "He turned back. We followed them back, but lost them at the boardwalk, but couldn't pick them up again."

"He went and got a boat," Larsen conjectured. "Did you ask around if anybody heard anything—noise, cries, anything?"

"Not a peep," Trask said.

Larsen sat down, reached for the phone. "Operator, get the number of the Fogg Bootery, in town here. Ring 'em and connect me right away. I'll want the manager there."

He hung up, said, "Go downstairs, boys. Tell Brinky to bring up that guy as soon as he's able to stand."

"You sure gave him a sock, boss," Trask chuckled.

"Hang around downstairs."

The plainclothesmen went out, and Larsen sat back, stuffed his pipe, lit up and stared absently at the graceful pumps. She was a beautiful girl. Pretty. No, beautiful. It was something like a dream; the dark river rolling by, the shadows—shoeless—her black curls clinging wetly to her head. He frowned. Murderess? He cleared his throat.

The door opened.

"Hello, Larsen."

Ferret-eyed Gatlin came in, full of vigor, his features tight, unpleasant, almost malignant.

"Where's the guy?"

"He'll be up," Larsen said, took a puff—added, "Any minute."

"When you went over the Clevedon, why the hell didn't you notify the district attorney's office?"

"You think I have nothing else to do but run to telephones all day notifying the D.A.'s office? Be your temperature."

Gatlin scowled. "You don't like me, Larsen!"

Larsen was annoyed. "Oh, don't be a guy like that, Gatlin. Grow up. You're not so important."

"Yeah? I represent the district attorney's office—"

"Homicides," finished Larsen. "I know. Also, you represent a big pain to me—and not in the neck. Every time the D.A. goes away on a vacation you see yourself through magnifying glasses. But to me you still remain something small—like a burr in the sock. I'm busy, Gatlin. Drag your tail somewhere else. Or go in and tell the chief what you think of me."

Gatlin flushed, but you couldn't down him. "I can tell you—to your face. You got the coat all right, but you didn't get the gun—your gun. And when the gun's found—your gun—and it comes to light that Storrs was killed with your gun—maybe you'll drag your tail somewhere. Out to the sticks, maybe. Or I hope. Unless you find the gun first and ditch it—"

Larsen stood up. "I suppose you also represent the dignity of the district attorney's office."

"Dignity my eye! You hate getting the razzberry, don't you?"

"I do," nodded Larsen.

The telephone rang. Larsen did not answer it.

"I'll turn the guy over to you for questioning after I've examined him and booked him. Hereafter when you come to my office—knock. Preferably—don't come."

Gatlin yanked open the door. "I'll see you take water yet, you big squarehead!"

Larsen answered the phone. "You're the manager of the Fogg Bootery?… Inspector Larsen, police headquarters. I have a pair of ladies' pumps here. Brown. A kind of snake or lizard skin, I believe. Inside it has 5-B-0096-S. That's stamped in blue, on the side, inside. Then on the heel, inside the shoe, there's D.S. stamped in gold. Is there any way of tracing the owner of these shoes?… Yes, that's right…. Good! Will you do that and call me back?… Thanks."

He hung up exuberantly, smacked his hands together, rubbed them briskly. He was still rubbing them briskly—and wearing a bright half-smile—when the door opened and Brinkhaus came in with the brown-suited man. There was a black and blue mark on the latter's forehead the size of a half dollar.

"Sit down," Brinkhaus said.

The man did not sit down. Brinkhaus slammed him into a chair so hard that the chair tipped, fell back to all fours with a thud. The swart stocky man scowled at Brinkhaus. Brinky's face remained blank, slightly curious. He turned to Larsen.

"Eduardo Dominguez," Brinkhaus said. "Aged 30. Spanish. Came to this country when he was eighteen. Got a record. A year ago he was collared for tryin' to make a gal in West End Drive. A nurse maid. Danish. He was indicted and did thirty days. I looked the case up. He was tried three years ago in El Paso on a charge of draggin' Mex girls across the Border. Acquitted. Again for the same stunt in California—and acquitted. Also known as 'Kid Spanish,' and 'Ed Domino.'"

Larsen nodded, leaned his elbows on the desk. "All right. Look here, Dominguez. I suppose you realize you're in a tough spot."

Kid Spanish scowled darkly. "Am I?"

"Don't try to hand me the run-around. We know how to handle guys like you. Why did you come to that apartment?"

"Can't I go to an apartment?"

"I suppose you think you can pull a gun on me, too. Maybe I can tell you why you came there."

"Maybe you can."

"To get a topcoat."

Kid Spanish retained his intense scowl. "That's what you say. I say, get my lawyer on the phone."

"Ain't that funny?" Brinkhaus said.

"How the hell did I know you were a cop?" Kid Spanish flung at Larsen.

"What did you think that motorcycle cop was?" Larsen said. "You get this, Dominguez. You had Rounds' key. You came to his apartment. I want to know where Rounds is. I'm not going to fool around with you. You're going to spring what you know, and you're going to do it in a hurry."

"Or else," added Brinkhaus.

"Where does the girl come in?" Larsen said.

"What girl?" Kid Spanish snapped.

"The girl who wore the coat you were after. The coat with the bullet hole in it."

Kid Spanish chuckled—but nervously. "You got a long way to go, Inspector."

"Was she a decoy for the mob?"

"You had my answer in the beginning. I'm not saying a thing. I want a lawyer."

Brinkhaus got behind him, planted a big hand on either shoulder, lifted Kid Spanish up and slammed him down again. Kid Spanish's teeth rattled. His dark eyes glittered. But he said nothing.

The telephone rang, and Larsen picked it up. He listened, nodded, said, "Yes, go on," and made notes on a pad. In a minute he hung up, leaned back, studied the pad.

"Doris Sandifer," he said.

Kid Spanish crouched.

"Number 498 Roseland Avenue," Larsen said. He reached for the phone again. "Hello, Sergeant. Larsen. Send a man to 498 Roseland Avenue. Have him investigate Miss Doris Sandler. Immediately."

He hung up and looked at Kid Spanish with dreamy eyes. "Are you going to talk?"

"You heard me."

"All right, Brinky. Put Davis and Shumacher on him."

Kid Spanish snapped, "Damn it, you guys can't—"

Brinkhaus heaved him out of the chair, rough-housed him to the door. The door opened. When it closed Larsen stared at it. He hated this. He hated to give a man the rough stuff, but sometimes you had to. The minute they started to squawk for a lawyer you had to get rough. Kid Spanish had a record.

Larsen picked up the shoes. They were light in his hands. He looked from one to the other. He foresaw another unpleasantness: law against a woman. And he remembered that she was very beautiful. His jaw hardened. He also remembered that old Charlie Storrs had been shot to death. Grimly he wrapped the shoes in a newspaper, put the package in his desk.

A minute later Brinkhaus barged in, his coat-tails flapping. "Now what d' you think?" he bit off.

"What?"

"A gal's body found floatin' at White Island. Gatlin got it, too, and breezed with the deputy medical examiner."

Larsen got his hat, put on a gray slicker.

HORAN drove the Packard official. Larsen and Brinkhaus sat in the rear. The siren moaned.

"This ain't even funny any more," Brinkhaus said.

"Who found her?"

"A clam digger. He hauled her ashore and left her there and then ran for a cop. Bennie Steinfelt reported it. Y'know, boss, there's two things I can hardly bear to look at: dead dogs and drowned women. Funny, I don't mind guys."

Noiseless brakes slowed the car to forty. Horan tooled it in beneath a shed, braked it to a smooth stop. Larsen and Brinkhaus climbed out, their slickers swishing.

Larsen said, "Wait here, Horan."

They went out on a dock, down a ladder to a float. Beside the float a dark green police launch had all lines cast off but one. A powerful motor was idling. Larsen went down first, and Brinkhaus followed.

"Let her go," Larsen said.

White Island was a mile long, half a mile wide. It faced the city broadside. At the east end was a long beach and an amusement park.

Larsen could see a ferris wheel, a roller coaster, a long boardwalk, several piers. There were no bathers, few others at this time of year.

The police launch tied up at the municipal pier, and Larsen and Brinkhaus climbed. At the base of the pier a police flivver was waiting. There was roadway round the island. Larsen and Brinkhaus climbed in the flivver and started off.

"How far?" Larsen asked.

"In a couple o' minutes," the driver said.

The car scooted up to a bluff, went down the other side with wet dust behind. There were flats below and little inlets and some houses built on stilts, like a Malay village. The road became level again, with brush on one side, the harbor on the other. There was a little group of people ahead, on the beach. The driver pulled up near several cars.

Larsen got out, and Brinkhaus paced him across a hard, grubby beach.

"Hello, Inspector," the deputy medical examiner said.

"Hello, Josephs."

"Well, what do you think of this?" Gatlin rasped.

Larsen ignored him. Larsen made a motion with his hand, and one of the cops drew back a blanket. Larsen stared, shrugged, shook his head.

"Well—well!" Gatlin snapped.

"It's not the girl," Larsen said.

Gatlin's face fell. For an instant he looked as if he were going to roar.

But Larsen was saying, "What do you say, Josephs?"

"Finger marks on the throat. I'm sure we'll find out that she was choked before she drowned."

"No identification, eh?"

"None. Except a ring, which might be useful later. Gatlin has it."

"Let me see it, Gatlin."

It was a diamond in a platinum setting, hemmed in by four small baguette diamonds.

"What finger was it on?" Larsen asked.

"Engagement."

"I know what this 'll turn out to be," Gatlin rasped. "You'll find that the jane you ran into down by the river was playing mama to the guy before this one came along. She got a guy to help her give this one the works."

Larsen looked around. "I see there are no reporters. Good." He gave Gatlin a smile of droll contempt.

"All right. You're so smart, what do you think?"

Larsen turned to the deputy medical examiner. "I'd like to hear the results of the autopsy as soon as possible."

They went back to the amusement park in the police flivver. Larsen entered a telephone booth, remained closeted for five minutes and then came out.

"They're still working on Dominguez," Larsen said. "Toby came back from 498 Roseland. The Sandifer girl has a two-room apartment there. Lived there for a year and three months. They don't seem to know much about her except that she never gave any trouble. The maid on the floor says the bed wasn't slept in last night."

"So what?" said Brinkhaus.

"So this: we get a boat."

They borrowed a small boat with an outboard motor. Brinky knew how to operate it. Larsen sat facing him, and they left the dock. They cruised past the wide bathing beach, heading around the eastward end of the island, keeping close to the shore.

Larsen said, "There was sand in the rowboat. It must have come from the sandy place." He pointed ahead. "This main beach ends there."

Where the main beach petered off low bushes grew, and as the outboard pushed along Larsen and Brinkhaus saw a rocky stretch, boulders where the tide-rips splashed. Upon knolls behind, summer houses looked toward the sea. There were little inlets and boats moored in some of them. Larsen explored the inlets.

"There's that point," Brinky pointed.

"Merkel and Trask followed the footprints out there. The gal swam from there to—" he swung his arm around—"Kilkenny's Wharf."

He drove the boat down the farther side of the spit of land, then swung left to follow the main shore. The sand ended at the base of the point, and there was a narrow boardwalk over salt marshes and jutting rocks. Ten minutes later they came to a cove, entered it and found a sandy beach that appeared to be deserted.

"Let's stop here," Larsen said.

Brinkhaus beached the boat, and they climbed out. A bluff, thick with foliage, rose sheer from the beach. They stood around looking up and down the narrow beach and up across the face of the bluff.

"There's a path," Larsen said.

They moved through the misty drizzle to a break in the foliage and started up a narrow pathway.

"House up there, Brinky."

"But give a look here," Brinkhaus said, nodding toward the wet earth. "Six ridges and a circle and an X."

CHAPTER FIVE

SLOVE STASH

THE HOUSE was brown with a green roof. Its color scheme mingled with that of the autumn foliage. There was a broad veranda.

Larsen went up three steps to the veranda. Windows, doors, were closed. Brinkhaus passed Larsen and knocked at the main door. The house had an empty sound. Brinkhaus looked at Larsen, and Larsen looked back at him, blankly.

No one answered the door.

Larsen and Brinkhaus had their hands on their guns in their pockets. Larsen made a motion with his head. They went around the side of the house, where the ground sloped away. They could not see through the lower windows. They went around to the rear. The door there was locked, too. Brinkhaus pointed to the ground. The familiar footprint was evident.

Larsen looked at Brinkhaus and made a motion with his shoulder. Brinkhaus nodded, stepped back, gathered his muscles and let drive. There was a rending sound. The door whipped open, hit a stopper, slammed back against Brinkhaus. Larsen kicked it open. They stood with drawn guns; then Larsen thrust Brinkhaus aside and stepped into a kitchen.

The interior was dim. Larsen went from the kitchen into a small butler's pantry. He kicked open a swing door and entered a dining room.

A woman stood at the bottom of a staircase in the hallway looking at him through the door.

"Come in here," he muttered.

She was lanky, loose-hipped. She had a wide red mouth and shingled brown hair, and she came into the living room with insolent languor.

"What's the idea busting into houses?" she said lazily.

"Why don't you answer knocks?"

"Why should I? I was sleeping."

"Sit down."

"Why should I? Who are you?"

Larsen and Brinkhaus turned back their lapels. Her face remained cold and expressionless. She said, "I'll stand."

"Who lives here?"

"What do you think I do here?"

"Always the snappy comeback, eh?"

"Well, why should I stand for you busting in here? Suppose you are cops?"

"Who's upstairs?"

"I was, but I'm down here now. You know what I am? I'm a recluse, a hermitette or what have you."

"Take care of her, Brinky."

Larsen moved slowly to the hallway, looked up the stairway, went into the living room, his gun moving where his eyes moved. He turned around slowly, warily. He returned to the hallway. He could see Brinkhaus standing by the woman.

Larsen turned, put a foot on the stairway, stopped and listened and looked aloft. He began climbing slowly on the soles of his shoes, careful of each step. The hammer of his gun was cocked. He reached the head of the staircase and stood with one hand on the balustrade. He saw an open door, a bathroom. To his left was another door, closed. He went up close to it, noiselessly, listened intently. He put his left hand on the knob, turned it.

He knocked the door open violently and jumped to one side. Nothing happened. Shades were down in the room. It was dark. But he heard a low moan.

Then he heard the quick stamp of feet below—on the veranda. He spun away from the open door. Below he heard the voices of men come in through a door suddenly opened. He sprang to the head of the staircase.

Three men were inside the door. He heard a crash. The woman screamed viciously. The three men below went into action. Guns leaped from their pockets, swung toward the dining room. Larsen fired. He knew Brinkhaus was in trouble because he knew he should have heard Brinky's voice, or the sound of Brinky's gun. His bullet caved in the chest of a man, sent him reeling against the front door. His head smashed a step below Larsen's feet. Larsen fired and crashed the droplight in the lower hall.

A gun boomed, and Larsen saw one of the men stagger from the dining-room door back into the lower hall. The man went reeling toward the living-room door, where the other had gone. Larsen ran down the steps. The wounded man turned on him, snarling.

"Drop it!" Larsen barked.

A gun boomed from the dining room again, and Larsen saw the wounded man pitch backward and slam against the door the other tried to close. The door banged open again, and the wounded man fell across the threshold.

Larsen reached the bottom step and flung a shot sidewise through the living-room door. A window went out with a crash. Two shots came from Brinky's gun, and Larsen, leaving the last step, fired another. A choked cry came from the living room. A man stumbled over the man lying in the doorway and fell flat on his face. His gun bounced from his hand. He clawed at the twisted rug.

The echoes of the gunfire petered off. There was a heavy, solid step and Brinkhaus appeared in the hallway. He looked at Larsen.

"O.K., boss."

"The woman?"

"She made a grab for my gun, and I had to bust her in the jaw."

Larsen took a few steps, bent down and turned over the man who had stumbled out. He was fair-haired, young, and had a blonde mustache.

Brinkhaus said, "Look, boss," as he knelt down and raised the man's foot. "Six ridges and a circle and an X."

"Grab a phone. Locate a doctor. Get the municipal pier station and see if the deputy medical examiner is still on the island."

While Brinkhaus telephoned, Larsen went into the dining room. The woman lay flat on the floor, unconscious. Larsen went into the kitchen, got a bucket of water and some towels. He carried them back into the dining room. Brinkhaus was looking vacantly at the woman.

"She would ha' been the fly in the ointment, boss. She kicked me in the belly first and then made a grandstand play for my gun."

"Was Josephs at the municipal pier?"

"Yeah. They're coming up in the police boat—the whole shebang." Brinky nodded toward the door.

Larsen looked aloft, said, "Douse the woman, Brinky. I'll be right down."

He went upstairs swiftly, paused at the top and looked at the open door. He moved toward it, reached in and found a light switch, flooding the room with light.

Bound hand and foot, gagged, toiling slowly in the bonds and groaning behind the gag—the Sandifer girl.

JOSEPHS, the deputy medical examiner, came in the front door, looked casually at the three men lying on the floor and took three ruminative puffs on a cork-tipped cigarette.

Gatlin, with his nose to the ground, his sharp, ferret eyes darting about, eager to pin onto something, scurried past Josephs. He hopped from one dead man to another. He straightened and looked sharply at Brinkhaus. Brinkhaus inclined his head slightly. Gatlin pivoted and saw Larsen standing in the dining room. He saw two women seated.

Half a dozen cops pushed in.

Gatlin set his jaw and stamped into the dining room. "Who are these women, Larsen?" he snapped.

"This," said Larsen, "is Doris Sandifer. This is Marge Mularkey. The three men lying in the hall are Joe Buff, Carl Shomberg and Ralph Rounds. Brinky and I fought it out with them. Miss Sandifer was a prisoner upstairs, bound and gagged. She's the girl I met down by the river that night."

Gatlin screwed up his nose. "Oh, she is, is she?"

Doris Sandifer shrank back in the chair. Her face was pale, drawn. Gatlin clenched his fists and made for her. Larsen put out a hand and stopped him.

"We can do this like gentlemen, Gatlin."

"Get out of the way."

"The girl's had a rough deal."

"Get out—"

"You heard me, Gatlin! I'm in charge of this case right now. Brinky and I broke this job." He moved and put his body in front of Gatlin. His eyes were dreamy. "I'm in charge, see?"

"All hog, eh?" Gatlin bared his teeth.

Larsen turned his back on Gatlin. "Now, Miss Sandifer."

She clasped her hands. "When you met me by the river I was frightened—afraid. I went to White Island—to this house—to get my sister Ellen. She was in love with Rounds. She was a little fool. I received an anonymous letter telling me about Rounds—what he was. He trafficked in women. He was the leader of this ring—he and Eduardo Dominguez. Schooners brought girls from Cuba and Puerto Rico, anchored twenty miles out. The girls were brought in at night in motorboats. Smuggled in."

Gatlin snapped, "Why didn't you tell the police?"

"I didn't want any scandal—for Ellen's sake. I thought I could get her away from him. She went into a rage when I told her. She didn't believe it. She said she was going to White Island and ask Rounds. She went one night. She didn't show up that night or the next day, so I went. I came here. She wasn't here. Rounds said she wasn't here. I didn't believe him. I told him what I knew. He was shocked, and he attacked me. I ran out, and he followed and chased me all over the island. Finally I reached the beach, kicked off my shoes and swam. That's how you met me. Rounds got a rowboat and followed. He couldn't swim.

"When I ran away from you, Inspector, I ran into him. He grabbed me, and we fought. He felt the gun in the overcoat and took it. He held it against me and forced me along. There was a policeman. I was terrified and screamed. Rounds fired, and the policeman fired." She touched her bandaged arm. "The bullet scraped my arm. Rounds took me to his hotel, threatening to kill me. He bandaged my arm and took me out again, about four in the morning, the back way. He brought me over here. I kept pleading for Ellen. I began to know that something had happened to her. I was bound and gagged here."

"Who sent the letter?" Gatlin rasped.

"It was anonymous."

"Where is it?"

"I—I tore it up."

Gatlin snapped, "I don't believe there was a letter."

Marge Mularkey said, "I wrote it. I was nuts about Rounds, and I wrote it. I wanted him. I didn't want this one's sister to get him. He was my kind—not hers. She came here all steamed up and asked him was it the truth. He was a little tight and began laughing. She threw a fit, and he made a pass at her. She began screaming, and he got her by the throat, damned near choked her. She ran out and fell down the hill. He ran after her. She ran into the water and began swimming. She got about two hundred yards and sank. That scared him. Then her sister here busted in, and Rounds was scared stiff. And you know what happened. He sent Kid Spanish after the coat he'd left in his apartment. Kid Spanish was the one picked the girls in Cuba and Puerto Rico."

The Sandifer girl was sobbing. "And—Ellen's—dead. O God, O God!"

Gatlin gnawed irritably at his nether lip. His hands opened and closed. He didn't know quite what to say. He spun on his heel and almost smashed into Brinkhaus.

"Well!" he rasped.

"I didn't say nothin'," Brinkhaus said.

Gatlin reddened with chagrin, stamped out of the room.

Brinkhaus made an awkward bow before Doris Sandifer. "I'm mighty sorry, Miss Sandifer."

"You've been good to me—you and Inspector Larsen," she said.

The Mularkey woman, lighting a cigarette, said, "You were good to me, too, Sergeant." She touched her jaw. "In a big way."

THE CRIMSON FIST

TO BRAND HIS OWN
SON A KILLER—OR
CHEAT JUSTICE. AS
SERGEANT BRINKHAUS
STARED AT THE PALE
FACE OF THE DEAD
WOMAN HE KNEW HE
MUST CHOOSE. AND HE
DID IT COURAGEOUSLY,
SETTING OUT ALONE
ON THAT BLOOD TRAIL
WITH A GRIM SMILE AND
FIGHTER'S GUNS.

CHAPTER ONE

CLUB TOMAHAWK

BREAKNECK HILL is really the name of a street. The southern grade is three blocks long, starting at Platt and dropping with a jolt to Brewery Lane, the northern boundary of the old breweries. It is proper and fitting that the farther down Breakneck Hill you go the lower in the social scale you register, and the very top is nothing to write home about.

Halfway up, the Club Tomahawk blinks its name in red globes of light. The globes show up well because the street is dark, narrow, and the roofs of three and four story houses seem to lean toward each other. A south wind brings the smell of the fruit markets. The fruiterers claim a north wind brings a worse smell from Breakneck Hill. Even Little Italy, off to the west, holds its nostrils.

Detective-Sergeant Otto Herman Brinkhaus came up the Hill. He came slowly, ponderously, at eleven o'clock of a warm summer night. Woolen-suited, he felt the tickle of perspiration. His polished shoes had a proletariat squeak.

He came beneath the red glow of the Club Tomahawk. A huge negro in a faded purple uniform showed a mouth full of white teeth in a slashed, battered face.

"How 're yuh, Brinky ol' man?"

Brinkhaus said, "I'm Sergeant Brinkhaus to you, Babe."

The negro laughed.

"Sho 'nuff! Sho 'nuff!" He made a mock bow, his eyeballs rolled whitely. "Yas suh! Yas *suh!*" He pulled open the door, leering at Brinky's profile.

The lobby was dim. It was hung in cheap maroon drapes. Tobacco smoke and a group of men filled it and a baby-faced blonde hung over the check-room counter.

"Your hat, big boy!"

"I'll keep me hat," Brinkhaus said.

The sound of a jazz band throbbed in the hot air.

Joe Niccolo turned laughing from a group and saw Brinkhaus and dropped his laugh but retained a thin, curious smile. Niccolo was darkly handsome. His hair was black, thick, wavy. He had broad shoulders. He wore a tux.

"Well, Sarge!"

"Hello, Joe."

Stolid, heavy-faced, Brinkhaus went past Joe Niccolo, pushed open the connecting door, let it swing shut behind him and stood squinting at the dancers. A waiter made a bow in front of him, led him to a table near the door. Brinkhaus sat down slowly, watching.

"Watcha drink, Sarge?"

"Anything."

"Shoo."

The only lights were on the tables—little red-shaded lamps that sprayed out lurid bars and angles of light. The air was close, damp with the breathing and perspiration of half a hundred persons. The connecting door opened a few inches. Joe Niccolo's face appeared there. He regarded Brinkhaus with curious eyes. The door closed slowly.

Brinkhaus watched. He watched the dancers shuffle past. His forehead wrinkled and his eyes squinted. Sweat stood out on his broad honest face. The music beat against him like a tangible force. He could feel the table tremble and through a gap sometimes he saw the rocking, heaving jazz band—six negroes working like madmen, stamping heels, rolling eyes.

Presently the music stopped, the players relaxed, the dancers teetered to their tables. And Brinkhaus watched. Then he looked at the ceiling. He didn't touch his drink.

Joe Niccolo came in, sat down facing Brinkhaus.

From somewhere out of his clothes
a gun appeared, magically.

"How come you're over this way, Sarge?"

Brinkhaus lowered his eyes from the ceiling. They were plain brown eyes in a brown face.

"Where's Hermie?" he said.

"Hermie?"

"Hermie."

Niccolo had teeth like polished pearls when he smiled.

"You're askin' me?"

"I'm askin' you, Joe. I come here and I'm askin' you."

"If Hermie comes in I'll tell him."

Brinkhaus looked at the ceiling, then looked at Niccolo.

"I ain't just makin' conversation, Joe."

Niccolo's smile got very small. He looked at his polished fingernails. When he bent his head the red glow played on his thick, wavy hair. He carried an aroma of perfume. He shrugged.

"I'm just tellin' you, Sarge." His dark eyes matched his white teeth in brilliance. Brinkhaus was unemotional.

"Hermie's here."

"Says who?"

"You ain't playin' ball, Joe."

Niccolo adjusted his stiff, immaculate cuffs.

"I got nothin' to play ball with, Sarge."

"You get Hermie down here, Joe."

"I tell you—"

"I'm doin' the tellin'."

Niccolo put his palms together piously, looked at the table and said, "I ain't takin' crap from you, Sarge. I told you what. Take it or leave it."

Brinkhaus stood up, grabbed his hat and started across the dance floor. His shoes creaked, his heels hit the boards with a hard, heavy thump. He reached a door and pulled aside a curtain. He turned and looked back. Niccolo was standing, looking at him.

BRINKHAUS climbed the staircase and reached a dimly lighted corridor. He heard laughter and noise at the rear end of the hall. He went toward it, his broad fists doubling but his face remaining unemotional. He reached the door and listened and the door shook as someone bumped against it.

Brinkhaus knocked loudly. He had to knock several times. The door opened and a fog-eyed girl stood swaying on her heels.

"Good evening, mister—or have we met?"

"Git out o' the way."

"I—I spose you bark too, huh? Go ahead, bark—like a nice doggie."

Brinkhaus pushed her aside and saw three men and two other girls. One of the girls was sprawled on a divan trying to drink from a glass which a man held. The man was really only a boy. His hair was tousled and his back was to the door.

A red-head said, "Who the hell let you in?"

The girl who had opened the door giggled. "He's Rin-tin-tin or somebody. *Arf! Arf!*"

The red-head was burly. He came toward Brinkhaus.

"I said—who the hell let you in?"

Brinkhaus looked at him quietly, then turned and went heavily across the room toward the divan. He laid his hand on the boy's shoulder. The boy turned, looked up, stood up and squared his jaw. His eyes were bleary and a curl of light brown hair touched his left eyebrow.

"You git," Brinkhaus muttered.

The boy's hands made white fists and his lips tried to form words. The girl on the divan kicked up her heels and shouted, "Whoopee!" The red-head hunched his shoulders and moved step by step, slowly, toward the divan, and stood back of Brinkhaus, his arms bowed, a threatening look on his freckled face.

"Git, Hermie," Brinkhaus muttered.

"What right have you got to bust in here and tell me?" the boy said. "I'm twenty-one! I know what I can do and I ain't goin' to take orders from nobody!"

"You git, Hermie."

A dough-faced youth put down his drink, sat down by a piano and began playing. He played with a lot of noise and sang in a loud, raucous voice. Brinkhaus turned and looked at him vaguely. Then he looked back at the boy, gripped the boy's arm with his left hand.

Red spots of anger flamed on the boy's cheeks.

"I ain't goin' anywhere! I got a right to stay here! I got a right to do what I want! Leggo my arm!"

"Hermie—" Brinkhaus shook his head wearily. "Hermie."

"Leggo!"

Downstairs the jazz band broke loose; its thumping, pounding sound electrified the walls and floor and a lamp on a table shook and glasses on a tray tinkled. The red-head got closer to the broad back of Brinkhaus and the dough-faced youth struck a final chord, swiveled the piano stool and looked at the others with a jovial leer.

"Git your hat and coat, Hermie," Brinkhaus said thickly.

"You leggo my arm."

Hermie swore and twisted away violently. Brinkhaus gripped with both hands. The red-head curled a lip and arched a short, chopping blow that stopped against Brinkhaus's neck. Brinky fell, carrying Hermie with him to the divan. They fell on the girl. She squealed and kicked and the boy caught one of the blows on the head and relaxed. The dough-faced youth stood up, hefting the piano stool and leering jovially. Two of the girls tiptoed to the door and let themselves out quietly and the third, kicking herself free of the divan, fell to the floor. The red-head grabbed Brinkhaus from behind, hauled him from the divan, whirled him around and sent him staggering across the floor. Brinkhaus hit a table full force, carried it against the wall. The wall stopped it abruptly and Brinkhaus flattened on the table, rolled off to the floor and carried a bridge-lamp down with him.

The dough-faced youth was swinging the piano stool like a pendulum. His jovial leer never faded. The red-head glowered and hunched his shoulders and watched Brinkhaus get up. The sergeant's fedora was battered in and there were three buttons off his vest. His face was a little blank and there was an absence of anger in his voice when he said:

"Go easy now. You guys are canned and go easy. I just want Hermie and he's goin' to go. Now go easy."

"You scram, you!" the red-head snarled.

Brinkhaus raised a broad palm.

"Don't be nutty."

The dough-faced youth laughed and let fly with the piano stool. It barged past Brinkhaus's head. It hit the wall with a terrific crash, gashed open the plaster and broke lathing, fell to the floor with a thud.

Brinky seemed to get broader, taller and darker. His hair-brush mustache bristled. He went across the room like a steam-roller, hit the dough-faced youth and drove his head against the music rack on the piano. The rack shattered. Chords banged. Brinky picked him up, shook him and slammed him down to the floor

The red-head went for a gun and Brinky crowded him, stamped a heel on the red-head's toes, made him howl. The gun was out but up in the air and the gun hand was throttled in Brinky's broad iron fingers. The gun wheeled, crashed out the ceiling light and the room was plunged into darkness.

The two men, spinning, hit the piano and knocked it over. It struck the floor with a thunder of wood and banging chords. The gun spun away in the darkness, struck a mirror and shattered it. The red-head got his teeth on Brinky's ear and Brinky gritted, got out his blackjack, chopped it once. He felt the red-head slide down his stomach.

He stumbled to the door, opened it, found a crowd of men listening there. Niccolo was among them.

"My God!" Niccolo exclaimed.

"I come for Hermie," Brinkhaus said.

He struck a match and went into the room. The divan was empty. He growled, "Hermie!"

He took the match around the room, stepped over the dough-faced youth, over the red-head. Hermie was not there. Brinkhaus returned to the door. He looked queerly at the faces there.

"Where'd Hermie go?" he said, looking at Joe Niccolo.

"Honest, I ain't seen him. I just came up."

There was dull red beneath the honest brown of Brinky's face. There was sweat shining like oil on his face. In his battered hat and his crushed hard collar, he looked almost ludicrous. Someone snickered.

"O.K.," Brinky muttered. "O.K., *wisenheimers*."

CHAPTER TWO

THE HIDEOUT

YELLOW-HAIRED INSPECTOR Peter Larsen said, "You look as if you've been up all night, Brinky," and carried his straw hat to the costumer. He went to his desk through bars of morning sunlight.

Brinkhaus blew his nose loudly.

"I been," he said.

"Been what?"

"Up all night. I called Mom on the phone and I git hell there too. I been places, all right, boss." His broad jaw looked oddly grim, there was a dead grimness in his plain words. Only his brown eyes remained placid as they stared at the window. "I'm in a jam, boss."

Blue-gray-eyed Larsen slit a letter half-way open, stopped, regarded Brinkhaus quizzically. Brinky gave him an apologetic look.

"Me boy Hermie," Brinky said.

"Oh!" Larsen nodded. "Oh—I see."

"Last night I went after him. I been warnin' him—in a nice way. So last night I went after him over to Breakneck Hill and I tried to git him out and there was a ruckus and he lammed on me. Plastered he was. Me Hermie! By God, boss, and him just a kid—just twenty-one! In Joe Niccolo's dump—with a dizzy dame—and 'Red' Corrigan and Louie Snekvik, and two other broads that could add chapters to any book on what a young gal oughta know!"

"You—got in trouble?"

"Me? No. No, boss, I wasn't on official business so I didn't go for me rod. I mighta cleaned up a bit but in a nice way. It ain't that. It's Hermie. It's—" His voice dropped, he shrugged, looked at his palms. "Hermie ain't home. Hermie didn't go home last night. I been huntin' high and low for him. I didn't find him."

Larsen said, "Everything will be all right, Brinky. He'll turn up. He was just scared."

"I seen it growin'," Brinkhaus said dully, thickly. "I seen him get smarter. I been watchin' and I shoulda knew, but it's only now, when I look back, that I see I shoulda knew. I don't want he shouldn't have his fun, but not in that crowd. I tailed him there through a hat-check I found in his room. You know that joint, boss. You know all Breakneck Hill. It's lousy. A kid ain't a man suddenly when he turns twenty-one. It don't happen as fast as that."

"Niccolo ought to know where he went."

"Niccolo plays dumb Indian. And how can Hermie run with that crowd on $23.50 a week, takin' off the $8.50 he gives Mom? That's it, boss. Dough. Dough for booze and them rotten women. Dough—and how the hell to get it. That's it! By cripes, that I should live to see the day when me flesh and blood'd run with the kind o' mugs I been fightin' for twenty-two years. It gits me where I swaller!" He raised a rugged fist. "I got to git Hermie before—before— Well, I got to git him!"

Larsen leaned back, interlocked fingers on his flat stomach. He had never seen Brinkhaus so crushed. He had never seen the old war-horse so up against it and showing it. The same dents were in Brinky's hat. His collar was a wreck, and his tie was half-undone. Dirt was on his coat. Last night he had had time for nothing but trying to find his son. His eyes were red-rimmed and there was stubble on his chin.

Larsen got up, went around the desk, patted Brinky's shoulder.

"Better take a snooze, old timer."

"How can I?"

"You've got to. Go home and see your wife. Take a sleep, a bath and a shave. Go on, Brinky."

"I got to listen to Mom bawl? Cripes, I can't stand women bawlin'. Me pal Ogglecarp was the same way."

"You've got to, Brinky."

Brinky's voice shook.

"What'll happen to me kid?" He turned a sigh into a grunt and got up. "Hell, I'm gittin' slushy. Excuse it, boss."

He turned and stamped out, his broad back rocking.

Five minutes later Larsen went downstairs. Hoolihan was waiting at the wheel of the police phaeton.

"212 Redfern, Hen."

Larsen sat in the rear with his first cigar of the day. The streets were bright with morning sunlight, the air clear like the sound of a bell. Bright fruits and green vegetables stood in sidewalk displays. White-gloved traffic officers saluted at intersections.

REDFERN AVENUE was west of Civic Park. 212 was a six-story apartment house with Ionic pillars supporting a gray marquee.

"I won't be long, Hen."

"Oke, boss."

Larsen spent money for his clothes. He looked it.

The lobby had pinkish pottery in it and a lot of fresco work that wasn't quite rococo. The elevator was a gilded cage, self-operated. Larsen took it to the fourth floor and walked down a broad corridor on mauve-colored carpet between blue-gray walls. 404 stared him in the face and he knocked, removed his hat, held it in both hands in front of his chest.

A negress opened the door. She was pretty.

"I'm Inspector Larsen. Tell Niccolo I'm here."

She went away with a spinning of short black skirt and a rap of high heels.

Niccolo came out in a flamingo dressing gown, strolling. His face looked newly shaven. Bright eyes matched his bright smile.

"Come in, Inspector."

Niccolo turned and strolled from the small reception hall into a living room with a beamed ceiling and many lamps, many chairs. A woman with russet hair drew a dark green peignoir closer and bent her head backward to avoid smoke that rose from a cigarette between her lips. The maid, clearing dishes from a breakfast room, looked up.

"You alone, Joe," Larsen said.

Niccolo looked at the woman. She swayed into a bedroom, left the door open. Niccolo closed it and poured ale from a bottle into a glass. He drank.

"To you, Inspector."

His eyes were steady over the glass's rim.

"How about Brinky's kid?" Larsen said.

"Kid? Man, you should see one of my rooms! This guy Brinkhaus does things up brown."

"He's dynamite, once he gets going."

Niccolo was casual. "What I say? How's tricks at headquarters?"

"Fine." Larsen looked around. "Nice place you have here."

"We like it."

"How's the Tomahawk doing?"

Niccolo shrugged smooth shoulders.

"So-so."

"You'd like to keep it doing—so-so. Wouldn't you?"

Niccolo lit a cigarette, smiled wryly.

"You're being nice as hell, ain't you?"

"I want to tell you something, Joe. Brinky's probably the best friend I have in the department. He's gold, all up and all over. He'd go to hell and beyond for me regardless of the consequences. I don't know how far I'd go for him—but pretty far, Joe. Pretty damned far. The old boy's hard up against it, and something's got to be done about it."

Joe sat down, leaned back.

"What am I supposed to say?"

"His kid's been hanging out at your dump—"

"It's no dump."

"All right, call it a dive. To me it's a dump. The kid's been hanging out there with guys and janes you know. The kid lammed on his old man last night and hasn't shown up this morning. The kid's at a bad age and I'm not going to have him rat on his old man through associating with the kind of guys you know."

"You're pretty strong, ain't you?"

"Don't be pious, Joe. I know what you are and so do you. Now, I want a line on the kid, the jane he's tangled up with, these eggs Red Corrigan and Snekvik and the whole shebang."

"I don't keep addresses, Inspector."

"With a good memory, you don't have to."

"Why pick on me if the kid comes into my place? It's a public place. Can I chuck him out? Can I help if he comes there?"

"No. But you played dumb to Brinky's questions last night and it gives off a smell I don't like. It's plain to see the kid has a crush on this jane, and if the jane hangs out at your dump I don't like her. She's no good for him."

"All right. But should I keep addresses of everybody comes there?"

Larsen said quietly, "Who's the jane?"

"Ain't Brinky big enough to find out himself?"

"He's big enough to handle you and a dozen like you. That's not the question. He's all shot and I want to crack this thing before he cuts loose and goes haywire. And if you want to continue doing business on Breakneck Hill you'll take a tumble and come through."

Niccolo got up irritably.

"You guys burn me!"

"This is not a waltz, Joe. It's business."

"I tell you I don't know!"

"You're crazy."

"I don't!"

Larsen rose wearing a cool, gray smile that stayed cool on Niccolo's hot dark eyes.

"You like this nice apartment, Joe. You like swank. A turn of the screw and I can dump you back into Dago Alley and the punks that run there. Remember, you're running on Breakneck Hill—and living here—by the grace of God and a good-natured department. We can be dirty, Joe."

Niccolo's lips got wet.

"I'm strictly kosher, Larsen. I run a place of business—"

"Monkey business."

Niccolo flushed, snapped, "I don't know where his kid went. The kid was onkdray and pulled a lam out of my place. That's all I know. What are you pickin' on me for?"

Larsen pursed his lips. "No spikka English, eh?"

"Gee, I told you—"

"Enough, Joe." Larsen's voice picked up briskly. "I gave you a chance and you waltz me around. I told you what Brinky means to me. I smell dirt. Think it over. Call me at five sharp tonight—or your joint gets crashed and I put the screws on you."

Niccolo stared feverishly but said nothing. Larsen went out quietly, took the staircase down.

LOUIE SNEKVIK strummed a guitar and hummed *En Cuba* to a pair of love-birds in a green cage. His eyes drowsed and his jovial leer was satanic in the morning sunlight. He was entirely dressed but for shoes and stockings. Bare feet were perched upon a radiator.

Red Corrigan came in saying, "Damn that banjo!"

"It's a guitar, stupid."

"To hell with you. To me it's a banjo. Was I drunk last night? Unh—unh!"

"Not only drunk but dumb—pulling a gat on Brinkhaus."

Corrigan growled. "There's a guy I'd like to give the works—with all the trimmin's. But was the kid soused? Floss found him asleep in the bathtub, all dressed."

"Well, wasn't I there?"

Corrigan blinked.

"That's right—you was."

"No, *you* weren't drunk!" Louie chuckled, rose, got water and seed for the love-birds; cooed to them gently, tenderly, then said, "Me, would I like to give Brinkhaus a belly-full? I'd like to hold a Tommy gun on him till it run dry."

Corrigan stared at the back of Louie's neck. His voice was low. "How about the kid?" he asked.

Louie whistled.

"Jake. Everything's sweet and lovely. Lookit these two birds, Red. D'you ever see anything as cute? Just look!"

"Ah, nuts on them birds! We got other things—"

"You just don't appreciate the little things in life." Louie wore a beatific smile, cooed to the birds. "Yes, Red, for a nice sure go at Brinkhaus, in a dark alley—late—I'd give ten years of my life. Well, maybe ten."

Corrigan was impatient.

"Come on, get your shoes on. The way you monkey around them birds— Some day, dammit, I'll drown 'em!"

"You drown 'em, Red," Louie cooed, "and I'll shoot you inside out. Call that baloney and find out, sweetheart."

"You're funny, you are."

"At the workin' end of a rod I'm funny as hell."

Corrigan looked at the back of Louie's neck. He said nothing. He got his hat and put it on and stood waiting in stone silence. Louie got into socks and shoes.

"The kid's gone over the fence for Floss. He's screwy. He played right into her hands. We handle this right Red, and it'll be upsy-daisy all around. You know him. You know that after a bender he can't remember a thing. That's swell for us. With Floss workin' on him especially."

Corrigan muttered, "If Joe Niccolo's don't rat on us."

"Dumb-bell, Niccolo can't afford to. I talked it all out with him. It's Joe's big chance. It's our big chance."

"But dagoes—and dames—"

"Hooey! I know dames and I know dagoes, but I'm beginnin' to wonder about the guts of the Irish."

"Cut that, Polack!"

Louie's eyes drowsed and his drop smile showed teeth spaced wide apart.

"You wouldn't be gettin' tough, would you?"

"Ah, nuts, Louie—what's the use of battlin'? Come on."

They got an old Cadillac touring out of a nearby garage and Louie drove on through the city; down the Post Road to the West Bridge and across the river. The road went along a high embankment east of which were railroad yards, and far beyond the squat shapes of oil storage tanks. Louis hummed something from *La Bohême* and smiled at the bright warm sunlight. They left the state highway three miles farther on and took a black-top road through wooded country. The road began to roll up and down and birds sang in trees and there was a lush smell of earth.

They rolled through a small settlement of one main street, crossed a covered wooden bridge, took the right turn of a fork and followed it for a mile. A lone farmhouse stood behind four elms, and Louie swung in, drove around to the rear and into a large barn where another car was parked.

The woman who had been drunk on the Tomahawk divan waited for them at the back door. She leaned with one broad hip higher than the other. Her hair was blue-black, cut Japanese fashion.

"Hello, baby," Louie said. "How's the kid?"

"Got a head."

"He remember anything?"

"Not a thing."

Louie grinned. "Swell!"

Hermie sat at the kitchen table in shirt sleeves, his elbows planted among empty breakfast dishes, his head between his hands. His face looked washed-out, dark half-moons were beneath his eyes. He looked bewildered. Floss put an arm around him, kissed his head, smiled over his head at Louie and Red Corrigan.

Hermie swallowed.

"What—what—"

"Now be calm," Louie droned. "Be calm, pal. It's all O.K. We're standin' by you."

"But—what happened?"

Corrigan wore a concerned look.

"You just gotta lay low and keep a stiff lip, buddy."

"But, God, what happened?"

Corrigan inhaled dramatically, looked Fat Louie. Louie nodded.

"It wasn't your fault, kid. The guys landed on you and you grabbed up a gun and it went off. One of the dicks got hit. Now, now, take it easy."

Hermie stood up, shaking.

"I—I shot somebody!"

"Sh!" Louie soothed. "They were lookin' for it. Your old man busted in with some guys on a raid. He slammed you and knocked you down. We tried—hell, you're our pal—we tried to defend you. We mopped up and got you out safe and—"

Hermie cried, "I didn't shoot pop!"

"No—no. It was some other shamus," Louie said.

"O God!" Hermie groaned. He sank back to the chair, his face shocked. "I must have been crazy!"

Louie patted his shoulder.

"You got us, Hermie. We'd do anything for you. We got you out of that scatter at the risk of our life. But what the hell. Nothin's too much for a pal. We—we're in bad too. But as I said—what the hell. We had to stand by a pal. Floss took you over and we covered your tracks."

Hermie's voice was clotted.

"I don't remember a thing." He looked up at them with a stricken face. "What am I goin' to do?"

"Just sit tight," Louie said. "We got friends. We'll see you through, kid—for your sake and Floss's."

"Pop'd kill me. Pop 'd—"

Louie droned, "I don't like to make any cracks against a guy's father, Hermie, only I seen things your pop did. I seen him burn guys with cigarettes. I seen him beat 'em with a chair till the chair busted. I know a dozen guys he's double-crossed. Maybe you ain't known that at home. But we know. Huh, Red?"

"I hate to say it, Louie, but that's right. He's always persecuted guys that ain't had a chance. And I used to like him too, oncet."

Floss said, "Leave it to me to take care of Hermie. I love Hermie and no guy is going to hurt him—only over my dead body."

"I'll go back," Hermie gritted, making a fist. "I'll go back and give myself up. I ain't goin' to drag you guys in. I'll take the blame. I'll go back—and face—pop."

Louie looked horrified.

"You wouldn't stand a chance! What, shootin' a dick—and then goin' back! You're a screw loose, Hermie!"

"I don't care. I ain't goin' to drag in my pals. I'll take what's comin' to me."

Louie purred. "Suppose they stick you away for ten or twenty years? What about Floss? She needs a guy like you—"

"I—I couldn't live without him," Floss said.

Hermie groaned and kissed her hand.

"I couldn't live without you, Floss."

"Besides," Red Corrigan said, "we helped you, Hermie. We're in a jam, too. You go back and it means we get hauled in too. We're all in it, kid. We all gotta stick together. Hell, it ain't a bad racket. You got to support Floss. You got to take care of her. You can make a coupla thousand a month easy—and honest, too."

Floss said, dramatically, "If Hermie got sent up—I'd kill myself!"

"O God!" Hermie groaned, and held her tightly.

Louie lit a cigarette.

"There's only one guy might come between you and Floss, Hermie. He's been after Floss. He hates her and he'd like to put the cross on her."

Hermie looked up.

"Who?"

"A big fella. Gus Hagehorn. He runs this town—almost. He lives on the north side. He's a bad egg, Gus is."

Hermie gulped. "He'd—kill Floss?"

"Even that, maybe," Louie nodded grimly. "Even that."

JOE NICCOLO was well-groomed in a dark suit with a faint pin-stripe. His tie alone cost eight dollars. His gray fedora cost fifteen. He leaned against a slot-machine in a room back of a south side bar. Smoke rose tranquilly from his cork-tipped cigarette.

"This sounds good," he said.

"Good!" Louie exclaimed softly. "Man alive, it's the biggest step you ever took! I tell you, Joe, we got the kid where it's all gravy and red meat. He'll act noble for Floss if he kills himself doin' it."

Joe Niccolo looked at his cigarette.

"And how about Floss?"

"For what we want her"—Louie patted down his palm—"just swell elegant. It means a jump of a thousand per cent for you in profits. It means a jump for Red and me and the guys that run with you and us. And, cripes, it's air-tight." He was close up against Joe Niccolo, holding Joe's lapels for emphasis. "We been playin' the kid for a month.

We got him all sewed up. Gus Hagehorn's been ridin' high and mighty and just askin' for this fall."

Joe Niccolo took a thoughtful puff.

"Larsen made a crack that if I don't steer him on Hermie he'll padlock the Tomahawk."

Louie chuckled drily.

"Let him. Let the bum do it. What the hell do you care about the Tomahawk when you got this big stuff starin' you in the kisser? To hell with the Tomahawk."

"H'm," mused Niccolo.

"But get this, Joe: we got to act fast. We got to act before the kid gets cold. He's hot now. We got to act while he's hot. And he's red-hot—for Floss—and Red and me."

"H'm," mused Joe Niccolo.

He turned, stuck a quarter into the slot-machine, cranked it, got nothing. He turned around and looked at Louie.

"It's got to be sure, Louie."

"Do I clown around with anything that ain't sure?"

"It's got to be damned sure, Louie."

"It's open and shut"—he smiled—"big fella."

Joe Niccolo expanded his chest, smiled. His dark eyes were bright and shining.

"Big—fella," he mused.

"Sure. Why not?"

Joe Niccolo looked almost benevolent when he laid his hand on Louie's shoulder. His head nodded—once.

Louie chuckled.

"You ain't dumb—big fella."

CHAPTER THREE

MURDER!

A DAY went by. A night. Another day. It took five pounds away from Brinkhaus. It put an awful grimness in the set of Brinky's mouth. It put a queer, fixed look in his eyes that hardly wavered, hour after hour. It put a coldness in his heart that reached out slowly to every corner of his being. It rolled emotion into a frozen ball and jammed it somewhere back of his rugged chest. It got Brinky.

He finished supper.

"I'm goin' back to headquarters, Mom."

He forgot to fold his napkin. That meant something. Mom looked at him.

"You ought to get some sleep, Herm."

"Shucks, I ain't tired."

She had cried herself out hours before, had turned into a quiet rock of patience and unrelenting hope.

"He'll come back, Herm. He's a good boy. I know him."

She was not as close to the warp and woof of crime as her husband was. She hadn't seen crime raw and unadorned. She couldn't realize that a good boy could be lured into the crimson fist of crime through the medium of degenerate men, case-hardened women. Brinky believed all things possible.

"I'll just go down and hang around," he said.

"You haven't slept in two nights."

She hadn't either.

Brinky got up and went across the room slowly and got his hat. His shoes were smudged. There was stubble on his face again. His suit needed pressing. That meant something.

"Don't worry, Mom."

He was at the door. She didn't cry. She was too white-faced to cry. She didn't say anything.

Brinky went down one flight of stairs, into the summer night. He walked with the slight rocking motion of a heavy man. Nobody knew it at headquarters. No one but Larsen and himself. That was the hell of it. Only the two of them scouring the city for Red Corrigan and Louie Snekvik and Hermie. Larsen knew what a blow it would be to Brinkhaus to have the news spread.

Nor had Larsen slept in two nights. The yellow-haired Swede had just finished shaving when Brinky trudged into the office.

"Nothin', boss?"

"Nothing, Brinky."

Brinkhaus sat down, stared.

"If only I could talk to him, boss. If only I could see him and talk to him. He's my kid. I love that kid, boss."

"I'd hoped to get some dope through Niccolo. We crashed his joint. Closed it. He took it quietly. That's what puzzles me—he took it quietly."

"Niccolo might be all right."

Larsen said, "I've got four of my best stoolies looking for Corrigan and Snekvik. I said nothing about Hermie. We find them and we'll find Hermie. Niccolo's either stubborn—or kosher. We can't press him too hard, because if we do— After all, this has got to be a quiet recovery."

"You're white, boss."

"I like Hermie too, Brinky."

There was a hum in the loud-speaker on Larsen's desk. The police dispatcher's monotonous voice sounded.

"A call just came in from Patrolman John Wiltshire, of the fifth precinct, on peg post between Anderman and Crosby Streets. An unidentified woman was found stabbed to death in an alley back of the old stables on Ludlow Street, near Gas, at seven-forty-five o'clock."

Brinkhaus moved forward in his chair, interest suddenly displacing despondency on his broad face. Larsen got up, went to the costumer, listened while the dispatcher's voice trailed off. He put on his hat.

"You stay here, Brinky."

"I better go."

They went downstairs, past the shooting gallery, into the garage, where Hoolihan was polishing the bright work on the phaeton.

"Ludlow and Gas, Hen," Larsen said.

"O.K., boss."

WHERE Ludlow meets Gas, south of Little Italy, you get the smell of the river, and on very damp nights an age-old smell rises from the abandoned stables, recalling the '90s and two and four team trucks, wet kegs and raw hides on the move. Around Gas and Ludlow is a honeycomb of alleys where the sun never reaches and the cobbles stay damp from the night mists. It is a swell place to do murder.

The tinted headlights of the city ambulance threw a red glow over the broken sidewalk. There was no street light nearby and a couple of cops moved around with pocket flashes. Deputy Medical Examiner George Josephs stood with hands on hips dictating to his secretary in a good-natured voice. District Attorney Dan Paddison was scouting furiously up and down the alley with a flashlight.

The phaeton arrived and Hoolihan swung two spotlights up the alley. Larsen got out and one of the cops pointed and Larsen went up the alley.

George Josephs said, "Hello, Peter. There she is."

"Knifed, eh?"

"Once. Just once. Through the heart."

Larsen bent over and one of the cops sprayed his flashlight up and down the body.

"She wasn't killed here," the deputy medical examiner said. He pointed. "There's a few drops of blood along the alley."

"Could she have crawled?"

"No. She died when she was stabbed. She was carried here, left here."

Larsen straightened.

"Where's Wiltshire?"

"Here, Inspector."

"How'd you happen to find her?"

Wiltshire said, "I always poke in these alleys for lush jobs. I fell over her."

"Hello, Pete," The D.A. said, coming down the alley. "This is sweet, isn't it?"

"Hello, Dan. Find anything?"

"Not a thing. Know her, Pete?"

"No. You?"

"Nope."

Brinkhaus bulked in the glare of the phaeton's spotlights. He bent over, palms on knees, arms braced.

"Know her, Brinky?" the D.A. said.

"I dunno. I—I think I seen her—once."

He remained as he was, bent over, for a long minute. He straightened quietly and his face was a brown, heavy mask. The lights' glare made his eyeballs glint. He dipped his head forward so that his hat brim made a shadow halfway down his face.

The deputy medical examiner said, "She was stabbed somewhere else and brought here. You can see that something—maybe a blanket or a towel—was held against the wound to absorb the blood. You can see the way the blood spread and caked. Then when she was carried in the alley a few drops fell."

"Wiltshire," Larsen said, "was there anybody around the street when you found her?"

"Not a soul."

"This is sure a lulu," the D.A. said.

Wiltshire said, "I guess there's the morgue bus."

"Well, look, Pete," the D.A. said. "I've a date. Got to run along. If anything sudden turns up phone me at the Hotel Storrs." He poked Brinkhaus. "How's things, Brinky?"

"O.K., Dan."

They carried the dead woman on a stretcher to the morgue bus. Two morgue attendants argued about a baseball game that day. The deputy medical examiner told Larsen about a new book revealing the affairs of Louis XIV and chuckled over a few choice morsels. One cop laid a bet with another on the outcome of an impending prize fight.

Brinkhaus waited by the police phaeton while Hoolihan rattled on about some new tricks of his two-year-old son. Brinkhaus nodded, said, "Unh," absently, from time to time. The ambulance and the morgue bus drove away. The D.A. had gone. George Josephs and his secretary drove off in a flivver. Larsen stood meditatively at the mouth of the alley, then came toward the phaeton, climbed in and dropped to the seat with a sigh. Brinkhaus followed and Hoolihan got into gear.

They went up through Little Italy, through the color, clamor and smells of Cherry Square; the pool parlors, social dubs, spaghetti stores; past stands of artichokes, spring onions, ripe tomatoes.

Larsen said, quite casually, "You knew her, eh, Brinky?"

Brinkhaus sat with hands clasped between his knees. He stared fixedly at nothing.

"Who was she, Brinky?"

Brinkhaus stared and swayed slightly as the phaeton wheeled around a corner.

Larsen said, "Hermie's, eh?"

A gust of wind clattered in the canvas top and they passed the shrill whistle of a peanut vendor.

Larsen laid a well-kept hand on Brinky's solid knee. "Remember, Brinky, that I'm a cop—but I'm your friend first."

Brinkhaus unclasped his hands, put one on top of Larsen's.

"I know, boss. I know. Thanks."

A ragged street minstrel played humoresque on a violin to fat women leaning on tenement-house window-sills. The stars were low brilliant chips in a powder-blue sky.

"I know, boss," Brinkhaus said thickly. "But me—me, I'm a cop. All over, I'm a cop."

Little Italy dropped behind.

"Was he in love with her, Brinky?"

"I dunno. I dunno just how they stood. He must ha' been seein' her lots, though. He's got a temper when he's started. And that drinkin'. He can't stand drinkin'. When a kid like him gets drinkin' and a jane like her gits to crackin' wise, a kid like him might git—dangerous. She must ha' been ten years older than him. Things mean different to a kid like Hermie than they'd mean to her—if I know me groceries. Hermie ain't got much sense o' humor."

He spoke without inflection. His voice was low, throaty, deadly in its even monotone. His lips scarcely moved. No part of him moved.

But one word he said with a phlegmatic catch of emotion. "Mom." Hoolihan swung the car into the headquarters' garage. Brinkhaus trudged behind Larsen to Larsen's office. Larsen was a little pale. But his voice was even.

"They'll identify her at the morgue—by morning, at least. We've got the night, Brinky."

Brinky had hard jowls.

"I ain't doin' right by the department, boss."

Larsen shook a hand.

"Forget it. We've got the night. Something's got to be done—quick. Action. Action law. Quick—"

"If Hermie—" Brinkhaus swallowed, groaned. "But, God, he's my kid!"

CHAPTER FOUR

THE CRIMSON FIST

THERE WAS one low lamp burning on the table in the farmhouse's living room. It was a dim light guarded by an old-rose shade. Wind blew in the elms outside.

Louie Snekvik lounged on a horsehair sofa strumming *Aloha Oe* on his guitar, crooning in a soft, languid tenor. He was dressed except for his shoes.

Hermie sat in a Boston rocker, next to the table. There were two bottles of Scotch on the table, glasses. The ash-tray was full of cigarette butts. Hermie rocked slowly and the rocker creaked and Hermie stared at the floor and heard the wind blowing in the elms, heard Louie's plaintive crooning. It made him think of Floss, of her white arms and soft lips. She had gone into town for dinner and to pick up news. Red had driven her in and come back again at eight. It was ten now.

Red kicked the kitchen door open and came in carrying a soup bowl filled with ice. Red glowered and banged the bowl down. He slammed cracked ice into a glass and broke the glass. He cursed and took another glass.

Hermie, trancelike, paid no attention.

Red filled half the glass with whiskey, finished with ginger ale. He drank it all down at two swallows and crunched ice vindictively between his teeth.

"Cripes, cut that bedroom music!" he growled.

Louie crooned on, laughter touching his voice.

Red leaned with his hands on the table, scowling across the lamp at the shadows that hid Louie. Red looked down at his hands. The lamp's glow made his hands look crimson. He grimaced, stood up, wiped his hands on his shirt, glared at the shadows.

"You hear, Louie!" he roared.

The guitar tinkled to silence. Louie yawned.

"You're gettin' temperamental as a chorus girl, Red."

"Nuts! I'm just gettin' fed up on this yammerin' o' yourn."

Louie sauntered nonchalantly across the room, switched on the radio. He listened.

"Here," he said, "is a guy talkin' on the peculiar habits o' the gnu. That suit you, Red?"

Red reached for the whiskey again. The red glow fell on his hands. His lips tightened. He growled and pulled the bottle away from the glow. He omitted the ginger ale.

Louie turned the dials.

"… and reporting police alarms for the past eight hours," came a stentorian voice.

"This should interest you, Red," Louie said.

Red Corrigan's eyebrows came close together.

Hermie came out of his trance.

The voice went on. "At 7:40 this evening an unidentified woman was found dead in an alley near Gas and Ludlow Streets by Patrolman John Wiltshire. She apparently had been stabbed through the heart at another place and removed to the alley by her assailant or assailants. Deputy Medical Examiner George Josephs reported that death was instantaneous. The woman is about five-feet-six and about thirty years of age. When found, she wore a green silk dress, beige stockings, brown snakeskin shoes, a brown cloth coat and a brown Empress Eugenie hat to match. Black hair, cut in an Oriental manner; brown eyes; two gold fillings in the upper right jaw. Any information leading to identification of this woman will be appreciated by police head-quarters. Telephone Centre 1000—"

Louie turned it off.

Hermie's hands were white-knuckled, his mouth agape.

Red Corrigan set the bottle down on the table, watched the lamp's red glow touch his fingers. He drew back, jammed his hands into his pockets.

"My God!" Hermie cried, and jumped up.

Louie said, "Easy, kid."

"It's—Floss!"

Red Corrigan muttered, "The heel got her!" in a grating voice.

Hermie spun on him.

"You took her in! Why didn't you watch her? What'd you let her alone for?"

"Gosh, kid, I didn't think."

Louie came over in front of Hermie.

"Sit down, kid. Hold your head. Give him a drink, Red."

Red Corrigan slopped liquor into a glass.

"I don't want it!" Hermie cried. "Floss is gone and—"

"You need it," Louie said. He pressed the glass to Hermie's lips. Hermie gulped it down, coughed.

Red Corrigan said, "T' think o' Floss, poor Floss. Why, she was the best all-around pal a guy could have."

"I'll tell the cops who did it!" Hermie cried. "I'll tell—"

"Easy now," Louie said. "The cops 'd like to find you, kid. Easy, Hermie."

"I don't care if they do! Floss is dead! What the hell does it matter?"

Louie gripped his arm.

"You remember that me and Red are in a jam, too, kid. When a guy bumps off a friend, we don't run to the cops. We ain't that kind. We settle our own troubles. Only guys with no guts run to the cops, Hermie. It takes guts to settle your own troubles."

"Gus Hagehorn did it," Hermie mumbled. "You said Gus Hagehorn had the finger on her."

Red Corrigan nodded. "Who else? There ain't no guy woulda bumped Floss off but Gus."

HERMIE began pacing the room, biting his knuckles. His eyes stared feverishly before him. Floss was gone. He wouldn't feel her white arms or her warm lips any more. He would have gone anywhere with her, done anything for her. She was dead and lying in the morgue now and Gus Hagehorn had done it.

Hermie was in a bad way. He felt he could never go back to his father, never walk the streets openly again. Louie and Red had taken him in and hid him from the police at their own risk. He had shot a detective. Louie and Red said so. He couldn't remember because he'd been very drunk that night. Now that Floss was dead he longed for Mom. He was a kid at heart and he longed for his mother.

"You need liquor, Hermie," Louie said soothingly. "It'll brace you up."

Hermie was white.

"I don't need liquor, Louie. I want to be stark sober."

"Don't he a goof!"

"I ain't a goof. I don't need liquor."

Red growled. "You gonna let this mutt Hagehorn get away with bumpin' off your woman? You gonna let this cake-slashin' slide?"

Louie dumped liquor into a glass and thrust the glass into Hermie's hand.

"Get that under your belt, kid."

Hermie went to the table and set the glass down.

"I don't need liquor. You're talkin' about guts, Louie. Only a guy without guts needs liquor. Where's Hagehorn live?"

Red Corrigan expanded, took in a reef on his belt.

"The kid's hunkydory, Louie."

"Where's Hagehorn live?" Hermie gritted.

Louie went to a sideboard wiping his hands on a handkerchief. He opened a drawer, drew out a .45 Colt automatic. He stood wiping the gun with the handkerchief. He laid the gun on the sideboard, closed the drawer. He strolled across the room. "There's a roscoe on the sideboard, kid," he said.

He sat down on the horsehair sofa, pulled on his socks, his shoes.

Hermie crossed to the sideboard, picked up the gun, held it tightly in his hand. Red Corrigan went into the bedroom and got Hermie's coat out of a closet. He took a long, thin clasp-knife from his pocket, wiped it off on a handkerchief and held it with the handkerchief until it slipped into the inside pocket of Hermie's coat, among a packet of old letters.

When he returned to the living room Hermie had gone into the bathroom.

Red Corrigan grinned and said nothing. Louie came up close to him.

"He'll get Gus—but he'll never get out o' that house alive."

"That's the way we want it, ain't it?"

Louie chuckled.

"You should ask!"

Hermie came out of the bathroom. Red Corrigan held his coat and Hermie shoved arms into the sleeves. They all put on hats and Louie turned out the living room light and they went into the kitchen. Louie paused to look at the love-birds, then motioned to Red and Red took Hermie to the back door. Louie turned out the kitchen light and they walked across the yard to the barn.

Louie started the car and sat behind the wheel warming up the motor. Red Corrigan and Hermie sat in the rear. Louie backed out, rolled among the elms and swung onto a dirt road. The settlement was dark when they drove through.

Red Corrigan said, "Cripes, we shoulda got Gus long before this. We sure shoulda."

Hermie hardly heard him. There was a cold white flame burning in his chest. There was a numbness in his brain. He was certain he was going to his death. He had no doubt about it. He didn't know just how it would happen but he was sure it would happen. He would vindicate the murder of Floss. He would kill the man who had killed Floss. Beyond that nothing mattered.

"You guys have been good to me," he said. "You and Louie. I want to thank you, Red."

"Aw, hell."

"It was through you I met Floss. She was wonderful to me. She was the first woman I ever loved. I couldn't love another."

"Poor Floss."

"I'm going to kill Hagehorn."

The summer night was cool and mellow. Mists came from the river, cool and strong in the nostrils. The stars twinkled and there was a moon. Floss used to rave about the moonlight. It was all over now. Hermie felt tragic and remote from worldly things.

The bridge lights shone ahead, the lights of the city beyond. They crossed the bridge and went up the Post Road. Hermie didn't bother about the streets. Louie turned many corners and Red Corrigan spoke in a low, dramatic voice, telling Hermie what to do, how to act. They were swell guys, Red and Louie. They were sticking by him, helping him.

He'd like to see Mom once more. And Pop. And the new baby. But he wouldn't have time. And he wouldn't want to see the look on Mom's face. Hermie never pitied himself. There was a man's job ahead of him tonight.

Louie pulled up in a quiet neighborhood, halfway between two corners. He let the motor idle.

Red Corrigan said, "Walk up here, kid, turn right the next block. It's the fourth house from the corner. Number 48. It's brown brick with a wooden veranda."

"We'll pick you up here," Louie said. "At the corner."

Hermie got out. "You boys better get along. Don't hang around and get caught."

"Nuts," Red Corrigan said. "We're your pals."

Hermie shook their hands. "Good-by, pals."

He walked away, turned right at the next corner and walked slowly, deliberately. He felt very cool and self-contained. He was going to die and he didn't care; when you felt that way you could feel cool.

HE DIDN'T see the car slipping past the corner he had turned. He didn't see Red Corrigan and Louie Snekvik leaving. He saw the brown brick house with the wooden veranda and shrubbery on the lawn. There were lights in the house. He didn't pause. He took the cement walk to the veranda, climbed the steps firmly, rang the bell.

A man opened the door. He was a gaunt, granite-jawed man in a black coat, a little black vest.

"I want to see Hagehorn," Hermie said.

"What's the name?"

"Brinkhaus."

The gaunt man looked. "I know Sergeant Brinkhaus."

"I'm his son."

"Come in. Wait here."

The entrance hall was done in dark-panelled wood, lighted by wrought-iron candelabra. There were high-backed chairs of dark, carved wood. The gaunt man disappeared and Hermie stood with his hands at his sides.

The gaunt man reappeared.

"In here," he said.

Hermie saw a large, luxurious room. A man's room, with massive furniture, thick rugs. A big man lay on the floor laughing and watching a child of two or three playing with building blocks. Hermie remembered when he had played that way. It was all so long ago and far away.

"Hello, hello," the big man rumbled cheerfully. "O.K., Buck, beat it."

The gaunt man went out, closing the door. The big man got up and grinned good-naturedly, scratched the back of his neck with one hand, shoved out the other.

"I didn't know Brinky's son was on the force. I must be gettin' behind the times. Have a seat, won't you?"

Hermie shook hands mechanically and Gus Hagehorn lumbered to a big chair, flopped down into it, reached around side-wise to take a cigar from a humidor.

The gun was in Hermie's hand.

"I'm not on the force, Hagehorn."

Hagehorn squinted at the gun, looked Hermie up and down, struck a match and lit his cigar.

"Humph," he grunted.

"I came here to kill you," Hermie muttered.

"Me? What the hell do you want to kill me for?"

"You know," Hermie said bitterly. "You know."

Hagehorn lounged back, crossed one big leg over the other, took two slow, ruminative puffs.

"This is the berries," he said. "Hell, I don't know what to say."

"Da," said the child on the floor.

Hagehorn said, "Be quiet, son."

"You killed Floss," Hermie muttered. "You murdered Floss."

"Oh, so it's Floss. And who, I oughta ask, is Floss?"

Hermie muttered. "Don't give me the run-around, you!"

Hagehorn considered his cigar. "Honest, kid, you hand me a honey to figure out. Floss who?"

"Floss McGirty, damn you!"

"I'm sorry, Mr. Brinkhaus, but I don't know her. What's she do? Where'd she hang out? Why'd I kill her?"

"Da," said the child on the floor, crawled to Hagehorn's knees, crawled to his lap.

"And that baby ain't goin' to save you!"

Hagehorn put his cigar between his teeth, took the baby in his arms, carried it across the room and laid in on a divan. He returned to the chair and resumed his seat.

"I don't hide behind babies," he said. "And I'm not heeled. You've got all the chance in the world to do your stuff. But as you go out"— he nodded toward the door—"Buck will get you. Sure as hell."

"I know," Hermie said in a low throbbing voice. "And I don't care. You killed the girl I loved, Hagehorn. You stabbed her to death— tonight—and left her in an alley near Gas Street. You've been wanting to do it for a long time. You did it—tonight. I'll get killed for killin' you. That's what I came here for."

Hagehorn smoked.

"I'm sorry, kid. Your old man is a swell cop—the swellest on the force. A white guy. I'm sorry as hell to see a son o' his go meshuga on a bum steer. It'll kill him. It'll break his heart. I don't know this woman. I've never known her. I haven't been out of this house since four this afternoon. Somebody's doin' you wrong."

"You lie!"

Hagehorn calmly laid aside his cigar, stuck his thumbs in his vest.

"All right, I lie. I'm unarmed. I can't defend myself. I lie. O.K. Cut loose with that roscoe and give it to me."

Hermie's hand ached on the gun. He saw courage here—hard, casual courage. He saw a big man—the biggest in his own way in the whole city. He saw something vastly different from anything in Louie or Red Corrigan. Corrigan had said, "Walk right in and let him have it. Don't chin." Corrigan had said, "Don't give him a chance. Slam him in the back if you can and empty the rod all the way."

You couldn't slam a guy like this in the back. You couldn't slam a guy who didn't crawl, who didn't mention his kid or his family, who sat there, big and comfortable, ready to take it. To hell with Red and Louie! You just couldn't do it! There was something wrong. Somewhere, there was something wrong!

HIS RIGHT elbow, pressing hard against his side to brace his forearm, pressed something hard against his body. He reached his left hand inside in his coat, into his pocket. His fingers felt something long and hard. He drew out a clasp-knife he had never seen before. He looked at it lying in his left palm. His gun drooped till it was pointing at the floor.

Hagehorn did not get up. He might have eased off the faint murmur of a sigh. He picked up his cigar and put it back between his teeth.

Hermie started, gripped his gun, expecting to find Hagehorn diving at him. But Hagehorn was tranquil.

Hermie laid the gun on a table. He pulled open the blade. It was dark with blood. It was four inches long.

"My God!" he choked. Red Corrigan had got his coat, had held it for him. Red Corrigan had driven Floss to the city.

Something like an animal snarl grated from Hermie's throat. He grabbed up the gun, swivelled, rushed toward the door. Hagehorn bounded and got him from behind, locked his arms.

"Nix, kid."

"Lemme—get—out! Lemme—get—"

"Nix."

Buck came and grabbed Hermie and Hagehorn wrestled the gun free.

Buck said, "Should I let him have it?"

"No. Just hold him."

Hagehorn, tranquil, went to a large, heavy desk, picked up a telephone.

"Police headquarters." He waited. "Hello, Brinkhaus there?... Gimme him." He waited. "Hello, Brinky, this is Gus Hagehorn.... Say, come over my house. Your kid's here. Screwy or something."

He hung up, chuckled. In the past minute sweat had come out on his face.

"Whew!" he said. And again, "Whew!"

BUCK let Brinkhaus in. Brinky came hard-heeled, his coat tails flying.

"Hello, Brinky," Hagehorn said.

Hermie stood white-faced by the table, his fists clenched at his sides. Brinkhaus stopped and looked at him. His chest heaved and his breath whistled.

Hermie said, "You better arrest me, Pop."

"What 'd he do, Gus?" Brinky muttered.

"Nothin' much. He busted in here all steamed up over a jane that got knifed. He had an idea I did it. Maybe now he ain't. There's the gat he had. There's a knife. He looked kinda surprised to find it in his pocket. It looked like a plant on him. I didn't know what to do, so I called you and held him. He was for steamin' off after somebody else."

Hermie said, "You let me go first, Pop. You let me go and when I've done what I got to do I'll walk in and you can pinch me. I didn't mean to shoot that detective. I didn't—"

"What detective?"

"That night at Joe Niccolo's."

Brinky growled, "You fool, there wasn't no one shot!"

Hermie swallowed. "There wasn't—"

"There wasn't no one shot. Who said there was a dick shot?"

"They—said I shot a detective. They said—Hagehorn was after Floss McGirty—and knifed her—tonight. They said—" He stopped and groaned and staggered a bit, gripping the side of the table. "Oh," he said. "Oh, God."

Brinky crossed the room and gripped his son's arms.

"Look here, son. Look here."

Hermie met his father's stare.

"Yes, Pop."

"You been flimflammed. By two guys and a woman."

"Floss was good. She—"

"So good that she let them mugs tell you you bumped a cop!"

"She— God, Pop!"

The truth broke over Hermie like a wave, drenched him.

Brinky said, "Where'd you get that knife?"

"I don't know. Just before— I felt it in my pocket."

"Corrigan's known for his knifin's!"

Hagehorn was laughing.

"By cripes, Brinky, it's as plain as the nose on your face! Corrigan and Louie Snekvik travel together. They're punks for Joe Niccolo. Joe's got yearnin's. They tell the kid I'm after his woman and then Corrigan—or who else?—slits her and they sic the kid on me. And plant the knife on him. They figured he'd get me. He could have. Hell, when he said Brinkhaus I thought it was you. And then when he said he was your son, I was off my guard. Those guys ain't dopes. Because they musta figured that after he'd bumped me Buck would nail him on the way out. Oh, no, them guys wasn't dopes a-tall!"

Hermie put a hand across his eyes. All the odds and ends fitted into proper slots. Floss had tricked him. She had known all along that he hadn't shot a cop. She hadn't told him. And Red and Louie had framed him, used him as a stepping stone.

"Oh, Pop," he muttered. "I'm a louse."

"About this, in here," Hagehorn said, "forget about it. You done things for me, Brinky. I've never been able to buy you, but you always gave me a break. I'm a big bum, I know, but I got limits."

"Thanks, Gus."

He didn't say any more. He put the .45 and the knife in his pocket. He took Hermie's arm and propelled him across the room, into the hall. Buck opened the front door. Brinky and Hermie went down to the sidewalk.

Hermie muttered, "Look out, Pop. They were goin' to wait by that corner. Better give me that gun."

"You ain't never goin' to touch a gun, son."

There was no car at the corner.

"It all figgers," Brinkhaus muttered. "It all figgers of a frame. Taxi!"

The taxi bounced across the city.

"Where we goin', Pop?"

"To Mom."

SHE WAS waiting at the top of the staircase. She began crying when they were halfway up. She was a plump but not uncomely woman for her years. She cried and laughed when Hermie put his arms around her. There were no words. She just held onto him.

Brinky backed out, closed the door. He went down the stairway very slowly. He stood for a minute on the curb. He walked a block and found a taxi and climbed in. He gave an address. His shoulders rode squarely and his thick neck was rigid. His broad hands were planted firmly on broad knees. He watched lights streak past.

Then there was a broad boulevard with more pretentious lights and wide lawns in front of fine houses and fine apartments. The taxi slowed down, pulled out of the main stream of traffic, stopped at the curb. Brinky paid his bill. Going up the walk to the apartment house with the Ionic pillars, he looked dumpy and slow-footed. The frescoed grandeur of the lobby made him look very plain and homespun. He took the stairway. His shoes had a proletariat squeak.

A door with 404 on it faced him and he knocked.

Niccolo opened it. Niccolo had a patch over his eye and a swollen jaw.

Brinkhaus said, "We tried once tonight to make you talk, Joe. Now I come alone."

He pushed in, unbalancing Niccolo. He saw Red Corrigan and Louie Snekvik standing in the center of the living-room. He shoved Niccolo toward them. His face was very brown and broad and his squatty fedora sat low on his forehead.

"I figgered I'd find you all here," he said. "Kinda countin' chicks before they're hatched, ain't you?"

He drew the clasp-knife from his pocket, snapped it open. He spun it hard and sank it into a polished table.

Red Corrigan stared at it. He stared hard because the shade of the lamp was reddish and it threw a reddish glow on the quivering blade. Corrigan's jaws seemed to bulge.

"It's a pinch," Brinkhaus said.

Louie cackled. "Yeah? And for what?"

"Gus Hagehorn's livin' and my boy is home with his Mom."

Red Corrigan dived to the table, wrenched the knife free, threw it across the room. A fierce sound tore from his throat. His hand shot beneath his left lapel.

Brinkhaus's rugged body remained rooted like some gnarled old tree. But his hand moved as if it were detached from the rest of him. From somewhere out of his clothes a gun appeared, magically.

Its muzzle roared.

Red Corrigan looked startled, then stricken.

Before he fell Louie Snekvik drew and Niccolo drew at the same time.

Brinky remained rooted. His gun shook and thundered and locked its thunder with Louie's but its lead was truer and Louie whimpered and slumped sickly. Niccolo's bullet shook Brinkhaus but never budged his feet. Brinky's third bullet smashed through Niccolo's chest and Niccolo stopped living like a candle snuffed.

Brinky muttered, "Maybe that's action for you, bein' you asked for it."

Blood trickled from the cuff of his left arm and he held the arm away from his side as he moved slowly across the room. He sat down at a secretary, lifted the telephone receiver. He called a number.

"Hello, Mom. This is Pop.... How's Hermie?... Yeah? Well, you see he gits to bed by the time I git home.... No, I ain't comin' right away. I got to do some telephonin' with headquarters. I got to tell the boss somethin'. Leave the coffee pot on and some hot water for me to shave. And git out that new shirt with the blue stripes for the mornin', and me new gray suit.... G'night, Mom."

MURDER BY BALLOT

HAD YOUNG HARRIS
DOUBLE-CROSSED
HIS PUBLIC OR THE
POLITICIANS—PLAYED
SQUARE WITH THE
FANS OR THE CROOKED
BOSSES? A CITY
ELECTION HUNG ON THE
ANSWER—A VOTE BOX
OF GUILT YAWNED FOR
BALLOTS OF BLOOD!

CHAPTER ONE

THE STUMBLEBUM CROSS

A T THE end of the fourth round "Young" Harris piled "Kid" Chico against the ropes and let him have a faceful of lefts and rights. The white-trousered referee hopped around close and Chico gasped at Harris, "You lousy heel!" and went into a clinch. They toiled like men in a slow-motion movie until Chico, crowding close, ripped a hand free and screwed in an attempted foul.

Harris locked in a clinch and turning his head, muttered to the referee, "Talk to this Dago."

The referee said, "What's the matter?" and Harris cursed and cut free and dropped Chico with a roundhouse.

The crowd roared and the bell clanged.

Chico got up; his seconds met him; Chico turned and slammed down to his stool.

The roar of the crowd petered off like a roll of thunder and typewriters rat-a-tatted in the press box.

Jabez Connor got up from a seat in the fourth row and plowed his way past six pairs of knees. At the end of the row he leaned down and said to Fairfax, "Want to see you, Ken. In Jack's." He put on his derby and walked heavily up the aisle. He had thin legs and a fat, beefy trunk that made him look top-heavy. His face was big, white-jowled, and small ears were plastered close to his head. He wore his derby at a slant and black-pearl studs adorned his plaited dress shirt.

He left the City Arena by the south exit, walked to the end of the building and went down three steps to an areaway in the building adjoining. He pushed open a heavy wooden door, followed a hallway and pushed open another door that led into a small, clean bar. The fight was coming over a radio and the barman turned from the instrument and brightened.

"Oh, hello, Mr. Connor. Some fight!"

Connor was heavily preoccupied. "Scotch."

"Yes, sir—yes, sir!"

Fairfax came in, wearing a worried half smile and leaned his elbows on the bar. "Out of the same bottle, 'Skinny.'"

Connor picked his drink up in his hand and nodded solemnly to a closed booth at the end of the bar. He walked toward it with his

He hit the window with a bang.
Glass and frame were shattered.

drink, opened the frosted glass panelled door and sat down at a table inside. Fairfax came with his drink and took a drag standing in the doorway.

"Close it," Connor said.

Fairfax was a white, thinnish man of forty with a dish-face and eyes so wide open and expressionless they looked like glass. He sat down and said, "To you, Jabe," and put his glass to his lips. Connor didn't drink but looked stonily at Fairfax who put his glass down.

"What's up, Jabe?"

"It doesn't look to me as if Chico had this fight in the bag."

Fairfax shrugged, said, "Cripes, do you want Harris to fold his arms?"

Connor took a drink without taking his eyes off Fairfax. "If you're trying to double-cross me, Ken—"

"Who's trying to double-cross you?"

"I don't know. The way Harris went after him in the fourth round it looked like blood."

"He's got to make a showing."

Connor remained cool without ever taking his eyes off Fairfax's pale, transparent skin. "This guy Harris has got to flop in the sixth round. I'm not taking any chances. I promised Chico's uncle and you promised me. Arbutti controls the votes on the south side and without those votes Payson can never be elected mayor. Chico's the idol of the south side and the apple of his uncle's eye. Get that. And I'm campaign manager and it's up to me to get those votes. I warned you that if you tried to double-cross me on this, you'd never stage another fight in the City Arena—or in the state, for that matter."

"But, geez—"

"O.K., O.K. You heard me. I don't like the way Harris went after Chico in this fourth round. Remember, if Harris doesn't flop in the sixth round—" He took a drink and said candidly— "I'm a pretty tough egg, Ken."

"Sure, Jabe, sure. But Harris is chucking it."

Connor said, "I never liked box-fighters that were working their way through college." He stood up. "See you deliver, Ken."

He moved heavily and opened the door and stopped to listen to the radio.

"... and Harris leads with his left, feints, changes over, leads with his right— Wham! A thundering smack to the beezer of Kid Chico! A be-a-utiful left-handed sock to the old beezer! Boy, is this champ a two-fisted fighter? Don't ask!... There he goes again—in fast—the old one-two punch! Boy, you can't see those mitts go, he's so fast. And what foot-work! Chico comes back, boring, head down, like a fighting maniac! Harris is measuring him. Harris gives ground, measuring him! Harris is almost against the ropes! No—no! Zowie! Folks— Oh, boy, oh, boy! Young Harris brings the old left up and slams Chico flat on his back! The crowd's gone mad! Hear 'em! Chico's on one knee, shaking his head. The referee's counting. One... two.... Chico's got his arms braced on the floor. He's waiting out the count. He's stopped shaking his head. Man, was that a sock! Seven... eight.... He's up! Chico is up! He dives in with—"

"Get," Connor said to Fairfax.

Fairfax went swiftly to the door.

The barman was shadow-boxing in front of the radio. A man was standing at the bar, his back to Connor. The man was broad and wore a suit of rough, drab woolen material. A flat-crowned fedora sat rigidly on his head, and the back of his neck was thick and solid with a semicircular hair-line. He was drinking a stein of beer and looking in the mirror behind the bar.

Connor yanked his derby down over one eye and went out with his fat trunk heaving on his thin legs.

"Clang!" went the bell ending the fifth round.

The barman straightened and smacked fist into palm. "Sarge, that guy Harris is a real champeen! Boy, did you hear that one?"

Brinkhaus said, "I got ten bucks on him. Now you got a chance, Skinny, see how fast can you put a head on this."

"O.K., Sarge. I always said Harris was the nerts and he is." Wet foam slopped over the stein and Brinkhaus got his square, hairbrush mustache slightly dampened.

" 'S good beer, Skinny. Where you git it?"

"Cholly Koenigfelt."

"Tell Cholly when you see him I said *prosit.*"

Clang!

Skinny went into a crouch before the radio. "They're off!"

JABEZ CONNOR did not return to his seat in the fourth row. He remained in the rear of the arena, his mouth closed over a fresh cigar, unlit. Fairfax went, light-footed, down the aisle, back of the pressmen and around to Young Harris's corner. "One-Punch" Brannigan turned a teak jaw.

The boxers' feet beat a tattoo on the canvas.

Harris saw Fairfax's white dish-face and squinted, and Chico let him have an uppercut that walloped Harris against the ropes. Harris bounced back with his hands working and tied Chico up in a clinch. Over Chico's shoulders he looked hard at Fairfax. One-Punch (one punch and he was usually out) frowned at Harris and then turned and looked at Fairfax again.

Someone in the crowd yelled, "Come on! What's this, a waltz?"

The referee broke them and hopped back, and Chico imitated the Dempsey crouch and sprang. But he wasn't Dempsey. Harris weaved and speared him on the ear, and Chico took a header through the ropes. Harris caught him by the legs before he went through and hauled him back and Chico corkscrewed upward and let Harris have it in the stomach. Harris chopped downward across Chico's face and Chico almost went to his knees—came up with a whistling fist that Harris slid neatly off his jaw.

Fairfax plucked at his batwing tie, caught Harris's eye again and scowled, moving his lips. Harris's face was white and grim, and there was a glitter in his blue eyes. His stomach was covered with red welts. He was caught off-guard and knocked to the canvas, his legs flying. He lay on his back, narrowing his eyes. The referee jumped over and began counting. Chico stood with a mad dark smirk on his face and the crowd had suddenly become quiet.

"Six... seven...."

Harris rolled over on his stomach, got to his knees, his lips taut. At the count of nine he was up. With both hands he smothered Chico to the ropes. His blows traveled swiftly, wet with sweat. He cut Chico down, cut him down ruthlessly. He stepped back and watched Chico totter from the ropes. He let him have a haymaker and sent him skidding on his back across the resin.

The roar of the crowd was deafening.

"Seven... eight... nine.... Out!"

The radio announcer screamed, "Ladies and gentlemen, Young Harris knocked out Kid Chico in two minutes and twenty seconds of the sixth round, thereby retaining his welterweight championship!" He flung up a hand. "Hey, Young!"

Harris ran over and leaned down to grab the mike. "Hello, folks. Glad I won. And this is to let you know that I retire—now—tonight—from the ring."

"What!" yelled the announcer.

"I wouldn't fool you," Young Harris said.

He turned and bumped into One-Punch.

"You dippy or somethin'?" One-Punch said.

"You can always say this about me, One-Punch: I always gave my public a square deal."

He shrugged into his bathrobe, climbed through the ropes and ran into Fairfax. He looked once at Fairfax's white, still face and then plowed up the aisle, flanked by his seconds, amid the thunder of applause.

When he reached his quarters Fairfax was behind him, and Fairfax clipped to the others, "Get out a minute." He closed the door after them and put his wide, expressionless eyes on Harris.

He said, "Do you realize that certain guys in Dago Town contributed a total of fifteen thousand to have Chico win?"

"Get out," Harris said, breathing slowly.

"You dirty crackpot, do you realize that Jabe Connor controls the political and fight game in this town and that I promised him a flop in the sixth?"

"Get out, Ken. I'm through. Finished. Washed up. I retire tonight as undefeated champion. That Dago was a pushover from the first round on. A stumblebum."

"You two-timing—"

"Yeah? How about yourself? You tried to two-time on the fight game and on the fans. You're a cheapskate, Ken. I'm through with you and the game, and I broke clean with my public to the end. You're not my manager. Get the hell out of here before I break your damned jaw!"

Fairfax quivered. He jumped up in front of Harris and started cursing. Harris caught him by the throat in one hand, carried him across the room, opened the door and flung him into a crowd of newsmen, handlers and hangers-on.

Yelping, Fairfax's hand went to his hip, half-drew a gun. But he didn't draw it all the way. He shoved the gun back in and a couple of men helped him up as the door slammed shut.

CHAPTER TWO

THE DEATH SEDAN

AGUARDO'S FANCY speakeasy was three blocks from the Arena, in an old brownstone. The barman wore a crisp little white jacket, a formal waistcoat and he had bored eyebrows. The waiters were elegant in dress and manner. Besides the bar and the main dining room, there were many private rooms.

When Fairfax came into the bar the barman said, "Should you come in, Mr. Connor said he would be in the regular room."

Fairfax unbuttoned his blue topcoat and said, "Scotch, straight, Felix."

When he downed the drink he took off his coat, draped it over his left arm, lit a cigarette, took a breath and went upstairs. He paused outside a door marked 6 and listened to the drone of voices inside. He laid his hand on the knob, turned it and pushed open the door.

"Well, there's the sweet son-of-a-so-and-so," Payson, the candidate for mayor, said.

Connor's fat trunk swayed on his thin legs. He had been drinking Scotch straight and fast. "You double-crossed us, Ken."

"Now, wait a minute, boys, wait a minute," Fairfax chattered.

Finck, the Fifth Ward Alderman, said, "And I drop two thousand on this dirty framed box-fight! Hey, Fairfax, you swine, I thought this was in the bag?"

Fairfax hunched his shoulders, "Cripes, didn't I drop all I could borrow? Didn't I drop seventeen thousand?"

"Yes, you did!" Connor mocked icily.

"I did!"

"How can you prove it?"

Payson's cadaverous face was hateful, and he slurred his words. "This puts me in a nice spot, doesn't it? I thought I had fifteen thousand votes in the bag. I thought I could count on all Dago Town to swamp my opponent, 'Hizzoner' Mayor Walsh. It's come to a fine pass when a man can't rely on the honesty and integrity of his friends— of those, rather, whom he considers as his friends. It's both regrettable and lamentable. It is a travesty on the honor of—"

"Oh, hell," Connor muttered, "don't go on all night."

The candidate for mayor snarled. "You, you big fat slob! You were the one promised those votes! You talked with Arbutti, and you had it all fixed! And when I came out of the Arena tonight there was Arbutti, red in the face like—like—like, well whatever the hell he was like."

Connor carried his drink over and faced the candidate for mayor. "Remember, Jackie, my boy, you may be the candidate for mayor on this ticket, but otherwise I run this city, and don't you call me a big fat slob!"

Payson simpered. "Excuse my glove, Jabez."

Connor turned on Fairfax. "I warned you tonight, Ken, in Jack's. I warned you."

"I know," Fairfax groaned. "I promised, and I meant it."

"Doesn't that just burn me up," Payson slurred.

Connor went on to Fairfax, "You've made dough in the Arena because I've backed you. I gave you backing all over the state. A turn of my finger and the Arena's doors are closed to you. Another turn and I queer you in the state and I can reach out and queer you in other states. So what the living hell do you mean by hauling off and pulling a fandango like this?"

"I tell you, Jabe—"

"Listen." Connor's voice got very deep. "It's two months to election. There's got to be a return bout—between Harris and Chico. There's got to be! And Chico's got to win. He's got to be made champion."

Fairfax gulped, shook his head. "I didn't tell you—maybe you didn't hear it yet—but Harris is through. Retired and—"

"Well!" cried Payson, brightening. "That's easy! We can stage another fight for the championship and throw it to Chico!"

"But wait," Fairfax said, choking, shaking his head. "Harris told me that he'd stay retired only unless Chico was matched for a championship bout. He said he'd go in then and polish off Chico in the first round. He called him a stumblebum, a pushover and a general ham palooka."

"Say," Alderman Finck said, "is that guy nutty?"

"He's gone noble," Fairfax said.

"Oh, yeah?" the candidate for mayor snarled. "Well, I'll be damned, I will, if any box-fighter is going to queer my chances for being mayor of this fair city!"

"By God!" Connor erupted. He plopped his glass on the table, tramped the length of the room once, heavily, pivoted and clapped his hands together and held them in front of his overhanging paunch. "That's it!" He began laughing, and his white jowls flopped against his high collar like balloons filled with water.

"Wh-what?" Alderman Finck wanted to know.

And Connor stated, "No box-fighter can throw in a monkey-wrench in the works of the mechanism—"

" 'The works of' is superfluous," Payson said drily. "Just 'a monkey-wrench in the mechanism' will do."

Connor subsided darkly and said, "What the hell." Then he spoke less oratorically, looking at Fairfax. "This guy Harris may have gone noble, but to hell with that. He's got to meet Chico again, and he's to take a flop in the early rounds."

"He won't," Fairfax said, worried. "You don't know that egg. He's through. He's been reading things in books and he's through."

Connor's eyes became chilled. "You fumbled the trick this time, Ken, and by cripes you've got to make good. Arbutti turned over fifteen thousand he'd collected from Wop sympathizers and you pocketed it. You put it on Chico to win—so you say. He lost and—so you say—you're broke. These Dagoes can be Indian-givers like nobody's business. I swore to Arbutti that Chico would win. He didn't. You promised he would. Arbutti and his friends'll be up in arms by tomorrow and on my neck. And I'm on yours. Hard. And I'll do more than bust you as a fight king. Get that, sweetheart."

"B-but what can I do?"

"You figure that out. In a month we want another box-fight for the championship. Chico fights Harris—or else. Dammit, the strength of our party hangs on this! We've promised sewer contracts, paving contracts! We've got to get in office!" He rocked over and grabbed Fairfax by the lapels of his coat, shook him. "You hear me!" he roared. "We've got to get in!"

THE WITHDRAWAL of Young Harris from the pugilistic game raised quite a furor in the sporting pages of the daily press. Some writers wanted to know why. Others wrote down that the game had lost one of the straightest, finest boxers in the history of the prize ring, and let the why and wherefore lie. Some said he was foolish; some said he was wise, nobody's fool. Harris didn't say anything. He was through.

Brinkhaus, grabbing a late snack in Billy Howser's beanery a week later, said, "Well, Billy, I got me ten back and five to boot. It's good I did, else Mom would have give me hell— Pass the red lead, Billy. 'D you win?"

"Didn't bet. I ain't a sportin' man since the frau went and give me them twins last spring. But was I bettin', me dough would ha' been on Harris. The fight game's lost a natcheral."

A stutter of shots came over the rooftops, up the alleys. Brinkhaus coughed and almost fell off the high stool. His hard heels rang against the brass rail.

"Four," Billy said, holding up four fingers.

With a great clatter of heels and a tossing of coat tails Brinkhaus went through the door. He galloped a block before realizing that a napkin was still tucked beneath his chin. He tore it off, jammed it into his pocket, ran another block and stopped and listened. He pulled his flat-topped fedora closer to his ears and licked his hairbrush mustache.

He took a right turn and started running again. He was a square-built, ungainly figure, and he ran with the peculiar sidewise motion found in the gait of a running dog. He puffed to a stop at the first intersection, blew his nose, gave a satisfied grunt and turned left. Every time his heels came down, two-hundred-and-five pounds punished the pavement. Reaching the next intersection he stopped again and looking left, saw a crowd on the sidewalk a block and a half beyond.

This time he did not run. He walked, fast, with the slightly rocking motion, from side to side, of a heavy man of medium height. His breath was noisy in his nostrils and made a faint whistling sound in the bristles of his mustache. He saw a couple of bluecoats in the light thrown out from the broad windows of the Cedar Garden Restaurant. Japan Street began to flourish here with restaurants.

He heard a woman's voice quavering, "Oh, a man's been killed!"

"Been murdered," a deep voice said bitterly.

A cop said, irritably, "Come on, come on, get away. Don't gang around like this."

Brinky reached the edge of the crowd saying, "Excuse it, missus," as he pushed his way through until he met the broad back of a uniformed officer.

"McFee?"

The cop whirled, dark; then relaxed. "Oh, hello, Sarge. Guy got it."

"Dead?"

"Than a doornail."

"Shucks," mumbled Brinkhaus.

"Murder just as sure as the nose on your face!"

Brinky absent-mindedly felt his nose, and the cop stepped aside revealing a man lying face down on the sidewalk. A crooked line of blood lay from his body to the curbstone. A woman who had been sobbing quietly suddenly broke into hysterics and Brinky stepped over and grabbed her arms.

"Sh, missus."

A man was holding her from behind. "She's my wife. I'd better take her away."

Brinkhaus turned back to the cop and said, "D'you git a ambulance?"

"They called one here."

Brinkhaus gathered up his coat tails and knelt down. He turned the body over, rested on one knee, took Billy Howser's napkin from his pocket and wiped blood from his fingers. The dead man's shirt front was soggy, and his jaw was smashed. Brinky got up, shook his legs to straighten out his pants.

"It's that fight guy," he said to McFee.

"What fight guy?"

"Fairfax. He useter manage Young Harris, the retired welter champ—"

"Ah!" piped up a voice.

Brinkhaus looked at a fat Italian.

"Ah, dat was what I said!"

"What you say?"

"Young Harris. To myself I say, 'Pietro, dat ees Young Harris, de fox-bighter.'"

"And who're you?"

McFee said, "He owns this joint here."

"So what now, Pietro?" Brinkhaus said.

"Joosta dat. Joosta Meester Young Harris and Meester whatcha call him Fai-r-fax come to ma ver' swell place and eat ma ver' swell food."

Brinky frowned. "Them two guys come in and chowed up?"

"Whatcha call chow? Like I say, Meester Young—"

"O.K., Pietro," Brinky interrupted. "I get you. Now when did Young Harris go out?"

Pietro went through a setting-up exercise, shaking his hands from the wrists violently. "Joosta what I said! Meester Young Harris— Look, boss. Geeve a da look now. Dese two gentleemen come in. Ukey. Dey eat—mooch. Ukey. While a dey ate dey have mooch argument. Ukey. Den ees over, dey gat op, pay de bill and go outta da place side by each. Ukey. Den: boom-boom-boom-boom! Ukey. Den—well, whatcha, t'ink—deesa genteelman ees croak' and de odder genteelman ees—" he looked around, shrugged— "gone!"

"You see the shootin', Pietro?"

"Nope."

"Anybody here see this man git shot?"

No one had. One of the men who had been dining called attention to the fact that curtains covered the restaurant windows halfway up.

Another man said, "I heard an engine roar just as the shots started, like as if a car was getting away fast."

"When I came here," a third man said, "I saw this man who is now dead get out of a tan Cord sedan with Young Harris. I did recognize Harris from pictures in the papers, of course. They preceded me into the restaurant. They were arguing. Harris particularly seemed upset and quarrelsome."

Brinkhaus asked humbly, "Who was first out here after the shots happened?"

"Mother o' God, me—me!" cried Pietro.

"You see the car?"

"No. Must be eet was go queek."

Brinkhaus sighed. "I better phone headquarters and git the morgue bus and maybe the D.A.'s office 'll want to come over. I'd appreciate it, folks, ladies and gentlemen, if you'd all kinda hang around in the restaurant here till me boss comes over and maybe a man from the district attorney and the medical office. Just make yourself to home. Like me missus always says, make the best of a bum predic-u-ment and the devil take the hindmost or somethin'."

CHAPTER THREE

HONEYMOON HORROR

YELLOW-HAIRED INSPECTOR Peter Larsen, in charge of the Portsend Detective Bureau, came crisp-footed into his office, threw hat and topcoat over a chair and reached for a telephone.

"Kilpatrick?... Listen, Kil. Either Fairfax or Young Harris owned a Cord sedan.... George A. Harris. Get in touch with the Motor Vehicle Bureau and see.... Get the license plate number, motor number, right away if you can.... Well, Fairfax was bumped off, and we're looking for Harris.... Right, Kil."

He hung up and stood for a moment nibbling his lower lip and wrinkling his fair forehead. He reached for the phone again. "Adams. Shoot out an alarm. We're looking for George A. 'Young' Harris, the retired welterweight champ. He left the Cedar Garden Restaurant, 444 Japan Street, at nine-five tonight in company with Kennard Fairfax, his former manager. Fairfax was murdered outside the restaurant—nobody saw it—and Harris got away in a tan Cord sedan…. Haven't got it yet. Kilpatrick's looking it up, and he'll have it in a few minutes. Meantime flash the alarm to all precincts and cruising cars, outlying police booths and blind stations, and follow up with the plate number when Kil reports."

He pronged the receiver as Brinkhaus came in reading a newspaper and saying, "Here's a guy that says that seventeen-year-old kid that murdered his mother, father and sister ain't really criminal-minded, but that all this was caused by a bump on his head and the position of the stars when he was borned. And here's a guy says there ain't really no depression; it's a state of mind. And if you think these here remarks are on the funny sheet, boss, you're wrong. Look."

The phone rang, and Larsen answered. "I see. Thanks, Kil. Will you give that to Adams too?… Thanks." Hanging up, he said, "It was Fairfax's car."

"Weather: fair and warmer. Huh? Oh, Fairfax's. Pietro, the spiggoty, runs that place. He admits when I git him in a corner confidential—he admits Harris tucked away seven highballs durin' supper there."

Larsen started a cigarette, his eyes faraway and thoughtful. "Twenty-four, his age, Brinky. Young and on top of the world. I always heard he had a temper. Temperamental. One of the reasons, I imagine, why he gave up the fight game. But why—why on God's green earth did he wipe out Fairfax?"

"I found he lives at the Donaldson Hotel. Maybe I should hoof over there."

"Do, will you? I want to stay here, in case something breaks." He dropped his voice. "You'd like to break this case, wouldn't you, Brinky?"

"Mom would sure like to see that new photygraph o' mine in the newspapers."

Larsen said, "Break it."

Brinkhaus walked down to Madison and Chilton and caught an uptown car. He got off at Leland and Western Avenue, bent back on his heels and looked up the front of the Donaldson Hotel. Then he tramped up beneath the striped marquee and entered the lobby. He spotted McCullen, the house officer, leaning at the cigar counter and went toward him.

"Hello, Mac."

"Well, Brinky!"

"Yeah." Brinky inclined his head. "Say, you heard yet about Young Harris?"

"No. What?"

"Fairfax got himself bumped off in Japan Street tonight."

"Fairfax? What's the connection?"

Brinky took hold of McCullen's arm. "Would it be askin' too much could I look in Harris's apartment?"

McCullen said slowly, "I see." Then he said, "I'll have to call up first."

"He won't be there, Mac."

"I know, but his wife may."

Brinkhaus blinked. "Huh?"

"He was married last night on the q.t., out in the county."

"Oh, m' Gawd!" Brinky's voice, chin and hands fell, and then he got out a handkerchief and mopped his face. "Oh, jeepers, look what I got meself into! And she don't know— Listen, Mac, like an old pal, go tell her while I go out and git a bellyful o' Cholly Koenigfelt's beer."

"Not me," McCullen said. "I'll call up and say you want to see her, and then you can go up."

Brinky took off his flat-topped fedora, fanned himself and looked around like a man seeking a means of escape. But his big feet remained rooted to the rectangular tile floor.

He swallowed. "O.K., Mac."

GOING up in the big mirrored elevator, Brinkhaus looked at himself in one of the mirrors. He straightened his tie, buttoned his coat and threw out his chest. He made his face grave. He squared his shoulders. When he got off at the eighth floor he walked with a solemn, ponderous tread, very stiff and erect, his big shoes creaking. Reaching a door marked 817 he raised his hand in a peremptory manner to knock, then gulped, sagged and dribbled his knuckles down the door.

A lovely girl opened the door. Brinkhaus thought her lovely and sweet, and she smiled, though behind the smile was a touch of apprehension. He made an awkward bow when she told him to come in. He started to sit down in one chair, then moved to another, moved to a third and wound up by remaining on his feet.

"Missus Harris." He cleared his throat. "You heard from your husband this evenin'?"

"N-no, sir."

He saw trunks, brand-new, with new labels on them, and handbags half-packed.

"Goin' places?"

Her voice was small. "Our—honeymoon."

"Uh—m-m-m. Where's your husband?"

"Oh, what is the matter?"

He stated the obvious—"I'm a p'lice-man"—and felt like a fool for doing it.

He felt he had to proceed, come what might. "I b'lieve your husband had a date tonight with Mr. Fairfax."

"Yes, yes?"

"Missus, Mr. Fairfax was murdered and—"

"George!"

"N-no."

She sank to a chair. "Oh, thank God!"

"But, Missus Fairfax, your George disappeared from the scene of the murder."

She was almost hysterically light-hearted because he had said George hadn't been murdered. "But what of it?"

"Uh—that's it. He disappeared. He went outta the restaurant with Mr. Fairfax; the folks inside heard the shots, and George drove away in Mr. Fairfax's auto. Now, now, missus—"

She had sprung to her feet, shaking. "Oh, no—no!" Her eyes widened. She sprang to a Governor Winthrop secretary and whipped open one of the drawers. "Oh!" she cried, and her hands flew to her face.

Brinkhaus heaved over beside her. His eyes slanted down into the drawer. He saw a box of cartridges. Policeman, he picked up the box, counted the cartridges. Seven gone. A full load for a .38 pocket-model Colt automatic. He dropped the box into his pocket and put hesitant brown eyes on the girl.

"Oh, no—no!" she said again, quivering. "He didn't do it."

"Missus, he had a gun. You went for this drawer, and the gun wasn't there. He bought a gun, didn't he?"

"Yes, but—"

"Why did he buy it?"

"We were going to drive to Mexico. He thought it might be dangerous down over the Border."

"Why did he go out with Mr. Fairfax?"

"Mr. Fairfax phoned him three times today, and finally George said he would go."

"Was he mad?"

She almost whispered, "He—was mad at Mr. Fairfax. But I made him that way. I never liked Mr. Fairfax. I never liked prizefights. And maybe I talked George into not liking them. He said he was through because the game was getting rotten; it wasn't fair any more."

"You know if Mr. Fairfax ever threatened him?"

"I—don't know. I do know, though, that since the last fight Mr. Fairfax was always calling him up and wanting to see him. Once George went out and met him and came back very angry, but he wouldn't say anything. Oh, what has happened, what has happened?"

"Don't cry, missus."

"Oh, Sergeant, George wouldn't do a thing like this! He wouldn't leave me—and kill a man—and run away! He wouldn't!" She threw herself on a divan and burst in tears, chest-racking sobs.

Brinky passed his hand over his head, shifted from one foot to the other and made motions like a conjurer with his hands.

"Missus—"

He laid a broad brown hand on her convulsing back, and sweat began to stand out on his honest brown face. He patted the back with clumsy tenderness and thought of the time his son Hermie had run away and he had patted his wife's back in much the same manner. And had felt just as awkward, as wordless, as knotted up in the chest as he felt now. "Missus—"

He couldn't get beyond that.

"He didn't kill anybody! Oh, please, he didn't kill anybody! We've just been married! Just last night! He didn't— Oh, he didn't kill anybody!"

"Uh—missus, you got any friends, any relations?"

"A sister—Louise."

He felt easier and sat down beside her, taking hold of her hand. "You got to brace up—uh—what's your name?"

"Lily."

"You got to brace up, Lily. I been in a fix like this once meself. I got a wife and kids, and I'm crazy about 'em, and I know how you feel. But I got to do me business. What's your sister's phone number?"

She sobbed it out, and Brinkhaus went to a telephone and transmitted the number. "Miss Cordine, will you come right over to your sister's right away?.... This is a friend. Your sister ain't feelin' well.... Thank you, ma'm."

He hung up and went slowly to the door. He went out slowly and, once in the hall, barged to the elevators. Down below he found McCullen waiting.

"Keep out an eye, Mac, should Harris turn up."

He went across the lobby like a squat, relentless army tank. When he got beyond the end of the striped marquee and the blue-and-gold liveried chasseur he slowed down and stopped beside a cement lamp post atop which glowed a wrought-iron lantern. From his pocket he drew a slip of paper that he had taken from the telephone table in the Harris apartment. A memorandum hastily scrawled in a woman's handwriting: *Call Triangle 1201 urgent.*

CHAPTER FOUR

TRIANGLE 1201

FELIX, THE elegant barman at Aguardo's, was completing four Old-Fashions when he looked up and saw the broad everyday hulk of Brinkhaus hesitating in the narrow doorway leading from the hall. Felix had become used to feeling on equal terms with nothing less than a congressman, only possibly an alderman, rarely a police lieutenant and never a sergeant.

He said, quietly, "There," to the waiter, and the latter trayed the four Old-Fashions and vanished behind tapestry curtains.

Brinkhaus came, creaky-shoed, to the bar, and Felix, bending to the custom of the establishment as regarded policemen, said, "Yes?"

"You got any of Cholly Koenigfelt's beer?"

"We do not serve beer."

"I don't want a drink anyhow."

Felix bowed and lifted superior eyebrows.

"I want," said Brinkhaus, "to know where Triangle 1201 is in this here new buildin'."

Curious, Felix said, "Triangle 1201?"

Lazy, quiet chimes behind the bar intoned the hour of eleven.

"This number is Triangle 1205," Felix said, indicating a monophone beside a pyramid of Perrier bottles.

"Now that that's settled, where is this here 1201?"

Felix signaled a passing waiter, commanded, "Summon Mr. Aguardo."

The most amazing thing about Aguardo was his haircomb. Smooth, incredibly black, it fitted his head like a lacquered casque, with daggerlike sideburns that reached halfway down his cheeks. He made an L-shaped bow.

"Sergeant Brinkhaus-s-s, I believe."

"Listen, Aguardo, I'm lookin' for a telephone. The number's Triangle 1201 and the address is 555 Columbia Street and this is it."

Aguardo straightened and struck an attitude like a man listening for the sound of a bird. "Tr-r-riangle wan-do-o-wan. You aire sure, ser-geant?"

"Yup."

Aguardo pressed a finger against his lip, looked at the ceiling, then said, "Wan moment, please."

He stalked off and disappeared behind the tapestry curtains. Brinkhaus heard footsteps mounting stairs. He blundered to the curtains, pulled them aside, saw a stairway and saw Aguardo's heels vanishing at the top.

He started climbing, taking two steps at a time to cut the number of squeaks his shoes made in half. He reached the top in time to see Aguardo make an L-shaped bow and then enter a door. Brinkhaus tiptoed down the corridor and looked quaintly like an elephant.

A door marked 6 stared him in the face, and he deliberated. The door opened smartly, and Aguardo bumped into him, fell back and knocked the door wide open. Brinkhaus saw Jabez Connor holding a drink and Jackie Payson sitting on a table dangling his legs.

"Evenin'," Brinkhaus said politely, walking in.

Alderman Finck whistled to himself and put his rotund smallness in front of a telephone.

Connor had started to scowl, but changed his mind and blossomed in a hearty laugh. "Well, well, good old Sergeant Brinkhaus, the arm of law and order! Yes, sir, I always said that if we had more men like Sergeant Brinkhaus on the force, we would have a very good force indeed. Haven't I said that, Jackie?"

"Haven't *I?*" slurred the candidate for mayor, sucking in one cheek humorously.

Aguardo bowed. "I weel go." And left.

Connor's overhanging paunch heaved from side to side as he came over and clapped Brinkhaus on the back. "My old friend—yes, my great and good friend Sergeant Brinkhaus!"

Brinkhaus said across the room, "Hello, Mr. Finck, I ain't seen you since the time Henny Williams' store burnt down." He thumped forward with his hand extended.

Finck gave him a scared smile and held his body stiff while he shook hands.

Brinkhaus went up on his toes a trifle and, looking down over Finck's shoulder, saw a telephone. He leaned against Finck and Finck lost his balance and knocked the table over. Brinkhaus said, "Gee, excuse it," and hastened to pick things up. Among them the telephone. Triangle 1201.

Connor's eyes wore a faint glitter.

Brinkhaus turned and said, "Should I ask, could I maybe find out who called George Harris's place this evenin'?"

Connor and the candidate for mayor exchanged glances, and then Connor laughed good-humoredly and said, "Sure. I did. The son of a gun went and got married and didn't let anybody know. I wanted to congratulate him. We all wanted to congratulate him. We wanted to throw a party for him."

Brinky said, "Headquarters wants to chuck a party for him, too."

Payson's eyes flickered and then narrowed, waiting.

"Fairfax was bumped off," Brinky said. "We're lookin' for Harris."

"For Harris?" Connor said, bending.

"He left Fairfax dead on the sidewalk in front of the Cedar Garden and lammed in Fairfax's car."

"Good gracious!" Connor cried. "Did you hear that, Jackie?"

Payson made an irritable mouth. "Yes, I heard it." He flung a quick look at Connor and took a drink. He turned to Brinkhaus. "This is extraordinary, to say the least. It seems incredible that George Harris, this city's chieftest exponent of the manly art of fisticuffs, should do unto death the man who raised him in the ranks—from the ranks—to a stellar role. Incredible! I am shocked beyond words."

For no reason at all Brinkhaus said, "Thanks."

The candidate for mayor stood up, struck an heroic attitude and was about to break into metaphors when Connor grated, "This is murder then! Murder!"

"Mr. Connor," Brinkhaus said, "the night of the fight between this here Harris and that spiggoty, Chico, around the fourth round you and Fairfax had an argyment in Jack's speakeasy, next the Arena there."

"Did we? I forget."

"I figgered it was funny you and him—him bein' Harris's manager and all—you and him should leave the scrap in the fourth round and go in Jack's."

"We were dry."

Payson sliced in wheedlingly, "My dear Sergeant, surely you can find nothing pertinent in the fact that our honorable Mr. Connor and Kennard Fairfax chose to quench their thirst in the fourth round of that remarkable bout?"

"It gits me why a manager should leave a fight where his man is scrappin' for the champeenship."

Connor boomed righteously. "Brinky, this coming from you pains me indeed!"

Brinkhaus made a meek face. "I was just askin'. I'm sorry, Mr. Connor."

Payson put an arm affectionately around Brinkhaus, walked him cleverly to the door. "You know, Sergeant, I've heard a lot about you. I admire you. One day soon I shall be mayor of this fair, proud city, with a great amount of power in my hands. I like to recognize worth, ability, honesty and that courageous spark which I find only too infrequently in men. But which, Sergeant, I find in you. And which I hope to reward some day soon. I know you would enjoy being made a lieutenant in charge of the homicide squad. I shall remember that. Now, if you'll pardon us, we are busy with affairs of state. But do drop in again—any time."

Brinkhaus trudged disconsolately down the corridor. At the head of the staircase he paused, turned and looked in the direction of the door. His face looked brown and heavy, a slow brown fire kindled in his eyes.

His lower lip popped out, and he growled, "Horsefeathers!"

BRINKHAUS was approaching headquarters at midnight when he saw Larsen and a couple of others come pounding down the steps and pile into the black phaeton. He broke into a run, shouting. The phaeton had started, but Larsen looked out, saw Brinkhaus and told the driver to wait. Brinky piled in the rear with O'Mara and Larsen reached back and slammed the door. Tires squeaked, and the car was off. Brinky pried his hat up off the bridge of his nose, reset the crown.

Larsen called back, "They found Harris."

"Yeah," O'Mara said.

"We're going out there," Larsen said.

Brinky asked, "Where?"

"On the Quarry Road. Motorcycle Patrolman Davidson called in that he'd found a wrecked Cord, license so-and-so, down in the quarry. Man in the car was all smashed up and dead, but Davidson got an ambulance anyhow, but it wasn't any use. The ambulance wouldn't take it so he called the county morgue."

"He sure it was Harris?"

"Yes. Harris."

Brinkhaus put his hat on carefully. "That's tough, boss," he said, watching houses streak past. "Tough on his wife."

Larsen twisted. "Wife!"

"They were married on the q.t. last night, and she's the sweetest little woman you ever saw."

"God, can you imagine that!" Larsen said.

The police car's siren moaned past a square, scattered late traffic. The sleek black car hit the Post Road north, traversed suburbia and went droning powerfully through dark rolling country. The smell of hay was on the wind. The pale cement road turned.

Where a filling station raised a beacon at a crossroad the police car turned left onto a black-top road, and the sound the tires made was different. Hills became sharper, grades more abrupt. The car passed out of some woodland and Larsen pointed to lights ahead.

A uniformed cop was making cars move on. The turn in the road was sharp, and on the right the earth sloped away. Below the stone quarry made a pale blur. Larsen, Brinkhaus and O'Mara climbed out and the driver remained at the wheel. They passed the morgue bus and then ran into Davidson.

"Right down there, Inspector."

"How'd you come to find it?"

"I was rolling along here when I heard a horn blowing, on and off. I looked back and there was nothing, and there was nothing ahead, so after a minute I stopped. And I still heard it. I began looking around, and I had a hard job, it was so dark. Then the horn stopped, and it wasn't till fifteen minutes later I found the car. And the guy was dead."

Larsen could see a lantern glowing down below, and a few flashlights.

"Who's down there?"

"The D.A. and George Josephs and a couple newspaper guys. Here, take this light, Inspector."

Larsen, Brinkhaus and O'Mara went down the hill. The car was a ruin of twisted metal among pinnacles and slabs of granite. Someone had taken off Harris's topcoat and thrown it over his face. Dan Paddison, the energetic district attorney, hopped through the beams of several flashlights.

"That always was a bad turn up there, Pete," he said. "They'll have to eliminate that some day. Harris was on the lam and probably going like hell, and he never made it—not that turn."

"Find a gun on him?" Larsen said, looking around.

"No. He must have chucked it away. Hell, I thought this was going to be a long drawn-out proposition, but it sure simplifies matters. I was afraid with another case like this I might get gypped out of my long-postponed vacation. He came rolling down the hill— Come on, I'll show you."

Paddison began climbing and pointing out the course the car had taken in its mad plunge down the hill to the quarry. Larsen and Brinkhaus followed. Eventually they reached the top and stood by the side of the road while Davidson kept shooing on traffic.

Brinky took off his hat, scratched his head, replaced the hat and went halfway down the hill again. He stopped and held his jaw and looked up the hill toward the silhouetted figures of Larsen and Paddison. He looked down at the moving flashlights that marked the wreck. He climbed the hill again, bending over and holding his little flashlight close to the earth. Reaching the top, he found Larsen standing alone and went toward him.

"Listen, boss," he muttered. "I ain't gittin' any flighty ideas, but a little bird's been tryin' to tell me that Harris didn't drive that car off here."

"Who did?"

"I dunno. But look along the side there. A car speedin' at this curve—did he go off, the car would skid and slew sideways. You give a look there. See them tire prints. They're nice and orderly. They go straight off the turn through the dirt and down the grade. They ain't messed up. You go twenty feet down the grade, and you'll find them tire prints still nice and orderly. Was a guy in control o' that car he would ha' used brakes. Brakes would ha' locked the wheels and there wouldn't be nice smooth prints, the way they are now. After about twenty feet the car skidded off a stump and from then on down it flip-flopped."

"And all that, Brinky, leads you to what conclusion?"

"Well, boss, it don't lead to any conclusions yet. But it begins to point, and it says to me, 'Herman, find out what Jabez Connor and Kennard Fairfax argued about the night Harris licked Kid Chico.'"

"The little bird says that, huh?"

"The little bird."

CHAPTER FIVE

BALLOTS OF BLOOD

JABEZ CONNOR walked up and down his office. Below in the street a newsboy was yelling, "Extry! Extry! Read all about the murder—" Connor closed the window with a bang. His first cigar of the day did not taste good. He tossed it into a bronze tray, thrust his hands into his pockets and went on pacing. His overhanging paunch swayed hugely from side to side, and his fat rubberlike jowls flopped against his collar.

He stopped short, went to the desk and read again snatches from *The Globe's* account of the murder and the death by accident of George "Young" Harris.

"... and it is believed that Harris in his mad flight failed to make the curve and was hurled along with the automobile down the treacherous slope to death among the jagged rocks of the quarry."

He pursed his lips, straightened, jammed his hands back into his pockets and went on pacing.

The door opened and a girl said, "Sergeant Brinkhaus to see you, sir."

"I'm busy."

"Yes, sir."

The door closed, and Connor mopped his forehead and dropped, exhausted, to a chair.

The door opened again; the girl said, "He says he'll wait."

Connor glared, then subsided, snarled, "Send him in."

He reached for a fresh cigar, lit it and leaned back. He felt the knot of his tie, brushed a hand across his forehead. When the door again opened Brinkhaus stood there, holding his flat-topped fedora and making a polite bow.

Connor was very businesslike this morning. "Good morning, Sergeant. I'm very busy, but what can I do for you?"

Brinkhaus closed the door. "I s'pose you read all about the accidental death of Young Harris, huh?"

"Yes." Connor nodded toward the newspaper. "Terrible, wasn't it? I suppose Harris, after he'd murdered Ken Fairfax—well, I suppose he was all worked up, nerves rattled, reason gone. I can't tell you how sorry I feel for his wife."

"I just been over there, Mr. Connor. They had to take her to the horsepittle, the poor thing."

Connor spread his arms benevolently. "If there is anything I can do for her, anything to ease the pain—"

"Maybe you could."

The blunt incision stopped Connor's mounting eloquence, and Brinkhaus creaked his shoes across the floor and planted his broadness slowly in an armchair. He put his hat on the desk and his hands on his thick knees.

He said again, "Maybe you could."

"Of course, of course. I'll see that she's well taken care of at the hospital—"

"She don't need that. Harris left plenty of dough, and she's got a sister lookin' after her. Nope, nothin' like that, Mr. Connor. Somethin' bigger, somethin' that oughta be wiped out of her mind, so the memory o' Harris won't hurt her and the kid she'll have next year. You wouldn't like to be the son of a murderer, would you, Mr. Connor?"

Connor looked bewildered. "No—no, to be sure."

"I was speakin' to her about the phone call you made. She didn't say you said anything about wantin' to chuck a party. She didn't say you said anything about congratulations."

"Of course I didn't. Not to Mrs. Harris."

Brinkhaus went on placidly, "She said you sounded anxious, and when Harris wasn't home you asked where you could find him and she didn't know. You were excited, she said, and she said you left word Harris should call as soon as he came in. That was at nine o'clock, just about the time Fairfax was killed."

Connor leaned forward. "Just what are you driving at?"

"I ain't drivin'. I'm just reportin' what I heard. I seen a guy this mornin' named One-Punch Brannigan that was one of Harris's seconds at the fight. He said that when Harris won and climbed down through the ropes Fairfax looked fit to kill him. That was funny comin' from the champ's manager. I also find out at the bank that Fairfax was flat broke at the time of his death. The day after the fight he drew out six checks makin' twenty thousand bucks. It seems to me he should ha' been puttin' a lot in, seein' as his man won. So what? So I figger that Harris was to throw the fight and then changed his mind, thinkin' it would be a swell idea to double-cross the guys that were tryin' to double-cross the fight fans."

"Oh, nonsense, my dear Sergeant!"

"Well, maybe. Just like I figure that Harris didn't drive himself off the road down to the quarry and git killed."

"This is really startling, Sergeant!"

"I figgered you'd find it that way, too, Mr. Connor."

Connor sat back abruptly, narrowing his eyes. The brown face of Brinkhaus was barren of any expression except one of bland placidity. His quaint old-fashioned mustache and similarly dated hair-comb recalled the tintype photo of another decade. He did not meet Connor's gaze, but stared blank-eyed at a corner of the desk.

Connor said at last, "I do not know why you insist, Sergeant, on taking it for granted that I am immensely interested in this case. True, I knew Harris—I knew Fairfax. I'm a big political gun, and it is natural that I should know varied types of men. I deplore, I am deeply grieved, over the unhappy fact that Harris had to murder his former manager—"

"That," said Brinkhaus modestly, "is what I'm gittin' at."

"What?"

Brinky's bland brown eyes rose to meet Connor's. "I'm gittin' at this: I ain't sure Harris bumped off Fairfax."

"But my dear man, the evidence—"

"You forgit, Mr. Connor, that no one actually seen Harris rub out this guy, Fairfax. The papers, sure, went right ahead on the assumption Harris did it because he was found smashed up in Fairfax's car and he'd ditched his gun."

"What better evidence could you want?"

"I happen to know what kind of a gun Harris carried. It was a thirty-eight Colt—"

"Exactly the kind of bullet that killed Fairfax."

"But nope. A thirty-eight—O.K. But the slugs that took Fairfax down were 130 grains, and the bullets that were loaded in Harris's gun, before he left home, were 95 grains." He tapped his pocket. "I got the box he loaded from."

Connor's voice was not enthusiastic when he said, "That is very interesting. You surprise me, really."

"I ain't surprised you yet, Mr. Connor. But here goes now: I want the guys that rubbed out Fairfax and wound up by rubbin' out Harris."

Connor stood up, looking insulted. "You come to me!"

Brinky nodded modestly. "Yup."

"Why—why—" Connor broke into scornful—but uneasy—laughter and swung his paunch from side to side during a turn up and down the office. "Why, this is ridiculous, to say the least."

"You made that phone call and I'll take Mrs. Harris's word for it that you were excited. You asked her again and again if she didn't know where her husband'd gone—"

"You take her word in preference to mine? Mine? My dear man, don't you realize that I run the insurgent party in this city, that within another year we'll be in power?"

"But I'm talkin' about murder now."

Connor became cold as ice and looked at his watch. "I have an appointment here in a few minutes. You will have to leave."

"I'm sorry to be in the way, Mr. Connor, but I can't leave."

"I think I made myself plain, Sergeant."

"Me, too."

Connor's rubberlike jowls jigged on his collar. "Get out!" He leveled a shaking arm at the door. "Out!"

"I can't accommodate, Mr. Connor. I come in here to git me some information. I ain't got it yet. I figger to stay here until I git what I come for."

"I gave you an answer, you damned clown! Now get out!"

"That's where you're wrong. I ain't a clown; you didn't give me an answer—and I ain't goin' out."

Connor snarled, "Very well, then *I'll* go out!"

The door opened, and Payson, Finck and Arbutti, the south side boss, trooped in. Nobody looked pleasant, and Payson, seeing Brinkhaus, actually scowled. Then he laid down his stick, tossed off his coat.

"You were just going, Sergeant? I'm afraid you'll have to. We have an important meeting this morning— What the hell's the matter with you, Jabe? You look as though there've been ghosts flitting about."

Connor said dully, "Brinkhaus has been clowning around again."

"Oh, has he?"

"Yes. Spreads himself here and wants to know who killed Harris and Fairfax."

Payson swivelled and shot at Brinkhaus, "That's all settled, Brinky. Don't be a pest. Come on like a good chap—scram."

"Not till Mr. Connor comes clean about that telephone call and why him and Fairfax left the fight in the fourth round."

The candidate for mayor scoffed irritably. "Oh, don't be an ass, Brinky. Beat it. We're busy."

Rocklike, Brinkhaus stood on big feet. "There ain't nobody in this here room big enough, politically or otherwise, to make me lam outta this." His voice was hardening now, and there was a smoky look growing in his eyes.

Payson, hot-headed, said incisively, "If you know what's good for you, you'll leave this office right now. Understand, we're not going to be pestered to death by a dumb cluck of a policeman. We're men of affairs and we're busy—now—and you vamoose."

Brinkhaus looked from face to face, then said slowly, "I come here, Mr. Connor, because you're the political boss. I tried to git it to you as nice as I could that I knowed who killed Fairfax and run Harris down that hill to death. But you right away git on your high horse. Now git this—all of you—git this: If I walk outta this room now, I walk straight to the guy that actually did the shootin'. I take no chances. He knows I'm after him when he sees me, so I have me rod out and I let him have it. And maybe you heard that when I plug a heel he stays plugged."

Connor pawed suddenly at his stomach and coughed. Payson, the candidate for mayor, tightened his mouth. Arbutti rocked on polished heels and twisted one end of a piratical mustache. Finck looked too innocent.

Payson snapped, "What the hell are you talking about?"

"You heard just what I said, Mr. Payson. These shenanigans are gonna be cleared up or I go right after the guy that did the shootin'. And I wipe him out."

Connor argued, "If you know the guy, then why did you come here with a song and dance?"

"Just because I figgered maybe you'd be white enough to give the wiper a break and a trial and maybe with political influence git him somethin' small—like fifteen years."

Connor shrugged and looked hopelessly at the candidate for mayor. Payson gnawed fretfully at his lip, and Arbutti had stopped rocking on his heels and was regarding Payson's back with narrow bloodshot eyes.

Payson went over and took hold of Brinky's arm. "Listen, Brinky, you play ball with us and you'll go a long ways."

"Maybe you'll be mayor for four years, and then after that I go back where I started from—and maybe back further. Ixnay, Mr. Payson. I told you what. Does the guy that killed Fairfax git a break, or do I go after him heeled and knock him over?"

Payson turned and looked at Connor. "You said you were boss of this political party, Jabe. What's the verdict?"

Connor's lip curled. "I can't touch it. We can't afford to touch it. The risk's too great."

Payson said, "Ah, hell, Jabe—"

"No!" boomed Connor. "I said no!" He looked feverishly at Brinkhaus. "Now get out and get your pinch over with."

Brinky said, "It'll be a kill, Mr. Connor."

"I can't help it."

Brinkhaus shrugged and moved reluctantly to the door.

"Wait a minute!"

ARBUTTI'S face was dark and passionate and his black eyes were in turmoil as they stared at Connor.

Arbutti said, "For cripes' sake, Jabe!"

Connor seemed to grow tall and cold, and his paunch seemed to grow in size. "Sorry, Arbutti."

Payson went over and snapped up into Connor's ear, "You can't do this, Jabe!"

"Shut up," Connor said heavily. "I told you the risk's too big for what we'd get out of it. We've tried our best, but it wasn't good enough, and he'll have to take it on the button. I didn't order this, and I'm not going to jump in over my head. It's a case here of every man for himself."

Arbutti ripped out hotly, "That's what you say! By God, you've got to jump in! You can't swing this election without the votes I pull in the south side. Without me, you'll lose in every district. Lay down on me now, Connor, and you might as well pack up and go away till election's over."

"We've got to, Jabe!" Payson snapped. "We can't afford to lose the south side!"

Connor was cold. "No."

Payson raised his fists. "Damn it, are you going to throw me over? I want that job! I want to be mayor of this damned town, and it's only with the Dago vote that I can get in! I'm going to be mayor! We can't lay down on Arbutti!"

"I don't touch it," Connor said. "It's too dirty for us to get out clean. I tried to stop it. I tried to warn Harris."

Arbutti jumped across the room and shook his fist under Connor's nose. "You're yellow, Connor! You're yellow as your belly is fat! By God, you can't do this! You've got to stick!"

"I didn't order that kill," Connor said.

"I didn't either," Arbutti said. "But it's done. And it's done because you passed the buck. Because you said you thought Fairfax double-crossed us when Harris didn't flop as he was supposed to. To hell with passing the buck now. We've got to stick. Get that, Connor!"

"Listen to me, you dirty Dago, you can't talk like that!"

Arbutti pointed. "Tell that copper what to do."

Connor's jowls were motionless. "I told him what to do. I told him to go after his kill. As far as that kill goes, I'm clean."

Arbutti stepped back, muscles twitching in his dark face and his lips growing thinner. Payson snapped, "Jabe, you're a wet blanket! You're turning me down as the next mayor of this town—"

"Jackie, don't be a fool. I'm older than you. I know just how far a racket can go. Chico went ga-ga when he killed Fairfax, that's all. He'll have to take it—along with his pals."

Brinky's eyes brightened. He said, "Well, I'll be goin'," and thumped to the door.

"No you won't!" Arbutti snarled, and a gun appeared in his hand.

"Hey!" Connor yelled.

"Stay back!" Arbutti warned.

But Connor said, "Put that gun away, you fool Dago."

Payson got a gun from the desk, stuck it in Connor's back. "Don't act rash now, Jabe. I'm saving you from yourself."

"Jackie, you're crazy."

"Am I? I'm going to be the next mayor in this town and Dago Town's votes are going to put me in. Just before I came here I was speaking with Larsen and the chief. They don't know a thing about Chico."

Connor said, "I've been a pretty ruthless politician in my day, Jackie, but I know where to stop. You don't know. You've just gone one notch too far. Drop that gun, Jackie."

Arbutti, his eyes burning on Brinkhaus, said, "Keep him covered, Jackie!"

Finck stood frozen in a corner, silent.

Payson said, "This is your gun, Jabe."

"I know it."

"And I'm tired of hearing that you run me and this political party. I'm going to be mayor and in order to be mayor I've got to get Dago Town votes, and in order to get those votes I've got to stand by Arbutti and his nephew, Chico."

Connor's voice was thick, "Jackie, you're through."

"Am I? No. I am going to kill Brinkhaus with your gun. Whereupon Arbutti will take Brinkhaus's gun and shoot you. Our story will be: 'Connor drew a gun on Sergeant Brinkhaus and both fired.'"

"You're mad, Jackie," Connor said.

"You, Brinkhaus," Payson said, "get away from that door."

Sweat stood out on Brinky's face. He moved and, clumsily, tripped over a rug. He went down like a log, rolled over and got tangled up in the rug.

"Get up, you big lummox!" Payson snarled.

Brinkhaus got up with the rug draped over one shoulder and, still seemingly groggy, tottered toward the window. He hit with a bang. Glass and frame were shattered and fell to the sidewalk below and Brinky's head and shoulders went through the aperture until it seemed he must plunge to the street.

Connor said, "Good God!" And, forgetting the gun in his back, he leaped over and grabbed hold of Brinky's legs and hauled him back into the room. Brinky fumbled and rolled over Connor drunkenly, and then suddenly from the folds of the rug and his coat flame burst, and the room roared.

Arbutti straightened, stood flat against the wall like a wooden soldier while his eyes stared fixedly, and his automatic stripped and drove seven shots into the floor. Then he slammed to the floor hard and was motionless limp and dead.

Finck hid his face in a corner, and Payson looked suddenly like a man gone mad. His hand shook violently. The gun he held blazed, and a shot clanged against the radiator. At the same time Brinky's gun belched, and Payson turned away with a sickly grimace and collapsed.

Brinkhaus got himself untangled from the rug and Connor's legs and heaved up to his feet, covering Finck.

"D-don't!" Finck cried. "I ain't done a thing!"

"Well, don't," Brinkhaus growled.

He lunged to where Arbutti lay, bent down and then rose saying, "Very dead."

Brinkhaus reached for the telephone and called Larsen. "Listen, boss, this is Herman…. Yeah, Brinky. Listen, boss. Take a squad and go over to Arbutti's house and pinch Chico for the Fairfax kill…. How do I know?… They told me—Arbutti and Payson and"—he looked at Connor—"Mr. Connor here."

He hung up, and Connor said, "You mean to say you didn't know—"

"Nope, I sure didn't. But when you guys got to finegling around I figgered I'd do some of it meself."

"O my Lord!" groaned Finck.

Connor looked at the door. "You win, Sergeant."

"When Chico and his pals kidnaped Harris so we'd think Harris bumped off Fairfax, it was just too bad. It's like me old pal Ogglecarp used to say: 'You can fool all of the coppers some o' the time but you can't fool all of the coppers some of the times, or it might have been some of the coppers all of the time.'"

Connor walked steadily to the door, laid his hand on the knob and used his other hand to turn the key.

"It's funny," Brinkhaus said, "but you got guts, Jabe Connor."

"And you're dumb," Connor said. "Like a fox—you are!"

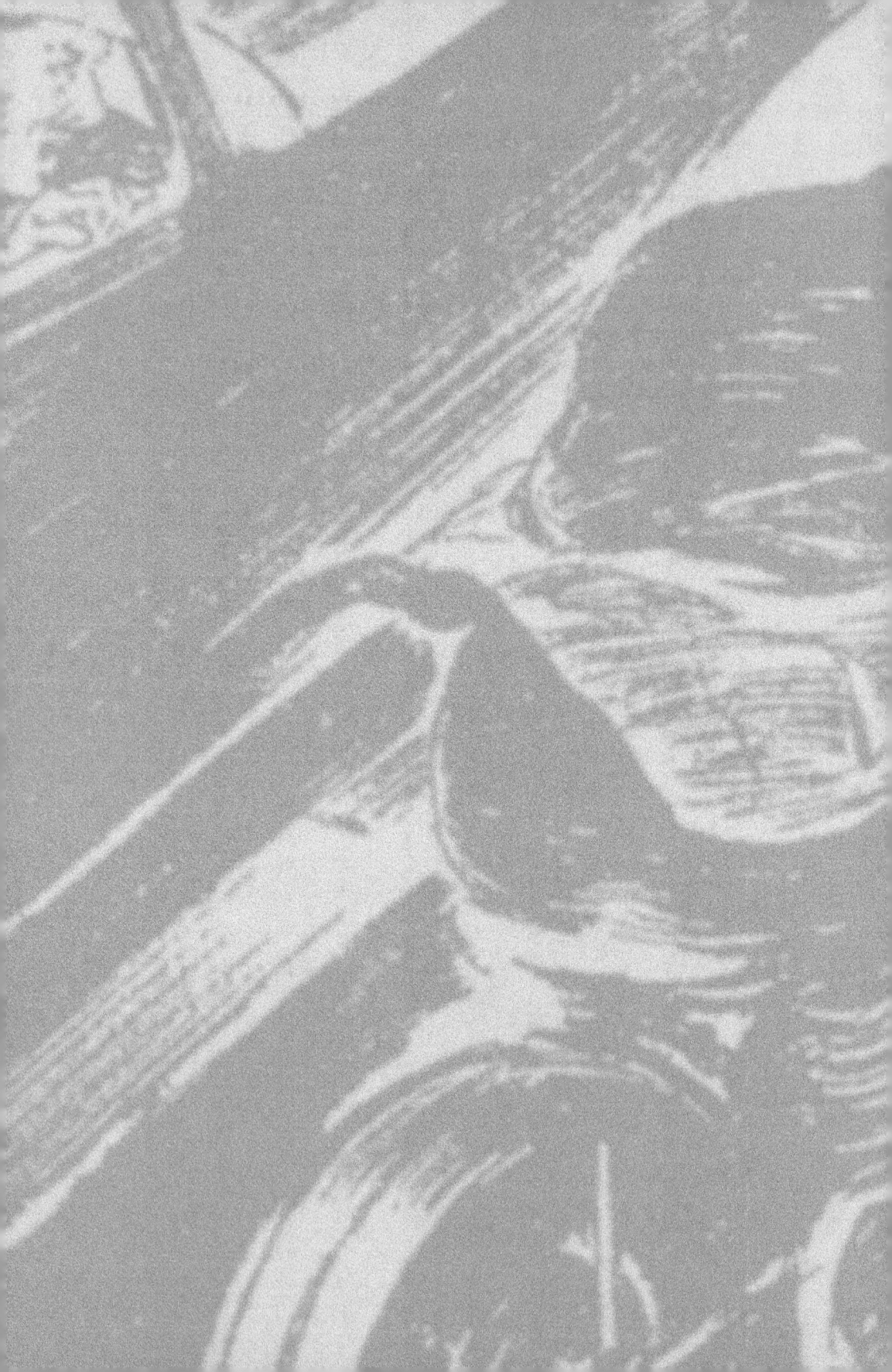

TAILOR-MADE CLUE

THERE HE LAY—BIG JOE
RUDNICKI—STARING
WITH SIGHTLESS EYES
AT THE SHAMBLES THAT
HAD BEEN THE HOT
SHOT CLUB. NO ONE HAD
SEEN HIM DIE, NO ONE
COULD FIND A CLUE—THE
TRAIL WAS COLD. BUT
BRINKHAUS SPECIALIZED
IN COLD TRAILS, AND IF
THERE WAS NO CLUE HE
HAD IT TAILORMADE.

CHAPTER ONE

THREE MISSING

THE PLACE was a wreck. A table stood upside down; the cloth that covered it was a sodden ruin. Amid a chaos of broken glass and shattered crockery an attenuated vase still stood erect and sprouting an artificial poinsettia. A chair that had been hurled, now hung from a wall-light. A rowdy foot had punctured the jazz band's bass drum. Glass ground underfoot glinted like tinsel on the dance floor. Splotches on the walls marked the death of flung bottles.

The Hot Shot Club was a shambles.

Flannagan, the owner, walked up and down near the archway leading to the lobby. Eight paces, then back again; then eight again. Completely bald, his head looked like an oiled skull. He held his head erect—but with an effort. In the unnatural silence of the club the drumming of his rubberless heels beat an endless monotone like the sound of jungle tomtoms. He was the only one who moved.

The waiters stood around like images. The guests—sixty-odd—sat on chairs detached from tables, from groups. One man sat dazedly in the center of the dance floor patting the left side of his face, though it was on the right side that a gash bled.

Members of the jazz band sat by their instruments. The saxophonist held his sax in position as if ready to play at a moment's notice. The drummer sat with his sticks braced on his knees.

A uniformed cop—Patrolman Traviglano—stood framed in the archway, his arms folded, his head turning from side to side like a robot's as his eyes watched the endless pacing of Flannagan.

Once he spoke. "For cryin' out loud now, Jerry, don't get all steamed up."

"Steamed up, eh? Steamed up, eh?" Flannagan's voice was tight like a drawn string.

Yellow-haired Inspector Peter Larsen came quietly into the lobby. Traviglano saluted casually and stepped aside and into the club proper. Larsen appeared in the archway idly drawing off pigskin gloves. A brown ulster had its collar up around his neck. A brown fedora sat neatly on his head. He stood cruising his blue-gray eyes around the club.

"Hello, Jerry."

"Hello, Inspector. Get a load of this."

Larsen nodded tranquilly.

Traviglano said: "Over there," and started across the dance floor. Larsen followed amiably toward a mound of chairs and an overturned table. Traviglano stopped, jerked his chin, said: "Pipe it."

"Brinky, you fool—stop!" The
police phaeton pulled up.

Larsen peered between the table and the mound of chairs.

"I didn't want to move anything," Traviglano said.

"Thanks, Mike. Move 'em now, will you?"

Larsen himself grabbed the table and slid it farther out onto the floor. Traviglano moved the chairs.

A woman choked an outcry.

Larsen dropped to one knee, felt the man's pulse. There was no pulse. He moved the eyelids with a forefinger. He saw the hole in the dress shirt and the darkness around the hole. The man was big, lumpy, fortyish. Alive, his face would have been bloated. It was not a good face even dead. There were many rings on his fingers.

"Jerry," Larsen said, rising, "did you get a doctor?"

"There was one in my guests." Flannagan signaled a man who was already on his way over.

"Floom is my name, Inspector. Death was instantaneous. He was shot through the heart."

Silence fell again and then sturdy shoes creaked across the floor and the squat, dumpy figure of Brinkhaus moved beneath the lights.

He said: "Josephs is here, boss. And Gatlin."

Deputy Medical Examiner George Josephs came in with his bobbing, happy walk. Rotund, immaculate in dress, he had round little bright eyes and cherubic cheeks.

"Well, well, Peter, what have we here?"

"A dead man," Larsen said.

"My, my!"

ASSISTANT DISTRICT ATTORNEY Wells Gatlin, small, dark, bitter-mouthed, streaked in importantly, shoved Flannagan out of the way, sideswiped Josephs and bent down over the dead man. He took one look. Then he straightened, pivoted, glared truculently all around and demanded: "Who did this?"

Larsen was in quiet conversation with Flannagan. Gatlin hopped to the center of the floor and shouted: "Who murdered this man? Quick!"

No one answered. A woman began crying. Gatlin rapped his heels across the floor and stood over her, his fists knotted.

"Madam, I will not be side-tracked by feminine tears. I am from the district attorney's office."

A man rose. "She's my wife. This—this has upset her. Quite naturally."

"And who are you?"

"My name is John Carveth."

"Who killed that man?"

"I don't know."

Gatlin snarled: "Oh, you don't know! I suppose you were in two other places when this happened. I suppose—"

"Please, please," sobbed the woman.

"Madam—"

Came Larsen's low soft voice. "Mr. Carveth, you may sit down. Mr. Gatlin, I am handling this investigation."

Gatlin tautened. "I am from—"

"Yes, the district attorney's office." Larsen nodded with mellow irony. "And I happen to be in charge of the detective division. Please mind your place until I've completed the investigation."

"You wouldn't be trying to be funny, would you?"

"No—anything but funny."

Brinkhaus and Josephs were kneeling on either side of the dead man.

"Direct to the heart," Josephs said. "Most direct."

"Close," Brinky supplemented. "Lookit the powder burn on the boiled shirt. I'm beginnin' to know this guy."

"Really!"

"Yeah. Oncet when me and Ogglecarp were pals we had to call on him oncet. Rudnicki's his real name—Josef Rudnicki—one o' them Slovaks or somethin' or a Polack maybe. He's in big time—or would you say he useter be? Yeah—'Big Joe the Beef' some called him, though he didn't like that monicker worth a damn."

"Oh, you mean Big Joe the Beef!"

Brinkhaus got up, his hard woolen pants clinging to his legs, his garters showing. "Boss—"

"Yes, Brinky," Larsen said, coming up.

"He's Joe the Beef. He's—" Brinkhaus stopped, stepped around Larsen and went creaky-shoed across the floor to a table at which two men sat. "Hello, boys."

The two men stood up, walked past Brinkhaus and did not stop until they reached Larsen. Larsen turned and looked at them. Their faces remained immobile. One was big and broad and thatch-browed. The other was quite as tall, slim and pale and strangely handsome, impeccably clothed in a tux with dull lapels.

This one said quietly: "Joe got it."

"Hello, 'Swan,'" Larsen said. Then he looked at the thatch-browed man. "Hello, Krieger."

"Joe got it," Krieger rumbled.

"You guys were with him?"

They nodded.

FLANNAGAN let the flood-gates open. "Joe was kind of drunk. Just kind of. At about eleven the place was jammed. Everybody's happy. This dead guy and these two guys are sitting right here—there was a table right here. A jane and a guy come in. I take a second look at the jane because she looks a knockout. Got an angel face and stands right out. The guy's with her is a bit soused. I get 'em a table way over there behind them palms. They're in here about ten minutes when the band cuts loose. The jane and the guy get up and dance and I'm watchin' the jane because she's such a swell looker and can she dance! Don't ask!

"A big crowd is on the floor when I see this dead guy push his way through and grab the girl by the arm. I can't hear what he says, the band is makin' so much noise. The young guy pushes this guy away and starts to dance again and this guy comes back at him and tries to get the girl away. I turn to call Buck, me bouncer; and when I look around again the young guy is takin' a swing at this dead guy. Other folks stop dancin' and shift. The jane yells. The lights go out. A guy roars and then—*bang*—a gun goes off.

"Then hell busts loose. Everybody starts crowdin' around. Women fall down and guys start swingin' on general principles. Things start to fly. People start makin' for the door and some get out. I finally find the light switch and turn on the lights and—and—here this guy is. And—and the young guy—and the jane—" he threw up his hands— "are gone. And lookit me place. Just look at it!"

Gatlin demanded: "Why didn't you stop him?"

Larsen said quietly: "Who turned the lights out?"

"I—I don't know," Flannagan gasped.

"Where's the switch?"

"Back in the hallway. Back there. The hall goes to the ladies' room and the men's room. I don't know who the hell turned the lights out. I wish to God I knew."

"How many people ran out?"

"Well, Inspector, they didn't go far. They only went as far as the sidewalk, and then after a coupla minutes Buck ran out and told 'em to come back or they might get in Dutch. So they all came back. All but the jane and the young guy. And—and another guy."

"Know him?"

"No. He come here alone. A little guy with eyeglasses on. And a sandy mustache. Harmless-lookin' guy. He danced a few times with one of our hostesses."

"His hat and coat in the check-room?"

"No. He didn't have an overcoat. He only had a hat. He didn't check it."

"Where was he sitting?"

Flannagan pointed. "At that little table—right by the hall that goes back to the rest rooms."

Larsen turned to The Swan and Krieger. "You know that guy came in with the girl?"

"No," said The Swan. "Never saw him before."

"I want the truth."

"You're getting it." The Swan's eyes were amber and steady in his pale narrow face.

Larsen clipped: "How about the girl?"

"I never checked up on Joe's women."

"What makes you think she was Joe's woman?"

"Because he went out after her. Give me a hard one."

Larsen smiled, humorlessly. "If you're thinking of going after that guy yourself—I mean you too, Krieger—think again."

The Swan's smile was equally humorless. But he didn't say anything.

Brinkhaus cleared his throat. "Boss—"

Larsen turned.

Brinkhaus was holding a hat and overcoat. "These are his, boss."

"Whose?"

"The guy with the gal."

Gatlin rasped: "I wish, Larsen, you would interrogate these people here so that I can."

"Go ahead."

Gatlin was caustic. "I thought perhaps you might object if I took the initiative."

"I don't intend quizzing sixty-two persons."

"What!"

"The only ones that interest me are the three that aren't here. Go ahead, Gatlin. Enjoy yourself."

CHAPTER TWO

OVERCOAT CLUE

DEAD. JOE THE BEEF was dead. Big Joe Rudnicki—forty-one years, three months and a day old. The underworld had known him as a man who went in strong for hard liquor, soft women and the mailed fist in the furtherance of his business. He'd plowed his way up from the bottom by means of the gun, brass knuckles, graft and an ability to take punishment and come back for more. He'd had guts. Plenty. Even the cops will tell you that. Each year he'd contributed two thousand dollars to the Fund for Policemen's Widows. Only those on the inside track know that he helped build the South side Orphanage. He'd lived a wild, tempestuous life; brute force had been supplemented by an uncanny ability to touch dross and turn it into gold. During the last year of his life rumor had been circulated that he was going soft. Some wiseacres had said, "The hotter the coal the quicker it burns out." Thereby springing an epigram worthy of the Chinese and, in the light of his death, quite prophetic.

Brinkhaus came into Larsen's office reading the morning paper. "Would I be asked," he said, "I'd say I never seen such slush in all my borned days. 'Big Joe Rudnicki, Don Juan of the Underworld.' I knew Joe. Kind of liked him. But would I be asked again, I'd say Don Juan 'd muscle over in his grave should he read slush like this. Joe was a bruiser. He had guts. It ought to end there— Nice day, boss."

Larsen was staring into space. "We've got to get the guy that did this, Brinky, before Joe's gang get him. They'll crucify him. I didn't like the look in The Swan's eyes. It meant something, I don't just know what."

"Looks like Joe was lookin' for a push in the mug when he grabbed that jane."

Larsen said: "I don't think it was premeditated murder. In fact, I'm sure it wasn't."

"Might ha' been. Them lights went out. The little guy disappeared. Everything went off like a clock. There wasn't a hitch anywhere."

Brinky folded his paper. "He left his hat and coat."

"What good are they? No labels in either."

"That's what I come in for early, boss."

"What?"

"To borry that coat."

Larsen squinted. "What's on your mind, Brinky?"

"Should you lend me that coat, I'll git started."

Larsen grabbed the phone, made a departmental call. "Harry, this is Larsen. When Brinky comes down give him that overcoat."

The day was bright with winter sunlight, sharply cold, the air clear as the toll of a bell. Brinky walked away from headquarters with his broad shoes a-creak, a woolen muffler that Mom had knitted and heavy woolen gloves that Mom had knitted also. He walked with the side-to-side roll of a heavy, stocky man. Five-feet-nine of him en-compassed two hundred and five pounds. The muffler jutted up from the back of his collar and almost touched the brim of his flat-crowned brown fedora. Over his arm he carried, neatly folded, a heather-colored overcoat.

In Plummer Street he visited a small tailoring shop. When he came out he boarded a street car and rode ten blocks, got off and entered another tailor's. From this shop he walked four blocks across town consulting memoranda he held in his hand. This was another tailoring shop, and from it he walked five blocks north to another. In two and a half hours he called on fourteen shops. At eleven-twenty he walked into the fifteenth. It was a large establishment on the second floor with broad windows overlooking North Harkness Street.

A man said: "Yes, sir?" and rubbed hands in anticipation.

"This coat," Brinky said. "By any chance did you make it?"

The man looked at it. He called a second man, and this man looked at it and galled a third. The three went into a close huddle and jabbered spiritedly, while Brinkhaus remained in the background patiently.

Then the first man turned around. "I believe we made this coat, sir."

"I'm Sergeant Brinkhaus, from police headquarters. Could you sorta check up and see who you made it for?"

The man measured the coat and called a fourth man. He talked rapidly and the fourth man disappeared into an office. In a few minutes the fourth man reappeared carrying some papers. He gave them to the first man and the latter came to Brinkhaus.

"This material was featured three months ago. We made sixteen overcoats of this material. According to measurements, there was only one man who could have had this made. His name is Paul Corson, the address 644 Hill Street."

"I'm much obliged, mister, thanks. And should I ask would you say nothin' about this, is it a promise?"

"Indeed, Sergeant."

THE EXPRESSION on Brinky's face was slightly less downcast than when he had entered. Down below, he considered a taxi parked at the curb, considered his forthcoming insurance installment, and walked three blocks to a street-car line. He changed twice before reaching Hill Street.

Number 644 was a five-story apartment house in a modest neighborhood. Alongside one of ten buttons in the lobby he saw the name of Paul Corson. He pressed the button, heard the door click open, entered. He climbed a staircase to the third floor and saw a woman standing in an open doorway.

"Good-day," he said. "Are you Mrs. Corson?"

"Yes."

"Is this your husband's overcoat?"

"Why—why—" She stopped and stared at him.

"The tailor says it is."

She laughed jerkily. "Why—why, yes. Yes, of course. Thank you so much."

She was small, dark-haired, pretty. Brinky seemed embarrassed.

He said: "You're husband ain't home, is he?"

"No—no. He doesn't get home until six."

Brinky said: "I'll leave it. Will you ask your husband to meet me tonight at about eight in Herbie Kettner's Coffee Pot, 55 Clove Street?"

"Why, yes—yes, of course."

"The name is Brinkhaus, missus. Thank you."

He went back to headquarters by way of three street cars. Entering Larsen's office, he found Assistant District Attorney Wells Gatlin pacing furiously up and down. Gatlin stopped short and glared at him.

"Where's that overcoat?"

Blinky blinked. "Whuh-what overcoat?"

"You know damned well what overcoat I mean! The one we picked up at the Hot Shot Club!"

"Oh, yeah. Oh, that overcoat. Well, Mr. Gatlin, I'm havin' it cleaned. I fell off a trolley car with it and got it all dirtied up. I'm having it cleaned."

"Having it cleaned! Who ever heard of such a thing!"

"I'll give it to you soon as I git it back."

Gatlin appeared about to be overcome with apoplexy. His lips sputtered wetly. "Damn my stars!" He spun and drilled Larsen with a dark look. "Is this the type of idiot you recommend as your right-hand man?"

Larsen himself looked puzzled, but he said, "I guess Brinky thought it was the best thing to do."

"Best thing! Bah! I said 'Bah'!" He whirled back to Brinkhaus. "You go get that overcoat immediately. Immediately!"

Brinky swallowed. "Well, I can't, Mr. Gatlin. It's being cleaned."

"As a representative of the district attorney's office, I demand—"

Larsen cut in: "Now wait a minute, Gatlin. Just wait a minute. Don't go off the handle. You'll get a look at that coat when it's returned."

Gatlin trembled with anger. "I know! I know! Your whole damned department is working against me! That's what! I'll bet that coat is right in this building! I'll bet!" He drew himself up. "All right! I'll find it!"

He stamped out, banged the door violently.

Brinkhaus said: "There ought to be some kind of medicine for a guy like him."

"Brinky—" Larsen's voice was low—"Brinky, what have you done with that overcoat?"

"I give it back to its owner."

"What!"

"Yeah."

Larsen jumped to his feet. "Then where is he?"

"Well, he wasn't there. I give it to his wife. A pretty little thing, boss. The guy is goin' to meet me at Herbie Kettner's Coffee Pot tonight."

Larsen looked slightly exasperated. "Why in God's name didn't you bring the man back with you? How did you find out who owned the coat?"

"Well, I went around to Ikey Goldfarb, the tailor, and asked him was the coat tailor-made. He said yes. So I went around to all the tailors. So one of them recognized it and I got the name that way. Paul Corson. I didn't want to git the woman all fussed up, so I left it there and told her to tell her husband to meet me."

Larsen dropped back into his chair.

Brinky shrugged. "The lady wasn't the one Corson brung in the night club, so I didn't want to—to— Well, it's the guy we want after all, so what the heck's the use o' gittin' his missus all het up? I hate to have doin's with women and like me pal Ogglecarp useter say—"

"That's quite enough, Brinky," Larsen said distinctly. "See that that coat is not lost. See that Corson meets you."

"Yes, boss." He dipped his head. "Yes, boss."

PAUL CORSON was a tall man of about thirty. He entered Herbie Kettner's Coffee Pot at exactly eight o'clock. Raw night wind had nipped his cheeks. He wore the heather-colored overcoat and stopped beside the cash counter.

"Pardon me. Is there a Mr. Brinkhaus waiting?"

Herbie said: *"Ja."* Lifted his voice: "Hey, Brinky, dot zhentlemans—" He pointed. "Give a look, please, mister; dot's Mr. Brinkhaus."

Brinky was standing, his broad head tilted to one side, his candid brown eyes watching Corson approach.

"Hello, Mr. Corson. Have a seat right in this here now booth."

"You're the man returned my coat?"

They were sitting down.

Brinkhaus nodded. "Yes. I'm Sergeant Brinkhaus."

"Sergeant—"

"P'lice headquarters."

Corson said: "Oh," softly.

Brinkhaus interlocked his stout fingers and kept looking candidly at Corson. "I didn't want to say anything to your missus first off. I figgered I oughter have a talk with you first. I figgered you'd know why I asked her you should come here. There was a man killed at the Hot Shot Club last night."

"Yes. I read it in the paper— Cigarette?"

"No, thanks. I cut out smokin' account of me missus said I was tossin' all night. You got a very nice missus, Mr. Corson."

"I think so myself."

"I understand you work in a bank. Assistant cashier, ain't it now?"

Corson's eyes were on guard. "Yes."

"I want to be as good as I can about it, Mr. Corson, but law is law, and even if Big Joe Rudnicki was a racketeer, the law is so writ that a dead man's a dead man and we cops have got to do somethin' about it. It was pretty tough when you clean outta that night club leavin' that there now coat behind."

Corson's face was becoming pale. His lips barely moved. "I see. I begin to see. You think that I was at—what's the name?—the Hot Shot Club?"

"Account of your nice missus, I'm sorry I got to say yes."

Corson bowed his head. "I'm sorry you're mistaken, Sergeant Brinkhaus."

"You don't look like a bad feller yourself, Mr. Corson. I'm sorry you're actin' like that."

"I can't help it, Sergeant. I wasn't there."

Brinkhaus sat back. "You mind comin' to p'lice headquarters?"

"Not at all."

CHAPTER THREE

"I KILLED HIM"

LARSEN, RUNNING a palm back over his yellow mane of hair, said: "Take that chair, Mr. Corson."

Corson sat down beside the desk.

Larsen shifted a powerful desklight so that its hot white beam drove mercilessly into Corson's face. Then he turned out the other lights in the room. Corson shifted uneasily and his lips tightened.

Gatlin blew his nose briskly, jammed the handkerchief into his pocket, smacked his palms together. His eyes were bright bale-fires in his dark, saturnine face. Brinkhaus looked meekly at him and shifted from one foot to the other.

Gatlin rose on his toes, smacked his palms down on the desk. His dark face shot into the glare of the spotlight.

"Mr. Corson, this is murder and Sergeant Brinkhaus claims that this coat you're wearing came from the Hot Shot Club. There's no earthly reason for your denying, or attempting to deny, that you were not there last night. As assistant district attorney of this county, vested with—"

"I was not at the Hot Shot Club, Mr. Assistant District Attorney."

"Oh, ridiculous! Ridiculous! My dear, dear fellow—"

Larsen interrupted quietly with: "Mr. Corson, you admit that it is your coat?"

"Yes, sir."

"And you claim that you were not at the Hot Shot Club last night?"

"I was not at the Hot Shot Club."

"Seems a bit paradoxical, doesn't it?"

"Yes."

Larsen said: "There's only one other answer. Another man wore this coat there."

Corson's face was white and set. He said nothing.

Gatlin snapped: "If you were not there in this coat, then who was?"

Corson's eyes glinted. "The only thing I can say is that I was not there. That can easily be proven by people who were there, I imagine."

"You can't crack wise with me!" Gatlin warned.

"I am not attempting to crack wise."

Gatlin's fist hammered the desk and his voice crackled. "This is murder! You understand? Murder! A man was shot to death last night! Murdered in cold blood! In the city of Portsend, county of Windmore, of which, as assistant district attorney, I am a representative vested with prosecuting powers, I ask—demand—the truth and nothing but the truth. Who wore your coat to the Hot Shot Club last night?"

"I cannot tell!"

"Piffle! Bosh! Do you realize that in secreting evidence—"

"Mr. Corson," broke in Larsen's mellow voice, "whatever sentimental feeling you must have, you must be aware of the fact that in acting the way you are you thwart justice and place yourself in a very undesirable position."

Corson raised a hand against the glare of the light. Gatlin knocked his hand down. Corson stiffened and his lower lip shook, his eyes glittered.

"I refuse to say anything other than I've already said!"

Gatlin snarled: "You listen to me, you damned fool—"

"Gatlin," Larsen cut in, pushing him aside. "This inquest happens to be in my office."

Gatlin whirled on him. "I don't give a damn where it is!"

"You heard me, Gatlin."

"This man is guilty! I demand the right to question him in any manner I see fit to!"

Larsen's voice became edged. "Gatlin, I repeat that this is my office. I add that you have no right in here if I choose not to have you!"

"Oh, is that so?"

"Try maintaining the dignity of the district attorney's office by taking the air. This man has not yet been booked. When he has been, and when I've finished with him, then you'll be at liberty to question him."

Brinkhaus, sighing, went to the door, opened it and stood looking innocently into space.

Larsen pointed. "The door is open, Gatlin."

Gatlin's face worked and his mouth drew down at one corner. His eyes burned with hatred and words fought for utterance behind his twitching lips.

A man appeared in the doorway. A young man. Tall and lean and with a pale, haggard face.

"Inspector Larsen?"

Larsen pivoted. "Why, yes."

The man walked into the office, drew his hand from his pocket, laid a gun on the desk.

"I killed Rudnicki," he said. "I killed him."

JUNE CORSON was Paul Corson's wife. She sat in an overstuffed armchair, her eyes red-rimmed, a crumpled ball of linen handkerchief moving spasmodically from one hand to the other. Corson stood by the open window staring down into the street.

Brinkhaus sat on a straight-backed chair, his overcoat open, the ends of a woolen scarf trailing haphazardly across the lapels. He looked at once uneasy and sympathetic. It was not warm in the room but none the less he fanned himself with his hat.

"O God. O dear God," the woman sobbed.

"Missus," Brinkhaus said, and then forgot what to say.

She sobbed on. "He's my brother, my brother. Allan is my brother. They'll hang him—hang him. O God!"

Corson turned from the window, grim-faced. He came over and patted her on the shoulder.

Brinkhaus said: "If we can prove it wasn't premeditated, there won't be no death penalty."

Corson said: "He could have got away. I told him to. I intended bucking you so that he would have a chance to get away. But he wouldn't. He gave himself up."

"It was best," Brinkhaus said. "When did he borrow your overcoat?"

"Yesterday morning."

Brinkhaus scratched his chin. "He won't tell us the gal was with him. We've got to find the gal."

"What's the use of dragging in the girl?" Corson asked.

"She'd be his star witness. She'd have to be. He won't tell. You'd best tell me who she was."

Corson said: "We never met her. He'd only talked about her. He never brought her around. We don't know who she is or where she lives. But he loved her. Lottie he called her. But he never brought her around. She'll show up. Maybe she doesn't even know he gave himself up yet."

"You get a lawyer for him yet?"

"Yes. I notified Walton & Arnholt."

"Good," Brinkhaus nodded. "They're the best in town but they cost like heck."

"I don't care. I'll spend every cent I have."

The woman sobbed. "Poor Allan—poor Allan."

Brinkhaus got up and moved closer to the woman. "Missus, I know it's pretty tough. These here things bust out like a rash when folks least expect 'em. Here you got a nice home here and I know it ain't nice havin' all this mess on your shoulders. He's only twenty-five and that's pretty young. You got to buck up, missus, and hope for the best. It's times like this when I wisht I wasn't no cop. If I can do anything for you, let me know."

"You're kind, Sergeant—you're so very kind."

"I'm a family man meself, missus." He made an awkward bow. "I got to be goin'. G'night."

Corson went to the door with him. "You're blamed white, Sergeant. We'll help all we can—but it seems so futile. You'll take good care of him, won't you?"

"Sure, mister. Sure."

WHEN BRINKHAUS walked dejectedly into Larsen's office the inspector was sitting back in his chair. He looked winded.

"Any news, Brinky?"

"Nope."

Larsen mopped his face. "The boy's stubborn as hell. I was after him. Davis and Shumacher were after him. And Gatlin. The boy's all shot—all nerves." He put away his handkerchief. "If we could only find the little guy Flannagan said ran out when it happened. Or the girl."

Brinkhaus went out and up two blocks. He bought two cheese sandwiches and a bucket of coffee. He returned to headquarters and went down to the cell-block. Hennessey let him into cell number 5.

Allan Cable crouched, then relaxed. "Oh, I thought it would be Gatlin again. God, keep that fiend out of here!"

"Um," said Brinkhaus. "I—I brung around some sandwiches and coffee, Allan."

"Thanks. I—I am a bit hungry."

"It'll brace you up."

Brinkhaus sat down and watched the boy eat. He waited until the last drop of coffee had been drunk. He did not smoke cigarettes, but he had brought along a pack for the boy. Cable said: "Thanks. Gee, you're swell!" He smoked nervously.

Brinky said: "You oughter tell us who the gal is, Al. It'd help a lot."

Cable gave him one look, then went on smoking.

"If she loves you, Al, she'd want to stand by you."

Cable cried: "Why should I drag her in?"

"You got to think, boy, that your life's at stake."

"I know it. I knew it before I gave myself up. I'll take the chance. That dirty rat grabbed her. I told him to let go. When the lights went off I—I just went crazy. I guess I was afraid he'd pull a gun on me. So I shot him. I don't repent it. He deserved it. And now that I know who he was—nothing more than a dirty gunman—I'm doubly glad I gave him what he deserved."

"I know, Al, I know. But a life's a life. We got to look at it that way. You killed a man. Even sayin' he deserved what he got, you should be willin' to help us try givin' you a break."

"Break, eh?" Cable laughed scornfully. "That man Gatlin wants to hang me. He wants to! He's worse than any gangster. Give me a break—" He stopped. "I'm sorry, Sergeant. You're different."

"You got a nice sister, Al. She's standin' by you. But the one we want is the lady friend you was with."

Cable's jaw stiffened. "If she comes, that's all right. But I got myself into this and I'll take what's coming to me."

Brinkhaus stood up. "Al, should you want anything, just ask for me."

Unexpectedly the boy gripped the old sergeant's hand. "I know you mean well, sir. But try to understand. I don't want to drag her in. I can't. I was drunk a bit and maybe I shouldn't have done what I did. But I've done it. I'll stand trial and hope for the best."

On the way out, after Hennessey had locked the cell, Brinkhaus walked down the cell-block with him.

Hennessey sighed. "Clean lad, Brinky."

"You got a kid, ain't you, Henry?"

"Yeah. 'Bout his age."

Brinky nodded. "Me too."

"Yeah," said Hennessey.

"Yeah," said Brinkhaus.

AN ANGEL-FACED GIRL was sitting in a chair beside Larsen's desk when Brinkhaus walked disconsolately into the office. Larsen stopped talking. Brinkhaus made a hesitant bow with his honest brown eyes hopping from the girl to Larsen.

Larsen said: "This is Miss Blakeney."

Starry eyes, slightly moist, trembled on Brinky; and Brinky bowed and said: "Miss Lottie Blakeney?"

"Yes," Larsen said. "Miss Blakeney, this is Sergeant Brinkhaus whom I've placed in charge of the investigation."

She half rose and made a demure little curtsy. She was beautiful, an ash blonde; slender and of medium height. A lapin coat was open far enough to reveal a flowered chiffon dress.

Larsen said: "Miss Blakeney is Allan Cable's—"

"Good, good," Brinkhaus said, and his tone, his manner, meant it. "I was just down to see Allan."

Larsen said: "Miss Blakeney tells me— You tell the sergeant, Miss Blakeney. Brinky, I'll be back in a few minutes."

Larsen went out and Brinkhaus pulled a chair up to face the girl, sat down and assumed a very fatherly attitude.

The girl said in a trembling voice: "It all happened so fast, Sergeant—it's still like a dream, like a nightmare. Allan and I went into that club. A man seated us. Then Allan and I danced. The man—this Joe Rudnicki, so the papers say—came over and said, 'I want to dance with that girl, guy.' Like that. Allan said, 'I beg your pardon, but you are not.' Then the man grabbed me and Allan shoved him away. The man tried again and Allan said, 'You're drunk. If you don't stop I'll hit you.' The man kept trying and Allan hit him. They grappled and then the lights went out. Then the shot. Then—then Allan had me by the arm. 'We've got to get out of here,' he said. I didn't know what to do. I went with him and we ran away fast. In the morning—we saw the papers."

She stopped, stared at the floor, her eyes glazed. Then she said: "Allan had borrowed his brother-in-law's coat. His own was being cleaned. He said. 'Gosh, Paul's coat—we left it there.' We didn't know what to do. He told Paul. Paul told him to run away. Allan didn't know what to do. Then—then he knew he couldn't run away. So—he gave himself up."

"Do you remember, miss, if this Rudnicki went for a gun?"

Her eyes raised to meet Brinky's. "When the lights went out I tried to do something. I grabbed Rudnicki's arm—his right one. I could feel he was trying to get his hand in his pocket. I said, 'Allan—Allan, look out!' He must have sensed what I meant. He shot him." She took a breath. "He killed him."

Brinky said: "That's good, miss. Remember that about Rudnicki's hand in his pocket."

"And Allan," she said, "when he decided to give himself up, made me swear that I'd stay out of it. But how could I?" Her eyes filled. "How could I?"

"Course you couldn't," he agreed. "There, there, now. Don't cry, miss— You work, miss?"

"Yes."

"Where?"

"The cigar shop in the Hotel Billings. Allan met me there—two months ago. He was saving to buy an engagement ring."

Brinky edged closer. "When you and Allan ran outside, miss, did you see a little guy with spectacles runnin' away too?"

"A little man?"

"Yeah—and with spectacles."

She shook her head slowly. "No."

"And you never before in your life seen this Rudnicki?"

"No—surely not. Why—when he came up to me—I—I didn't know what to say, to think."

Brinky nodded. "Yeah, I heard Rudnicki useter to do that, take a kinda shine to a gal and git fresh with her—I'm glad you turned up, miss. You're gonna be a big help to Allan. Keep in mind kinda that I'm your friend." He patted her hand. "Just remember me should you want something."

"Oh, thank you, thank you, Sergeant."

Larsen came in and Brinkhaus rose and said: "I'll be gittin' along downstairs, boss."

He went downstairs to Sergeant Connolly's office. Connolly was the gun expert. Connolly said: "Yup, it is the gun. It is the bullet." He held up a slug. "This, Brinky, was ejected from this gun. It killed Rudnicki. Positively."

It was a .25 Colt automatic, pocket model. Brinky picked it up and examined it.

"If you're looking for the number," Connolly said, "it's been filed off."

"Yeah, I notice."

Brinkhaus picked up a magnifying glass and examined the gun closely. "Mind if I borry this gun?"

"It's the gun, man. It's the gun. Open and shut. It's the gun that killed Rudnicki."

"Mind if I borry it?"

"You mean to stand there and tell me that I'm a liar!"

"No," Brinky said. "Only could I borry it?"

Connolly laughed. "Sure, go ahead."

Brinkhaus said: "Thanks," put the gun in his pocket and went to the door. He turned to say: "How is Mrs. Connolly's varicose veins?"

"Better, thanks, Brinky."

"Good. Should you remember, give her me regards and tell her I ain't forgot what swell liederkrantz she had there that night."

CHAPTER FOUR

ANGEL FACE

THE SWAN, pallid, his amber eyes dreamy, regarded his likeness in the Palladian mirror. His skin seemed almost transparent. His eyelashes were long and curved upward. His ebon hair had a precise part down the center. At first glance his face seemed weak, effeminate; after a while you became aware of the rigid jaw, the straight lines of wide narrow lips. His hands moved so gracefully that you were hardly aware they moved at all. By moving his head a bit he could also see the reflected image of Brinkhaus.

Brinky was sitting on a vis-a-vis couch, coat and overcoat open and thumbs hooked in lower vest pockets. Light from a parchment-shaded lamp brought into sharp relief his quaint haircomb of the '90s.

"O' course, Swan, it was a helluva accident. Big Joe had no right a-tall, though, to go crashin' into another guy's party. He musta been pie-eyed."

"Plastered," said The Swan to Brinky's image. "We always had that trouble with Big Joe. Get him on a party and you never knew when he'd go meshuga. Still, he was a swell guy in many ways. He's getting a honey for a funeral."

Brinky wiggled his fingers while still keeping his thumbs in his vest pockets. "Who's takin' Big Joe's place?"

"Where?"

"As the brass hat o' your mob."

The Swan regarded his own image. "I don't know yet. We haven't talked about it. There's Krieger and 'Maxie-waxie' Klein and 'General George' Onkman. We'll see."

"I expect you will, Swan."

"What's that—a crack?"

"Oh, no-o. I just kinda figgered you was some groceries yourself in this mob. I like you, Swan. You don't act like an egg. I figger if you was boss of this scatter we'd have less back-alley jobs."

The Swan's chest expanded. "Thanks, Brinky. There's a swell chance I may handle the reins."

Brinky looked gloomy eyed at the carpet for a long minute. Then he said, without looking up: "You ain't seen 'The Professor' around town lately, have you?"

"The—who?"

"His name's Jehle. He uster be private secretary to 'Long Tim' Coose, what ran things in Philly three years ago till a rival bunch of big shots rubbed him out. I ain't sure, only I heard The Professor was in town."

"Never heard of him."

"It don't matter. I was just thinkin'. I just heard he was in. They say he's some groceries with a gun and I just like to keep checked up on the red-hots. Well...." Brinky slapped his knees, rose, yawned. "It's near ten. I'm up past bedtime."

The Swan turned from the mirror. He smiled graciously, bowed and indicated a decanter and glasses. "Have a nightcap."

"Don't mind if I do."

They touched glasses.

Brinky said: "I got a hunch, Swan, you're gonna be the next kingpin o' this mob."

"I'll do right by you, Brinky."

"Yeah, Big Joe was past his prime. The mob needs new blood. Here's to you, big fella."

They drank and Brinky smacked his lips. "Thanks, Swan." He went to the door. The Swan hastened to open it.

Brinky screwed a thumb into The Swan's ribs. "And I expect by and large the mob's takin' orders from you right now."

The Swan chuckled drily, flexed his lips, said nothing.

LEAVING the opulent apartment house, Brinky trudged up the broad avenue until a bus came along. He boarded it and rode as far as Union Circle, got off and walked down South Broad Street. He stopped in front of a pool parlor, opened the door and looked in. He closed the door, walked a block and stopped at the next corner and waited. In a few minutes a man came out of the pool parlor and walked toward him.

"Hello, Brinky."

"Hello, 'Soup.' Anything?"

"Geez, Sarge, I been snoopin' all around."

"O.K., O.K. And what now?"

"I ain't heard of him bein' around."

Brinky's voice dropped. "I got a hunch the mug's in town. We ain't got no pictures of him because he was never mugged here. But it sounds like his work. Keep on your toes, Soup, and fall down on me and I'll put a pinch on you."

"On the up-and-up, Sarge—"

"O.K., O.K."

Brinkhaus walked on and then cut over into Little Italy. He checked up on two more stoolies, then crossed Cherry Square and entered a speakeasy."

"Gimme a glass o' Cholly Koenigfelt's beer, Tony."

"Hey, Sarge, headquarters rang up and said you should ring if you come in."

"Thanks."

He called the lieutenant. "Brinky, Sam…. Huh?… Yeah, I got it: Southern one-o-four-o. Thanks, Sam." He hung up, then unpronged

the receiver again and said: "Southern one-o-four-o." He waited, then
said: "Brinkhaus.... Oh, hello, 'Big-nose.' What's 'at?... I see. Listen,
Big-nose, you ain't givin' me a bum steer?... O.K., thanks.... Yeah, I'll
see can I git you a job on the highway commission."

He left the booth, returned to the bar and drained a mug of beer.
"How's your little gal's measles, Tony?"

"Swell, Brinky, thanks."

Brinky had an address: 909 Clermont Street. Twenty minutes after
leaving Tony's he entered Clermont Street from the north, turning
from Hawk. Clermont is level here. Once it was a pretty good neighborhood and in those days the city saw fit to pave it with expensive
red bricks. The bricks outlasted the goodness of the neighborhood.
The frame houses still stand, but the little front yards no longer sprout
flowers and the low iron railings have gone to rust and ruin. An enterprising meat packer started the decadence by buying up a square
block at the south end of the street and the winds in Clermont Street
are mostly southern.

Number 909 was a gray frame house of three stories. Its front door
was flush with the sidewalk. Brinky opened it and entered a musty
hall where a gas jet flowered yellowly against a scarred wall.

He climbed to the top hallway. Here another gas jet burned. The
wind moaned across the roof and the hall was damp and cold. Brinky
counted doors. He pulled his gun from his hip holster, shoved it into
his overcoat pocket. He left it there while he drew off the woolen
glove from his right hand and held it in his left.

He rapped at a door. He did not put his bare hand back into his
pocket. He waited patiently while he heard a chair scrape. He heard
a bolt rap open. He saw the door open to a crack. He did not move.
There was something shining in the crack the open door made.

"Go ahead, open it," Brinky said. "Nobody's goin' to eat you, mister."

"What do you want?"

"Did you open the door wide, we could talk better."

The door opened, bit by bit, and a small man with matted gray hair
and thick-lensed spectacles peered nearsightedly at Brinkhaus.

"Yes, yes, what is it?" he asked in a piping voice.

Brinky walked in, ponderously, and the little man backed up but
kept his left hand in the pocket of a faded bathrobe. With the change
of light and shadow the thick-lensed spectacles hid his eyes.

Brinkhaus said: "I seen you last about two and a half years ago, mister. You think back and you'll remember what I said. I said, 'Professor, I'm givin' you a break, so take it and lam outta Portsend and give her a wide berth.' That's what I said. Maybe you ain't got the memory for faces that I have. Git your pants on, Professor."

"Why, really—why, really—"

"And take care o' that left-handed rod in your pocket there. Gimme it. There's no tellin' what the hell you might do with it. Come on, gimme that roscoe."

The man piped: "What do you want me for? Why—why do you want me? I haven't done anything."

"Maybe you think goin' around takin' cracks at light switches in night clubs ain't nothin', huh? Like I said now, dammit, gimme that rod before it gits away from you."

"B-b-but—"

Brinky's right hand plunged to his wrist. The gun appeared. Brinky got the wrist. The man tried to leap backward. Brinky's heavy shoe pinned his foot to the floor.

"E-e-e-e!" yelped The Professor. "Oh—oh—ouch!" he cried.

The gun fell to the floor and Brinky said, placidly: "That's nice now, that's nice." He flung the man away. "Your pants."

THE PROFESSOR limped into Larsen's office yammering: "I—I can hardly walk, sir. He—he bashed me on the foot."

"It was like this," Brinkhaus explained. "A piany fell on it, boss."

Larsen stood up. "Who is this man, Brinky?"

"Oscar Jehle's his real name. He's got others. One o' them's The Professor. Git Flannagan over here from the Hot Shot Club and see wasn't this the guy was sittin' near the light switch. If he ain't, I'm goin' to the tall timbers."

"What reason have you for arresting this man?"

"Well, the first reason was I didn't believe Allan Cable plunked Big Joe in the heart."

"Connolly swears it's the gun and the bullet."

"There's somethin' else I'll be gittin' around to."

Larsen, always just, said, "I still don't see why you arrested this man."

"Boss, ain't you ever had a hunch that you figgered might be good and might be goofy? And ain't you felt like you wanted to keep it to yourself till you found for sure it was good? Git Flannagan, will you?"

Larsen got Flannagan.

The night-club owner took fifteen minutes to get over. "That's the guy," he said. "That's the guy was sitting at the table where you go to the light switch."

Larsen said: "You'll stick by that, Jerry?"

"Ab-so-lute!"

Flannagan left and Brinkhaus looked a little less worried. The Professor looked very worried.

Larsen said: "You threw that switch, Jehle."

Jehle's eyes rolled behind his thick-lensed spectacles. He made fluttering gestures with his hands. "N-n-no, I—"

"Don't be stupid. Flannagan identified you. We can get others—the girls you danced with, for instance. If you didn't throw it, why did you lam out when Rudnicki was killed?"

Jehle blubbered but didn't say anything. Brinkhaus made an apologetic bow to Larsen and Larsen stepped aside. Brinky planted his two hundred and five pounds in front of Jehle.

"You always had a hand in the dope traffic, mister. That's why I told you to lam two and a half years ago. When did you git back here?"

"Four months ago."

"Who come with you?"

Jehle's eyes bulged. He shrank back in the chair.

Brinkhaus turned to Larsen. "Boss, I got a friend, Billy Kiley, on the Philadelphia cops. I called him on long distance tonight and he give me the low-down on Jehle. Dope's Jehle's long shot, but he always gits the backin' of a mob. And he always has a gal with him. Billy says the gal usually gits a job in a swell hotel drug store or cigar stand— mostly the best in town. The customers go there and they usually ask for a kind of cigarette nobody every heard of. I figger we know who come with him."

"Who?" Larsen said.

"Lottie Blakeney."

"Lottie—"

"Yeah," said Brinkhaus. "Allan's lady friend."

Jehle's face became a frozen mask of terror.

Brinkhaus said: "Allan's shieldin' the gal. Al never plunked Big Joe. I took that rod apart and found pink face powder in the works. It's been there a long time. Like it was carried in a gal's pocket-book all the time. The gal's a moll. I described her to Billy Kiley and he said it sounded like the moll they was callin' 'Angel Face' down in Philly. She's a cokey herself."

Larsen said: "Brinky, you amaze me!" He turned to Jehle. "What have you got to say?"

Jehle chirped: "Nothing. I have nothing to say. I won't say anything. You can't make me. Notify my attorney Abe Klotz."

"Ain't it funny," Brinky said, "that Abe Klotz is The Swan's mouthpiece too?"

"I—I won't say anything."

Brinky said: "Boss, I'm goin' to git the Angel Face."

CHAPTER FIVE

THE PROFESSOR TALKS

HE BECAME a spendthrift. He hopped a taxi instead of a proletariat street car. He sat in the back and watched the lights of the city whip past. His woolen muffler rubbed against his chin and one end of it dangled down the front of his overcoat. He got out in front of the Hotel Billings, crossed the broad sidewalk and went in through the revolving door. The lobby was almost empty. His hard heels made a loud noise on the marble floor.

He spotted the cigar counter. The girl was closing up. She saw him coming and a sweet smile overspread her face.

"Hello, Sergeant Brinkhaus."

"Hello, Miss Blakeney. The boss over to headquarters would like to know could you stop by for a few minutes."

"This late?"

Brinky looked apologetic. "He sent me over to ask you."

"I'm so, so tired, Sergeant."

He nodded. "Yeah, it must be a hard job, workin' here late like this. I said to the boss, 'Shucks, boss, Miss Blakeney'll be worn out this late.' But he said I should come. It's for to help out Allan maybe."

She shrugged, smiled her sweet smile. "Of course, then."

He waited placidly while she locked drawers, turned out lights. He waited while she took a cash box over to the desk. She came back and said: "In a few minutes. I'll get my coat."

"Yes, miss."

He roamed abstractedly in front of the desk. Heard the scratching of the night clerk's pen on paper. Heard the voice of the switchboard operator. He stopped roaming and squinted at a fluted Doric column. He went over the desk.

"Please, mister, I'm Sergeant Brinkhaus."

The clerk looked up.

Brinky said: "Would you ask the operator what the call was she just put through?"

The clerk went over to the switchboard, came back. "It was from the ladies' retiring room. The call was made to Westend 999."

"Thanks very much."

Brinkhaus left the desk, drew a notebook from his pocket, turned to the S's. He saw: Swan, Westend 999. He closed the book and put it away and his expression became oddly pious.

The girl appeared, smiling. Brinky bowed politely and they went outside and got into a taxi. It was late. The city empty it reechoed the more so to sounds.

"Allan—how is Allan?" the girl said.

"Sleepin', poor kid."

"Oh, I, hope—I do hope he'll get out of this. I love him so."

Brinkhaus blinked in the darkness. He watched the street ahead, kept his eyes on street corners. The girl's voice came to him as from afar. It was a sweet voice, soft and melodious. Once he saw her eyes as they passed close to a street light. The eyes burned brightly. Brinky returned his watchful stare to the way ahead. He sat on the edge of the seat. He removed the woolen glove from his right hand and held it in his left. For no reason at all he had a vision of Mom waiting up for him by the dining-room table. He wanted her to use the living room, but times were hard and it cost too much to heat the living room. There would be something hot waiting in the oven and a kettle whistling on the back of the kitchen range.

He gave a sigh of relief when they swung into Civic Square and turned down a narrow street where the green lights of police head-quarters shone. The girl had stopped talking.

The cab stopped and Brinkhaus got out, helped the girl to the sidewalk. Three men came quietly out of the shadows.

"O.K., Sarge, take it easy."

Their hats were yanked down over their eyes, their coat collars were turned up. Steel glinted in their hands. A gun pressed hard against Brinky's back. The girl jumped away and one of the men took her arm and said: "Get in there, sugar." She hopped back into the cab. The man held a gun on the driver. "You be nice, kid."

"Um," said Brinkhaus.

One of the men said: "Keep 'em up, Sarge." He joined the other man and told him: "Get in. I'll ride the running board. Tell that driver to get started."

Brinky stood rooted to the pavement, his hands raised. He watched the taxi drive away, saw the man with the gun standing on the running board. Then Brinky turned and barged up to the headquarters garage. He almost fell over a parked motorcycle. He could feel that it was still warm. He hadn't ridden a motorcycle in eight years, but he started it. And blew the siren.

He rode it like a cowboy out of the garage. At the second corner he saw the taxi parked and the driver standing in the road. He stopped.

"Where'd they go?"

The driver pointed. "See that tail-light? A seven-passenger tourin'—dark gray. Plates—F-4066."

"When the squad car comes, stop it. Tell 'em."

He kicked his feet free of the ground and the motorcycle hooted up the dark street. He saw the red light disappear to the left. One end of his muffler trailed behind him like a pennant. His coat tails stood out straight in the wind. He got up nerve enough to take one hand off the bar. He yanked his gun and unlocked the safety.

FLEET STREET was a wide thoroughfare, a main drag with street-car rails gleaming coldly in the winter night. The motorcycle's siren wailed. Brinky stuck his jaw out against the bitter wind. He did not take his eyes from the red tail-light ahead. He had a feeling that if he should turn his head to the side the motorcycle would trick him.

But he kept the siren going. Out of the tail of his eye he was sure he saw, now and then, a uniformed cop. His heart was up in his throat. The motorcycle was a demon beneath him and he marveled that he was still sitting on it. He gave it a little more gas. He found that the faster he drove it the smoother it rode.

The street-car rails ended. Brinky was glad of that. Smooth cement lay beyond—a road that went north and east, that would join the Post Road diagonally a few miles beyond. He wondered if other cops had taken up the chase but he was afraid to turn his head. His head seemed locked in one position—with eyes front.

They hit the Post Road. There was a police booth at the intersection and a cop was standing in the doorway. Brinky fired his gun in the air. The touring car pounded on the straightaway. Two miles beyond the intersection, where wide fields began, a spurt of red flame shot from the touring.

Brinky held his breath. Nothing happened. He turned out all the lights on the motorcycle. He took the hand that held his gun and one of the handle-bars and raised it. He fired. The red light went on, winking around a wide bend. Flame spurted ahead. There was a crash. Glass pelted Brinky's face. That was close. They'd smashed the headlight.

He forgot about riding the motorcycle and consequently began to handle it like an expert. He got more speed out of it. He rode one-handed and raised his gun again. It boomed. The red light went out.

He became aware of a pounding sound close behind him. He looked around and saw a big car. It crept up alongside him because he retarded the throttle. He saw Larsen's face.

"Brinky, you fool—stop!"

"Can't, boss!"

He spurted ahead again. Two jets of flame leaped from the car ahead. Metal rang on the motorcycle and Brinky felt a shock in his left leg. The machine wobbled. He straightened it and kept on. Back of him, and to one side, a machine gun stuttered. Pain suddenly knifed his leg, the reflex of the first shock.

"Um," he said.

A wide bend in the road, and then the lights of a filling station. The car ahead left the highway, skidded up to the pumps. Brinky began braking. Fifty yards from the filling station he stopped and saw the police phaeton pull up beside him.

He got off the machine and started up the side of the road. He could see four men crouched by the station pillars while gas was being run into the tank. Larsen came up beside him with a gun drawn.

Butchman came with a Tommy gun. Groves had a sub-machine gun and Little carried his revolver.

"What started it?" Larsen said.

"I was bringin' in the gal. She phoned Swan from the hotel. These mugs met us in front of headquarters and she lammed with 'em."

Little fired. A Tommy gun in the hands of one of the men by the touring car cut loose. Lead chipped cement and Groves, getting set, let fly with his Tommy gun. One of the four men wilted and sank to the ground. The filling-station man, in a white suit, ran for cover. Another ran around to the front of the car and started in to the wheel. Little had his gun raised. It belched and the man fell back out of the car and lay flat.

The other two deserted the car and ducked among the pillars of the filling station. Brinkhaus, limping ahead, fired past the red ethyl pump. The two men ran away from the station and made toward the woods on the other side of the crossroad. Brinkhaus fired again. One of the men fell down. The other turned and opened fire with the Tommy gun. Little stopped running and looked oddly at his left arm. He shook it and blood dripped to the road.

Groves started running fast, cursing. He stopped short, braced himself and started his sub-machine gun. The fourth man fell down in a ditch.

A muffled shot sounded in the car. Larsen walked past everybody, his gun leveled, and pulled open the car door. The woman fell out. She was dead—by her own hand.

Brinkhaus limped past the pumps. He stepped over Krieger and went on toward the crossroad. Butchman came running up beside him with the Tommy gun.

"Now you be careful, Brinky!"

They stopped.

A voice said from the ditch: "I'm done for," weakly.

Brinky sat down in the middle of the road—suddenly. He looked around dazedly. Butchman reached the ditch with his gun leveled. Then he lowered it. He went down and dragged out The Swan. The Swan couldn't walk. He was shot in half a dozen places.

Larsen's shoes rasped across the cinders of the station drive and he came rapidly to the center of the road.

"Brinky...."

"Huh."

"What's the matter?"

"I just figgered I'd kind of take a rest."

"You want to catch cold sitting on that cold road?"

"That's right." Brinky tried to get up. He sat down again. "Nope, boss, there ain't no use. This here leg o' mine is actin' up like hell."

THE BRIGHT white light on Larsen's desk shone mercilessly on the face of Jehle, The Professor. They had taken off Jehle's glasses. His hair was matted and sweat poured down his cheeks. Around him were men—many men. He was hemmed in. He tried to dodge the glare of the light. He couldn't because the men pressed so closely around him.

"She's dead," Larsen said. "She killed herself. When she saw there was no chance she killed herself. And she killed Big Joe, didn't she?"

Jehle gasped: "Water—water!" and clawed at his collar.

"She killed him, didn't she?"

Jehle's eyes rolled. "Yes—yes. She killed him."

"Get that, Williams," Larsen clipped to the stenographer. "Now, Jehle—go on."

"Water—water."

"Afterwards. Go on."

"The light—take away the light."

"Afterwards."

Jehle moaned. "She killed him. She had the gun in her pocket-book. Cable ran out with her. She told him she did it to save him. He took the gun—and the blame."

"Why did she kill him?"

"The Swan. He got her to do it. The Swan wanted Big Joe out of the way. Said Big Joe was getting soft. Krieger agreed with him. The Swan got on to our dope racket—mine and Lottie's. We had to come through—and he promised us twenty thousand on top of that.

"She met Cable at the cigar counter. He was to be the fall-guy. She made love to him and she knew he was the kind of guy would take the blame. I was to take care of the lights. When Cable and Lottie came in The Swan and Krieger were to dare Big Joe to go out and make a pass at the girl. They knew Big Joe would do it. It never failed. So he did. And Lottie let him have it and made Cable beat it with her.

"When Brinkhaus went for her tonight she must have sensed that the game was up. I was to drop by the hotel at eleven. I didn't because Brinkhaus had me. She must have thought that was wrong too. So she called The Swan. And The Swan and some boys came down, as you said, and sprung her from Brinkhaus.... Oh, give me a drink, give me a drink!"

Larsen said: "Somebody get him a drink."

"Well!" exclaimed Gatlin.

"I hope," Larsen said with mellow irony, "that some day you'll get to realize that Brinky is the best right-hand man a chief of detectives ever had."

Gatlin scowled, snorted, disappeared, the door banging shut after him.

A voice in the shadows said: "Who's all right, gang?"

"Gatlin's all right!" they chorused.

"Gatlin?"

"Yeah," they chorused. "In a horse's neck!"

THE DEVIL'S SLOUCH

THREE DISGUISED
FIGURES SLUNK OUT
OF THE HOSPITAL AND
A DYING COP GASPED
A MESSAGE THAT LED
SERGEANT BRINKHAUS
INTO A SHAMBLES OF GUN
SMOKE AND DEATH

CHAPTER ONE

THE AMBULANCE RUSE

AT HALF-PAST nine the red-tinted beams of the ambulance lights arced across Plummer Avenue. The Plummer Memorial Hospital rose six stories, boxlike, on green grounds a block square. There was an incomplete checkerboard of lighted windows in front. The marquee lights were dimmed. Visiting ended at nine sharp.

A pedestrian stopped to let the ambulance cross the sidewalk. Long, sleek, maroon, the machine purred up the slight incline toward the receiving entrance on the right side of the building, lights ahead showed a sort of porte-cochere.

The man at the wheel wore a blue uniform coat, a hard blue cap with a brief patent-leather visor. The man at his right wore a white uniform coat with a stand-up collar, open, and a white visored cap raked jauntily down over his eyes. In the rear, a man similarly garbed sat athwart the opening there, one arm hooked on the safety-strap.

Leeming, reading a newspaper in the little cubbyhole just inside the receiving entrance, heard the engine's purr in the lush fall night, saw the tinted glow moving beneath the porte-cochere. He yawned. He was drowsy, only half-awake. He got up and poked out and stood in the receiving entrance as the sleek maroon side of the ambulance slid by, stopped. He reflected that there had been an emergency call from the waterfront only a short time before; the ambulance had made good time.

He sloped down the single step to the cement drive, saw the white-garbed figure back out of the rear of the ambulance. He yawned, rubbed his weary eyes.

"How many—"

The man in the white suit turned. He turned swiftly, neatly, with the true precision of a machine. Leeming was sleepy and unprepared for the short, dark thing that chopped downward. His flight into darkness must have been as instantaneous as that of a snuffed candle. He showed no reflex. For a moment he stood rigid, trancelike, like a robot, then his knees gave way, his legs became soft like dough and he crumpled. His body made a muffled dull sound on the pavement.

The man who had struck him shoved the blackjack away inside his coat. He was short, broad, powerful; the length of his arms was apparent as he reached down, their strength was obvious as he lifted Leeming easily.

The chauffeur came around the back. Holding the body, the broad man said, "Quick... the others!" Then he bent his way through the receiving entrance, shoved into the little cubbyhole and laid Leeming on the floor. For his short, long-armed bulk he moved with surprising speed.

The chauffeur was taller. He appeared bearing a half-clad man who was bound, gagged, unconscious. The broad man threw him a blank, tense look, went out, passed the third man lugging another body and swung into the rear of the ambulance. The chauffeur had come back and was waiting for the third unconscious man. The broad man went with him and when the four unconscious men lay on the floor of the little cubbyhole the broad man jerked his jaw. His two companions moved out. The broad man turned out the lights, stepped out, closed

A quick, sullen look came
into the broad man's face.

and locked the cubbyhole door and turned on his companions. All wore gloves.

His voice was low, clipped: "Okey." He raised his arm, tossed the key far out into some dark shrubbery. He led the way down the passageway until they came to an open service elevator. The three crowded in. The man in the chauffeur's uniform closed the door, worked a handle and the elevator rose slowly, silently. The three men said nothing. Thus far they had worked with a precision that implied everything had been planned ahead.

At the fourth floor the elevator stopped, the door opened. Dim lights glowed over a desk beyond. A girl was writing there. She was dressed in white and had a tiny white cap perched atop a mass of auburn hair. She looked up, stared at the elevator, looked down again. The men did not get out. There were rapid footfalls. A nurse appeared from the front of the building, went on past the elevator bank to the rear. The girl at the desk laid down her pen, turned off the bright desk-light, yawned.

The broad man stepped out and his two companions followed. The three men turned left and entered a corridor that made a dim-lit, cool tunnel toward the front of the building. The men's shoes made little sound. They paused before a door marked 407. The broad man pushed in, ducking his head low.

The room was bathed in a low, soft glow. There was a narrow bed in the center footed with large rubber wheels. The broad man's face was an indistinct shadow between the white of cap and uniform. The man in the bed was sleeping.

SHUMACHER stirred in his armchair, rose, yawned and made a half stretch with his solid arms. He was an oldish man, his hair white and thick and his face kind in the half light.

"He's been sleeping," Shumacher said.

The broad man said, "So!" in a thick but quiet voice, and slouched apelike to the head of the bed. He motioned to the other two. The man in the chauffeur's uniform moved, gripped the footrail of the bed and between them they worked it on its wheels until it was headed for the door.

Shumacher said, "Hey, begging your pardon, but is this guy supposed to go somewhere?"

"Yes," said the broad man. "Downstairs for treatment."

Shumacher blinked and teetered back on his heels. The two men worked the bed toward the door while the third went out in the hall and looked up and down. Shumacher pulled at his lower lip, let it pop back, then ambled toward the door.

"I know," he said, "but I ain't heard anything about this. You better clear me, doc. I better get a slip or something signed by the head floor nurse."

The broad man laughed quietly.

"I'll send one up."

"I know, but gosh...." He shrugged, put an arm out and leaned against the wall. The heel of his hand clicked the pushbutton that flooded the room with white, brilliant light. He was quite as surprised as the others. He hadn't meant to put the lights on. But he saw, then, the quick, sullen look in the broad man's face. His oldish face got grim.

"Now listen! Now wait a minute!"

"I told you it's all right!" the broad man snapped.

"I don't give a damn! You wait here! You just wait here till I get the head floor nurse!"

He started to push past the bed that was partway through the doorway. The broad man stopped him with a long, hard arm. Shumacher swung away, his eyes popping.

He choked, "I—I've seen you somewhere—before—"

"Oh, yeah?"

The broad man shifted with amazing speed. In the fraction of a minute he had Shumacher's back against his chest, an iron arm around Shumacher's throat. Shumacher's mouth was open like a man screaming, but no sound came forth. The man in the chauffeur's uniform pulled the bed into the hall. The other man in white came into the room swiftly, closed the door.

"I've—seen—your—mug—"

The broad man said: "Okey, kid; let him have it."

Steel flashed. There was a short, quick, hard thrust. Shumacher said, "Oh-o-o," quietly, and the broad man bent with him to the floor as his companion withdrew the knife, stepped to the bathroom, wrapped the knife in a towel and thrust it into his pocket.

"That get him?" he said.

"Yeah," breathed the broad man. He gestured. "Scram now!"

They went out of the room, closed the door, walked swiftly toward the elevator. They saw the auburn-haired nurse halfway down the corridor beyond the elevator bank. She was talking rapidly to the head nurse. The bed with the sleeping man was in the elevator and the man in the chauffeur's uniform was standing at the controls.

"Jeeze!" he whispered.

"Let 'er go," the broad man said.

The elevator descended to the basement level. They did not bother to roll the bed out. The broad man went out ahead with his cagy, ape-like slouch, his hand in his pocket, on a gun there, his eyes white and cold and steady. The other two carried the man from the bed. He was awake, but he didn't say anything; he seemed in a stupor, his head lolling. They laid him in the ambulance.

The man in the chauffeur's uniform got behind the wheel. The other two piled in. The ambulance clicked into gear, followed the driveway to the street in the rear, turned left. At the first main artery a traffic light showed red.

The ambulance siren wailed. Traffic stopped. The ambulance shot by the main drag. Its siren picked up again. Cars slewed out of the way. Traffic cops whistled, stopped adverse traffic, waved the ambulance past. It went across town like a bat out of hell.

"This," said the broad man, "is the nuts."

CHAPTER TWO

A CORPSE IN BED

HERMAN BRINKHAUS, sergeant of detectives out of Police Headquarters, did not wear rubber heels. On the other hand, his shoes did not creak. Their broad, solid heels struck the tiled floor of the hospital corridor loudly, echoing. He could not afford many luxuries on his salary—and he had a wife and two kids—but he spent seventeen dollars for his shoes. His feet were too broad for stock sizes. The shoes were like the man: broad, thick-bodied, substantial, capable of taking a lot of punishment; plain, unostentatious.

The cop on the beat was then in 407.

"Shumacher got it, Brinky," the cop said.

"Yeah," said Brinkhaus. He blinked in the white glare of the bowl-light on the ceiling. He held his brown Homburg in his hand and his broad everyday face began to show signs of emotional congestion. Then he made a hardly perceptible movement of his broad, thick shoulders and sent a bleak stare around the room and saw nothing, asked nothing.

"Poor Henry," he muttered.

Dr. Linkholt had a reminiscent stare on the body.

"I came in at nine-fifty to look at the patient. I found—this. I could hardly believe my eyes."

Johnny Pell, Brinkhaus's aide, breezed in, dampered down his spirits and muttered, "Well, I'll be...."

Johnny Pell was young, lean, and a year in plainclothes; he was hard as nails. "What son of a so-and-so did this?" he demanded.

Brinkhaus said nothing. He got down to one knee. It was hard, looking at the dead face of old Henry Shumacher. Coat, vest, shirt, had been cut away. The room got very quiet and there was no sound but the muffled, stifled sobbing of the auburn-haired nurse. A couple of orderlies stood around like images. The night superintendent, a stout red-faced woman, kept fanning herself with a handkerchief. Brinkhaus touched Henry Shumacher's hand, almost shook it. He sighed wearily.

"Okey, Henry," he muttered.

Rising, he felt his hairbrush mustache that bunched squarely beneath his short, broad nose; touched a mutinous cowlick.

"So now what happened?" he said thickly.

The cop on the beat gestured with his memo book.

"I got it all here. At twelve past nine there was a call for an ambulance. A guy called and said there was an accident on Front Street in front of Martin's Dock. Out the ambulance goes. Down in front of Martin's Dock it's dark. There's a car parked. When the ambulance gets there the guys get off. Three guys get 'em in the dock—socko! So that's all they know. The ambulance arrives downstairs. A guy there named Leeming walks out, and what? Socko! And that's all he knows. This jane here, this nurse here, sees two guys in white uniform get out. There's another guy with him dressed like the ambulance chauffeur. She don't think anything of it. They walk down the hall. A little later she's up the other end of the hall talking with the head floor nurse. They see the bed being rolled down. Then the two guys in white uniforms come out of this room and they all go down in the elevator. They don't think anything's wrong, these women; only the head floor nurse says she ain't been told about a removal from 407, so she calls downstairs, on the phone. They say no. Just then Dr. Linkholt comes out of the passenger elevator. He goes down the hall with the head floor nurse after him. He walks in."

Brinkhaus stared at the floor. "Where's the hospital men that went with the ambulance?"

"Being looked after. Say, were they socked!"

"They get a look at the guys?"

"Nope. They were socked and their clothes swiped. These mugs sail in here like they own the place and there you are."

Brinky looked at the doctor. "Was—was Henry dead when you come in, doc?"

"He was dying. He managed to gasp something out. It was: 'I remember that devil's slouch.' That was all."

BRINKHAUS kept staring at the floor. "Then the only one who saw these here men was"—he raised his placid brown eyes to the crying nurse—"this young woman."

She raised a white, tear-splotched face. "Yes. But I—I was busy. I saw the white uniforms—I didn't give them a moment's attention. It seemed so natural—after all, we see so many white uniforms...." She made a hopeless gesture.

Brinkhaus nodded, considered this placidly. The only indication now of inner torment was made apparent, if you looked sharply enough, by the tiny blister-like beads of sweat on his leather-brown forehead. His voice was slow, thick, almost guttural, methodical in its careful choice of simple questions.

"If you seen these men, miss, would you recognize them?"

"I—I don't think so. It was dim in the corridor. I'd been writing, you see, under a bright light, on white paper, and looking up as I did, kind of quick, you understand, things seemed blurred. I saw only the white suits. And then I went off to find Miss Corliss to consult her about the diet for 415. She was in the back of the building—"

"I met Miss Tenant in the rear corridor," said a small, spare, bony woman. "It was about 415's diet, the woman wouldn't eat and she abused Miss Tenant. We talked about conferring with the doctor. When I saw the bed coming down the hall I said to her, 'Who is that?' She said, 'There was some talk about Dr. Fougard making an examination of 407. Fougard was to come earlier, but he's been busy.' I wasn't alarmed, but I was curious. It's frightful!"

The night superintendent was caustic. She said: "Rank carelessness on this floor!"

"I never heard of anything like it!" declared Dr. Linkholt.

Brinkhaus said a thought aloud: "Poor Henry knew them mugs, poor Henry...."

Nurse Tenant was standing, her handkerchief a crumpled damp ball in her hand.

"It—it was my fault!" she cried softly.

Brinkhaus was gentle, even though his voice was thick.

"There, there, miss; these things happen, kind of. I can see how you stand. Don't you worry now."

The night superintendent was harsher.

"I dare say it will cost Miss Tenant her position!"

Brinkhaus shook his head.

"Madame, was I you, I'd learn to act as horsepittles are supposed to: kind, sort of. You just try to go easy on the girl. How long's she been a nurse?"

"Eight years with us."

"Been a good one?"

"I must say she has been. We've never been afraid to put her on the most unpleasant cases. She—well, she has stamina, but all that should not condone this awful negligence! And after all, sir, I am to be the judge of that."

Brinkhaus was placid.

"Henry was my friend. It's my friend that's dead. Firing the young lady won't help that. You think it over. Mind I kind of ask you to give her a break."

Johnny Pell, standing in one corner, bent a narrowed-down, curious eye on Brinkhaus. He could never figure the sergeant out. What the devil was behind all this sob stuff in reference to the nurse? It was goofy, Johnny Pell thought; and yet, he found himself thinking, there seemed to be a purpose behind it.

Brinkhaus was saying: "Well, Johnny, I guess we're done here. 'S matter of routine, we'll get a fingerprint man over." He addressed the gathering at large: "Whoever's boss around here, you keep this room shut off and don't let anybody monkey around that bed downstairs. The district attorney's man 'll be over any minute, and I figure you'll see a man from the medical examiner's turning up. He'll decide about the disposition of the body. Well," he sighed, "I'm sure glad Henry's wife died last year." He looked sorrowfully at his dead friend, said, "I'd sure hate to have to break it to Henry's wife." He looked up, spoke to the cop: "You park here, Loftus, till it's all washed up."

The night superintendent sniffed. "H'm," she said, "this seems, if you'll allow me, like a very sketchy police investigation."

Brinkhaus beckoned to Johnny Pell, ignored the rasp-voiced woman. The two detectives left the room, pushed through a hushed group of nurses and orderlies in the hall and went toward the elevator. Brinkhaus jerked a thumb over his shoulder.

"I wonder if that super there is married."

"Why?"

"Was I her husband, I'd jump in the river."

CHAPTER THREE

A FEMININE SUSPECT

THE NEWS of Henry Shumacher's death snaked throughout the police precincts of Portsend like chain lightning. It crackled in the marble corridors of the new eleventh in the swank West End, and it hit with no less force the ramshackle station house of the ninth which hunches in miserable Fruit Street on the tattered hem of Little Italy. It broke up penny ante games in station-house back rooms; it droned over the radio receiving sets of roving cars. Like lightning, it set fire where it struck.

Detective Henry Shumacher had been killed. A cop had been killed. Pedestrians may be beaten and robbed, citizens may run into scattered gangster bullets, banks may be robbed, even a mayor might take a dive because of a hoodlum bullet. But kill a cop—and that is another matter. It is the most heinous offense an erstwhile gunman could think of. Somewhere in the background of the sputtering knowledge of Shumacher's death there was also the report that one John Doe had been carried bodily from the Plummer Memorial Hospital. But this little morsel was as inconsequential as the chance obituary of a Balkan pretender to a vest-pocket monarchy.

Within an hour after the fateful news the entire police force of Portsend was, literally, up in arms. Plainclothes men in pairs sacked the lower levels of the city. Bums were picked up. There was the scuffle of feet in dark alleys, the thud of fists for those who acted recalcitrant. In pairs, grim-lipped men with shields beneath their lapels slapped their way into speakeasies, rounded up suspicious characters or characters they thought were suspicious. A cop had been killed. This fact created a police state of mind. Every policeman was outraged, as wrought up as though one of his own family had been murdered. They were loud in their grim threats of vengeance. The grand old man of the Department had been knifed to death. They would comb the city, haul in the culprits and see them in the chair.

Not so Herman Brinkhaus. He was neither loud nor dramatic. He was not that kind of man. To him Henry Shumacher was not the grand old man of the Department, but one who had been a simple and close friend; a crony who had played pinochle and poker with him, a man from whom he had borrowed money when Mom had had their first kid. Brinky did not climb upon the bandwagon.

He was alone when he plowed his placid way into the central room at police headquarters. He walked with the slight side to side motion of a stocky, heavy man. His Homburg sat uncompromisingly on his box-like head; tilted neither to right nor left nor slouched down over his eyes in the approved manner of those who hunt. In his square-cut suit of hard woolen material he looked as much as anything like a neighborhood butcher or grocer.

The room was alive with voices, with pressmen and detectives and reserves. Questions struck Brinky with the rapidity of slugs from a sub-machine gun.

"Hello, boys," he said, and barged on through, his side to side motion more apparent from the rear and quaintly comical, too. While everyone talked of Henry Shumacher, his fine record, his tragic death, Brinkhaus talked not at all and thought mainly of the missing John Doe. There was something fatalistic, and at the same time tender in his attitude toward his dead friend. Henry had lived a life of duty, had died on duty, like a true cop. That made a fine epitaph. There was one way to go about getting his killers, and it had nothing to do with postmortems, flag-waving, tall language. And there was another life in danger: the lost John Doe's.

"Well, Brinky," said Inspector Peter Larsen.

Entering the office, closing the door, Brinkhaus moved his palms out side-wise, let them fall back to his sides and sat down. He sighed once and then fixed his honest brown eyes on Larsen's shiny flat-topped desk.

Larsen said, "I picked it up at home over the short wave and came right down." He still had his hat on. He was a tall greyhoundish man with a fine, upright face and a mane of yellow hair, eyes as blue and clear as a glacial lake. "I know," he said, "what Henry meant to you, Brinky."

"Uh—thanks, Peter."

These two men understood each other thoroughly, which was why the long moment that followed was a strictly silent one.

Larsen looked at his pipe-bowl.

"What do you think?"

"A job pulled by brains and nerve, boss. A sweet job. I don't figure they meant to let Henry have it. But he must ha' recognized somebody.

He tried to crowd 'em. What could they do? It was they let him have it. Folks at the horsepittle say there was no row, no noise. That means it took two guys. One held Henry choked off, the other let him have it."

Larsen leaned back, made a pyramidal framework of his hands. "They'd read the papers. They knew that when this unidentified man regained his memory he would talk."

BRINKHAUS nodded. "Yeah. But it wasn't they did all that just to keep him from telling who took that shot at him. Would ha' been easier just to let him have it there in the horsepittle. Them mugs were after something else, something this feller knows. Now when Henry died he said something. He said, 'I remember that devil's slouch.' Now that 'd mean, did you ask me, Peter, that it wasn't just no ordinary slouch. It was a kinda slouch that was big enough to make Henry remember without maybe even remembering the guy's face or his name." He sighed. "It's too bad them gallery pictures we have can't move."

There were sounds in the hall, and a moment later the door opened and Lieutenant Stickney, plainclothes, shoved Nurse Tenant into the room. She was white-faced except for red splotches on her cheeks, and a red splotch on the side of her jaw. Propelled by an ungentle shove, she sank into a chair, breathless, her head drooping.

Stickney was a tall, burly man with a nose like a parrot's beak, and white jowls, small red lips that could snarl over tiny white teeth that seemed out of place in that large, fleshy face.

"I snagged this jane over, Inspector." He dropped a warm, blue look on Brinkhaus. "Brinky was there, but apparently he went just to see what the inside of a hospital looked like."

Larsen was quiet-voiced.

"Who's the woman?"

"Irene Tenant's her name. The night super had a peeve on about her and she looks wrong to me. So I snagged her over."

Brinkhaus, his eyes lowered, twiddled his thumbs.

"Why, Stickney?" Larsen said, offhand.

"Well, she was sitting about fifteen feet from the elevator these three mugs came out of. Yet she says she didn't notice what they looked like. It's screwy, too, that when they were wheeling the lost memory

case out she was up the hall talking the ears off the head floor nurse."
He chuckled. "Or keeping the head floor nurse out of the way!"

"How did you get on this case?"

"I was in the neighborhood. I just ran over. I ask if any detectives
have been around and the super said, 'Well, there were two men here
who I suppose were detectives, but they acted like children.'"

Brinkhaus slapped his knees.

"Well, I guess I'll go around the block and get me a hamburger
and java."

"Wait," Larsen said; then to Stickney: "What grounds have you
got for bringing this woman up here? I'm eager to know, because of
course this case is blind as a bat so far, and I'd like to tell the press we
have a suspect."

Stickney blinked.

"Ain't I told you?"

"Not quite. What you've told me seems to indicate that you were
influenced by the opinions of the superintendent. I want to be fair,
Stickney, but I want all tangible reasons."

"That's all I got," Stickney said. He blustered on: "Ain't it enough?
There she was only fifteen feet from the elevator, and, my Gawd, she
doesn't remember what they look like!"

She cried out: "I told you that I'd been writing on white paper
under a very brilliant light. When I looked up I was blinded for a
minute. I saw white suits and I thought naturally they were house
men."

Larsen looked at Brinkhaus.

"Sergeant, you were the first detective on this case. You investi-
gated to your satisfaction?"

"Yes, sir."

"You thought at the time, and you think now, that we have no right
to hold this woman for questioning?"

"Yes, Inspector."

"Do you want to change your mind?"

"No. I think I'm setting where I want to."

Larsen stood up, went to the door.

"Lieutenant, I want to speak to you alone. Outside."

Stickney grinned, flung a contemptuous look at Brinkhaus as he
went out behind Larsen.

He said, "Now listen, Inspector. We can hold this dame over night, just long enough to give the press something to write about. I'll land on this case like a ton of brick and—"

"**JUST** a minute, Stickney," Larsen said. "I brought you out here for another reason. When a man lands first on a case, it's the custom of this department to let him handle it. It's the sporting thing for others in the department to throw all information his way. By acting under the influence of this hospital super you showed plainer than words that you agreed with her that a couple of boobs hit the case first. I don't like that, Lieutenant. It's bad police manners. You bring a nurse here on a flimsy bit of gossip and expect me to overrule a department custom. I can't do it. I disapprove of your grandstand play, and in conclusion I must remind you that my duty prevails upon me to let Brinkhaus remain in charge of this investigation. I'll call you if I want you."

He turned, opened the door and reentered the office. He motioned Brinkhaus into an adjoining office separated by a glass-panel door.

"Brinky," he said, "you are at liberty to change your mind about holding this woman."

"Peter, am I still in charge?"

"Yes."

"Then suppose I see her home. I'll get that hamburger and java on the way back."

Larsen gripped him.

"You're sure you don't think this woman is any way guilty?"

"Boss," said Brinky, "I figure the dumbest thing we could do would be hold this little woman. I ain't saying exactly it's Stickney's fault, because he was dropped on his head when he was very young. So"— he nodded toward the connecting door—"I'll be taking the little woman back."

Larsen nodded. Brinkhaus entered the larger office and looked at the bowed head.

He said, "It was a mistake, Miss Tenant. I'll be seeing you back, if that is you don't mind."

On the way down the corridor with the nurse he ran into Stickney. Stickney was a younger man, a self-styled high-pressure dick, son-in-law of the president of the board of aldermen and therefore—politics having a finger in the police pie—a lieutenant not by the grace of God or merit but by the turning of the political screw. Brinky told the girl to go and wait before the elevator. He stopped and regarded placidly the uppermost button of Stickney's vest.

"Was I you, Lieutenant, I'd think maybe once or twice before trying to show me up before the boss. And going on, mister, being as you're new on the boss's staff, I'd think a lot of times before using your mitt on a woman's jaw."

"You're sore, Sarge! You can't take it any more!" Stickney cackled. "I'd like to know, I would, why you ain't in harness instead of plain-clothes!"

Brinky was placid. "Well, you see, when they changed over into the new uniforms I didn't have the dough to buy one, so they let me wear my everyday clothes. I hope I won't be seeing you."

He left Stickney and made his methodical, heavy-heeled way down the corridor. He went down in the elevator with the nurse. Johnny Pell was looking fretful in the central room. Brinky told the girl to wait a minute and went over to Johnny.

Johnny Pell said, "What's screwy going on? Is that mug Stickney trying to do some claim-jumping?"

"He fell on his head once. So what, Johnny?"

"Well—62 Andover Street. A small apartment house, walk-up. A one-room apartment, number 22."

"And then what?"

"No pictures. In the bottom bureau drawer—sh!"

They waited until two patrolmen had passed by. Then Johnny Pell drew out a notebook.

He said in a low excited voice: "In the bottom bureau drawer I found a hundred dollar bill. It was crisp, Brinky, and folded four times. The number seemed familiar, so I wrote it down. Here it is. So when I come back here I looked up the records. It's one of the numbers we got three months ago after that textile factory bankroll grab!"

Brinky dropped his eyes, his voice.

"Swell work, Johnny. You just keep that under your hat. It's only an opener. You say the address is 62 Andover Street?"

"Yeah."

"Plank your pants here till I ring you."

Brinkhaus turned, rejoined the nurse and they went out to the sidewalk. At City Hall Square they found an idle taxi.

Brinky was saying. "You got to excuse the lieutenant, miss, for dragging you up here. He's young and kind of ambitious. It ain't his fault."

She laid a hand on his arm. "You're so good—so good. Please don't bother seeing me home. I'll take this taxi. I'll be all right."

"Sure. I know this driver. Hey, Benny, take this young lady to—" He turned to her.

She said, "Number 62 Andover Street."

CHAPTER FOUR

THE FOURTH CARD OF A FLUSH

THE MONO TEXTILE MILL lies in the southwestern part of the city, flush with the upper river. South Broad Street is its address, though Front Street, leaving the river and making a loop behind the buildings, borders most of the property. At nine next morning Brinkhaus got out of a rickety police flivver and thumped his substantial heels up the main entrance. It took him a few minutes to get to a man named Jonas Burnham.

"My name's Brinkhaus," he said. "I'm from the cops. Is it right I'm thinking you were the man carried that payroll three months ago?"

"Will I ever forget it!"

"H'm," agreed Brinkhaus. "Was kind of an experience a man don't forget. Well, Mr. Burnham, if I remember it right, there was four guys."

"Yes. Four masked men."

"So wearing masks, you couldn't ever identify 'em."

Burnham wagged his head grimly.

"No. That was the trouble. There was no way I could tell. I looked over all the pictures in headquarters."

Brinky inched forward on his chair, laid a broad forefinger on Jonas Burnham's knee.

"Think back now, Mr. Burnham. Close your eyes and try to kinda like see the whole thing again—the street, the car up the street, and the masked guys. Don't try to go and picture them without the masks. Just kinda like try to work up a picture of them with the masks on."

After a moment Burnham, his eyes closed, said, "It's all plain. I can see the street, the kind of day it was. I can see how the men acted, the way they blocked me, and I can see how they went away, fast, how they moved—when the guard dropped—"

"Now! Now, Mr. Burnham! Was there anything about the way any o' them moved that you remember?"

There was a moment of silence. Then Burnham cried out:

"Yes! Yes! Only now—not until now—" He opened his eyes. "Yes, sir," he said. "I would remember one's walk. It was a kind of fast monkeylike slouch."

Brinkhaus stood up. "Thanks, Mr. Burnham."

Outside, Brinky made squeaks in the flivver as he climbed in.

"Johnny," he said, "it's a known fact, did you ask it of me, that where there's one bad apple you'll find others."

Johnny warped a hard grin off his lips.

"So now I suppose I'm supposed to break down and ask something."

"Meaning nine times out o' ten where you find one crime you'll find others back of it kinda.... Git this buggy started. I aim to mope around that horsepittle."

Johnny slammed into gear.

"Why the hell don't you lay your cards on the table and grab the pot?"

"I got to fill a suit, Johnny. I got only openers yet."

"Nuts! Bluff it!"

"Once I played poker with Henry and I tried to bluff. It cost me just four dollars and seventy-five cents. I'm an old hand, Johnny. You got to have the cards— Oops! Say, would you mind going around them corners instead of cutting across the curbs?" He relapsed into thought.

"The guard that was with that payroll man was buried just three months ago today."

"What's that got to do with it?"

"Just when you hit that bump, Johnny, I got an idea. No—don't stop. Git to that horsepittle and do you know you're heading the wrong way on a one-way street?"

Brinkhaus entered the hospital meekly, his hat in his hand and a respectful bow for the girl at the information desk.

"Miss, I'm Brinkhaus from the cops. I'd like to see the person that's head of the office force, could I?"

"Yes, indeed, Sergeant Brinkhaus!"

"Thank you, miss."

HE WANTED, he explained to an austere woman, to look over the files of persons who had been patients in the hospital during the past three months. The austere woman obliged with a card-index. Brinkhaus took out an old-fashioned pair of steel-rimmed spectacles, hooked them on his ears and looked more the neighborhood store-keeper than ever. He spent fully ten minutes with the card-index, considering finally a solitary card relative to a patient named James Johnstown, aged thirty-seven.

"Can you figure this out for me?" he asked the austere woman.

"Yes. James Johnstown, as you see, entered the hospital on August 12 and occupied Room 402. His occupation—none. His address, 1245 Inland Avenue. An emergency operation for appendicitis. No living relatives or dependents."

"Thank you. Now can you find out who the nurses were on that floor while he was here?"

She said she could and returned in a short time with a list of names. He pocketed the names, bowed, knocked a book off the desk, replaced it and made his solid-heeled way out of the office.

"Look," he said to Johnny, pointing, "you are parked smack up against a fire-hydrant."

"If you ask me, it's a hell of a place to put a fire-hydrant."

"Okey, okey," Brinky said. "Let's mooch along."

Johnny swung the flivver into traffic, cutting off two cars and making the brakes of a third squeal. Brinkhaus gripped the side of the car, gritted his teeth, subsided then and sighed and looked paternally at Johnny.

"What you find out?" Johnny asked, going through a red light.

"Maybe the third card to a straight flush. When I git five and fill it maybe I'll call. Look now—buzz this buggy over to Inland Avenue and see can you stop at 1245 without tearing them brakebands off. And for crying out loud, Johnny, we ain't in England; git over on the right-hand side o' the street!"

Johnny whanged the flivver to Union Circle, took Wellsworth northwest to Laurel Drive, cut due north a block and then swung west on Inland Avenue past fine apartment houses.

Number 1245 was a tan brick apartment house of nine stories. The facade was severely modernistic. The lounge was dim, cool, large, with a small desk at one end. A man sat beside the desk absently regarding his hands.

"Begging your pardon, I'm Brinkhaus from the cops." Brinky dropped his shield on the desk. "You got a tenant here named James Johnstown?"

"Yes, sir, we have."

"What apartment?"

"Number 515. Shall I ring?"

"No; no, don't ring. And kind of forget a cop was here."

"I see." The man nodded. "Of course."

Brinkhaus took the elevator up. When he alighted at the fifth floor, he paused to fish into an inner pocket. He put on his ancient spectacles, propping them far down on his nose. This made him look very innocent and he heightened the effect by assuming a bland expression. Hand thrust in his coat pocket, he went down the hall to 515, knocked.

A tall young man in a dressing gown opened the door. He was smoking a cigarette through a long black holder. His face was thin, wedge-jawed, and black hair shone like lacquer. His eyes were quite as black, keen, narrowed down.

"Yes?"

Brinkhaus cleared his throat.

"Well—huh—well, sir, I come in answer to an ad I seen in the paper—"

"To a what?"

Brinky nodded.

"Yes, sir. Begging your pardon"— he withdrew his hand from his pocket—"did you lose this and advertise for it?" He thrust a plain gun-metal cigarette case into the man's hand.

The man's face showed hard amusement. He chuckled.

"No. No, I didn't lose this."

"Gosh," Brinky said. "It said apartment 515 at 1285 Inland Avenue."

"Yeh? Well, this is 515 all right, but you got the wrong address. This is 1245. Here." He passed the case back, took a drag at his cigarette, stepped back and toed the door shut.

When Brinky climbed into the flivver and planked himself down in the creaky seat, he said, "Okey, Johnny. Make it headquarters now."

"So what you been doing?"

"Well, I think I got me the fourth card in that suit I'm drawing to."

Johnny cut in ahead of a speeding roadster. The roadster's brakes complained. "What's the fifth, Brinky?"

"The fifth," said Brinky, "would be this John Doe feller. That red light you see ahead, Johnny, ain't an ornament."

CHAPTER FIVE

THE GIRL IS GRILLED

THE PORTSEND *Daily Progress*, a wisecracking sheet that reaped boundless joy in taking cracks at the bureau, found plenty of subject matter in the case of the man stolen from under a cop's nose at the Plummer Memorial Hospital.

On the third day following the crime Cullen sailed into Peter Larsen's office with a chip on his shoulder. Cullen was the city editor, one hundred and twenty pounds of dynamite, bad manners and conceit.

"Now!" he yelped, hit the desk so hard that a glass fell over and Cullen himself skinned his knuckles. "Now, my dear, dear Inspector Larsen, one John Doe on the night of October 11, this year of grace, was found unconscious in an alley off Commercial Street by one Patrolman Nicodemus O'Reilly. Hearing screams, Patrolman O'Reilly, who was quenching his thirst at the rear door of a nearby speakeasy, wiped the beer suds from his mustache and hastened in the direction of the screams, beating his nightstick on the pavement. Rounding a corner, he saw a machine get furiously under way. He yelled. The machine did not stop. It got away, and Patrolman N. O'Reilly found this man on the sidewalk. The man had not been robbed. Thirty-eight dollars and forty cents were found in his pockets. But no identification—none whatever. He became automatically a police charge. Little attention was given the case. A cop was detailed to stay with him in the hospital until he should recover consciousness. Then—*then*, my dear Inspector Larsen, a case of little importance becomes the talk of the town. The unknown is taken right from under a cop's nose. The hospital night super indicates, in an interview, that the detectives who arrived on the scene acted like a couple of morons. She also indicates that one Nurse Tenant might be implicated, yet I find out that you yourself refused to question this woman. I also gather that your right-hand man, Sergeant Brinkhaus, spends his time getting lots of fresh air in a police flivver and doing not much of anything else. My paper demands apprehension of this nurse and proper questioning! Bums, small fry, have been hauled into precinct houses for questioning; there has been a lot of police ballyhoo about our late and lamented Detective Shumacher; but there has not, Inspector, been any questioning of Nurse Tenant! This I, my paper, demand!"

Larsen was cool, stiff.

"Cullen, I have an able man in charge of the investigation. I refuse to be bullied or intimidated by you or any threats you see fit to make. I refuse to give, at this time, any news of the progress of the investigation because it may retard that progress. I promise definite intelligence within the next twenty-four hours."

Cullen snarled, "I didn't come here for promises. I came here for—"

Larsen stood up, cut in: "You came here to hang a threat over my head. I don't like that. You will please get out."

"Out, eh? Why, by God—"

Larsen had pressed a button. A uniformed man came in.

"Show Mr. Cullen out, Combs."

At exactly this time, at 10 a.m. of the morning of the third day following the murder of Henry Shumacher, Brinky stood in a darkened theater in the West End. With him stood Jonas Burnham, the man who had carried the payroll on August 12. The picture was a newsreel showing the funeral procession of the guard who had died in his attempt to save the payroll. It pictured curbs lined with people, cops urging the people back.

"Watch close," muttered Brinky.

"Yes," breathed Jonas Burnham.

And at length he gripped the sergeant's arm.

"There—there! Oh—he's gone now!"

Brinkhaus yelled up to the motion picture operator, "Show that over again!" He reset his spectacles on his nose. He urged Burnham closer to the screen. In a minute the newsreel was reshowing.

"There—there—you see!" cried Jonas Burnham.

"I got it," Brinkhaus muttered. "Thanks for coming, Mr. Burnham."

WHEN he returned to headquarters he walked with the same solid tread, unhurried but steady, and his boxlike brown face was placid as it always was. He found Larsen pacing the office floor.

Larsen said, "Brinky, I'm afraid we've got to have action in this case. I've played along with you, I've backed you up against departmental gossip and against the advances of the press. There's a whispering campaign going on against us. The killing of a cop means something!"

Brinkhaus smiled sadly.

"Yes, boss, I'm only beginning to kinda realize that Henry's dead."

"Very well, then." Larsen raised his chin. He was one of the few who realized Brinky's worth and the quiet houndlike way this plain man followed a case. But he was being pushed. "Suppose," he said, "we grab that nurse."

"I'd kinda hate to do that, boss. I'm mooching along pretty good. Suppose you walk downstairs with me."

In the bureau of criminal identification Brinkhaus went to work. Larsen stood behind and watched the stocky detective go through file after file of pictures. Brinky was unperturbed. Rocklike, neither adverse criticism nor threats could move him. He cared not a hoot for the press. Larsen, a younger man, had come up swiftly in the way of career men. Brinkhaus had seen him rise, seen Larsen pass himself, but there was no envy in the old sergeant's heart. Twice he had saved Larsen's life at the risk of his own; but it was in the nature of the man that he should have forgotten this. But not so with Larsen.

"I want to stand back of you, Brinky. I believe in you. But the press, our own men, the D.A.'s office, are yelling for blood. I merely want to clear you—get you in the clear."

"Now this here nice-looking gentleman," said Brinkhaus, indicating front and profile of a man, "is one of the birds that stuck up the Mono Mill payroll three months or so ago. His name, I see, is Mr. Jacob Kruse, alias 'Slugger,' alias 'Jake the Punch.' Not a nice-looking guy to have in the family, huh?"

Larsen stood back on his heels.

"What the devil are you knocking around that Mono Mill case for? It's a dead issue. Lieutenant Stickney was on that and—"

"Maybe these here high-pressure ideas lose a lot, boss. According to record here, Jake the Punch was picked up a year and a half ago for breaking a guy's jaw in a labor riot. I see he was borned in Johnstown, Pa. That helps."

"Brinky, what the devil are you driving at? This man was no suspect in the Mono Mill job."

"I know. Yup, I know. Which is why it's a dead case."

Larsen, despite himself, got angry.

"Now look here, Brinky. Cullen of the *Progress* was in this morning and he gave me hell! I'm not going to have you going haywire on some half-baked idea. Cullen was here and—"

"I figured he'd come," Brinkhaus said, making notes. He never got angry with Peter. "Fact, I knew he'd come."

"How did you know?"

Brinky shrugged, said nothing. And then Larsen knew. Cullen was hand in glove with the president of the board of aldermen. Lieutenant Stickney was the president's son-in-law. Stickney had eyes on Larsen's job. Larsen's hands clenched. If Stickney, despite orders, should turn up this case it would mean a blackball for Brinky, for Larsen himself. An agitation would be started. The *Progress* would print a glowing tribute to Stickney. The board of police commissioners, prompted by the tribute and by the president of the board of aldermen...

"Brinky," Larsen said, "has Stickney been bothering you?"

"Me? Nope."

Larsen gripped him.

"I want the truth! It means a lot to me! I've got to know—for my own sake! You won't be doing yourself a favor. You'll be doing me one."

Brinky blinked.

"Well, boss, all I know is there's been a guy sort of tailing me around. I ain't looked close enough so I can't swear it was Stickney."

Larsen's jaw tightened. When Brinky did not want to say anything, you could not yank it out of him. In a department rife with jealousy and forever alive with envy, Brinky remained close-mouthed. Larsen got in front of him.

He ground out resentfully, in a low, passionate voice, "I don't know what Stickney will do. You and I have been close together, Brinky. He may go over my head. He has the politicians behind him. Adam Ghorman is his father-in-law and president of the board of aldermen, and Ghorman pulls the strings that move the mayor, too. I am asking you pointblank, Brinky: do you think if we put this Nurse Tenant through a sweat that we'd get something out of her?"

Brinky considered this, bending over and regarding the polished toes of his seventeen-dollar shoes.

"Peter," he said, "being you asked me, I will say that did we git her over here we'd git nothing out of her. I been thinking things over. I been mooching along, smelling here and smelling there. I been asking a few questions. Once I git my suit filled, boss, I'll land on this case like a ton o' brick. But it ain't ripe yet, it ain't ripe."

"Then you don't think this nurse is guilty?"

"No, Peter."

They heard heavy footsteps. A cop appeared.

"Inspector, the commissioner's looking for you."

COMMISSIONER PENTCOST was a spare man who wore rimless noseglasses. He had a high, brittle voice—

"Inspector Larsen, the progress of this—er—case doesn't suit me. You seem to have made an issue of one Nurse Tenant."

"I did not make the issue," Larsen said.

"Very well, we will lay it to circumstances."

Larsen shook his head. His eyes were level, hard blue.

"We may as well lay it to Lieutenant Stickney." Before Pentcost could interrupt, Larsen whipped out hotly, "Am I in charge of the homicide division or is Lieutenant Stickney?"

"Inspector," Pentcost said coldly, "I have weighed matters. There is the pressure of the press. There are opinions gathered within the bureau— Inspector, it is my opinion that this woman should be detained at headquarters for thorough questioning—"

Larsen towered.

"I am in charge of the homicide bureau. When I took charge it was at a time when the press was flouting the practice of third degree methods on women as well as on men. I cleaned that up. Getting this woman over will mean hours of sweating and coercion. I'll not be a party to it!"

"Why?"

Larsen thought of Brinkhaus.

"Because I don't believe she is guilty."

Pentcost said, "It is my duty then to assert my position. Lieutenant Stickney will go for the woman."

Larsen's "Thank you" was taut, bitter. He turned on his heel and strode out. He could not let Brinky down. He believed in the sergeant, and he could not let him down.

The evening edition of the *Progress* had news to print! It carried a grinning picture of Lieutenant Stickney. The lieutenant had gone over Larsen's head in a wild stab toward sudden success. He had the powers-that-be at his back. He made a grandstand play. Police head-quarters throbbed and bustled with the news, and newsmen swarmed like flies through its echoing corridors.

The placid equanimity of Herman Brinkhaus remained unruffled. While telegraph wires buzzed and the shouts of "Extra! Extra!" rang in the streets he watched the twilight hour from a window; smoked a two-cent stogie and waited. Larsen had gone off duty, white-faced, grim, realizing what a wall of politics he had run into. Rumors crackled.

"If Stickney busts this case he'll get Larsen's job. Yeah, and Brinkhaus'll go pounding pavements in the sticks. Why didn't he grab the jane when he had the chance? He's a sap—a sap where a jane's concerned!"

In a bare room bright with light, Stickney and two men worked on Nurse Tenant. Questions shot at her—barked and snarled about her ears. She tried to get up. They shoved her down. For a while she was cool, composed. Then she became defiant. But the questions assailed her, and in a red haze she saw Stickney's little teeth flashing between his thin snarling lips. Then a man held her. He stood behind her and held her arms and two fierce white beams of light blazed against her face. Perspiration soaked her body, made her hair cling to her forehead. She fainted. They brought her to, and then she fainted again, and again they brought her to—but it was only to snarl and hurl more questions and fresh accusations into her face. Then she fought. They held her down and Stickney roared:

"You helped kill Shumacher! You helped kill Shumacher!"

The lights blazed. Eyes came and went, glaring. Harsh voices demanded her to admit she killed a man named Shumacher. "Or we'll lay hands on you if you don't! You'll never get out of this room alive!" She jumped up and tussled, but again that was futile. Their fingers dug into her arms. She laughed wildly, hysterically.

"Yes! Yes! Anything," she screamed.

And then she fainted.

Stickney ran out of the room for more water. In the hall he ran into Brinkhaus. The sergeant was making his way placidly along, holding a sheaf of papers before his bespectacled eyes.

"Well!" snarled Stickney. "She's gonna come clean! She's gonna confess! How do you like that?"

Brinkhaus said nothing. He simply walked around Stickney, pursued his placid way down the hall and entered an empty office. Sitting down, he resumed reading. A letter had just arrived from the Johnstown, Pa., authorities; it had come via air mail and special delivery. He finished reading it, tucked it away in an inside pocket and grabbed a phone.

"Hey, Adolph, is Johnny there?… Good. Tell him he should get the flivver out."

CHAPTER SIX

BRINKHAUS CHECKS A CLUE

GOING AROUND City Hall Square, Johnny said, "Do you smoke them lousy cheroots because you like 'em or to save money?"

"First off," said Brinky, "I smoked them to save dough—it was when Mom was having her youngest—and then I got to like 'em. The address, being you didn't ask, is 1245 Inland." He pointed. "That cop ahead there ain't waving at anybody, Johnny. It means you should stop."

The ride to 1245 Inland was another horrible experience for the peace-loving sergeant. It included three skids, the breaking of seven traffic rules, and it concluded with a four-foot slide pungent with hot rubber. For a moment Brinkhaus remained sitting, to get his breath.

Then he said, "Thanks, Johnny. It was a swell ride. No you don't," he cut in, when Johnny hopped out after him. "You stay right here. And that," he added, pointing, "that thing your right mudguard is parked against is a fire-hydrant!"

He turned and made his way up to the entrance of the apartment house. The lounge was sprinkled with shaded lights, and here thick carpets muffled the fall of his substantial heels. He entered the elevator and got off at the fifth floor. Stopping before apartment 515, he listened for a long moment. Then he knocked.

When the tall lean man with the lacquer-black hair opened the door he saw a medium-sized, stocky man holding a Homburg under his left arm. He noticed the coarse brush of hair with the mutinous cowlick on the right side, and he also noticed the inoffensive but direct look of a pair of large brown eyes. Then he recognized the man who had made a call once before about a cigarette case.

He chuckled nasally, gestured.

"Where's your glasses? And don't tell me I advertised again!"

"Begging your pardon, Mr. Johnstown, I'd like to kind of mooch in and have a talk with you."

Mr. Johnstown seemed not averse to a little joke, but the limit after all was the limit. He tilted his chin.

"Run along, my man. I didn't lose anything."

He stepped back and gave the bottom of the door an idle kick. The door surprised him by hitting Brinkhaus's foot and whipping open again.

Mr. Johnstown's eyes snapped.

"Damn it, I told you—" He stopped. Brinky had raised his right arm from the elbow only. In his palm shone the shield of his calling.

"I'm Brinkhaus from the cops," he said.

A woman with a slender figure made more beautiful by tight-fitting silk, moved a hand languidly and shot two streams of smoke from her nostrils.

"What *is* going on there, Jim?"

Brinkhaus walked in, stopped, bowed toward the woman. He held his hat down in his left hand, carelessly crushed in his broad thick fingers.

Johnstown, eyes narrowed to a quick glitter, said, "It's nothing, Mona. Just an H. Q. man pulling"— he chuckled—"a kind of Dracula. Will you sit down, Mr. Brinkhaus?"

"Thanks. I'll stand. I been sitting all day."

"This is—ah—Mrs. Johnstown…. Mona, you'd better go in the other room."

"Missus," said Brinkhaus, with his quaint bow, "you'd better sit down right there."

Johnstown snapped: "Now look here! I don't know what you're doing here, but I'll not stand for—"

He stopped. Brinkhaus had not interrupted, but there was that in his brown, imperturbable eyes that quite silenced Johnstown. The sergeant remained standing on his big feet, his arms at his sides, his face almost blank of any expression. But something about him, some air exuded, silenced Johnstown.

He clipped, "Well, have it your way, then. Sit down, Mona." He crossed the room to a table, got a cigarette, turned with renewed anger and snapped, "Well, what do you want?" You could not see his eyes. You saw only two dark glitters.

Brinkhaus asked: "What's your business, Mr. Johnstown?"

"I asked you a question, didn't I?" Angry, Johnstown flung himself into a chair, lit his cigarette with a vengeance. "You walk in my place. You clown around. Now what's *your* business?"

Brinkhaus considered the man with a bland look, then turned to the woman, ducked his head. "Before you were Mrs. Johnstown, you were Mona Barbour, isn't it?"

The silk dress moved, catching, throwing off, rapiers of brilliance. "Why, yes." She leaned back languidly. "Yes, of course. Now perhaps you can read my palm. Do you pull things out of the air? Perhaps you can tell me my future." She laughed softly, mockingly.

IT ROLLED off Brinky like water off a duck. He looked around the large, opulent room, saw wealth in every chair, in every drape. He seemed to forget where he was. A minute passed and he said nothing, did nothing but roam his eyes absent-mindedly about the room. The man and the woman exchanged glances. Johnstown fretted where he sat, bit his lip. The woman became impatient because the room was so silent and because Brinkhaus remained like one in a trance. Was the man an idiot?

"Well?" she blurted.

Brinkhaus suddenly looked at the man.

"When did you leave Johnstown, Pa.?"

"Johnstown!"

"It's in Pennsylvania," Brinkhaus said, modestly.

"What the devil are you talking about?"

"Johnstown, Pa."

The woman jumped up.

"He's crazy, Jim! This man is crazy! I'm not going to listen to nonsense like this!" She started across the room toward a connecting door.

Brinkhaus did not budge, but he said, "Miss Barbour."

"Mrs. Johnstown to you!" the man barked, on his feet.

Brinkhaus said, "The lady can't hardly lug around a name that don't exist."

The woman spun, her eyes wide and her face shot with awe. "What *do* you mean?"

Johnstown's voice was clipped: "Steady, Mona. This cop is playing hide and seek."

But the woman was shaking. She could not help it. Fright welled up in her eyes. Johnstown's mouth was hard, taut, and there was an ugly sidewise jut to his jaw.

Brinkhaus said, "I'm looking for the guys who killed my friend Henry Shumacher. It begins right here. Your name ain't Johnstown. It's the name you been using, but it ain't Johnstown. You gave me your fingerprints the other day on that cigarette case. I sent 'em to the Washington Bureau. They had a record, but they referred my request to the burg where them prints was first made into a record: Johnstown, Pa. So Johnstown sends me a full record, all the trimmings—including, if maybe it'd interest you, a photy-graph...."

The woman clapped knuckles to her lips, against her teeth. She moved with great caution to a chair and sat down on the very edge of it. Johnstown seemed to grow taller, leaner, harder. He tossed off:

"Well, what about it? What the hell do I care if you raked up my record? A Johnstown record can't hang me in this state; it can't even cause me a pinch. I'm strictly kosher on that score, Brinkhaus. I've been living a life of ease—turning over a new leaf. I thought my record might crop up some day, so you don't worry me. I did time for the little stunts I pulled in Johnstown. That's all washed up. I paid my debt to"—he leered—"society."

"You did maybe in Johnstown, but not in this state. That horsepittle job was a neat one, engineered by a smooth guy that I figure took no hand in the actual snatch. But he knew how things were run at the horsepittle. He had inside dope. You were a patient in that horsepittle a few months ago. You met a nurse there and three days after you walked out of the horsepittle, this nurse chucked her job. I seen her picture in the office that was taken along with a dozen other nurses on the lawn one day. She's in this room now."

The woman kept her knuckles against her lips.

Johnstown snapped, "To hell with you! It's all a lot of talk! You haven't a thing you can hang on me!"

"It happens," Brinkhaus said, "that another gent came out of the Johnstown stir same day you did. You were cell mates. This guy is in town now. He was one of the mugs pulled the Mono Mill payroll snatch and killed the guard. You know him. His name's Jake the Punch. This woman here gave you the lay o' the horsepittle and Jake the Punch and two other heels pulled the job."

Johnstown moistened his lips. His voice crackled— "And why the hell should I want to swipe a guy out of a hospital?" he cried.

"That's why I'm here," Brinkhaus said slowly, hoarsely. "To find out. Git your hat and coat on. The woman too. I got a car waiting downstairs. Some things I can figure out, but not all. I'm a peaceable man, so you better come quiet."

The woman cried through a network of fingers, "I'll not go! I just won't go! Jim, I'm not going!" Her voice shook, her body shook. There was horror in her wide eyes.

Johnstown muttered, "Pull yourself together. I told you this cop is playing hide and seek. He's screwy. Get your things." He was cool as ice, but his face was white, drawn, and the glitter of his eyes was fierce.

She shrank back.

"No! No! I'll not go! Why should I have to go?"

Johnstown nibbled his upper lip, flung a glance at Brinkhaus. "Let her stay, copper. I'll go with you."

"She's got to go," Brinkhaus said simply.

She jumped up, her hands clenched.

"I won't! I won't go!" she cried desperately. "You can't make me go! I'll scream! I'll not go—no—no!" She turned on Johnstown. "That's final, Jim!"

Brinkhaus said, unexpectedly, "Okey, miss. You, Johnstown—you git your things on."

The man seemed relieved. He threw a queer look at the woman as he went past. He looked puzzled. He got his hat, a topcoat.

"I won't be long, Mona," he said.

Going down the hall, Brinkhaus walked behind Johnstown. The elevator dropped them to the lounge and outside, in the street, Brinkhaus said to Johnny Pell:

"Johnny, this is Mr. Johnstown. Take him to H.Q. Take him in a taxi, Johnny. I'll use the flivver."

Johnstown's lips tightened. "Look here—"

"Use the cuffs, Johnny. Keep quiet till I git to H.Q."

Johnstown's eyes opened—bulged. His face for a brief moment looked ghastly. Then his right wrist was manacled to Johnny Pell's left.

"Brinky," Johnny said, "I been holding something out on you. When you drive that buggy, the foot brake don't work. You got to use the emergency."

CHAPTER SEVEN

THE GIRL STEALS AWAY

WHEN JOHNNY Pell and Johnstown had gone, Brinkhaus drove the flivver a matter of twenty yards, then stopped, climbed out and lit a two cent stogie. He leaned against a tree and waited. He waited ten minutes.

The woman came swiftly out of the apartment house, reached the curb and looked anxiously up and down the street. Presently she hailed a cruising taxi. Brinkhaus heaved into the flivver, started the motor. He saw the green taxi roll past. With a shiver, a rattle and a jerk the flivver left the curb and swung into traffic. At the next block the green taxi turned left and Brinkhaus, running through a light that turned red, blushed for shame and thought of Johnny Pell. An eastbound motorist called him a name.

The way led south through a sedate, quiet district, and then the taxi struck Waterford Avenue and later hit Union at an angle. Union was noisy with trolley bells and radio stores and emptied finally into Union Circle. Here the taxi swung due south into South Broad Street and began to skirt the edge of Little Italy. It left South Broad and cut diagonally across Brick Square, a dark and dismal neighborhood, and then it swung down into Stable Alley, a narrow thoroughfare where in the old days hundreds of truck horses had been stabled. Now it boasted intermittent lights, blue or green or purple, and fantastic speakeasies, spaghetti joints and the dark haunts of a free and easy existence. There were plenty of taxies. There was the blurred sound of jazz bands. The ninth police precinct....

Brinky saw the green cab stop. He had a fleeting glimpse of the woman as she alighted, sped across the sidewalk and disappeared. He parked the flivver and went ahead on foot. The cab got into gear and moved off as he came abreast of it. At his right was a narrow cobbled alley between two shabby red brick buildings that rose three stories into the starlit night.

He stopped for a moment, took a few drags at his stogie and tossed it away. He thought of Henry Shumacher, of the old days when he and Henry had pounded adjacent beats in this same neighborhood. It had been a good neighborhood then, but time had had its way.

He made his way slowly into the alley, a shadow hardly distinguishable from the shadows of the alley—broad, patient, careful of each step he took. A man who rarely laid his hand on his gun, he now freed the .38 revolver from its holster on his right hip and warmed it in his palm. He found a dead-end to the alley—a high board fence that fronted on the next street. He stood for a moment in the shadow of it, thinking. He was not brilliant and took a lot of time thinking.

Standing with his back to the board fence, he waited half an hour. Then he heard a door open, saw a blur of motion appear from the building on his right. He did not move. He heard hurried whispers, then the sound of the door closing, and he saw the blur move ahead toward the mouth of the alley.

He moved then, and the woman was standing on the curb beckoning to a taxi when Brinkhaus came up behind her and took hold of her arm.

Her "Oh!" was startled.

He turned her around without a word and walked her back into the alley. "Miss," he said, "this thing you feel against your back is a gun. Keep your mouth shut." He moved her along until he came to a door in the dark wall of the brick house. His voice was a low, hoarse whisper: "You know how to get in here. Go ahead."

Presently she reached high up on the frame of the door, pressed a button four times—three short, one long. In a moment Brinkhaus saw a crack of light at the bottom of the door, heard the sound of footsteps coming down a bare wooden stairway. A bolt clanked, the door opened, the woman collapsed.

"Pick her up," Brinkhaus said. His gun was raised, steady, unwavering. "Pick her up, bozo, or I'll let you have it."

The man's mouth hung opened with surprise, but he stooped, picked the woman up in his arms.

"Git in," said Brinky's low, guttural whisper.

THERE was nothing the man could do. He had his arms full, and when he turned and entered the door there was the feel of a gun against his back. Yellow light showed a steep, narrow staircase up which he creaked. A shabby hall was at the top. There was the sound of low voices, and diagonally across the hall a door was part-way open. As they moved toward this door, Brinkhaus lifted a gun from the man's hip pocket. A breathed oath came from the man's gritted teeth. He kicked open the door and moved into a large, tattered room.

A man was sitting on the small of his back, feet propped on a coverless table littered with bottles, glasses. But Brinky's eye lit on a man who was swinging across the room toward an old scarred bureau where more bottles stood glistening darkly. He was a short, broad man, powerfully built, round-shouldered and with a distinct ape-like slouch at once swift and sullen. This man stopped in his tracks.

"Jake the Punch," grunted Brinkhaus. He did not command the men to raise their hands. There was no need. In his square-built solidity there was something oddly inimical, and the unwavering dark muzzles of his guns spoke louder and more plainly than words.

"B'jeeze!" growled the man with the slouch.

"Lay the woman down," said Brinky.

A youth rose from an iron bed, smiled hesitantly. There was a soiled bandage around his head. Brinkhaus knew he was John Doe. The youth was haggard, sallow, and the expression on his face was both curious and blank.

"You sit down," Brinkhaus said.

The boy obeyed meekly, and then seemed to lose all interest in the scene. He slumped and stared vacantly at his hands. The man whose feet had been propped on the table now sat straight in his chair, his hands poised outward, palms down, fingers hooked. The girl was placed on the bed. The room reeked of liquor and stale tobacco. Not a window was open.

"I'm Brinkhaus from the cops."

They started. A sharp intake of breath hissed in the room. The men remained like images, but unlike images they were tense, coiled like springs. From the hand that held the gun he had taken from the man downstairs, Brinkhaus dropped his police whistle. He took one backward step and eyed the unarmed man.

"Take that, open the window, blow it."

The three men seemed outraged, hurt, as though the sergeant were imposing on their good nature.

"You heard me."

Jake the Punch said, "Nix, Con! Don't you!"

"I ain't," said Con.

Brinkhaus did not argue. He considered their refusal for a moment and then lifted his broad brown chin to the youth. "You, son!"

The boy looked up.

"Pick that whistle up and blow it out the window."

The boy did not hesitate. He looked a little puzzled, but he rose promptly and crossed the room.

"Stop that, Harry!" growled Jake the Punch.

The boy turned around promptly and went back to the chair, sat down, and again lost interest in the action. He lowered his eyes and studied his hands.

Still Brinkhaus was calm, solid, unruffled. He began to move inch by inch, his guns level, covering the men, and reached the side of the bureau. On the very edge of it stood a telephone. Slowly, cautiously, his guns trained steadily on the men, he used his right elbow to knock the phone over. The receiver rolled out of the hook. For a brief moment he stepped away because hands had begun to move nervously. He could hear faintly a noise like static in the receiver that lay on the bureau. He moved nearer and said in a loud voice:

"Operator. Call the ninth police precinct. Tell them to send a squad to 238 Stable Alley. Tell them to break in the door in the alley on the north side." He repeated this three times.

The woman on the bed sat up, brushed hair back from her forehead, stared horrified around the room, then cried, "No—no! No—no!" and tottered to her feet, reeled toward the door.

"Git back, miss," said Brinkhaus.

The sound of his blunt voice seemed to rob her of strength. She slumped to her knees. On her knees, she moaned and rocked from side to side, ringing her hands. "Let me go! Please let me go!" She struggled up again, reeled toward Brinkhaus, her body bent forward. "Please, I didn't do anything!"

"Stay back!" Brinkhaus warned.

Her face was anguished, red, and she tottered before him, implored with her hands when words refused to pass her lips. The hair on his nape stiffened. She was pitching toward him, slumping, groaning. He took a heavy sidewise step as the man at the table twitched. Those clawing hands moved like a flash of lightning.

THERE was almost a look of sorrow on Brinky's face as the gun in his right hand blazed. His body did not move—only his hands moved from the wrists in a peculiar way so that they seemed detached from the rest of him. A gun clattered to the floor and the man at the table grimaced sickly, quietly, tried to rise and then fell across the table, unbalanced it and crashed with it to the floor.

The man named Con dived for the gun that had fallen. Motionless, only his hands moving in that detached way, Brinky gave him a fleeting look, then saw Jake the Punch in motion. Brinky actually sighed as his right-hand gun belched a second time. The slug turned Jake the Punch completely around. The woman threshed on the floor, screaming wildly. Echoes slam-banged and the room shook, plaster dribbled from the ceiling. Jake the Punch careened against a window, shattered the glass there, recoiled and went hurtling backward over a chair. In all this chaos of sound and motion Brinkhaus remained rooted like a tree in a storm. There was no hate in his eyes, no lust of blood or glory in his heart; there was, on his face, only a sorrowful, almost wistful look, as if he regretted all this.

While Jake the Punch fought to disentangle himself from the chair the man named Con got his hand on the gun on the floor and fired without rising. It was a blind, unreasonable shot. It stopped the threshing of the woman on the floor and she lay out straight on her back with a look of wonder in her eyes.

"My God!" screamed Con.

"Yeah," said Brinkhaus.

The gun in his left hand shook; interlocked with its blast was that of the gun in his right hand. "Ugh," groaned Jake the Punch. The man named Con reeled to his feet, his face shocked. He closed his eyes and gritted his teeth, his lips bared. He started backward, gathering momentum until, when he hit the wall behind, the force was so strong that he was knocked forward on his face. He twitched there, his fingers clawing the dusty boards, cluttered oaths and vague prayers bubbling from his lips.

"Ugh," Jake the Punch said again. He was bent way over, holding his stomach, weaving back and forth, his feet dragging. The boy sat on the chair, gripping its sides, his face white as snow, his stark eyes watching the motions of Jake the Punch. Little wisps of smoke were in the room, a smell of old dust mingled with the smell of gunpowder.

Jake the Punch suddenly fell forward. He fell so hard that the room shuddered.

Brinkhaus did not move. In all that fire and crossfire his broad substantial shoes had not budged an inch. His guns still remained level, though there seemed to be no need. Yet he stood there in a kind of brown trance, and there was sweat on his face, growing, beads of it trickling down the brown cheeks like beads of silver. He was no killer. He had never killed wantonly, had never used his shield as an excuse.

The sobbing of the woman roused him. He stirred, shoved one of the guns into his pocket, passed a damp palm across his eyes.

"I'm shot," the woman breathed. "Oh, God, I'm shot!"

He bent down beside her. He saw a dark splotch growing beneath the bosom of her dress. He knelt there holding her in his arms, cradling her.

"There, there, miss—there, there."

There was noise on the steps, hard, quick heels. The door burst open and men in blue with drawn guns, swept into the room. A uniformed sergeant stopped short.

"Holy smokes, it's Brinky!"

Brinkhaus lifted the woman. "Sweep up, Hal. Grab that boy over there and don't rough him. He ain't had nothing to do with this. Look out—I got to git this gal to a horsepittle."

CHAPTER EIGHT

BRINKHAUS GIVES THE FACTS

NURSE TENANT lay in an armchair, her head back, her face white. An electric fan blew in her face, made her hair move. Her cheeks looked hollow. From time to time a man laid a cold cloth on her forehead or held smelling salts to her nostrils.

In shirt sleeves, his hair tousled, Lieutenant Stickney sat at the desk. He read and reread a paper in his hand. He looked grimly at the woman from time to time.

The door opened and Commissioner Pentcost came in. He wore evening clothes. He had been summoned from a banquet.

He said, "The press is downstairs like a pack of hounds straining at a leash. They're waiting for the confession."

Stickney stood up. His lips were tight and there was a strange look in his eyes. "I had this taken down." He passed Pentcost the sheet of paper.

The commissioner adjusted his rimless nose-glasses. The transcript read:

> I killed a man named Shumacher. I did it with my own hands. Why did I kill him? I don't know. But you say I killed him, so you must know and I must have killed him. I killed him with these hands you see. Who are the three men who carried out the man? I don't know. I met them in the hall and said I wanted to kill Shumacher so they helped me. I killed him. I killed a man named Shumacher.

Pentcost frowned. He tossed the sheet back on to the desk, took off his glasses, frowned again. He pointed to the sheet: "Not that, Stickney. That is no confession. It's the result of hysteria. We don't dare give that to the press."

The door opened and Larsen poked his head in.

"Where's Brinky?"

"What are you doing down here?" Pentcost asked.

"I had a phone call from Brinky—" He came in, grim, cool as an iceberg. His blue glance took in the unconscious woman, the disheveled Stickney. He said, "Mr. Commissioner, if I am to remain in charge of the homicide division, I recommend the transfer of Lieutenant Stickney."

"Inspector," said Pentcost, "this is no time—"

He stopped. In the ensuing silence they all heard the hard, heavy footfalls in the corridor. Brinkhaus appeared in the doorway, ducked his head, said, "Hello, Peter. Well, I got here."

He came in, closed the door, took off his hat and put on his steel-rimmed spectacles.

"Adolph's getting the news from the ninth downstairs now," he said. "The guy Johnny brought in—that Johnstown guy—engineered the whole business. I'm sorry I couldn't bring in Jake the Punch and his two pals, but they got dead on me. The woman got shot in the mix-up—"

"What woman?" cut in Larsen.

"Name of Mona Barbour. She used to be a nurse at the Plummer Memorial until Johnstown had his appendix took out there. They kind of struck up, so a few days after he leaves there she chucks her job and goes to live with Johnstown. She's tired of working and Johnstown's got dough. It was just after Johnstown engineered the Mono Mill payroll grab. Little while ago who should turn up but this jane's kid brother, the same John Doe that was carried out of the hospital. He ain't dumb. He sees the lay of the land, and he sees his sister's headed for no good. He tries to git her to go home with him—out in Arkansas—but she's tasted the walnuts and wine and she won't go. Then he starts to git a line on this bird Johnstown's racket and he threatens, at last, to turn him up. Johnstown don't want to bump the kid off account of he's the girl's brother, but he slaps Jake the Punch and two other guys on him for a shellacking. They beat hell out of the kid, so hard he goes goofy—and that's when he's found that night by O'Reilly.

"So then he's in the horsepittle. Johnstown knows the kid'll talk for sure when he comes to. He gits the lay of the horsepittle from Mona and send his three heels after the kid."

"But how," demanded Pentcost, "did you get on the trail of this Mona and this—ah—Johnstown?"

"Well, first off I kind of wonder about this poor gal here. I git Johnny to frisk her apartment, and he finds a hundred-dollar bill hid away that we find was part o' the Mono Mill payroll snatch. So I mooch around and find things out about her. She's heavy in debt, what with doctor bills for her folks in Indiana, and she's three months in arrears at the apartment. I am figuring that was she in debt like that, why'd she be hanging on to a hundred-dollar bill. Then I find out this Mona Barbour used to room with her. This Mona Barbour was a nurse, too, at the Plummer. I mooch around the horsepittle records for the last three months and I find that of all the patients a man named James Johnstown was the only one that gave no occupation, no relatives, and I find this Mona Barbour was his nurse. She left the horsepittle three days after Johnstown did. It was finding that bill that led me to the Mono Mill. I put the payroll man in a trance, and after a while he remembered one of the heels had a special slouch. I took him to a newsreel o' the guard's funeral. He saw a guy with the same slouch in the crowd. We got a record of him here. It was what I was after. I was trying to hook up this horsepittle job with the Mono Mill job because o' that there bill. And how'd the bill git where it was? Mona Barbour told me, little while ago. She got it from Johnstown in the horsepittle. She give it to Nurse Tenant the day she went to go with Johnstown. 'I won't need it,' she says. 'I'll be in the dough now.' And Miss Tenant says, 'I'll save it for when you change your mind and come back.' This poor gal here didn't know a thing about that horsepittle job."

"And John Doe?" asked Pentcost.

"He come to. In the noise of the shooting in that room he come to. He's at the horsepittle with his sister. She's dying. I got her there quick as I could, but the poor thing— Well, her brother'll help burn Johnstown."

Stickney picked up his hat and coat. He looked like a sick man as he left.

Larsen took off his hat.

"We are ready for the press," he said. And the way he said "we" excluded all others in the room but Brinkhaus and himself.

Nurse Tenant stirred in the quiet room, opened her eyes. She stared for a moment and then her eyes closed and she sighed faintly, smiled.

That was because Brinky was holding her hand, patting it, saying, "There, there, miss. Everything's jake now—everything's jake."

THE GREEN WIDOW

SERGEANT BRINKHAUS WAS SATISFIED TO LET "THEM SMART ALECKS CLOWN AROUND," HE HAD TO SEE A WOMAN ABOUT THE GREEN WIDOW

HERMAN BRINKHAUS, sergeant of detectives, out of police headquarters, made his prosaic way down Edgemont Street at 11:30 of a windless, cold night. Edgemont Street, a thoroughfare of fine shops, was deserted at this hour, and the methodical fall of the stocky sergeant's large, substantial shoes echoed with sharp clarity from block to block.

Ahead, a block ahead, he saw a uniformed figure standing beneath a corner street lamp. He knew it would be Patrolman Huneker, on peg post, eight blocks of Edgemont Street north and south where crime broke seldom but when it did there was hell to pay.

"Hello, Hen."

A red weathered face cracked in a good natured grin. "You're keeping bad hours, Brinky."

"I was on my way home on the Lattervale trolley, so I got off and walked down to see you."

"What's up, Brinky?"

Brinkhaus shrugged. "Nothing, Gus."

He pulled off his right glove, thrust his hand into his pocket and drew out a small roll of bills.

He said, "I took the boys for a little dough at pinochle in the back room tonight, Gus, and here's them five bucks I owe you. I figgered I'd better pay it back before Mom takes a notion to go through my pockets."

"Hell, Brinky, you didn't need to worry about that!" But Huneker took the bill, shoved it into his pocket.

"I'll be seeing you some time, Gus," Brinky said, and turned away.

But the sound of hurrying footsteps stopped him and he lingered on the curb, looked east on Harrow Street and saw a shape coming

"Somebody h'isted
the Green Widow!"

toward them. The footfalls were irregular. They were sharp, staccato; they were the high, hard heels of a woman in haste.

A voice cried: "Officer—officer—"

Huneker spun his nightstick sharply, stretched his legs in a fast walk up Harrow. Brinkhaus went after him. The woman had broken into an irregular run.

Brinkhaus caught up with him. The woman stopped running, but she walked rapidly toward them and they could hear the sound of quick breathing.

"A man—in the gutter up the street—near Westover—"

She stopped but still poised for flight. In the dim light between street lamps they saw that she was young, colored, neatly dressed.

"Ah came up Westover and turned the co'ner and there was the man and—there was blood all oveh him—"

"O.K., Gus," Brinkhaus grunted, and broke into a run.

Huneker joined him and the two men, both heavy, pounded their feet on the wide sidewalk, crossed Lynn Street and galloped on toward Westover. They reached the corner, split up; one crossed the street and the other looked down Westover.

Huneker called: "See anybody, Brinky?"

"Nope. You?"

"No."

They stood for a moment looking at each other across the silent square. Then, far distant, they heard a crash. Unmistakably it was the crash of glass. Huneker reared around. But Brinkhaus was already on the run back toward Edgemont Street, and in an instant Huneker followed, drawing his gun. They reached Edgemont, looked up and down. In a nearby side-street they heard the blast of an automobile engine quickly accelerated.

Huneker said: "Down the street—" and pointed as he ran.

Brinkhaus barged past him, his coat tails flying. Midway down the block he stopped, and Huneker, coming up out of breath, stopped also. Glass lay on the sidewalk. Plate glass out of a shop window. In the window glowed a green light. It shone on a small black velvet pedestal and there was no other object in the window. A brass plate had been riveted to the building, beside the window; it bore a simple legend: *Simonson, Jeweler.*

Huneker pointed: "Somebody h'isted The Green Widow out of Simonson's."

BRINKHAUS had run to the next block, stopped beneath the street lamp there. His drawn gun glinted as he turned about. The last echoes of a departing car had died away. The sergeant craned his short, stocky neck, swiveled and struck his heels sharply up Edgemont. Huneker was standing on wide-spread feet and methodically going through a repertoire of low, bitter oaths.

"Like babes in the wood we were!" he complained.

"Was I you, Gus," Brinkhaus said, "I'd ring in right off. They'll have to notify Simonson."

"Being took by a skirt!"

"Well, then you park here, Gus, and I'll ring in for you."

"Been on this beat now for six years and never...."

But Brinkhaus was on his way. There was a call-box at Edgemont and Clark and he rang in, gave the details in a flat, dull voice, hung up and started back down the hill.

"I'll get holy hell for this," Huneker said. "You watch, Brinky. I was took like a sap, I was.... Look, I been hearing this Green Widow was worth ninety thousand bucks! Bucks, Brinky! I was just looking at it half an hour ago—the way it laid there, big and green in the green light—and not another stone in the whole window. I'm asking you now... ninety thousand—"

"Gus, begging your pardon, but suppose now you move your foot over."

Huneker moved and Brinkhaus bent down and picked up a small handkerchief.

"Turn on your flash, Gus."

Huneker switched on his flashlight. It was a lady's handkerchief, white, plain, still folded. Brinky unfolded it and searched for an initial. There was none.

"What's that on it, Brinky?"

"Lipstick, I guess. This ain't worth a damn, Gus. We got to start from scratch."

A PRECINCT car arrived with a sweep of spotlights and a squeal of brakes. A bullet-headed precinct skipper swung out and the man at the wheel whipped one of the spotlights around so that it sprayed blinding radiance on the shattered shop.

The skipper stared at the glass on the sidewalk and listened stonily while Huneker related what had happened. In the end he toed a piece of glass.

"Tough, Huneker." He strode up to the window, stared for a moment at the velvet pedestal, then wheeled sharply. "This ain't going to be so hot. The assistant district attorney is batting for the D.A. and he's hell on the department. You know that. He's going to jump all over us for this." He frowned. "Why the hell didn't you tell the jane to wait and—" He shrugged. He was a level-headed man and could realize how Huneker had been so easily duped. He looked at Brinkhaus. "Any ideas, Brinky?"

"Got to start from scratch."

They turned at the sound of an approaching motor and saw headlights coming down Edgemont. A black sedan drew up and Simonson, the jeweler, stepped out. He was a tall, lean man, well dressed.

"Crashed, eh?" he said.

Huneker said: "That green emerald you had in the window—"

Simonson cut in: "What else?"

"Why, there was nothing else. Leastwise—"

"Door forced?"

"Uh—no, but—"

"I see." Simonson strode to the shattered window, looked at the pedestal, at the little depression on top where The Green Widow had lain. He asked for a flashlight and sprayed it back of the pedestal, back of a velvet drape; made a thorough search with his fingers. Then he went to the door, tried it. It was locked.

"That's all right, gentlemen," he said, turning. He lifted his lean, smooth-shaven face, and a twinkle appeared in his eye, a smile plucked at his lips. "You see"—he nodded cursorily to the broken window—"it was not the genuine Widow."

Huneker, angered, exclaimed: "What!"

"Soft pedal," the precinct skipper clipped.

Huneker blushed. "I—I beg your pardon." He chuckled. "I guess I ought to be happy." He beamed. "I am!"

Simonson was fifty or so, but well preserved, good humored. "Naturally," he said, "I should hesitate to leave the genuine stone in the window overnight. The one in there tonight was a perfect imitation. Worth only about two hundred. The window, of course, is insured. So you needn't worry, Officer. I can be thankful my shop wasn't forced."

The precinct skipper said: "Huneker's on peg post but I'll shoot a man over from the house to stay in your store till you can get the window fixed."

"Excellent!" Simonson jangled keys, opened the heavy door, switched on lights inside. He ran his eyes over the showcases, around the store. It was a small, narrow shop. It was known that Simonson dealt only in the finest gems, that he was an expert, a lover of gems as well as a dealer in them. "Everything's all right, gentlemen."

"Try your safe, maybe," offered Brinkhaus.

"Might as well." Simonson went to the rear of the shop, called back: "Nothing's been touched in the store. Obviously the thief was after The Green Widow."

Brinkhaus said: "Anybody been in lately asking to buy it?"

"It's not for sale, you know."

"I didn't know."

"Not for sale. One of my treasures. I picked it up in Siam four years ago. Originally there were two, identical. The other was lost fifty years ago, never recovered. A Siamese prince then named this one The Green Widow. I'll show it to you," he added brightly, proudly.

The precinct skipper drifted up and joined Brinkhaus and Huneker, craned his neck from a distance. Simonson opened his safe, unlocked an inner compartment, took out a square black box. The cover clicked open as he held the box out.

"The thief, you see, thinks he has this one," Simonson said.

Huneker came closer. "Me, I couldn't tell the difference."

Simonson chuckled, lifted the gem with thumb and forefinger, rocked on his heels. "You see, gentlemen, this one…" He paused, squinted at the large green stone. He screwed a glass into his eye, stepped beneath a light. His face hardened, paled. His hand shook. He turned and stared wild-eyed at the men.

The precinct skipper said: "What's wrong?"

"This," said Simonson, "is the imitation!"

Huneker groaned: "Oh, Gawd!"

CHAPTER TWO

INSPECTOR PETER LARSEN was a tall man with a yellow mane of hair. He ran Portsend's detective bureau. Sitting at his broad desk next morning, he read the entire account of the sensational jewel robbery in Edgemont Street. Finished, he sat back, started a thin brown cigar, and was inhaling the first pleasant drafts when the door opened and Assistant District Attorney Wells Gatlin came in.

"Morning, Gatlin," he said.

"I guess you read about that boner in Edgemont Street last night, huh?" There was a mean, wicked glitter in Gatlin's shoe-button eyes. He was a small man, bitter-mouthed, rasp-voiced. He rolled his eyebrows, waved his head from side to side. "And I see that prize tomato of yours is mixed up in it. Day by day, night by night, I am continually amazed that such block-headedness should go unbooked of justice."

Larsen puffed. "Accident, Gatlin. These things happen. Brinky and Huneker were accosted by a young Negress who told them a man was lying—"

"Nuts! I've heard all that already. Y'know"—he jammed his hands into hip pockets, warped his tight-lipped mouth—"I could understand a couple of kids falling for a line like that. But I can't—" He sighed, nodded. "Yes, I can, I guess; I guess I can understand. Considering the apes, I guess I can understand—"

The door opened and Brinkhaus walked in looking at a newspaper. "Morning, chief. I see here where that bill was put through and it means I got to fork over an assessment of $650 for the new curbing and paving up my street. Morning, Mr. Gatlin. Nice weather we're having."

"Yes. It was a nice night, too, wasn't it?"

"Well, I could have stood it a little warmer."

Gatlin smirked. "Oh, then it wasn't hot enough, eh?" And then he bared his teeth in a malicious grin. "Maybe I got it wrong. Maybe the gentleman seen in Edgemont Street wasn't Sergeant Brinkhaus after all."

Brinkhaus stared at the newspaper. "It was," he said placidly.

"Gatlin," Larsen said crisply, "Brinky and I have a few things to talk over. Will you drop in later?"

Gatlin chuckled dryly, went to the door. He pointed: "You notice the way the paper kidded your department, don't you?" He chuckled again, left the office.

Brinkhaus sat down, made a face, stared at his hands. "Boss," he said thickly, "I'm asking you if maybe you can't lend a hand about Gus Huneker. The razzing the paper gave him this morning, and what I just heard downstairs, Gus is liable to be suspended for a spell. He can't afford it, Peter. It wasn't his fault at all. This woman come running up and, shucks, there was nothing me and Gus could do but what we did. Gus has got a big family. It was my fault as much as his, but Gus gets hell because it was his beat. Any chance, boss?"

"I don't know, Brinky. I'll see. It's a wrong neighborhood to have anything go wrong. The emerald's worth ninety thousand."

"Insured?"

"Yes. But this man Simonson is a nut on emeralds, apparently. And especially this one. He feels that even the insurance money will not repay him for the loss of the prize of his collection. I want you to go down to his shop, Brinky. He has a clerk there. Quizz the clerk."

Brinkhaus put on his Homburg and went down to the central room. But he paused at the door, turned about and made his way downstairs to the laboratory. Craike, the expert in charge, was donning a white jacket, and Brinkhaus said:

"Phil, there's some stuff on this handkerchief I picked up in Edgemont Street last night. Looks like maybe it was stepped on, though first off, last night, I thought it was lipstick. See can you analyze it, and I'll be seeing you."

He left the laboratory, cut through the pistol range and entered the headquarters garage. Johnny Pell, his aide and chauffeur, was on the losing end of an attempt to polish the bright work of the shabby flivver.

"Down to Edgemont Street, Johnny. To Simonson's there."

BRINKHAUS reset his Homburg dead-level on his head and held on to the side of the car as Johnny Pell snaked it wildly through traffic. They headed west on Central Boulevard, turned south at Civic Park, and took a ramp to Park Boulevard. They crossed the Post Road and hummed down Edgemont Street. Glaziers were putting final touches to Simonson's new window.

"You wait here, Johnny," Brinkhaus said.

He entered the store and found a young man running a cloth over one of the showcases. The man was thin, pallid. He wore horn-rimmed glasses and said, "Good morning, sir," in a soft, quiet voice.

"I'm Brinkhaus from the cops. Could I now see Mr. Simonson?"

The young man appeared to become a little nervous, but he said: "Yes, yes, of course. Just wait a moment."

Simonson, standing, was a tall and well-groomed man, grave-faced but alert. "Officer Huneker," he said, "dropped in a few minutes ago to say again how sorry he was. Naturally I am sorry, too." He shrugged, made a wry little smile. "It may be difficult for you to understand how I feel about the loss of The Green Widow. I am, you see, a lover of gems. I loved The Green Widow as much—and this may sound absurd, but it's nonetheless true—I love The Green Widow as much as some men love their children. Jewels have their fascination. It's like that." He tapped once more on the desk, left his fist resting firmly on the surface, stared at it.

"Huneker is like that, Mr. Simonson. He's kind of proud that during all the time he's been on this beat there ain't been a break— except this one. I come down specially this morning to kind of ask you not to go too hard on him—"

"I had no intention, Sergeant. I suppose I could raise a lot of trouble, but on the other hand doing that sort of thing might impede the progress of the search. The stone has been stolen. The thing is, get it back." He slapped the desk. "I'd rather pay forty thousand dollars for its recovery than receive the insurance money on it."

Mention of so large a sum did not rouse Brinkhaus. He said: "So then you forgot to change the stones last night before closing?"

"No." Simonson leaned back. "My clerk, Mr. Hazley, changed the stones. He took the genuine Widow out of the window at five last evening. He took it, as he always has taken it, to the safe. He must have become confused. He'd broken his glasses that afternoon and perhaps that was the reason. At any rate, he must have returned the genuine stone to the window instead of the imitation."

"How long's this Mr. Hazley worked for you?"

"Five years."

"Married?"

"Happily." Simonson leaned forward, half-shrugged, broke a wry smile. "My dear Sergeant, you're not suspecting Hazley?" He raised a palm. "Don't—please. The poor chap's nervous as it is." He dropped his voice, spoke earnestly: "I might add, Sergeant, that he's not too well, either. I should hate to have you be rough with him. Lungs, I think. I offered him a sum of money to go away for a year—the Southwest somewhere. But"—Simonson spread illustrative palms—"he's proud, Sergeant."

"Where's he live?"

"They have a small apartment at 344 Western Avenue." Simonson leaned forward, level-eyed. "I want to make it plain, Sergeant, that I shan't stand for any rough stuff against Hazley. The chap's in no condition. I believe him. I have no patience with the error he made—but there were extenuating circumstances. He'd broken his glasses. He is nearsighted—blind, without them, almost."

Brinkhaus regarded his hat for a long moment, then shrugged. "I just got to do my duty. I ain't rough, Mr. Simonson." He put on his hat, turned and made his way into the store.

Hazley was rearranging stones in one of the showcases. He flicked Brinkhaus with a covert look.

Brinky said: "Just as a matter of routine, Mr. Hazley, I suppose you were home at 11:30 last night, huh?"

"No. I was at the Park Social Club. That's a little club I belong to out in our neighborhood. Last night was our semi-monthly meeting."

"There late, huh?"

"I—yes, I guess I was. I think I left at about one."

Brinkhaus pulled on his woolen gloves. "That's very good, Mr. Hazley."

Hazley's nervous hands moved rapidly inside the showcase and he kept his gaze averted. Brinkhaus gave him a lingering look then turned and plodded to the door, opened it, and went out into the street.

"What you find?" Johnny Pell said.

"I'm having a hard time, Johnny, getting away from scratch." Brinky settled into the squeaky seat, nipped the end off a rank Wheeling stogie, jammed the stogie beneath his squarish hairbrush mustache. "Just in case, Johnny, suppose you drive over to the Park Social Club."

"I gotcha."

Johnny Pell ground industriously at the starter button and after a while Brinkhaus said:

"Was I you, Johnny, I'd turn on the ignition."

CHAPTER THREE

POLICE HEADQUARTERS hummed with excitement. The so-called Diamond Squad went through the city like an ill wind, turned dubious pawnshops upside down, examined closely the pawnbrokers' books. Bureau files were raked for colored criminals. Negroes and Negresses tagged with the slightest record were hauled on to the carpet, grilled, released if they gave authentic alibis, slapped into the holdover if their memories seemed negligent. Precinct plain-clothesmen went on the walkabout, elbowed their way into nether haunts, cruised the shanty back-alleys of Darktown Flats.

The able cartoonist of the *Standard* took an uproarious slap in the noon edition; depicted a uniformed cop and a stocky detective listening to a girl's tearful story while, directly behind their backs, a man was robbing a pedestrian.

"I never wore a derby in my life," said Brinkhaus, otherwise unmoved.

Chief of Police Pentcost, a man easily abashed by the super sales talk of the district attorney's office, gave Patrolman Gus Huneker a pedantic tongue warming and suspended him for a month without pay. It was the first blemish on an otherwise perfect record, and Huneker took it hard.

Though Brinkhaus was not suspended, newsmen chided him in person and through news columns. Even brother officers joined the bandwagon. Peter Larsen, his immediate boss, was a man who held his tongue in any storm; he held it now. Wells Gatlin, the assistant D.A., drummed questions at the suspects in the holdover for two solid hours, and came out hoarse and with no point gained. Brinkhaus didn't even question the suspects.

At about two that afternoon he had a talk with Craike, the laboratory expert. Following this he hauled Johnny Pell out of a penny ante game and they went down to the garage. A new flock of suspects had been hauled in for questioning and again Brinky had refused to join in the grilling.

"Seems to me you're passing up a lot of chances," Johnny Pell said, starting the flivver.

"I'll let them smart alecks clown around, Johnny. I ain't never gone in for grilling guys just to make a show at being busy. And regarding this address, which maybe you ought to know, it's 344 Western, and how is your missus' swollen glands?"

"Better."

Johnny drove the flivver around City Hall Square, went straight through a safety zone, jumped a stop light and cut off a car on the right turn north into Spruce Avenue.

"This footbrake," Johnny said, "don't work so well. I can use the emergency in a pinch only that ain't so hot either."

"Pretty soon," said Brinkhaus, getting his breath, "I'm going to take up walking."

Johnny Pell brought the flivver to a stop in front of 344 Western by cramping the right front wheel against the curb.

Brinkhaus entered a small apartment house and climbed three flights of stairs and rubber runners muffled his footfalls.

He rang a bell on the right and in a moment a small, brown-haired woman opened the door.

The sergeant had his hat in his hand and an unruly cowlick bobbed once as he made a brief bow. "I'm Brinkhaus from the cops, missus."

"Yes?" she said anxiously.

"Could I come in a minute?"

Her round brown eyes searched his broad, placid face. "Well—well, of course. Yes, come in." Her voice was quick, a little breathless, and her round eyes did not leave his face.

Entering a small foyer, he was led into a small comfortable living room that had a distinct odor of cleanliness.

"Sit—sit down, sir."

He let himself down into a mohair armchair and the woman took a straight-backed chair nearby, sat on the very edge of it, folded her hands in her lap.

"**I SEEN** your husband this morning. He don't look well."

"He—he isn't."

Brinkhaus frowned compassionately. "Hard, ain't it? Once my boy Hermie was took sick with malaria and I say it wasn't pleasant around the house for almost a year. Mr. Simonson seems to think a lot of your husband."

"Yes, he does," she said quickly. "He's been wonderful to Charles and me. He—he wanted to send Charles and me to Santa Fe for a year. Charles wouldn't. It—it's hard to accept things like that, Mr. Brinkhaus. For Charles it is, anyhow."

Brinkhaus pushed out the crown of his hat, recreased it again. "You find it lonesome like in here when Charles goes out to them club meetings?"

Her eyes shimmered. "Yes—a little. But I read—I read."

He nodded slowly, his face gentle and kind. "My wife reads a lot when I'm away on night duty, too. I kind of mooched around the club this morning, just to check up on your husband. Not that I suspected him, missus, but it was police routine. Yes, he was there till one o'clock—from nine till one." He paused, looked at his cigar, which he had let go out because he knew most people hated the smell of the brand he smoked. "You were in all that time, I suppose, Mrs. Hazley?"

"Yes. Yes, I was in."

He looked at her. She was pretty, he saw—small and well formed and a little pale and, he imagined, in her middle twenties. After a while he looked down at his hands.

"The best check-up I had on your husband," he went on, "was at 11:35. That was now at exactly about the time the robbery was staged."

"Surely you didn't suspect Charles—"

"No, missus. You see, at 11:35 the club operator says Charles come up to her desk and asked her to ring this number here. She rang and rang and there was no answer." He looked at her and repeated blandly: "There was no answer, Mrs. Hazley."

"Oh, then. Yes, I stepped out. I had a headache and I stepped out for a walk. I walked up Western to Spruce and then back again."

Brinkhaus stared at his hands. "That would be, say, about a twenty-minute walk."

"About. It was twelve when I came in again. I remember because the chimes on that clock on the mantel were ringing."

He nodded. "I see. Then you come in at twelve."

"Yes. I remember."

"Missus, at twelve ten the club operator tried to get you again. She couldn't get you."

The woman's hands gripped the edges of the chair and her eyes widened, a half grimace caught at her face. "But I tell you I was home—"

"Missus," Brinkhaus said quietly. He said no more, but sat and shook his boxlike head slowly from side to side.

She gasped: "The phone must have been out of order—"

"I figured that way, too. So I asked the phone company if it was. They said no, not so far as they knew."

"But—"

"You were in at twelve thirty, missus. The third time the club operator got an answer."

Color fled from her face and she sat shaking on the chair. "You meant—you tried—to trap me!" she panted.

He was placid: "So where was you then?"

"I—I was out."

He nodded patiently. "That's been settled, Mrs. Hazley."

She ripped her hands from the sides of the chair, started to rise—then grimaced, settled back again, dropped her head. He did not urge her just then.

And presently she looked up, her eyes swimming. "You can make it very hard for me, for Charles," she said.

"I always try to make this here kind of thing as easy as I can, Mrs. Hazley."

"Then please believe me—please let me keep secret where I was last night."

He shook his head slowly. "I can't, missus. I'm a cop."

She put her head in her hands and Brinkhaus, remaining motionless, waited with a vast patience.

"All right," she said at length, and raised her eyes. "I went to a man's apartment. Charles didn't want to go to the club last night. I urged him to. I—I then went to this man's apartment. But if you tell Charles—please, it won't do any good. It 'll hurt him. He's sick. He needs me. I was a beast to do what I did!"

"So what was the man's apartment?"

She said: "His name's Dan Muir. He's"—she dropped her head—"a good friend of Charles's, too." She began sobbing.

"Don't be scared, missus." He patted her shoulder a few times. "I'll just check this up and then that's all there'll be to it. Where does this Dan Muir live?"

CHAPTER FOUR

DAN MUIR lived in an apartment hotel at 2020 Laurel Drive. The sergeant got Muir's apartment number from the desk clerk and rose in a silent elevator paneled with glass and chronium. The sixth floor corridor was painted gray, had mouse colored carpets. The doors were gray and studded with chronium knockers.

"Yes?" said a tall, dark man who had opened the door numbered 608.

"You're Mr. Muir?"

"I'm Muir."

"I'm Brinkhaus from the cops."

"Oh...." Blue eyes studied Brinkhaus sharply; then Muir said: "Sure, come in."

It was a man's apartment—large, roomy, with a lot of big, heavy armchairs. The men sat down. "Cigar?"

"Well... yes, I guess I could. They look good."

Brinkhaus lit up from a match held by Muir and Muir said: "I suppose I should be uneasy, Officer, but I'm not." He grinned. "Should I be?"

Brinkhaus leaned back. "Nope." He took a long puff. "I just come around to ask if you entertained a woman last night."

"Yes, I guess I did."

"Who was she?"

Muir slapped palms on his knees. "That's an embarrassing question, Officer."

"I figured it would be, Mr. Muir. I'm kind of embarrassed myself, kind of. But I got to ask it. I got to clear things up. You got my word of honor that I ain't out to crack any scandal or anything like that. I'm just checking up."

Muir looked up swiftly. "There's nothing between us, Officer. She was lonesome and pretty ragged, if you get me. Nerves. She came over and—and I tried to cheer her up."

"Who?"

"Well, if you must know, her name's Mrs. Hazley."

"Good. Now when did she come and when did she leave?"

"She must have got here about nine thirty. After a while I had some food sent up. She was frightened. She was afraid of even the waiters, and hid in the other room. We had some food and something to drink and time flew and before we knew it it was twelve o'clock. She went, then. Wouldn't even risk taking the elevator. Conscience-stricken. Walked down the fire stairway. I told her not to be foolish. We're old friends. I've known her husband for twelve years—her for fifteen, since we were kids. What are you trying to hang on her, Officer?"

"Nothing, Mr. Muir. I'm just checking up. Little by little I got to check off my leads. My father used to say that in cutting a road through the woods you come first to the little trees, but you got to get them out of the way just the same." He stood up. "Thanks for bothering with me, Mr. Muir. I ain't had such a swell cigar since I went to Otto Horndorfer's clambake five years ago."

HE WENT downstairs, lingered in the lobby for a while, then asked to be shown the way to the steward. A bellhop escorted him and for a few moments Brinkhaus talked with a short, fat Swiss. Finally the Swiss called a waiter who was in the act of donning livery.

Brinkhaus said to the waiter: "The steward here says you were the man hauled all that food and ginger ale up to 608."

"Yes, it was me."

"Supper for two, huh?"

"That's right."

"How many bottles of ginger ale?"

"I can look it up."

In a few moments the waiter returned and said: "Took up six bottles, all told. Two to begin with, two later, and two after that."

"What would you say now is the only use for ginger ale?"

"Me? Rye highballs."

Brinkhaus dipped his head toward the waiter, toward the Swiss steward. "Thanks."

Returning to the street, he found Johnny squatting and eyeing the right front wheel.

"Now what, Johnny?"

"Oh, nothing. There's a blister on that tire there—been there for three days now and I'm wondering if maybe we'll get a blow-out sometime."

Brinkhaus took two slow puffs on his cigar. "Johnny, I'm going to take a little walk. I think walking's good for a man at times. Be seeing you."

Edgemont Street saw him next.

"And what can I do for you, Sergeant?" Simonson said.

"Well," said Brinkhaus, "I just want to ask Mr. Hazley two simple questions."

"Really, don't you think he's been sufficiently persecuted?"

"I ain't persecuting anybody, Mr. Simonson. These here two questions are simple and they don't concern Mr. Hazley. And I'll ask you, Mr. Simonson, to leave us alone. It won't take a minute."

Simonson said curtly: "Very well." He strode stiffly into the office, closed the door.

"Well," Hazley breathed, "what is it, what is it?" He dabbed at his face with his handkerchief, kept wetting his lips.

Brinkhaus said: "Does your wife touch liquor?"

"No. Never took a drop."

"Better speak the truth."

"I am."

"For instance, if you went home last night you'd ha' known she'd been drinking if she had been drinking, wouldn't you?"

"I tell you, sir, my wife has never touched liquor!"

Brinkhaus nodded. "Okey. Now tell me how much money you got in the bank?"

"Nothing. Not a cent. Every cent I make we spend—for doctors, for living."

"That's all, Mr. Hazley. Good-day."

CHAPTER FIVE

MUIR OPENED the door of 608. He had an overcoat slung over his arm. He said: "Well, hello. I was just about to go out."

"I won't take long. Can I come in?"

"I don't suppose there'd be any use in my objecting. Come in."

"You're what I call a downright sensible man, Mr. Muir."

They walked into the living room but did not take chairs. Brinkhaus rubbed the underside of his left arm against the crown of his hat and said: "You did a lot of drinking last night, huh?"

"Well, Mrs. Hazley was kind of in the dumps and—"

"Uhuh. I asked the waiter downstairs. He said he brought up six bottles of ginger ale. Said he brought up the last pair at eleven o'clock."

"Of course," Muir said affably, but his sharp blue glance trained steadily on Brinky's downcast, thoughtful eyes.

"To use six bottles of ginger ale two folks would have to drink one hell of a lot of liquor, wouldn't they?"

"I said we did."

"I remember. Say about three highballs to a bottle. Six times three 'd be eighteen highballs. Nine a piece, or being conservative, say twelve for you and six for the lady."

"What in the devil are you driving at?"

"Trying to clear up some snags, Mr. Muir. Even if a woman is used to drinking, six highballs 'd kind of now make her tight. If she wasn't used to drinking, six highballs 'd make her tighter than hell. Huh?"

Muir's eyes narrowed. "Will you please explain yourself?"

"I guess I'm dumb, but I'm trying hard. I'm trying hard to make you see, Mr. Muir, that if Mrs. Hazley drank six highballs she would have gone home kind of on her ear."

"Well?"

"I don't think she went home on her ear."

"Go on."

Brinkhaus shrugged. "I figure I got to know where you were between eleven and midnight last night."

"I was here."

"Who can prove it?"

"Mrs. Hazley."

Brinkhaus sighted down the crown of his hat. "And then of course you can prove that she was here."

"Naturally."

"Mrs. Hazley's husband'll probably knock your story into a cocked hat or something."

"I don't see how."

"He can swear, I expect, that when he came home last night his wife was stark sober. As a matter of fact, Mr. Hazley just said that his wife never touches liquor. That being the case, when she went home last night she would have been drunk and he would have smelled the liquor."

Muir leaned back on his heels, tightened his lips, stared hard at the sergeant.

Brinkhaus said: "The Edgemont Street jewel robbery took place at 11:35. You can't prove where you were between eleven and twelve."

Muir said sharply: "I've nothing more to say."

"I'm being easy as I can on you and the woman. If you dished me up the truth I could go a long ways to help you. I could—um—keep the woman's name out of it."

"Do you mean to stand there and say that Mrs. Hazley and I connived to rob that shop…. Nonsense. You know damned well a Negress was involved—"

"Wasn't, Mr. Muir." He drew the little handkerchief from his pocket. "I picked this up at the scene. First off, I figured, hell, it was lipstick, the street being kind of dark there. Next morning I seen it wasn't. So I had it analyzed. This smudge you see here, Mr. Muir, is a kind of stain actors use to make themselves look like darkies. That woman was a white woman operating as a decoy."

Muir took a backward step and his eyes shimmered, he snapped: "I don't believe it!"

"We'll go pick up Mrs. Hazley and then mooch over to headquarters. I hate to do it, but I offered to make a deal with you and you give me a waltz-me-around-again-Willie."

Muir stood motionless, staring, for a long minute. Then his jaw set. He put his overcoat on savagely, snatched up a pair of gloves.

"Come on," he snapped. "Do your damnedest then!"

TWILIGHT was falling rapidly when they alighted in front of the Western Avenue address.

Mrs. Hazley opened the door and a little cry caught in her throat. Brinkhaus motioned Muir to enter, then followed and closed the door.

The woman gripped Brinky's arm. "Don't! Please don't!"

"Missus, I ain't enjoying this a bit but I got to do my duty."

Hazley stepped into the foyer from the living room. He had just come home, had removed his coat and stood in vest and shirt sleeves.

"What—what's this?" he asked.

"In," Brinkhaus said.

They went into the little living room, and Hazley threw a puzzled look at Muir. Muir did not look at him but kept his eyes straight ahead, his jaw firm. In the momentary silence that ensued Mrs. Hazley's breath was plainly audible.

Hazley cried: "What is this?" in a cracked voice.

"Mr. Hazley," Brinkhaus said, "will you now just step outside the door for a minute?"

Hazley backed to the foyer door, bit his lip, flung a hostile look at Muir, a baffled look at his wife. Shaking, he stepped out and closed the door.

Mrs. Hazley, her eyes fixed on Brinkhaus, groped her hand for the back of a chair, got hold of it, steadied herself. "What do you want?" she gasped hoarsely.

Muir cut Brinkhaus off, saying: "I tried to prevent this, Helen, but there was no way I could. I did my best." He spoke in a low, sure voice. "This policeman has tried to implicate us in that Edgemont Street jewel theft. It's silly, because you were at my place—I had to tell him that, Helen—and we both know we were there."

She flung a frightened look at the closed door. "Of course—of course, I was there—I was there."

Brinkhaus was becoming grim. "You can't prove it."

"Nor can you prove," Muir said, "that we weren't there."

Brinkhaus looked at him vacantly, said: "I figured I proved it to you, Mr. Muir, that the la-de-da you handed me wouldn't hold water. Was I both you folks, I'd start in using my head. I got you, got you guilty as can be, in action and in talk. You ordered all that ginger ale up last night to make believe you was getting tight. But you didn't get tight. It was just a stall, and it was a good one. Only it didn't just work. The two of you hooked together to lift The Green Widow—"

The door opened and Hazley stood there, shaking, his mouth warping. "So that was the game!" he cried, glaring at his wife.

"Oh, no—oh, no!" she pleaded. "Please, Charles—"

"And you!" Hazley flung at Muir. "My friend! My very good friend!" His teeth chattered and his lips gleamed wet, his body trembled with frenzy but he did not move from the door. "You—you vile rat!" he rasped out.

Muir's face remained stony.

The woman reached out a hand. "Charles, please, Charles, don't excite yourself. You know that if you do—"

He snarled: "If I do! If I do! What the devil is it to you what I do.... So, my dear wife, it was you—you and my old friend Dan Muir. No wonder—" He stopped short, thinned his hueless lips. "I see now. When I came home for lunch yesterday, my glasses—they were on the desk there while I washed in the bathroom—and when I came back, they were on the floor, broken. I—thought they had slid off. I see differently now. You knocked them off!" he shrilled.

Muir broke in: "Charles, pull yourself together. Helen did nothing of the sort. I—I asked her to my apartment last night. She came over." He shrugged. "I'm—sorry—you had to find out. But there it is. We committed no robbery."

"No! But you—"

Brinkhaus chopped in placidly: "Mr. Hazley, when you came home last night, your wife was all right, huh?"

"What do you mean by all right? She was here. Sitting right in that chair. We sat and talked and for a while she sat on my lap."

"She was sober?"

"Of course she was. Stark sober."

"You didn't even smell no liquor like?"

"Not a breath of it."

Brinkhaus smacked his gloves across his left palm. "All right, Mr. Muir, Mrs. Hazley; you got to come along to headquarters. Get your things on, missus, and dress warm because it's getting colder out."

She choked: "You're not—"

"I got to kind of pinch you and Mr. Muir for that jewel stick-up. And while I think of it, you better take a handbag and some extra clothes along. I got an idea they'll keep you over for a while."

MUIR said crisply: "Go ahead, Helen. Just stick to your story and everything will be all right. Get your things. We'll see this thing through."

Hazley's frenzy had died down. He dragged his feet into the room, slumped to a chair. He ran his hands through his hair, then let them drop and hang limply toward the floor. He wagged his head slowly from side to side.

His voice was dead, flat: "I—I can't believe it. I can't believe it. I can't believe you'd trick me like that, Helen. We always seemed to mean so much to each other. I"—his voice broke—"just can't believe it."

She went and touched him on the shoulder. "Charles, I—"

"Don't, Helen. I guess I can't blame you. I don't blame you. Excuse me for—for talking the way I did. But at first it was—it was such a shock. Please go and leave me here alone for a while. I want to think."

She went from the room but returned in a moment, her face grave. "Charles," she said, "where's that gun?"

"I don't know."

"You do. You always kept it in your bureau drawer. It was there day before yesterday."

"I—I don't know where it is."

She turned and looked at Brinkhaus. "Officer, I can't leave him here alone. I can't. He'll—"

Muir said: "Take me down, Mr. Brinkhaus. After all, I'm supposed to be the master mind. You can see the shape he's in. It would be criminal to leave him here alone. Come on, let's go."

Brinkhaus said stolidly: "Mrs. Hazley has got to come along. I offered to make a deal with you. This here situation ain't one I like and there's still chance to spring the truth. I'm after that emerald and I got to get it."

"But, man, don't you see, we haven't got it!" Muir cried.

"Nope. I don't see. You got to go along, Mrs. Hazley."

She snapped: "I won't!" and stood straight, trembling. "I tell you I can't leave my husband here the way he is. I'd never forgive myself. I refuse to go!"

Hazley stirred. "You needn't worry about me. There's no use trying to argue with the law, Helen. I'll be all right. I promise. I swear to you I have no intention of doing away with myself."

"You'd better," Muir urged, "get your things, Helen."

She turned at last and went into another room and reappeared in a few moments dressed for the street. She was grave-faced, round-eyed. Muir took her arm and led her out into the corridor.

Brinkhaus joined them and they went down the stairs, into the darkened street. The sergeant got between them, took hold of their arms and began walking them east.

He said: "I'll give you the next three blocks to think it over, then it's all off. That husband of yours looks pretty bad. He might write a farewell letter and then bump himself off—"

The woman stopped. "Officer, I tell you—I'm afraid—I can't explain—but I feel that he—"

"I know. You come across with the truth and we turn around and go back to him. You don't, and we go ahead to headquarters."

She sobbed: "I do love him! I want to—"

The vicious bark of a gun shattered the silence of the street and Brinkhaus took a half-step forward, stopped, blinked, said: "I'm hit. Duck, you two!"

The woman flung herself into a hedgerow choking: "Charles must have—"

Muir landed beside her saying: "Quiet, Helen!"

BRINKHAUS shook himself, took a heavy sidewise step, thudded against a tree. He was trying to draw his right hand from his pocket but seemed unable. It was lodged there. It felt as if lead weighed it down. He muttered something vague, reached around with his left hand and thrust it awkwardly into his right-hand pocket and got hold of his gun. His right arm was numb all the way down.

He broke suddenly into a heavy-heeled run at sight of a dim overcoated shape scurrying across a lawn. He plowed his way among the trees, his gun gripped in his left hand. He crushed through a hedge like a steamroller and saw again the running figure.

His hoarse voice called: "Stop!" But the figure darted on, only half-seen—and Brinkhaus fired and the echoes of the shot spattered up and down the avenue. He jumped from the lawn down into a cement driveway. From the corner of a garage a gun muzzle blazed and in the confined space the echoes banged violently back and forth. Back of Brinkhaus, a window was shattered by the shot.

The sergeant ran to the side of the house and pressed along in its dark shadow. He listened and after a moment heard the twang of wire, the sound of clothing being ripped. He started off, made the garage safely, went down along its sidewall and came to a wire fence behind. Beyond, somewhere, he heard drumming feet.

He pried his way through the wire. Pain began to knife and slash at his right arm and he gritted his teeth and felt an odd sickly warmth rising through his body. His big feet crunched on cinders, then rang on flagstones, then thudded dully on a hard lawn. And then he was in another street, on the run, and up the street, on the other side, the figure was fleeing.

Brinkhaus crossed and plugged on, zigzagging among the lane of the trees. The warmth was rising to his head, flooding it, and his eyes felt heavy, his body felt waterlogged. His feet seemed to drag at the ground, and when another shot rang out from ahead he did not stop or swerve but kept plugging on. Lead snicked off dry winter branches above his head and a twig fell on his hat, bounced off.

"Tried to get Muir, I guess, before," he mused wearily, "and was a bum shot... got me. Well, Brinky, old horse, you're insured anyhow. Mom... and Hermie... and the little one. It was tough about poor Gus Huneker... good cop... all about a lousy emerald."

He dragged to a stop, propped himself against a tree, raised his left arm and fired three times. He reeled away from the tree and slouched on with short, leaden footsteps; and beneath a street light he came upon a figure lying on the sidewalk, face down. And ten feet beyond the figure, a gun. The figure was groaning hoarsely.

A cop came running up demanding: "What the hell's the matter? Stick 'em up— Oh, it's you, Sarge!"

"Go call an ambulance—quick kind of."

"Okey, Sarge!"

The cop turned and ran up to the nearest house.

Brinky dropped heavily to one knee, pocketed his gun, turned the body over saying: "Well, Charles, you kind of made a—" He stopped, grunted. "Uh," and stared.

He rubbed his thick fingers across his eyes, took them away and bent down closer to the body on the sidewalk. He winced and groaned as pain seared his right arm. He moistened his lips. Then he chuckled weakly.

The man lying on the sidewalk was Simonson.

BRINKHAUS came to in a hospital hours later and Inspector Peter Larsen was sitting at the bedside. Larsen leaned over and patted the sergeant's big, thick hand.

"That was swell work, Brinky."

"He was a bum shot, Peter. How is he?"

"Didn't pull through."

"I'm sorry, Peter."

"Simonson had the emerald all the while," Larsen said. "He was almost broke, and he had many offers for The Green Widow. It's hard to understand the man. He was madly in love with the stone and could not bring himself to sell it.

"But he needed money. And the emerald was heavily insured. He had made one imitation, and so he made another. And when young Hazley changed the stones that evening, he merely replaced one imitation with another. Simonson had planned with Hazley's wife. The insurance money would have carried him through."

"Gosh, Peter, I kind of liked that little lady."

"You'll like her better when you hear. Simonson went to her and made her the proposition. He offered her five thousand dollars to help him, enough to take her husband away to a climate that would help him. She had courage, Brinky. She went through with it. It was she who broke Hazley's glasses.

"Then that night she stained her face with the dark stuff and acted as the decoy to get Huneker out of Edgemont Street. Simonson was waiting around the corner. He broke the window, got the imitation stone."

"Her and Muir give me a fancy story. I never did believe it."

"He's an old friend of the family. When Mrs. Hazley found out that we were suspecting an inside job, she went to Muir and begged him to help her establish an alibi. He did. He had a woman in his apartment that night, but she wasn't Mrs. Hazley. I've seen the woman.

"Simonson was no criminal really, but he lost his head, got panicky. When he saw you taking Mrs. Hazley away he lost his reason. He shot you."

"I kind of feel sorry about the woman."

Larsen said: "In his confession, Simonson merely mentioned a woman—no name. Muir was the one came to me with a plea of mercy for Mrs. Hazley. Officially she's not on the records. She's home with her husband now. I filled out the story with her help. I saw conditions

there. My report, still to be completed by you, is that you trailed Simonson, he tried to escape, he shot you and you shot, and killed him."

Brinkhaus let out a vast sigh of relief. "Peter, that sounds like a
hunkydory report and I don't guess I got much to add to it."

"I reason that way, Brinky. Is there anything you want now?"

"Well, Peter, I guess I'd just like to see Mom."

THE LEMON

THE LIMP BODY THAT HAD BEEN THROWN ON THE WIDOW'S DOORSTEP SENDS SERGEANT BRINKHAUS SCOURING THE DARK CUL-DE-SACS OF DEATH STREET

SHE WAS young. The conductor helped her from the street car because she carried a baby. The baby was wrapped, muffled, in a fuzzy pink blanket. The young woman held the baby close to her breast, reached the sidewalk. She was well-dressed in plain, inexpensive clothes, a pert little hat; though it was cold, she wore sheer stockings, trim black pumps.

The street light on the corner bathed her upturned face with a harsh radiance. Her lips moved as she read the street's name. Her face was white, too white, and a little drawn at the mouth. Turning left, she walked up the narrow street with a rhythmic clicking of high heels on cement.

She saw, presently, the glow of twin green lights. She walked more rapidly, came into the radius of the green glow, climbed the broad steps. The double-swing doors were heavy and she had to shove her body weight against them and shoulder her way in backwards. And then she was in the bleak central room of police headquarters. She paused, a little hesitant now, and eyed the uniformed fat man behind the high, severe desk. He was droning monotonously into a telephone. She did not move again until he had hung up the telephone receiver.

He had a fat, rubicund face, wore steel-rimmed spectacles. "You want something, madam?"

"I—I'd like to see Sergeant Brinkhaus."

The fat man jerked an illustrative thumb. "Upstairs, next floor. It says Detective Division on the door."

"Thank you."

She walked away. The fat man craned his neck, puckered his forehead. She climbed the staircase, reached the corridor above. She found a ground-glass door panel that had Detective Division painted on it in black letters. She knocked.

A voice said: "Come in."

She hesitated, looking anxiously up and down the corridor, drawing in her under lip. Then, as she reached toward the knob, the door was opened from the inside.

"Oh..." said Johnny Pell.

"Are—are you Sergeant Brinkhaus?"

"No. You wanna see him?"

"I—I'd—"

"Who's it, Johnny?" asked a thick, guttural voice.

Johnny Pell swung the door wide. "Come in, madam."

There were five desks in the long, narrow office. The office was dim except for a cone of light sprayed downward from a green-visored bulb. A flat-topped desk stood in the glow. Brinkhaus sat at the desk. But for the unruly cowlick above one temple, his coarse black hair was combed neatly backward. A coarse black mustache bunched squarely beneath his broad nose. Squinted eyes made his broad face appear slightly quizzical.

Brinky had dumped
out all the papers and
stamped on the flames.

"Yes, missus?"

"I—I'm Mrs. Bannon," she said in a throaty little voice. She added: "Walt Bannon's wife."

"Oh, Walt Bannon," said Johnny Pell, nodding.

"Sure enough," said Brinkhaus, getting to his feet. He looked around the office. "Kinda cold in here, missus." He moved, turned on another light, picked up a chair and planked it down alongside a steam radiator. "Sit down over here, it's warmer kinda."

Her voice was suppressed, scarce above a whisper. "Thanks, Sergeant," she said. She sat down. Her eyes darted about the floor, rose at last to meet Brinky's gentle brown look. "I—I'm worried."

He looked concerned—a plain, amiable man, as broad in the body as he was thick. "What's up, missus?" He turned, caught hold of a chair and pulled it over. He sat down facing her, leaned back comfortably, interlocked his fingers on his stomach. "About Walt, huh?"

She nodded, grimaced, seemed about to cry. He put out a thick-fingered hand.

"Now, missus...."

The simple gesture seemed to iron out the grimace. Johnny Pell came nearer, his eyes bright and round with interest, not a muscle moving on his tight-muscled young face.

"You see," she said, "he—he hasn't come home." She looked at the clock on the wall. "And now—now it's half-past nine."

"What time's he usually come home?"

"Five. And if he doesn't, he always—always—telephones me."

"Maybe he's on a job."

She shook her head. "I called the office. They said he left there at five sharp. I called them at seven—and again at nine. They hadn't any word from him. I—I feel something is wrong. I couldn't wait any longer. He—he always used to speak of you. That's why I'm bothering you."

"You ain't bothering me, missus."

HER LOWER LIP trembled. "Maybe I'm foolish, Sergeant Brinkhaus—but I can't help it. Maybe you know how Walt is. His—his crusading spirit. He gets himself into trouble sometimes—by his lone-handed investigations."

Johnny Pell threw in: "A great guy. He sure turned up the dirt on those municipal sewer contracts."

She reached out toward Brinky's knee. "Can't you—find him?"

Brinkhaus spread his broad palms. "Sure, missus." And then he dropped his voice: "Was he prying into anything special?"

Her tone was hopeless: "I don't know. If I only knew! But he was always close-mouthed about what he did until the thing was done. And that's it: I'm not sure!" Her voice broke: "And I'm so worried— so miserable! I *know* he would have telephoned me if he thought he'd be home late. I know!" There was a touch of panic in her voice.

Brinkhaus got to his feet, dropped a comforting hand to her shoulder. "You ain't ought to worry like that, missus. Walt could always take care of himself. It's like my missus—she's always worrying, too, and her old enough to know better. Still I suppose now if she didn't worry, that'd make me sore, too. I bawl her out for it, but the same time I kinda like it. Me, I know Walt. He ain't no fool. Prob'ly fell onto a case and he's so busy he ain't had time."

He looked at Johnny Pell. Johnny Pell's expression was not particularly buoyant. Johnny looked worried. And a little too grim at his hard mouth to be nonchalant.

Brinky said: "Johnny, go down and git the car out. We'll take Mrs. Bannon here home. Then we'll scoot and git Walt home."

Johnny's "Okey" was tossed off abstractedly. His mind was elsewhere. But he pivoted, grabbed up his hat. He threw a sharp, keen-eyed glance over his shoulder, went out.

Brinkhaus took the woman downstairs. He wore, now, a brown Homburg of hard felt; it rode uncompromisingly on his squarish head, above his broad squarish face. His brown eyes, usually placid and deceptively blank, radiated an amazing twinkle. He lifted a homely, naive buoyancy out of a growing sense of doubt. His big, polished shoes did not creak as they went down the staircase. They represented his only luxury: made to order, seventeen dollars a pair. He had to have them. No stock size was broad enough to encompass those tremendous feet.

His mood, genuine or otherwise, was none-the-less adroitly insinuated into the woman's sense of hopelessness. By the time they reached the flivver, she was livelier, hopeful.

Brinky took Johnny aside, said: "Now this woman's nervous, Johnny, so I'm telling you, for crying out loud, don't ride this flivver like a cowboy."

By concentrating his mind on nothing but the operating of the car, Johnny managed to maintain a safe and sane speed. He acknowledged every stop light, did not drive in the wrong direction on one-way streets, and he turned corners with singular discretion. Brinkhaus, pleased, lighted a three-cent stogie.

Nancy Bannon lived in a small bungalow on the north side. It was a dark, quiet street. The bungalows were all of a type; they did not crowd each other and in front of each was a little yard, a length of green hedge, a gate made of pipe and wire.

Brinkhaus was the first to alight from the flivver. His weight, never handled on his toes, made the footboard creak. He helped Nancy Bannon out. Wind clicked overhead in the leafless branches of a maple tree. Brinkhaus opened the gate. It grated on its hinges.

"You just stay home and keep you and that there baby warm, Mrs. Bannon. Boy?"

"Yes."

"I got two. My missus wanted a girl last time but—"

Nancy Bannon's footsteps faltered.

Brinky gripped her arm. "Easy now, missus!"

But she broke away from him, flew to the little veranda; fell to her knees on the top step. She held the baby tighter, as though in fear of having it snatched from her.

She moaned: "Ooh—ooh!"

Brinky's heavy feet thumped on the steps, his big knees landed on the boards.

Johnny Pell came swiftly—light, fast on his feet.

Brinkhaus grabbed the baby as the woman collapsed. The blanket became undone. He fumbled with it, got it securely around the baby and stood up. The bundle in his arms whimpered. He rocked it, muttering: "Sh! Sh!"

Johnny Pell's flashlight swept up and down, steadied as he bent over. His left hand probed. Then he straightened. His eyes glittered, his mouth was hard, muscles bulging at either corner.

He rasped under his breath: "Head bashed in!"

"Any—any chance, Johnny?"

Johnny shook his head violently. "Not a chance!"

Brinkhaus rocked the baby. "Johnny"—he nodded toward the unconscious woman—"git her inside. She'll git a death o' cold. Git her in, Johnny—git her in."

Walt Bannon, with his head bashed in....

CHAPTER TWO

INSPECTOR PETER LARSEN appeared in the doorway of the Detective Division office. He was head of the division—a tall, blonde, severe man, quietly, inoffensively brusque. He slapped a pair of gloves across his left palm.

"That reporter Bannon, eh?" he said.

Brinkhaus nodded.

Larsen said: "I was out in my car—picked the news up on the short wave." He walked across the office, muttered: "Killing a man of Bannon's reputation is as bad as killing a cop! Any details?"

Brinkhaus sighed. He seemed not to have heard Larsen. "I don't never want to see that again," he mused aloud.

Larsen half-turned, lifted one quizzical eyebrow.

"Oh...." Brinkhaus cleared his throat, blinked. "I was thinking about Walt's missus."

Larsen's face softened. "That's the hell of it, Brinky."

"Well...." Brinky got up, dipped his head. "I guess we can't go on mooning about that."

"Dead when you found him, eh?"

"Out cold. He was laying on the veranda. He never walked there. He was brung there. Had his head bashed in somewheres and the dirty bums, with the lousy sense o' humor they got, they hadda bring him home." He gestured feebly, grimaced. "It's that kinda stuff makes me sick at my stomach, Peter." He paused, went on: "Doc Josephs came out from the medical examiner's. Doc said he was dead about three hours. That'd mean he was knocked off about seven. Mrs. Bannon turned up here about half-past nine after leaving her house at nine. That'd mean Walt was dumped home between nine and ten."

"Any leads?"

"Next door neighbor said about half-past nine she was putting her kid to bed and went to pull the shade down account the street light outside shined in the window. Said she noticed a car parked in front o'Bannon's bungalow. Didn't think nothing of it, o'course. Said it had only one headlight burning. Said it looked like a big touring car, curtains closed.

"At about twenty to ten Gus Meyerholtz was moping along on his motorcycle, regular patrol. He seen a car mooching along with only one headlight. Well, you know Gus; he's got a reg'lar mania for a guy should have two headlights. He swings around. It's on Morningstar Drive, half a mile from Bannon's house—and the car was headed for the city. So Gus rides alongside and yells they better hurry up and fix the dead headlight. And by God if Gus don't make 'em go right to a filling station and buy one. That satisfies him. His bad temper's over and he waves the guys good-by."

"Did he get the license number?"

"He wasn't worrying about it. No; he didn't. He didn't even git a look inside. The driver just yelled from the car and told the guy at the station to fix up the headlight. The guy put in a new bulb. Gus didn't hang around. He waves and scoots off looking for more violations. Gus hates to waste time. It was a touring car; he remembered that."

"How about the filling station man?"

"Well, he says it was a Packillac touring—maybe a coupla years old. Dark blue. He don't remember the license. He got a peek at the driver's face, though. Description ain't worth powder to blow them to hell, but he says he'd know the guy if he seen him again."

"Better tour him through Rogues' Gallery."

"Did." Brinky shrugged. "Nothing there like this guy was. Homer— Paul Homer's the gas man's name—said the guy wasn't 'specially tough looking. Just an ordinary kinda guy—"

There was a sharp rap on the door. Larsen opened it and Harry Borg came in. Borg was managing editor of the Portsend *Telegraph*, the newspaper Walt Bannon had worked for. Borg was small, natty. His eyes were sharp, direct, and a sandy mustache followed the crooked line of his upper lip.

"Sorry about Bannon," Larsen said.

"Me, too," Brinky muttered.

"Save it," Borg clipped. He wasn't intentionally insolent. He was disturbed, nettled, in an unpleasant frame of mind. One of his best boys had been murdered. "Got a cig, Pete?"

Larsen gave him one. Borg lighted it with a nervous gesture, snapped smoke through his nose, let a portion of it ooze between teeth suddenly bared, clamped. His eyes flashed. He snapped: "I sent his wife to the hospital!" There was a kind of restrained madness in his tone, a glaze in his eyes. He was an innately sensitive man who showed the world a tough, caustic front. He lashed out: "If you gazaboes don't turn up the sweet son that rubbed Walt out, I'll ride your department ragged! That's a promise and I don't care if you don't like it!"

"Wait a minute, Harry," Larsen said. "Just a minute, old egg."

"Yeah, just a minute, Harry," Brinkhaus said earnestly. "Remember now it was me his wife come to first off. Seemed like as if, with all the phoning she did your paper, some guys there would ha' figured something was wrong."

Borg dropped his chin, muttered: "I wasn't there. The dumb cluck that answered the phone figured Walt was on a bender."

He shrugged. "I'm sorry about that crack I made."

LARSEN said: "Isn't there anything—don't you know of anything he might have been after?"

"I know this," Borg rasped. "He found something. He hooked onto something. But it wasn't anything he'd been working on. He just fell into something. Either that—or it's an old score settled. Mapes was the last to see him in the office. Walt said, 'I'm toddling home.' Mapes saw him go out. Walt didn't seem hopped up about anything. He was sucking a lemon—you know him, he was always doing that. Always carried a couple of lemons in his pocket. He used to make our eyes water just by sucking 'em. He'd grin—poor guy. He was one of the swellest—" Borg stopped, tautened; rasped: "Nuts! I've got to get back to the office!" He slammed out.

The door was reopened almost immediately and Johnny Pell came in, jerked a thumb. "What's Borg steamed up about?"

Brinkhaus sighed bleakly. "Walt."

"Oh, yeah, now." Johnny leveled a forefinger as he came smartly forward. "Walt was in Death Street after five yesterday."

Larsen's eyes sharpened. Brinkhaus merely leaned a little forward.

Johnny's mouth was hard. "I dropped in the newspaper office and found out that Walt usually caught the Far Hills trolley that left Beacon Square at 5:05. A reporter there named Kensey used to take it with him sometimes, but not last night. But I found the conductor. Walt took the trolley, as usual. But he didn't go all the way to his neighborhood. He got off at Wilton and Death Street. Said to the conductor: 'I forgot. Got to get a bottle of good cheer for a friend. I'll grab the 5:35.'"

"Did he go up Death Street?" Larsen asked.

"Yep. Conductor saw him head up Death Street."

Larsen swivelled. "Brinky—"

But Brinkhaus was already on his way to the clothes-tree. His brown eyes did not gleam, he did not set his jaw. His broad brown face merely appeared very thoughtful. He worked his way into his overcoat, used both hands to put his hat on.

"I'll mooch around Death Street," he said.

Johnny Pell opened the door, followed Brinky out. Johnny Pell looked very snappy in a belted ulster, a flap-brim fedora. His jaw, shiny from a recent shave, stuck out. His eyes glittered. Johnny always gave the impression that he was eager, primed for trouble; which in fact he was.

Brinky squeezed into the flivver beside him and Johnny hurtled it out of the H.Q. garage. The morning was bright, cold, and Johnny pumped the choke, raced the engine. The wind whistled. Brinky pulled a woolen muffler from his coat pocket, wrapped it around his neck; he drew on a pair of woolen gloves that Mom had knitted.

Johnny took the first left turn on the inside and forced a taxi against the curb.

"Yuh hog!" yelled the taxi driver.

Johnny glared at him, muttered: "Imagine the guy!" Still glaring back at the driver, Johnny sailed past a red stop light. Brakes of another car squealed on the right.

"Oomp!" grunted Brinkhaus. "Now listen, Johnny, there ain't no fire, there ain't no riot."

Johnny said: "They must have put that stop light there overnight. I don't remember it."

Brinkhaus shut up like a clam. He held on to his hat with one hand, gripped the side of the car with the other. He did not breathe naturally until Johnny pulled up in Death Street, parked alongside a No Parking sign. Brinky climbed out, looked at the sign, looked woefully at Johnny. With a faint show of exasperation he picked up the sign, marched a distance of ten feet along the curb, planked the sign down.

Johnny, who was blissfully lighting a cigarette, did not even notice it. Brinkhaus made no comment.

Death Street was not really the name. It said Smith Street on the rusty signposts, but everyone called it Death Street. The nickname harked back to the early history of the street, when the railroad had a grade crossing there, when the street was known as a tenement district. Many had been killed at the grade crossing. Now the railroad, electrified, tunneled beneath the street, the whole neighborhood.

But it was still a narrow street, incredibly crooked. The tenement families had moved on. The red brick buildings now housed a few garages, a few warehouses, but mainly the street was devoted to wine, women and song. Jazz bands thumped at night, electric signs winked seductively. The brick buildings were old, the oldest in the city. Many of them were no longer red. Enterprising hosts to the trade had painted the fronts in brown, gray. It was a short street, three blocks in length, but it contained the bulk of Portsend's night clubs and bars. Six months ago a floor in the Race Club had caved in.

Six persons had met death, scores had been injured.

Johnny Pell said: "It don't look so hi-de-ho by daylight." He snapped smoke from one side of his mouth. "You take one side, huh, and me the other."

"Lotsa them won't have nobody there this hour," Brinkhaus said. "We better go call on Ruby John. Up a block. Number 85. He's got his office there."

"Let's go. Nick Popopulis'd like to run this street."

Number 85 Death Street was a three story brick house painted tan. The ground floor was a smoke-shop and bowling alley combined. The smoke-shop occupied a space twenty-by-twenty feet in front. A railing separated it from the bowling alleys in the rear. A couple of men were bowling. The crash of ball into pins was deafening.

The man behind the cigar counter wore a green eyeshade.

Johnny Pell clipped: "Ruby upstairs?"

"I'll see."

"Never mind."

BRINKHAUS and Johnny opened a door at the side, entered a hallway and climbed a narrow staircase. On the second floor was a glass-paneled door bearing the legend *O'Kelly Enterprises*. Johnny Pell shoved open the door. A typewriter was clicking. The office was spacious and furnished with half a dozen desks, only two of which were occupied. A youth hammered the typewriter. A very sleek young man sat at a broad desk that faced the door, squarely, and both Johnny Pell and Brinkhaus knew that the top drawers, right and left, contained loaded .45s. The young man sitting at the desk was not a clerk.

He said curtly: "Hi, police."

"Ruby," Johnny Pell said.

The typewriter stopped. The youth rose and walked across the office to a closed door. This door looked like wood and was, but the wood sheathed a core of two inch steel. He opened the door and spoke into the office.

"Okey," said a heavy voice.

"Okey," said the youth, turning.

Ruby John O'Kelly was sitting behind a massive desk. "Hi, Sarge. Hi, Johnny."

Brinkhaus said placidly: "Guess you had a killing up the street last night, huh?"

Ruby John was a big man with a shock of red hair, pink jowls. His face was big, shrewd, and his voice blunt. "News to me," he said. He was scribbling among a mass of papers, busy with affairs. He was a business man, powerful in his domain. He was the kingpin in Death Street—collecting rents from every bar and night club in the street and levying an added tax.

"I'm speaking o' young Walt Bannon o' the *Telegraph*," Brinky said patiently.

"Oh, that," Ruby John said, writing on. "I read about it. Tough. I'm sorry to hear about it. He was a good kid. What happened?"

"He got his head bashed in."

"Not in this street, Sarge."

Johnny Pell snapped: "Suppose you take care of that writing business later, Ruby. We happen to be talking to you."

Ruby stood up, said pointedly: "I'm not taking any cracks from a cheap H.Q. dick. If the kid was bumped off in this street I would have heard about it. Scram. I'm busy."

"Tie that tripe outside," Johnny said. "You're not big enough to talk down to me, baby."

"Ain't no sense arguing," Brinky put in.

Ruby John sat down, growled: "That's wise. Now I'm busy. Drop in again sometime."

"I wasn't going yet," Brinkhaus said.

Ruby John tossed his pencil on the desk, sat back. "You cops, you cops!" he complained.

"Walt came up this street a little past five last night," Brinky said. "He came up to git a bottle o' hooch, on his way home. He never did git home. His body was tossed to the veranda of his house at nine-thirty last night. It was carted out there in a dark blue touring car. We got a tip on that. We got a guy can identify one o' the birds in the car. It's murder, Ruby, and you boss the street and you know when a job's pulled off. I came here first to kinda save time. I know it ain't your fault if something goes wrong in some speakeasy in this street, but it's your fault if you don't open your jaw."

"Finished?" Ruby John said.

"I said my say."

"Okey. Now I'll say mine and I won't be long-winded about it. I don't know a damned thing about the kill and I don't believe Bannon got the dose in Death Street. You guys are trying to make it tough for me at a time when I'm bailing out of Death Street and the whole business."

Brinky leaned forward. "Says which?"

Ruby John drew a cigar from a vest-pocket, used a penknife to carefully snip off the end. "Bailing out. I'm through. Selling all my interests in Death Street—everything. Getting out."

"A guy'd have to have dough to buy you out, Ruby."

"Nick Popopulis has plenty dough, Sarge. This time next week he'll be the brass hat of Death Street."

"Boy, ain't that a bit o' news!" Johnny exclaimed.

"Nick is turning over four hundred thousand this afternoon. He couldn't lick me out of Death Street. For a long time he couldn't buy me. But I decided to sell at last. I'm washed up."

He struck a match, lighted his cigar, tossed the match away. He sighed: "And I'm sorry about Bannon. You're up a wrong alley."

A crackling sound started in the office. Brinky jumped up, pounced on the wastepaper basket into which Ruby John had negligently tossed the match. The sergeant yanked out some burning papers, stamped on them. Ruby John heaved his bulk toward a fire extinguisher, but there was no need of it. Brinky had dumped out all the papers, stamped out the flames. He rose from behind the desk with one hand in his pocket and a particularly blank and innocent look on his broad homely face.

"Whew!" he breathed out. "Got a nip o' something, Ruby?"

"Sorry, Sarge. I don't keep any booze at the business end."

"Okey. Come on, Johnny; we gotta git along."

Brinkhaus and Johnny Pell reached the street, began walking.

"Why the sudden up-and-go?" Johnny asked.

"I hadda git outside and think. I mooched something out o' that basket. Got it in my pocket here."

"What's it?"

"A lemon."

CHAPTER THREE

LARSEN TOSSED the lemon in the air, caught it, gazed down at it where it lay couched in his palm. He raised slightly amused eyes toward Sergeant Brinkhaus.

His voice was gentle: "After all, Brinky, a lemon is only a lemon. You can't suspect Ruby John because you found a lemon in his waste basket."

"I do," grunted Brinkhaus.

"Why?"

"Well, I asked Ruby for a drink. He don't carry no liquor in his office and he was telling the truth. I once heard he don't. But I asked him anyhow. Only reason he'd have a lemon in there'd be if he had liquor and soda around. Which he don't."

Larsen thought this over, turning the lemon round and round. "It's too farfetched," he said. He asked: "What do you suppose all these little pinpricks are on the skin?"

"You got me, Peter. I been wondering myself—"

A cop opened the door, said: "Popopulis out here."

"Me," said Brinky, in answer to Larsen's quizzical look, "I asked the Greek over. Send him in, Hen."

Nick Popopulis was small, chubby, olive-skinned. He wore a voluminous polo coat, a low-crowned derby slanted over one ear. He carried a stick.

"So what, so what?" he drawled, grinning, his eyes lazy.

Brinkhaus said: "I hear you're buying into Death Street."

"And I'm sore because my mug ain't in the papers about it. So what, so what?"

"Deal all kinda sewed up, huh?"

"In the bag," Nick swaggered. "Ruby I guess got tired of holding out. I been after that street for a coupla years. I'm gonna make it a hot number. With Death Street now, I'll have the north side sewed up, and you better tip them south side mugs that it ain't gonna be roses if they bounce down my street. Have a cigar, gents. Fifty-centers. I can't stand cheap ones."

"Four hundred thousand, huh?" Brinkhaus asked.

"That's the figger, Sarge. Four hundred grand. Outta my pocket, gents! And ten years ago I was hawking papers in Union Station. Treat me right, guy, and you'll be riding in a Rolls. Didja see my new Rolls? Say, a guy wants to write my b'ography—wants to write the story o' my life!"

Larsen said a little sadly: "You're a pretty smart man, Nick."

"I guess I'm kinda wise. I'm putting up a new ten story apartment house out on Inland. Calling it Grecian Towers. Gonna cost two hundred thousand—chicken feed." He snapped his fingers.

Brinkhaus, wrapped in thought, said: "Okey, Nick. You can go. Thanks for coming around."

Larsen nodded toward the closed door after Nick had gone out. "He'll get a grand funeral one day."

"When they shoot off their mouth like that, boss, they're ripe for it." He scratched his broad jaw, shook his head. "I can't figure out why Ruby's selling."

"Maybe he's one big shot who is wise," Larsen ventured. "Besides, he's getting old. He's getting out before he's too old. Brains, Brinky. Catch." He tossed the lemon.

Brinky hefted it, sighed, shoved it into his pocket. He was puzzled. He was not quick-witted, nor brilliant. Thought was labor for him. But he was tenacious, he was obstinate. He said stubbornly:

"Walt was in Ruby John's office last night."

Larsen shrugged, spread his palms. "Have it your own way. Only this: don't spring your suspicions while any newspaperman is within earshot."

Brinky stood up. "I'll wait till I hang it on Ruby." That dull, solid persistence was in his tone.

Larsen knew. Peter Larsen knew that once Brinkhaus set his mind on something neither argument nor coercion could make him deviate one inch from his chosen course. The news that Ruby John O'Kelly was selling out his gangdom concessions surprised Larsen, but not greatly. Ruby was resigning, undefeated. He had been a great underworld character, in strong with the political machine. No cop had ever hung a rap on him. Men had died mysteriously, several times Ruby John had been suspected, but never had he been brought to trial.

AN EVENING tabloid spread his picture. Brinky, eating sauerkraut and frankfurters, wetting his mustache in a mug of Cholly Koenigfelt's beer, studied the big face gravely, read Ruby John's valedictory. He was resigning, said Ruby John, with honors. Making way for a younger man. Going to buy a little vine-clad house in the country and raise flowers.

"Pfooey!" muttered Brinkhaus.

Cholly Koenigfelt said from the bar: "He's one guy is wise, Brinky. Getting out while the getting's good. A shmart feller, ja."

"I ain't saying yes or no. Only thing I'm saying, it don't look right. I can't lay my finger on it, Cholly, but it don't reason out."

"I hear he's giving a big dinner tonight. Dot so?"

"Yeah," Brinky grumbled.

He finished eating, polished off another mug of beer, said: *"Auf Wiedersehen,* Cholly," and went out into the dark street. His hand, in his pocket, was clamped around the lemon. It was a distance of four blocks to headquarters, and he walked heavily, his rubberless heels ringing on the pavement in the empty streets. His head bent, his eyes downcast, he entered the central room and was plodding methodically across the floor when Sergeant Keefe called:

"Hey, Brinky."

Brinkhaus looked up. The sergeant was pointing to a man sitting on a bench. The man rose. It was Homer, the filling-station operator.

"Uh, hello, Mr. Homer," Brinkhaus said.

Homer looked frightened. "I think I seen the guy."

"What guy?"

"That was driving that car last night."

"Where?"

Homer gulped. "It sounds goofy, Sergeant, and first off I thought I was cracked. I went home and thought about it, and the more I thought, the more I thought about this feller's face—well, finally I says to myself, I says, it looked like the guy. I—I seen him in City Hall today."

"Huh?"

"In City Hall. I'm thinking of adding onto my filling-station and went down City Hall to see about a permit. You gotta have a permit, you know, to add on like that. I seen the guy walking across the main hall."

"Going out?"

"Nope. And this is why I figgered I was cracked. It looked like the guy worked there. He didn't have on no coat or hat and he was carrying some papers in his hand."

Brinkhaus teetered back on his broad heels. "Um," he mumbled. And then he said: "You sure it looked like the guy was at the wheel o' the car?"

Homer nodded vigorously. "Right now, after thinking it over all day, I'm dead sure!" He added: "If he ain't, he's the guy's double then."

Brinkhaus felt a warm glow moving through his body. It was worthwhile information, yet it did not reveal to him the killer of Walt Bannon. He was wary of coincidence. It might have been the killer's car that had stopped at Homer's filling-station. He had a hunch it was. But you cannot take a hunch into court. He thought of poor Walt Bannon lying dead on the windy veranda, of Nancy Bannon in the hospital, almost out of her mind. And his hand tightened around the lemon.

Homer was rambling on: "Of course, I seen doubles before. There was a guy during the war that looked just like me but he was a white-collar guy, he was. One o' them guys reads secret writing and like that. Yeah. A brass hat mistook me for him once. I got quite a kick out of it."

"Listen," muttered Brinkhaus. "You come with me now."

He piloted Homer toward the door. Midway, he stopped and stared curiously at the man.

"Huh?" said Homer.

"Nothing," Brinkhaus grunted. "Come on."

CHAPTER FOUR

RUBY JOHN did things right. There were thirty persons at his table in the Roundhouse Club and he presided, red-faced and beaming, at the head. At his right sat Alderman Ken Martin, a

young man well on his way in the political catch-as-catch-can. Commissioner of Parks Mike Mulvaney was there; he had a pious mane
of white hair, a long sacerdotal face. Magistrate Joseph Oberdorfer
sat next to Queenie Meloy, a musical comedy star, and kept patting
her hand avuncularly. Tod Riley, the lightweight champ, stuck strictly to water. At the foot of the table sat Nick Popopulis wearing a
collar too high for him, and black pearl studs. He was saying to State
Senator Mojecki:

"And look at the sparkler there, Sam. A honey, huh?" He held his
hand up, wiggled it, and grinned like a fool. "Twenty grand, Sam. A
week's income." And he scoffed, adding: "Pfft! Chicken feed. Stick
around me, Senator.... Ruby John's a great guy, ain't he? I guess I never
understood him proper." And in an aside: "He dresses lousy, though.
Take this suit here I got on. Two hunnert bucks—not counting this
vest."

Nick kicked back his chair, said: "I could go for that Meloy dame
in a big way. I think she likes me."

The night club was crowded with others not connected with Ruby
John's party. The bar was beyond a chromium archway. Three bartend-
ers shone, scintillated in starched jackets, wing collars, brilliantined
hair. A couple of precinct detectives wandered about.

Brinkhaus and Homer climbed to a balcony. Homer was pop-eyed,
awed and confused by the lavishness of the scene below. They sat
down close to the gilded railing, and Brinkhaus said:

"That big table there. Most o' them are dancing now but they'll sit
down soon."

Homer nodded. His eyes were dazzled and he found it difficult to
systematically scrutinize each face below. After a while the music
stopped, laughter bubbled, conversation hummed, droned. Homer
plucked at Brinky's sleeve.

"Th-there."

"Where?"

"Other side o' the table, about the middle. On the right o' that lady
wearing the green dress."

"That young feller?"

"He's laughing right now, and sitting down."

"Okey."

They stood up, went downstairs, reached the hallway below and
walked through the draped foyer to the front door. The door was not

locked. Brinkhaus led the way into the street. Cabs and limousines were parked alongside the curb and chauffeurs stood in groups, tapping feet on the cold pavement, talking.

Homer was choked with excitement. "Ain't—ain't you going to pinch that guy?"

"He'll keep," Brinkhaus said, piloting Homer down the street as far as the main boulevard. "You see, Mr. Homer, it still is only a co-incidence. You can't haul that kinda stuff into court. Now you go ahead home and don't mention this to nobody. I'll be seeing you again."

He stood on the windy corner after Homer had departed. He nibbled at the end of a three cent stogie, lighted a match, cupped the flame in his hands. Then he began retracing his steps up Death Street. The street glowed, vibrated at night. He paused in front of number 85, heard the crash of nine-pins going down. He sighed, whistled a few bars off-key, pushed open the door and entered the smoke-shop.

A dozen-odd men were bowling. The man with the green eyeshade was behind the counter.

Brinky leaned on the counter. "Who's upstairs?"

"Nobody."

"I'd kinda like to go up."

"There ain't nobody up there," the man insisted.

"Locked, huh?"

"Sure."

"Suppose you and me go up and you open the door."

"Honest, I can't do that, Sarge."

Brinkhaus moved slowly to the side door, opened it, turned and looked at the man. "Come on."

"Listen, boss. Ruby John's up to the Roundhouse—"

"You want I should go up and shoot them locks off?"

The man complained: "Aw, gee…" But he opened the cash register, withdrew a bunch of keys. "I'll get dutch for this."

He kept muttering and complaining as they climbed the stairs. Brinkhaus said nothing. He waited patiently while the man stalled at the lock. When the door was finally opened, he walked in and switched on the lights. He sighed, crossed the outer office, entered Ruby John's private office and turned on the lights there. He stood for a moment moving his eyes about, drawing slowly on his cigar.

Then he said: "Okey. Sit down."

"B-but I gotta tend store—"

"You sit down there and keep your mouth shut for a while."

The man sat down, grimaced, pouted.

Brinky went to the desk, rummaged among a mass of papers there, picked up one after another, laid it down again. His face was blank, expressionless, even a little dull. He withdrew the lemon from his pocket, peered closely at the many pin-pricks on the yellow skin. He gathered up every paper in sight, plucked several calendars from the wall. Sitting down at the desk, he rummaged through his pockets, pulled out several packets of matches. He laid his cigar carefully on the edge of an ash-tray, jerked his chair nearer the desk.

CHAPTER FIVE

RUBY JOHN was the life of the party. It was almost midnight and he was still going strong. He wore a cone-shaped paper hat atop which a little bell jingled. His face was flushed with liquor and merriment, and he had just sent around a ten dollar gold piece to every guest, as a souvenir. And he sat beside Queenie Meloy, patting her regal back.

It was at this time that a headwaiter bent over Ruby John's shoulder and whispered. Directly opposite, another waiter was bending over the shoulder of a young man who a moment before had been laughing, singing. The messages were delivered simultaneously. And instantly the glances of Ruby John and the young man met, held, steadied.

Ruby John was the first to rise. He swung his bulk hugely around the end of the table. His jowls sagged, his mouth hardened. He reached the young man and towered for a brief moment beside him.

He muttered: "Come on."

"Whuh—what do you think—"

"Come on. Keep shut. Let me talk."

The young man stumbled at the heels of Ruby John. Ruby John flung aside paper streamers, elbowed his way roughly, his jaw hardening in the midst of his flopping jowls. Horns and noise-makers blared and screeched about him. He struck down a toy balloon savagely. Two young men in tuxedos fell in beside him.

One said: "What's up?"

"Leave this to me," he growled.

He had just enough liquor on board to be headstrong, reckless. Plowing his way through the crowd, he reached the chromium archway. He clawed irritably at more paper streamers. And then he caught a picture of himself in a mirror. He was still wearing the cone-shaped hat. He tore it off, stamped it underfoot.

The young man bumped into him, reeled away.

"Stay on your feet," Ruby John muttered. "Pull yourself together. This is a snap."

The young man was quite drunk. His lower lip drooped. He looked sick and uncertain and his knees kept wobbling. Ruby John hauled him through the crowd in the bar. They reached the corridor and went down it to the foyer.

Brinkhaus and Johnny Pell were standing there. One end of Brinky's muffler had worked out of his coat, was dangling on the outside. He wore a slightly apologetic expression.

He said in his thick, husky voice: "Sorry, Ruby, to go busting up your party but—"

Ruby John blurted: "You ain't busting up no party o' mine, copper!"

Gimlet-eyed, Johnny Pell pounced on his arm. "Cut it, mug!" he rasped.

Ruby John tugged. "You bum, leggo—"

Johnny Pell bared his teeth. "Fat-head, we're trying to make this quiet!" He jerked his chin. "Get your hat and coat."

The intoxicated young man started to duck back toward the hallway.

"You!" Brinkhaus barked.

Johnny Pell leaped, caught hold of the young man's arm. "Your name Swain?"

"Uh—ah—why, y-yes."

Johnny Pell shoved him toward the check room. "Get your duds."

The young man spun around several times, fell against Ruby John. He panted: "John—John—"

The two men in tuxedos appeared magically and one snapped: "What's up, Ruby?"

Johnny Pell sang out: "Okey, Brinky. We'll take 'em without their duds."

He grabbed Ruby John's arm. "Out, big shot."

One of the tuxedoed men shouldered Johnny roughly, rasped: "Lay off him, copper!"

Johnny struck with his blackjack and the tuxedoed man went down. Brinkhaus jammed his gun against the back of the other tuxedo and its occupant dropped a half-drawn gun to the floor, broke into a nervous, idiotic little laugh.

But Johnny was ruthless. The idiotic laugh was chopped short by a descending blackjack.

"Stop that, Johnny!" Brinkhaus said.

Johnny glared. "No palooka's going to yank a gun on this burg's police department!" He swivelled, slapped his hand against Ruby John's arm, tightened the fingers. "Grab the drunk, Brinky, and let's get out of here before a flock o' conscientious objectors pile on us."

"Oke, Johnny."

They manhandled the two men through the door, hustled them across the sidewalk. Swain was heaved into the front seat. Brinky nodded Ruby John into the rear seat and climbed in beside him. Johnny, behind the wheel of the flivver, stepped on the self-starter. The car backfired once or twice, then jolted off, rattled and vibrated down Death Street between lights, red, green, blue, that winked seductively.

After a few minutes Big John growled: "So what's the bad news, copper?"

Brinkhaus shrugged. "Murder, John."

"No kidding."

"I wouldn't kid you, John."

Swain looked around, his mouth wide, his face ghastly.

The jolting of the flivver made his lips flutter as though robbed of every muscle.

Ruby John drawled: "Still trying to hang it on me, huh?"

"If we don't hang it on you, John, you still won't enjoy all that dough you made."

"Jokes!"

"Nick Popopulis ain't much of a joke, I'd say, was I asked."

Ruby John stiffened.

Brinkhaus sighed, said: "But I guess we'll hang it on you. And Mr. Swain there."

"Me!" cried Swain.

"You just happened to drive that there car that brung Walt Bannon's body home.... Johnny, that's the second red stop light you piled through. There ain't no fire, there ain't no riot. Everything is hunky-dory."

"It sure gets me," Johnny Pell complained, "the way they stick up new stop lights here all the time."

INSPECTOR LARSEN said to the Commissioner of Buildings and Structures: "I regret to report that your confidential secretary, Amos Swain, is to be indicted along with Ruby John O'Kelly and two others, for the murder of Walter Bannon, the newspaperman."

The commissioner frowned, shook his head bitterly. "Terrible, terrible, Inspector! I always trusted Swain implicitly. What are the details?"

"The murder apparently was an accident. Swain and the others may get off with a manslaughter rap. It took place in Ruby John's office. They beat Bannon up. Your secretary, it seems, got panicky—lost his head. He hit Bannon with an iron doorstop. He and two of O'Kelly's men drove the body to Bannon's home. Swain was at the wheel. But Swain—Ruby John—the others—will be safer in jail than on the streets. The Greek—Nick Popopulis—would surely crucify them.

"Bannon was apparently on his way up Smith—they call it Death—Street, to get a bottle of liquor to take to a friend. He happened to see Swain duck into number 85. Knew he was your secretary. Naturally, Bannon had a nose for news. He listened outside the door, in the hallway. The man who watched the cigar stand on the ground floor sent up a warning to O'Kelly—and they jumped Bannon, yanked him into the outer office. They tried to find out how much he had heard and suspected the worst. He refused to tell. They locked him in O'Kelly's private office and the gang of them went into a huddle in the outer office, discussing ways and means.

"Bannon apparently knew he was on the spot. Sitting in the private office, he couldn't phone because the phone there was an extension from the one in the outer office, and the switch in the outer office was off. Though he'd listened in the hall, he had picked up no details. He only suspected some connection between Ruby John and your office. He figured they would try to beat the truth out of him. He was not a well man, and he didn't know how much he could stand.

"He always carried a lemon or two in his pocket. We must reason that he found a clean, unused pen point in the desk, inserted it in a holder. It was a long chance, but he was in a tight spot. There was a big paper calendar hanging on the wall. He punctured the lemon many times with the pen point, wrote on the calendar with lemon juice. He wrote: 'Ruby and Swain of Department of Buildings and Structures in cahoots. This may be my swan song.' He added the time, the date, and signed his name.

"A hard-working sergeant of mine, Herman Brinkhaus, was on the case. He found the lemon in O'Kelly's office and associated it with Bannon. But that was not evidence. A filling station operator, who had put a bulb in a headlight of the car Swain drove, gave Brinkhaus an idea by happening to remark about a man he knew during the war who was an expert on secret writing.

"Well, Brinkhaus—we call him Brinky—got into O'Kelly's office last night and went over every piece of paper in the place, looking for secret writing. And he found it. You may know that lemon juice writing remains invisible until you hold the paper over a flame, when the writing appears in brown. It clinched the case, and your secretary, confronted with this evidence, gave the other details.

"He knew about your secret conference in which it was practically settled that a month hence you would condemn every building in Death Street. The buildings were to be razed, the street widened. He went to O'Kelly with this news and O'Kelly saw a way of topping off his fortune in a grand way. And he cut Swain in on the profits, naturally.

"He got four hundred thousand dollars out of the Greek for complete control of a street that in a month would be a white elephant!"

The commissioner said: "By Godfrey!" And then he said: "You know, Larsen, I should like to meet this man—er—what's his name—Brink—"

"Brinkhaus." Larsen strolled to a window, smiled, turned about. "I'll tell him. I saw him about twenty minutes ago sneaking down a side street with a bunch of flowers under his arm. I think he was taking them to Walt Bannon's wife."

STRANGLE HOLD

**BRINKHAUS WANTED
TO KNOW WHAT WAS
BEHIND THAT DOOR;
THE MURDER TRAIL
THAT HE AND DAN
WERE FOLLOWING LED
STRAIGHT TO IT**

CHAPTER ONE

ON THE EIGHTH FLOOR

IT WAS ten past three when George P. Hessler entered the ornate, crowded lobby of the Exchange Building. He was a stocky man, well groomed, and carried a snakewood stick. There was a look of bitter concentration in his eyes; his white mustache, neatly clipped, was drawn resolutely downward at one corner by the determined warp of his mouth. He looked straight before him as he strode through the shifting crowd in the lobby. People bumped and shied off his solid shoulders. He growled, muttered under his breath.

His face indicated that under ordinary circumstances he might be an amiable and genial man; but now he appeared strictly purposeful, blind to all things but that which he held fixed in his mind.

He reached a bank of four elevators. One car was open, and this he entered, stood in the center of it, champing on his mustache, glowering. Four other persons entered the car. The starter clicked something in his hand, and the operator closed the doors. The car started smoothly upward.

"Floors, please?"

George P. Hessler growled:

"Simmons, the attorneys."

"Eight, sir."

"Six," said a woman.

The occupants of the car looked at Hessler, exchanged amused glances. He thumped impatiently on the floor with his stick, sighed, inhaled, exhaled loudly and as if with vast remorse. He blew his nose, and was thrusting his handkerchief back into his pocket when the lights went out, the car stopped.

The operator worked his controls.

George P. Hessler snapped:

Dan spun and drove at the door. Edgar's gun dropped to the floor.

"Well, what's the matter?"

"Power's off. Be calm. Just a minute."

"Disgraceful!"

The stick stumped. The occupants of the car moved about uneasily. The operator tried to use the phone, but could raise no one. His hand remained on the controls in the darkness, and he said again:

"Be calm. Power'll be on in a minute. Don't get excited."

"Is anyone excited?" demanded George P. Hessler irritably.

A woman said haltingly:

"Is there any danger?"

George P. Hessler said distinctly:

"No danger, madam. Probably some amateur electrician." He was silent for a moment, and then his voice rasped: "Operator, can't you get in touch with—haven't you a phone?"

"All the power's off, sir."

"Bah!"

Again the stick rapped the linoleum floor.

"I should have walked up." He added: "Probably would have been good for me, anyhow." A loud sigh followed. "Incompetence! Rank incompetence!"

A woman's voice quavered: "It's so dark in here!"

"Tut, tut," came George P. Hessler's gruff voice. "No danger. Only it seems to me that some provision should be made—"

The lights flashed on.

"About time," growled George P. Hessler.

The operator worked the control, and the car began rising slowly. It stopped at the sixth floor to let out a woman. It rose again, passed several, oozed to a stop at eight. The door slid open and George P. Hessler sailed out, made his way hard-heeled down the corridor.

His jaw was thrust out, his eyes glittered, and he gripped his stick rather like a cudgel.

The two shots boomed, slam-banged violently in the corridor. George P. Hessler stopped walking. He came to a stop gradually, dragging one foot after the other and looking dumbly back over his shoulder.

He saw a door moving slowly shut; the door worked on a pneumatic hinge and above it he saw a red globe marked "Fire Exit." Directly beside him a glass-paneled office door opened, and a man looked at him.

George P. Hessler looked back at the man and stood teetering soggily from one foot to the other.

The man said: "My God—what's the matter?"

"Huh," grunted George P. Hessler.

It was the last sound his lips made. He fell suddenly, as if up until that moment he had been upheld by props and the props had been knocked from beneath him. He fell so hard that his hat flew from his head, rolled in a complete circle and came back to stop against his head.

His hair, snow white, fell across his forehead with the limpness of damp cornsilk.

A girl appeared in the doorway.

The man turned on her, cried: "He's been shot! Get—get—" He jabbed an index finger towards a telephone. "Get—" Then he brushed the girl aside and ran to the phone himself, rang the manager's office.

Other doors opened and people ventured into the corridor. A slab-cheeked, oldish man in gray tweeds came striding hatless down the hall, demanding, "What's—"

Men and women pointed and made little outcries.

The slab-cheeked man walked on, reached the body. He did not kneel down. He put his hands on his hips, gnawed at his lower lip. He glanced up shrewdly at the girl standing in the doorway.

"Who did this?"

"I—I d-don't—"

"I saw him first," her companion said, coming from his office. "I heard the shots—opened the door. He was falling. I—I don't think he was coming here. We're in perfumes—"

"Of course not," the slab-cheeked man said. "He's one of my clients. D'you call the police?"

"The manager—"

"Good enough."

The slab-cheeked man knelt, probed with a hand. He stopped probing, rubbed his jaws, said, "H'm," reflectively.

Then he reached down. He gently closed one eyelid, then the other. The eyelids remained closed.

He rose; his face was wrinkled with a mixture of bitterness and remorse—but his voice was clipped, vacant. "Yes, of course. Dead."

HERMAN BRINKHAUS, sergeant of detectives out of police headquarters, pried his way into one of the four compartments of the revolving door and was ejected forcibly into the lobby by the man who followed in the next compartment. He regained his balance, removed his hat, which had been bounced down onto his nose, and placed it back dead-level on his head again.

"Say, ain't this a swell dump, though?" said his companion.

"You have to push me that way?"

"Hanh? Oh. Oh, I'm sorry, Brinky."

A uniformed patrolman jerked a thumb. "Eight, Brinky. Hi, Dan."

"Hi," said Detective Dan McCauley. "Eight, you said?"

"Yowssuh."

Dan nudged Brinkhaus. "Eight, Brinky."

"Yeah," said Brinky.

The two men headed toward the elevator bank. Dan was six paces ahead; Brinky followed at his customary lagging gait, a broad, plain-looking man of medium size with a hairbrush mustache bunched up beneath his broad nose. Dan was almost as tall as men come—young and towering, with shoulders broad as a church door and a jaw that looked as if it could take punishment.

He had a windy blue eye and a loud voice, and he had been in plainclothes just one month. Brinky was breaking him in, a fact that had caused several wisecracks to issue from the district attorney's office, among them the observation that it was a case of the blind leading the blind.

The elevator car stopped at the eighth floor, and far down the corridor Brinkhaus saw a group of civilians and a few uniformed policemen. Dan was off ahead, striding long-legged, with his snowplow jaw in the air, his chest out and his arms swinging.

"Hi, guys!" Dan greeted the policemen; and to the uniformed sergeant: "Hi, Sarge." His eyebrows bent, he jerked a finger downward, said out of the side of his mouth: "Who's this?"

The slab-cheeked man said:

"You're from the bureau?"

"Yeah, from the bureau. I'm McCauley. This is my partner, Sergeant Brinkhaus. Who killed this guy?"

"Just a minute, Dan," Brinkhaus said. He looked around placidly at the crowd. "Anybody see this happen?"

The slab-cheeked man said: "My name is Simmons, of Simmons & Simmons, attorneys. We have offices on this floor. This gentleman—Mr. Couse—occupies this office. He heard the shots, he said, and opened the door and saw Mr. Hessler going down. Hessler's the name. I dare say he was on his way to see me."

The uniformed sergeant held up two fingers. "Shot twice, Brinky."

Brinkhaus bowed towards Mr. Couse. "You see anybody in the hall?"

"No. I saw this man looking down that way. I looked too. I didn't see anybody. I—I saw that fire exit door closing, but didn't connect the two until several minutes later."

The building manager said: "You see, just before the shooting occurred, the power was shut off. The elevators were stalled wherever they happened to be for at least three minutes. There was a lot of dashing about, and then the starter downstairs decided to look at the switches. The room is off a corridor back of the elevators. He found that all the switches had been thrown off. He threw them on and"—the manager spread his hands—"the power simply went on again."

Dan McCauley's eyes widened. "Can you tie that?"

Brinky was kneeling beside the body. "I guess this old gentleman was followed here. I'd say by two guys. One chucked the switch off while the other beat it up the fire stairways. He reached this floor before the elevator did....H'm. Two shots—smack in the back. Them guys knew where he was going—and they knew why." He sat back, scratched the top of his head, looked up at the attorney Simmons. "Know why he was coming to see you?"

Simmons was standing spread-legged, his hands thrust in the pocket of his tweed jacket. He shook his head briefly.

"No. No, I don't." He sighed, blank-eyed. "I can't imagine. Of course, there are any number of things he might have come for."

"F'r instance?"

"Oh"—Simmons shrugged—"advice on legal matters involving a transaction of business. Advice on taxes. But I can't imagine why—specifically."

"Know him personally well?"

"No. We saw each other only on business. He's a very wealthy man. Made it in advertising. Got a wife—a son—so on." He frowned, said in a lowered voice, gesturing with an index finger. "I suppose you—the police—will break it to his family."

Brinkhaus sighed. "Yeah, we usually git those nice jobs." He rose. "He come in his own car or—"

"Not in his own," Simmons said, "I went down to see. His car isn't about."

Brinky said to Dan: "Buzz the morgue, Dan."

"Okey, Brinky, I'll buzz the morgue," boomed Dan.

Brinkhaus said: "I'll take possession of his dough and things." He knelt down, went through the dead man's pockets, took out a wallet containing sixty dollars, a watch and chain, two rings from the man's hands. From the overcoat pocket he took a silver cigarette case and a piece of crumpled paper.

Still kneeling, he unfolded the paper until it became a green oblong. He peered down at it.

"This is funny," he said. "Here's a check for five thousand made out to cash."

Simmons leaned forward. "Who signed it?"

"Him," Brinkhaus said. "Mr. Hessler."

"Is it endorsed?"

"No."

The attorney and the sergeant of detectives looked at each other for a long moment.

CHAPTER TWO

NOTHING TO GO ON

MRS. HESSLER sat sobbing now. She sat in the spacious, rich living room of the Hessler home; she was a tiny woman, with tiny black patent leather pumps worrying the carpet. She was a gentlewoman, Brinkhaus knew. And Brinky sat poking the index finger of his right hand into the palm of his left. His face looked dull and glum and sad, congested; he bent 'way over to look at the dull black glow of his seventeen-dollar shoes. A maid moved about in the drawing room adjoining.

Dan McCauley stood by a French window, chewing on his lip, staring slit-eyed into the garden. His face looked hard as nails, but he made it look that way because he was really soft inside. The sight of the white-haired little woman, the sound of her sobbing, made the big young man writhe inwardly.

Brinkhaus rose at last and went across the room and stood beside Mrs. Hessler. He laid his broad, hamlike hand on her shoulder. He patted the shoulder. He took the hand away and shoved it into his pocket. Looking up, he saw Dan gazing at him. Dan jerked his chin towards the door, his lips formed silent words: "Let's scram before I go nuts!"

Brinky looked at Mrs. Hessler: "Uh—well, we'll be gitting on, Mrs. Hessler."

Dan McCauley came lunging over from the window, flattened a palm against the air, said out of the side of his mouth: "We'll get them babies did him in, Mrs. Hessler. Me and my partner, Sergeant Brinkhaus here." He went on to the doorway, towered there, waiting.

Mrs. Hessler stopped sobbing and stared bleakly at the floor.

"Poor George. He never harmed anyone...."

"Um," muttered Sergeant Brinkhaus, looking at his hat; and then: "Well, when your boy comes in, Mrs. Hessler, ask him to shoot over to headquarters. Maybe he'll know something. Well"—he made an awkward gesture—"'g'-by, ma'am."

Brinkhaus and McCauley went out, walked down the veranda steps, took the long cement walk to the street. Dan said: "I'm burnt up! This kinda stuff burns me up!"

Walking, Brinky had the side to side roll of a heavy man. His narrow-brimmed hat rode uncompromisingly on his boxlike head, and beneath its brim his brown, pacific eyes stared straight ahead.

They took a bus to City Hall Square, walked two blocks and entered the central room of police headquarters. The central room was quiet, claustral, with the uniformed man at the desk droning like a prelate into a telephone. Brinky and Dan went upstairs to the bureau, found Chief Inspector Larsen sitting behind a broad, flat-topped desk. The yellow-maned chief of the bureau laid down his pen, sat back.

"**HESSLER,** huh?" he said, drawing a long forefinger across his lower lip.

"We been out to see his missus," Brinkhaus said dully. He sat down, held his hat in his hands. "She ain't got no idea at all. I asked the maid. She ain't, either."

"One thing, though," Dan barged in, "this maid says for the past week the old man and the kid was hardly civil to each other."

Larsen said: "Where was the boy at the time?"

"Out!" barked Dan. He took a turn up and down the room, barked again: "Out!" His bushy brows bent and he went on: "The maid says about two-thirty this afternoon there was a phone call for the kid. Some dame. The kid put his hat on and left. He left in his roadster."

Brinky added dully: "I told Mrs. Hessler she should tell him to shoot over here when he comes in."

Larsen sighed. He picked up the wrinkled check, gazed at it. "What's your idea about this, Brinky—any?"

"I got a hunch, Peter. I got a hunch the old gentleman wrote it out. Then he either changed his mind or somebody else did."

"Somebody else did what?"

"Somebody else changed their mind. The old gentleman made the check out and whoever he made it out for refused it. That—or Hessler himself changed his mind after making it out.

"I asked his lawyer, but the lawyer didn't know nothing. On the way on out to Mrs. Hessler's I stopped off at Hessler's office. The staff threw a fit. They liked him. His manager didn't know nothing, either; said Hessler left at a quarter to two."

"Did he receive a phone call before he left?"

Brinky shook his head.

"No. The manager said, though, that Hessler was kinda absorbed all day—hardly talked at all, and scowled a lot to himself like he had things on his mind."

Larsen put the check down, wagged his head.

"This is—well, this is out of a clear sky. I don't like it. I—"

The door whipped open and Assistant District Attorney Wells Gatlin came in. He was a small, dapper man with sharp little black eyes, a small, bitter mouth. He kicked the door shut, puffed his meager chest and drew down one corner of his mouth. His eyes flashed.

He rasped: "Thanks for notifying the district attorney's office!"

Brinkhaus raised his palms. "Well, you see—"

"Oh, I see all right! Maybe it's some new rule I haven't heard about. A murder pulled in a big downtown office building and I get notified of it an hour later from the morgue! What's this, a new rule? Is it?"

"Ah, calm yourself," Dan said from the other side of the room. "It was open and shut. There was nothing there to see. The guy was bumped off and the guy or guys that killed him lammed and nobody saw them."

"That's what *you* say!"

Dan flipped a toothpick neatly from his teeth, said offhand: "Ask my partner, Brinky."

Gatlin laughed scornfully. "Ask your partner Brinky!" he rasped.

Dan slung his legs across the office and shoved his big face down close to Gatlin's. "Was that a crack?"

"Just a minute," Larsen said, rising, leaving his fingertips on the desk. "Just what is wrong, Gatlin?"

"What's wrong! Damn it, haven't I told you? The district attorney's office was not apprised of—"

Brinkhaus muttered: "Was my fault, Inspector. I didn't see any need, so I just—"

"You see?" piped Gatlin, straining; he pointed at Brinkhaus, still looked at Larsen. *"He* didn't think there was any need. I always thought it was a matter of custom, of routine, that—"

Larsen sighed, offered: "You've free access to Brinky's notes if you want them."

"I don't want them!" snapped Gatlin; he added spitefully: "They probably would be unintelligible anyhow."

"That," boomed Dan, striking the desk, "is a crack!"

Gatlin whirled. "Suppose it is?" he cried.

"Cut this," Larsen bit in. "Both of you." He paused, went on to Gatlin: "As I said, Sergeant Brinkhaus's notes, if you want them, are here. I'm getting tired, Gatlin, of your histrionics. Tired. D'you mind going?"

The door opened and a clerk said: "There's a Mr. Wallace Hessler out here—"

"The boy," Brinkhaus muttered in an aside to Larsen.

"Send him in," Larsen said, and sat down.

GATLIN stood smouldering in a corner, and Dan stood in another corner chewing on a match and eying him from a vast and scornful height. Brinky sat in a chair, quiet, stolid, a ripple of a frown on his forehead, his placid brown eyes watching the doorway through which, in a moment, young Wallace Hessler entered.

Larsen said: "Good day, Mr. Hessler. This is Sergeant Brinkhaus, and there's Detective McCauley—on the case. That is Mr. Gatlin, of the district attorney's office. Sit down, please."

Larsen leaned back, flicked a look at Brinkhaus.

Wallace Hessler was tall, fair, in his early twenties. He evidently had been made aware of his father's death, for a bit of a shock still remained in his eyes, and it was obvious that he kept his lips taut with an effort.

Brinky leaned forward, bracing one elbow on a knee. "You got any idea of anybody had a grudge against your pa?"

"No, I haven't."

"You got any idea where your pa might ha' gone this afternoon?"

"I'm afraid—I haven't."

"You got a phone call about two thirty this afternoon, didn't you?"

"Why—yes."

"Where'd you go?"

"Why, to see a friend. A girl. I had been waiting for the telephone call. I drove the car, picked her up and we went to the Lenox Grill, tea dancing."

"What's her name?" Dan barked from the far side of the room.

Young Hessler looked up. "Florence Somers."

Brinkhaus asked: "She live near you?"

"No. She lives at the Monterey Hotel on Ocean Pike."

Dan said: "What time'd you hit the Lenox?"

"At three."

Gatlin snapped: "What's this girl do?" He left the corner and came over to stand in front of Hessler. "What's she do?"

Hessler colored. "Why, she's an entertainer—a dancer—at the Wigwam Club."

"A dancer, eh?" Gatlin sneered.

Hessler stood up, tall and lean. His fists clenched. "Am I expected to stand for insults?" he said in a low voice that shook.

"Who insulted you?"

"Your tone—"

Brinkhaus had risen. He moved Gatlin aside and said to Hessler: "Were you and your dad on the outs kinda?"

Hessler's lips tightened, his eyes clouded and became evasive.

"Yes, we were. I feel rotten about it—the way he died and—"

"What was it about?"

Hessler clenched his fists and stared at the floor, his mouth working.

Gatlin snapped: "What was it about?"

Hessler looked up, shrugged. "Silly thing. I had a little disagreement at college and came home. I wanted to leave college and go to work with Dad in his advertising business. He wanted me to finish college. I—I refused to go back."

"When'd you make that up?" Gatlin sneered.

"It's true!" Hessler cried, his eyes burning.

Gatlin leveled an arm. "Was your allowance cut?"

Hessler inhaled deeply and red color flooded his face, his lips twitched.

"Yes, it was." There was a moment of silence and then he suddenly cried: "You're as much as intimating that I had something to do with—"

"If the cap fits," Gatlin droned ironically.

Brinkhaus turned to Larsen.

"I guess we don't need Mr. Hessler any more, Peter." He turned back to the boy. "Thanks for coming around. You can go now." The sergeant's broad brown face was expressionless, his round gentle eyes rested vacantly on young Hessler. "Yeah, you can go, Mr. Hessler."

Hessler bowed briefly, turned, strode out of the office.

Gatlin hummed to himself, sauntered elaborately to the door, turned and said casually:

"Well, good day, master minds."

He sauntered out.

Dan barked: "Hey, what's that mug acting so happy about? Hey, was that the birdie he gave us?"

"Well," sighed Brinkhaus. "That's that. I can see Gatlin is gonna ride that kid, and that's what I want."

"Hanh? Why?" blurted Dan.

Brinky said: "So we can work our own angles without having Gatlin there getting under our dogs all the time."

CHAPTER THREE

THE ROOM IN THE MONTEREY

AT TEN that night Brinkhaus walked down South Broad Street and came to Brick Square, which lies on the tatterdemalion west hem of the ninth precinct. It was a cold night, brisk, with pale scud driving across the moon.

Brinky inhaled. When hard put in a mental way, the homespun sergeant walked the quiet back streets at night, aimlessly. But tonight he had a destination, a purpose.

He planked his seventeen-dollar shoes across Brick Square, followed a winding narrow street that gradually drew nearer the hum and clangor of night life. He came into Stable Alley from the west; it was a narrow thoroughfare where in the days gone by hundreds of truck horses had stabled. Now it boasted some of the drabbest and some of the swankiest speaks and clubs in the whole city of Portsend. The cobbles remained; the same sidewalks, half the width of an ordinary sidewalk; the brick houses, dull red, very narrow or very broad.

Up the street it said *The Wigwam*, in lights that one moment were red, the next blue, alternately, all night long till dawn split. It was the cream of the swank. The doorman looked like a cigar store Indian and spoke like an Italian—which he was.

"Hello, Pio," Brinkhaus said.

"Same t' you, Sarge; an' how-a you feel, yes?"

"Sure."

"So, yes!"

Brinky climbed the seven stone steps. The doors were open. The blue glow in the lobby was weird. The hat check girl, dressed like a squaw—her name was Sonia Wilenski—reached for his things, but Brinkhaus shook his head. Joe Barnelli came into the lobby through a draped doorway. He was tall, with fine olive skin, a clean-cut jaw, handsome black eyes. He was young, not over thirty. His evening clothes were the last word. A dark, gentle smile came to his face and he held out a hand. His voice was low, liquid:

"Stranger."

"Hello, Joe."

They shook. Their hands parted, and Joe, his heels together, his body straight, looked quizzically down into Brinky's face, while his lips formed a silent question: "Trouble?"

Brinkhaus shook his head, said:

"My credit good for a stein of beer?"

Joe laughed softly, took Brinky's arm and piloted him through the drapes, down a corridor, into the bar. A dozen-odd men had feet on the brass rail. On through, an archway gave into the long dining and dancing room, with its white linen, its soft lights, its polished floor. Almost everyone wore evening clothes.

Brinky and Joe leaned on the bar. Joe took water and Brinky took a stein of beer.

"Business good, Joe?"

"Fair."

The quiet gaze he had placed on Brinky was polite and friendly, but the depths of his dark eyes were still quizzical.

Brinkhaus took a long drink. Foam frosted his mustache. He wiped it off with a handkerchief.

"Joe"—the sergeant set his mug down—"could I maybe see Florence Somers quiet-like?"

Joe smiled with an I-thought-so expression passing across his eyes and vanishing as he lifted his chin and said:

"Okey, Brinky. She goes on in fifteen minutes. I'll"—he nodded towards the rear—"let you use my office. I'll send her there."

Brinky went into Joe's office, took off his brown hat, placed it on the desk. He looked at his hands and his forehead wrinkled. The heavy walls muffled the sounds in the bar, made them seem distant, like the sound of a sea-shell held to the ear. He heard the jazz band start; it too sounded far away. He sat on the edge of the desk, looked down at a silver-framed portrait of a large-bosomed, smiling woman: Joe's mother.

The door opened and the girl came in, round-eyed. Her hair was raven black, casque-like.

She wore a Shantung silk robe over her dancing tights, and soft-soled silver slippers.

Joe smiled at Brinkhaus, then drew back into the hall, closing the door.

"Yes?" the girl said.

"You know I'm Brinkhaus, from the cops, miss. Sit down here."

SHE KEPT her round eyes fixed on him while she moved across the room, let herself down quietly into the chair he had indicated. She held the robe tight at her waist, looked up at him steadily, searchingly, with the faintest pucker between her penciled brows.

Brinkhaus held out both palms and stared gloomily at them. "O' course, you know about old Hessler being knocked off this afternoon. We had Wallace over to the bureau, just as a matter o' form kinda. He said 's how you and him went dancing this afternoon at the Lenox. For tea, or something."

Her quiet, restrained voice said:

"Yes, for tea."

Brinkhaus took his gaze from his hands and placed it gently on the girl's lovely face. "You ever meet the old man?"

She shook her head. Her "No" was very quiet.

"O' course, at the time the old man was killed you and Wallace were—um—dancing at the Lenox."

"I suppose we were."

Brinky looked up at his palms again. "You and him—well, in love sorta?"

"Just friends. He's a nice boy. I like him."

"You worked here long?"

"About two months."

"When'd you meet Wallace?"

"Oh, about six weeks ago."

"Here?"

She nodded.

He looked at her again, making a frank appraisal of her face. She colored a bit, her lips shook, her eyes flickered and finally wandered away. She stared across the room for a long minute, then turned suddenly to him and said:

"What's the matter?"

He smiled. "Ain't anything the matter, miss. Just routine. I didn't want to pester you, but I hope you don't mind. You can go now, thanks." She rose and walked swiftly to the door. She opened it, turned to look at him, seemed about to start back into the room again; but then she went out rapidly, closed the door, leaving a faint perfume in the room.

Brinkhaus looked at his hat, put it on, went slowly to the door, his head bent and his eyes thoughtful. He made his way back into the bar, saw Joe at the far end.

Joe wore a faint, enigmatic smile. Brinkhaus went up to him and said:

"Thanks, Joe."

"Have another stein?"

"Not now. Say, Joe"—he dropped his voice—"how long's she worked here?"

"Two months."

"Suppose you kinda seen her on the stage or something and then give her a job here, huh?"

"No. I got her from the Acme Agency. They supply talent all over town. She's made a hit here. Wait and see her dance."

Brinkhaus waited. He saw the lights diminish, saw a spotlight spring to life on a balcony, make a white pool on the dance floor.

Flo Somers cartwheeled out. The crowd applauded.

She was, he saw, an eccentric dancer, able to stand on one leg and spin the other round and round. Joe stood beside him, tall and debonair, drawing on a cork-tipped cigarette, a shining light in his eyes. Brinkhaus saw how hard she worked. She did not smile much. As the music speeded up, she made several missteps. He could see the chagrin in her eyes. Joe frowned, puzzled. Doing a back handspring, she fumbled and flopped. Her face went scarlet. Her jaw set and she worked harder.

Brinky thought he saw tears in her eyes. She finished the number and cartwheeled off. The crowd applauded, but she did not reappear. The orchestra members craned their necks. Finally the music stopped and the master of ceremonies went to the loud-speaker microphone, announced the next number.

Joe smiled wryly.

"That's the first time she made any slips."

Brinkhaus said: "Well, I got to git along, Joe."

BRINKY climbed down the seven steps, passed the Italian dressed as an Indian, and walked on down Stable Alley. Every now and then the blare of a jazz band burst from the open doorway of some night club. Lights winked up and down the street, taxicabs sped, braked sharply.

He stopped at a corner, drummed his heel on the curb, then walked several steps and heaved his broad, substantial bulk into a cab. He gave an address, sat back and lighted a three-cent cigar. His head was buzzing with thoughts.

He remembered that his wife had asked him to bring home a special kind of cough syrup for Junior, and he stopped long enough to make the purchase in a corner drugstore. He reentered the cab, drove on, and figured that he would have to cut down on lunches during the week in order to pay the installment due on the new dining room suite. He looked out and saw that he was passing Bayside Park, hard by the harbor embankment. The lighted windows of fine apartment hotels reared into the dark. The cab cut through the park and came to a stop in front of the Monterey Hotel.

The vastness and grandeur of the lobby dwarfed Brinky. The luxury of the appointments made a sharp contrast with the frugal plainness of his clothes. But his shoes did not squeak. They were his one necessary luxury. There was a ball going on, and the sergeant had to weave and wind his prosaic way among men and women in evening clothes. But he reached the desk, passed it, took a narrow corridor and opened a door whose panel was of ground glass.

Burgher, the house dick, was twiddling his thumbs behind a small hardwood desk.

"Well, Brinky," the big fat man said.

"Hello, August."

"You got a smelling look about you, old horse." Burgher's tremendous apple cheeks beamed. He was a bald man, with a large conical torso. His jowls hid his collar. "So what, so what, eh?" A pearl-handled penknife clicked open and Burgher pried at a hangnail.

"See can you git me the number of the room Florence Somers is in."

"Simple, Brinky—simple as simple…. Operator. Listen, a Florence Somers—what room's she in?… I get you. Thanks, Hilda." He hung up. "Apartment 1101."

"Uh, thanks, August. Now—uh—"

There was a metallic ring on the desk mingled with a low, rolling chuckle in Burgher's throat.

"Go ahead, Brinky."

Brinkhaus picked up the pass-key and said:

"Thanks. I'll bring it right down."

Brinky was the only passenger that rose in the chrome-and-onyx elevator car. The car made little sound. Lighted buttons winked on and off. The operator wore a blue suit trimmed with silver, a high collar, white spats.

"Eleven out."

"Thanks," said Brinkhaus.

The hall runner received and swallowed silently the fall of his broad, heavy heels. The doors were pale gray and had knockers of German silver. It was a long walk to a far wing. But at last Brinky stopped before a door numbered 1101.

He put his ear to the panel, listened for a long moment. Then he used the pass-key.

He entered a spacious, oblong foyer, came face to face with his image in a narrow, beveled mirror. A wide entry led into the living room. One light glowed. He turned on others, moved about, and was unable to hear his own footfalls.

He looked into a white-tiled pantry, a black-and-white-tiled bathroom, a large bedroom that was redolent of faint perfume. Returning to the living room, his brown eyes moved swiftly about.

He sat down before a gray secretary, rifled the pigeonholes, then the drawers. There was a flagon of liquor which he moved aside, off the gray desk blotter. Quickly, his thick finger moving with surprising speed, he examined the contents of the desk.

Apparently he found nothing of consequence, for when he had finished he sat staring vaguely at the desk and drummed his fingers on his knee. Then he replaced the objects, lifted the flagon to place it back on the blotter. It tipped and liquor spilled out over the blotter.

He righted the flagon, muttered under his breath. He used his handkerchief to pat the spilled liquor, then undipped the blotter from its binder and found fresh ones beneath. He hastily rolled up the soggy blotter and thrust it into the inside pocket of his overcoat.

He returned to the center of the room and was standing there rubbing his jaw when he heard a sound at the corridor door. He whirled, lunged into the bedroom. He heard a man clearing his throat. He pressed into a closet, worked his way behind a rackful of clothes and held his breath. He heard a chair knock against something else and then there was silence. He let his breath out carefully, waited in the dark closet.

Ten minutes later he opened the closet door on a crack, listened intently. He heard nothing. He opened the door a little wider, peered into the bedroom. It was empty. He eased his way out, left the door ajar and moved on his toes.

Approaching the doorway to the living room, he bent forward, putting one ear towards it. Then he moved on. The living room was empty. His breath flowed out in a long, slow sigh.

He went into the room, saw that the chair in front of the secretary had been removed. He crossed to the desk and saw a square of hotel stationery pinned to the center of the blotter. He read:

Phone me as soon as you come in.

Brinkhaus did not touch the note. The writing was in dark, firm script, straight up and down with no flourishes and with severe vertical lines. There was no name signed.

He went downstairs, returned the key to August Burgher, turned down a drink of rye, and left the Monterey Hotel.

CHAPTER FOUR

GATLIN'S ONIONS

WELLS GATLIN said: "If I were asked, I'd say he's probably planted in one of those German beer gardens slopping himself full of beer."

Dan McCauley leaned back expansively in the swivel chair and with elaborate precision removed a toothpick from his teeth. "More power to him."

"Of course, you'd stick up for him!"

"Okey. Why shouldn't I? You think maybe I'd stick up for you?"

Irritable, Gatlin made a spitting sound, and then suddenly smacked the desk.

"I tell you, that kid's guilty! He's shown it! I just spent two hours out at his house and I demand his arrest. I found his allowance was cut—and not just made smaller. It was cut out entirely!" His black shoebutton eyes glittered. "And he's scared. And this, you dumb ox"—he jabbed fiercely at space with his index finger—"I found him packing his grips. And do you know what he said? He said he was going to spend the week-end with a friend in the country. And take his mother. Of course, she backed him up. But she looked scared. She had to back him. He's her son, isn't he?"

Dan looked very bored. He said:

"Nuts. I'm just holding down the desk till Brinky gets back."

"*When* he gets back!" Gatlin rasped. "I know him. Spends his time drinking beer and eating pretzels with all those old Dutch cronies of his."

The door opened and Brinkhaus plodded in.

"Hello, Dan. Hello, Gatlin," he said.

Gatlin snapped: "That kid, Brinkhaus, I've been raking him over the coals and we've got to grab him. I want you to pinch him and slam him in the hold-over overnight. I found him packing his bags."

Brinkhaus was undismayed. He blew his nose and said:

"Oh, we can wait till tomorrow, we can. No hurry."

"I tell you he was packing his bags!" Gatlin shrilled.

Brinkhaus sat down, laid his hat on the desk. "Sorry I can't back you up kinda, Gatlin. I got a little routine business to do tonight. Wait 'll tomorrow."

Veins stood out on Gatlin's forehead as he cried:

"Do you realize he may be gone by tomorrow?"

"If he goes, we'll git him back."

"Me," drawled Dan, "personal."

"Sure," said Brinkhaus. "Dan 'll git him."

Dan thrust thumbs into his vest, swelled. "Betcha."

Gatlin suddenly looked haggard.

"My God! Here I work my head off grilling the kid. I find out he's nervous as hell, evasive, scared. I find him getting ready to go places. I come here and tell you, and what happens?"

Brinkhaus spat into a cuspidor, looked up at Gatlin and patiently waited for the answer.

"Bah!" snarled Gatlin. "I'll call the chief up and have him detail a man to go with me and make the pinch." His eyes bulged, he tossed up his chin. "That's what I'll do! I'll do it now! If I can't get any cooperation out of the bureau, I'll go over your head! There!"

He spun, strode to the door, whipped it open. He vibrated in the doorway, said:

"For the last time, will you cooperate with me?"

"Y' see," Brinkhaus said apologetically, "I'd like to, but I got routine duty to do tonight."

Gatlin slammed out.

Brinkhaus spat, and Dan produced a fresh toothpick, inserted it alongside an eyetooth. He sighed. "Gatlin can't take it, Brinky. He'll bust a blood vessel some day."

"Gosh!" Brinkhaus stood up, withdrew the blotter from his overcoat pocket, threw it on the desk. He removed the overcoat, carried it across the room and laid it on the steam radiator.

He turned on the steam.

Dan said offhand: "What about the dame?"

"Kind o' worried."

"Yeah?" Dan picked up the blotter. "You think maybe that bozo might be right about the kid?"

Brinkhaus shrugged. "Dunno. I got a hunch—no."

"Then where's the dame fit in?"

"I'm trying to work that out."

"Hell, if the dame's guilty, then the kid is."

Brinky sighed. "She's a nice little gal, Dan."

"Say, where the hell did you get this blotter?"

"Oh, I just picked it up and forgot to chuck it away."

Dan exploded: "Chuck it away!"

Brinkhaus turned from the business of drying his overcoat. "Huh?"

Dan bared his teeth in a hard grin. "Pipe this!"

Brinkhaus crossed to where Dan was holding the blotter spread before him. Dan was pointing to the side that had been face down on the apartment desk.

He said: "Read that. Read it backwards."

Brinky followed Dan's moving forefinger, his lips forming each letter as he read backwards. He stopped, looked up at the tight-muscled face of Dan.

Dan said with a hard little laugh: "George P. Hessler!" He jabbed the blotter. "Hessler blotted his signature on this!"

"Oh-oh," said Brinkhaus. He added: "It was face up then. The maid… straightening things… turned the fresh side up and—"

"Hanh?"

"I'm just thinking."

"Well, hell, let me in on it. Don't I work here?"

Brinkhaus dropped into a chair heavily. His face sagged, and he looked gloomy, a reminiscent gaze came into his eyes. "I kinda liked that gal, Dan. It's tough. I kinda liked her." He drummed on the desk with his fingers, licked his dry lips. "But we gotta take her in."

"Okey. Where'll we grab her?"

"The Wigwam. She goes off at one."

IT WAS exactly midnight when Brinky and Dan McCauley got out of a cab in front of The Wigwam. Dan took the seven steps easily with his long legs. The doors were closed. He hit one of them a punch and it flew open. He strode in. The door banged shut behind him and almost knocked Brinkhaus back down the steps.

Joe Barnelli was lighting a cigarette in cupped hands. His eyes gazed above the cup of his hands at Dan McCauley.

No muscle in his face moved—nor in his body; none that was visible.

Dan's hat was on the back of his head. He grinned broadly, good-naturedly, as he swung his rangy legs across the lobby.

"Hi, Joe. We come to get it, kid. Hey, Brink—"

Turning, he saw Brinkhaus coming in, dusting off his hat, which had been knocked from his head in the encounter with the door.

"By cripes, Dan, you'll kill me yet."

"Hanh?"

"Hello, Joe. Hey, Joe, see can you make it quiet. I gotta drag out that Florence Somers."

"Yowssuh, Joe," Dan said with great good humor.

Joe Barnelli dropped his match into a sand-filled urn, inhaled, let the smoke dribble from his nostrils. "Sorry, Brinky. She left."

Dan stood 'way back on his heels, his grin broader than ever. "Giving us the merry-go-round, Joe?"

Joe Barnelli shook his head, said:

"That's on the level. We had to call off her midnight show. She left about a half hour after you did, Brinky. She"—he knocked a speck of ash from his cigarette—"was kind of busted up." He raised his soft dark eyes, placed them provocatively on Brinkhaus.

Dan growled, started past Joe Barnelli. "The hell! We'll fan the joint."

Joe was cool. He put a white hand flat against Dan's chest and said quietly, soberly: "Don't horse around, copper. Play ball."

Dan glowered: "Pitch to me, Joe."

"I am, Dan."

"Don't be a couple o' bush leaguers," Brinkhaus said. "I'm taking it you're on the up and up, Joe."

"Ever see me when I wasn't?"

Brinkhaus said: "Come on, Dan. She ain't here."

Dan joined him and they strode to the door. Dan turned to raise a hand, bawl out:

"No hard feelings, Joe?"

"Am I a kid?"

Brinkhaus and Dan reached the sidewalk, climbed into a taxi.

"Monterey Hotel," Brinky said, and started a three-cent cigar.

"Phew!" coughed Dan.

"Want one?"

"Nah! It 'd stunt my growth. What's it, cabbage?"

Brinkhaus shrugged. "Broccoli, maybe."

"Say," Dan muttered confidentially, "d'you think Joe was playing ring around the rosie?"

Brinkhaus shook his head, puffed. "Joe's a white man."

They got out in front of the Hotel Monterey, crossed the broad sidewalk and entered the vast lobby.

Dan expanded, craning his neck.

"Hot-cha, ain't this a swell dump, though!" he exclaimed. "When I get married, maybe I can muscle in on a honeymoon here."

They rose in the onyx-and-chrome elevator to the eleventh floor, and Brinkhaus led the way down the quiet corridor. He used the knocker on the door of number 1101, stood with his hat in his hand.

He said under his breath to Dan: "I hate to do this, Dan. She reminds me o' Mike McGonigle's daughter that got knocked off in them election riots ten years ago."

"Who, the daughter?"

"No. Mike."

"Work that dingus again."

Brinky used the knocker a second time, waited patiently, with his chin resting morosely on his chest.

Presently he said: "You stay here. I'll go down and git a key off a August Burgher that's the house dick here."

Dan waited, pacing up and down, and in a few minutes Brinkhaus returned with a pass-key. He unlocked the door, and they entered the apartment.

"What I mean," exclaimed Dan, "this dame ain't none o' the hall-bedroom girls. This lay-out must cost dough-re-mi."

Brinkhaus had switched on the lights. He made his way into the bedroom, reappeared in a moment, saying: "She skipped."

"Hanh?"

"Skipped. And in a hurry. Coat hangers all over the floor. Okey"— he was on his way to the door—"this ain't no place for us."

They went down in the elevator. Brinkhaus returned the key to Burgher, thumped his heels out of the office and stopped at the lobby desk.

"When did Miss Somers leave?"

"Leave? Why, I didn't know she had left!"

"She jump her bill?"

"No. It was paid in advance. The custom on the apartment side of the hotel."

Brinkhaus swiveled. "Come on, Dan." He reached the sidewalk and said to the doorman: "You know Miss Somers?"

"Sure."

"See her leave tonight?"

"I believe she did."

"Where'd she go?"

"I don't know. I believe I hailed a passing cab for her."

"Bags?"

"I believe yes."

Brinkhaus walked to the curb, looked up and down the wide boulevard. He was a little out of breath.

"Hey!" Dan muttered.

"Huh—what?"

Dan was pointing. "I just seen Joe Barnelli duck into the park over there. Come on."

They ran across the street, Dan far ahead.

But in the darkness of the park they lost Joe Barnelli.

Dan bared his teeth, ripped out:

"That spaghetti bender's giving us the run-around, Brinky. The run-around!"

BRINKHAUS and Dan McCauley entered the central room of police headquarters at a quarter to one. A couple of detectives were standing around, and the man at the desk said:

"Your mug oughta be red, Brinky. Gatlin talked with the chief and got a plainclothes Johnny to make a pinch. That kid, you know— what's his name?—"

"Where is he?"

"Down the hall."

Brinky's face was red—a very dull red. It wasn't from chagrin entirely, because he had hurried. But he struck his broad heels down the corridor and plowed into a large room at the end.

Gatlin was perspiring. He evidently had been doing a lot of talking, for he stood panting and taking swigs at a tumbler of water.

Wallace Hessler sat on a chair, gripping its sides. His hair was tousled, his tie loose, and there was a hunted look in his eyes. He seemed to have gone to pieces, and he breathed heavily.

Gatlin planked down the tumbler, glared truculently at Brinkhaus, his eyes snapping.

"Well—well, I suppose you've been polishing the seat of your pants on some speakeasy chair while I—while I—"

"You watch," said Dan, pointing. "Some day you're gonna get yourself all tied up in a knot and gag to death."

"Go to hell!"

"Much obliged, only I don't go to your house when you ain't home.... Lookit him, Brinky; he's gone ga-ga on us."

Gatlin pointed to Wallace Hessler. "Well, I did it. We're holding him in the hold-over."

Hessler jumped up, his fists clenched. "I tell you I had nothing to do with it! I didn't!"

"Why, then," snapped Gatlin, "were you packed and ready to lam out?"

"I wasn't lamming, as you call it! I—I was just—"

"Ah, just! Just what? And why?"

Hessler tensed, his wet lips closing, his eyes bulging.

"All right!" he cried. "I'll tell you! I was thrown over by—by a girl. By a girl I—" He stopped, went limp. "Oh, what the devil!" He clapped knuckles to his forehead.

Brinkhaus said, "Florence Somers?" quietly.

Hessler slumped to a chair, sobbed out: "Yes! Yes!"

Gatlin cried: "You planned to bump off your old man and run away with the girl. You got your old man bumped off and then the girl chucked you! Ha!"

"That's not true!" screamed Hessler. "It isn't true! It's a lie!"

"You loved her kinda?" Brinky asked.

Hessler's face became contorted.

"I hate her now! I was a fool! What is she? A common—" He broke off, flushed with embarrassment, hid his face in his hands.

Brinkhaus sighed.

He had rather liked young Hessler on first sight, but he saw now that the young man, up against it, hadn't the will to carry on. It made Brinkhaus grimace.

Gatlin was saying bitterly: "And he didn't want to go to work. I found that out—from the maid. He just didn't want to do anything but dance around night clubs and use his old man's money. A lounge lizard, that's what!"

Brinkhaus guessed that this much was true.

Gatlin finished dramatically: "He'll break yet! We'll find he planned the killing of his old man!"

"I didn't!" screamed Hessler. He leaped up, wild-eyed, sprang towards the door.

Dan stopped him, held him, said under his breath: "Easy, baby—easy."

"See!" cried Gatlin. "Ha! I'll show you," he yelled at Brinkhaus, "if I don't know my onions!"

Brinkhaus was placid. "I ain't never raised onions. I don't like the smell o' them and I don't like the taste o' them. Detectiving is my job, not knowing about onions—was I asked?"

CHAPTER FIVE

"RED HOT!"

AT EIGHT next morning Joe Barnelli got out of a big four-poster, kicked his feet into green slippers, put a black silk robe over his blue silk pajamas and went through his Spanish type living room to answer the doorbell.

"Morning, Joe," Brinkhaus said glumly. "C'n I come in?"

"Sure. Ever see the time you couldn't?"

Brinkhaus entered carrying his brown fedora before him. Joe telephoned downstairs for breakfast, went into the bathroom and held his head under the cold shower for a moment. He came back drying it briskly with a towel.

"You got me up early."

"Got myself up early," Brinky said, twiddling his thumbs. "Say, Joe, we seen you last night out front o' the Monterey."

"Yeah, I was there."

"What's the idea o' playing hide-and-go-seek with me? Ain't I always been your pal?"

Joe shrugged. "Sure."

"Didn't I bounce you on me knee when you was a kid?"

Joe grinned. "Sure. And you muscled apples for me out of Nick Gargotti's fruit stand." He turned, balled up the towel, pitched it neatly into the bathroom. "So what, Brinky?"

"I'm thinking maybe you're kinda dampering down on all you know."

"Yeah?"

"This gal Somers pulled a fade-out."

Joe nodded. "Yeah, I phoned there. I know."

"What else do you know, Joe?"

Joe held his palms upward, shrugged. "Nothing."

Brinky frowned at his hands. "I kinda thought maybe you'd know where she came from. She must have a home or something. When a dame gits in a jam she usually runs to her ma. That's what I was thinking, Joe."

"Sorry I don't know, Brinky. Maybe the agency I hired her from 'd know."

Brinkhaus looked up. "That's an idea." He stood up, brushed his hat against the underside of his left arm. "Joe, I'd feel low as hell if it turned out you was pitching me drops when I'm asking for straight balls."

Joe was tall, quiet; he smiled faintly, warmly. "What a swell bum you make me out."

Brinkhaus went to the door, turned. "Joe, what d'you think of this Wallace Hessler?"

Joe shrugged. "He's all right, I guess. I guess we guys that come up from the gutter naturally hold a grudge against guys who live on the old man's dough. But what the hell, he's okey, I guess."

Brinky said: "Thanks, Joe."

He went down in the elevator, stood on the curb outside in the bright crisp morning. Florence Somers had vanished. Young Hessler was in the hold-over, shattered, hurling invective at everybody—even at his mother, who had come down this morning to comfort and reassure him. Had Florence Somers vanished so that she would not have to testify under oath that she had been with young Hessler at the time of the murder?

Brinkhaus walked to the nearest drug store, entered and thumbed a telephone directory. He wrote down an address, came out, boarded a bus and rode across town to the business and theatre district. He got off, walked down a side street and entered a narrow, five storied building. The lobby was small, shabby. He eyed the directory board, then walked into a small, ancient elevator and was lifted to the third floor.

Getting out, he walked down a narrow, dark corridor, saw Acme Theatrical Agency on a ground glass panel and walked in.

A girl was typing in a small, cluttered office. A connecting door, open, led to an inner office.

Brinkhaus said: "Morning, miss. I'd like to see the boss."

"Name?"

"Sergeant Brinkhaus from the cops."

She got up, flounced to the doorway, said:

"Sergeant Brinkhaus from the cops, Mr. Weyland."

"Send him in, sugar."

Brinkhaus entered the inner office, saw a tall, beak-nosed man sitting behind a large desk. He had his hat on, a pearl-grey fedora with a rakish brim. Two young men, nattily dressed, stood at one side.

"Morning, Sergeant," Weyland said breezily. "Park the limbs. And what can I do for you?... Wait outside, gentlemen," he added to the two men. They went into the outer office and Weyland explained: "Two hoofers looking for a job. So?"

Brinkhaus sat down, looked glumly at his hands. "I was thinking, Mr. Weyland, you'd have the address, the home address, of a girl you handled a job for here."

Weyland leaned back expansively, optimistically.

"I might. Who?"

"Well, you see, this gal disappeared last night. I figure maybe if I knew where she came from, I could git a line on her. Name's Florence Somers."

"Oh, Flo Somers. Worked at The Wigwam?"

"Yes."

"Just a minute."

Weyland rose, went to a steel filing cabinet, thumbed a card index, withdrew a card. "Yes, she did give us an address. Most don't. Comes from Cleveland."

Brinkhaus said: "Good. I'd thank you, Mr. Weyland, if you'd just write the address down for me."

"Glad to."

Brinkhaus, waited patiently while Weyland wrote down the address on a slip of paper.

Weyland passed it across and Brinkhaus folded it, slipped it into a vest pocket. He dipped his head.

"Thanks. And good day."

In the outer office he dipped his head towards the girl. "Good day, ma'am."

REACHING the street, he stood on the curb, withdrew the slip of paper, unfolded it and squinted down at the address. But instantly the importance of the address was lost.

Brinky's eyes widened. There was no mistaking the script, the severe vertical lines. It was script such as he had seen in Florence Somers' apartment the night before.

Weyland was the man who had come into the apartment, left the note, departed.

Brinkhaus crossed the street, entered a drug store and found a telephone booth. From it he could see through the plate glass windows, watch the doorway of the building across the street. He rang headquarters.

"Dan McCauley there?" He waited, kept his eyes on the doorway across the street. "Dan?... Brinky. Grab a cab and shoot down to 380 Mulholland. It's a drug store. I'm inside. If I ain't here, shoot back to headquarters and stand by.... Hot? Red hot, Dan!"

He went up to the head of the counter, near the plate glass windows, and ordered a malted milk. Fifteen minutes later the door whanged open and Dan came in, his unbuttoned overcoat flying behind him and his hat on the back of his head. He looked like a man primed for action.

But Brinkhaus said: "Sit down."

Keeping his eyes on the doorway across the street, he explained to Dan what had occurred. He added: "And now we'll just park here and wait till he comes out."

Dan was impatient. "Hell, let's go up and take him."

"On what evidence?...No, Dan. I'm an old cop. I learned how to be patient. Wait a guy out, give him rope. I ain't never liked the third degree. Git a guy with the goods is best."

It was twenty minutes later that Brinkhaus saw Weyland appear in the doorway opposite. With him were the two hoofers.

"Hoofers me eye," muttered Brinkhaus.

"Hanh?"

"I was just thinking out loud," Brinky said as he got off the stool. "There he is. The big, heavy guy. That's Weyland."

"Who's the others?"

"Dunno. Take it easy. They're gonna take that black sedan. We'll give 'em a start and then grab a cab. There's a cab standing up a couple o' doors."

They waited until the black sedan drove off. Then Dan opened the door, swung out, and Brinkhaus followed. Dan walked up to the taxi, said to the driver:

"Police. Tail that black sedan with the trunk on back."

"Oke."

The black sedan headed south, turned right into the Post Road, weaved through heavy midtown traffic. At Union Circle it went halfway around the monument and headed down South Broad Street through the bleat and blare of radio stores and the rumble and clang of produce trucks. At a congested traffic stop, the cab was half a block behind the sedan. Next to the cab stood a huge black town car with an open drive and a liveried chauffeur. The tonneau was empty.

"Come on," Brinkhaus said. He got out of the cab, climbed into the back of the town car and showed his badge to the surprised chauffeur. "We're on a tail. Snake ahead and pick up a black sedan with a trunk on back. I'll point it out. Tail it."

The traffic moved. The chauffeur spurred ahead, and in the middle of the next block Brinkhaus was able to point out the black sedan, adding: "Not too close."

At Fessenden Street the sedan turned left, wormed among parked produce trucks. It turned right into Plum Street, went through a warehouse district and then entered a rundown residential section of frame houses. It stopped presently, and Brinkhaus, pulling down the right hand curtain, said:

"Pass it and turn left at the next block."

The chauffeur swung into a narrow street.

Brinkhaus said: "Keep going. We'll jump off. And thanks.... Come on, Dan."

They dropped off, reached the sidewalk and turning about, walked back to the corner. Brinkhaus had to hold Dan back while he peered cautiously around the corner. The car was still in the same spot. It was empty.

Brinkhaus said: "Them houses have back yards. Count the number of houses from that one to the corner then we'll go around back."

Both men counted, and Dan said: "It's the sixth from this corner."

"Okey. Through the block now."

They crossed the street, walked on, turned right and walked up the street that paralleled the one on which the car stood. They found a fence with a loose board, pried the board out and forced their way through the aperture. Standing in the vacant lot, Dan counted the backs of the houses they faced. Dan pointed. "That one."

They hopped a wire fence into the back yard of the third house from the corner, kept close to the backs of the houses as they moved on. Picket fences divided each yard and these were easily negotiable; in a few minutes Brinky and Dan were in the back yard of the house they had picked out. The house was, like the others, two storied, frame, with a basement and a shallow areaway, so that half the basement was above ground and half below.

They dropped down into the damp areaway. The door and windows were locked. Dan used a big pocket knife to carve through the window to the lock. It took him fifteen minutes. But he got the lock open and cautiously, quietly raised the window. They climbed into a cool, damp-smelling basement, stood close beside each other, listening.

Then Brinky put a hand on Dan's arm, whispered:

"Mind, now, Danny boy. Take your time. Let me do the talking."

"I gotcha, Brinky. Let's go."

CHAPTER SIX

SKIN GAME

THEY REACHED the main hallway and stood in the semi-darkness.

Through the glass panel of the curtained doorway they could see the sun shining outside, but in the hallway there was no sunlight. Dan was like a hound dog on a leash; Brinky was the leash, restraining him. Listening, they heard voices, faint and far away. They looked aloft. Brinky motioned.

They climbed the staircase. It was narrow, with an old banister polished by the passage of many hands over a long period of years. Brinky paused on the top step, used a hand to hold Dan back. The voices were nearer, but still indistinct.

Brinky moved up past the last step, stood in the second-floor corridor, his brown eyes shifting from closed door to closed door.

Then both men tensed at the sound of a woman's short, vibrant cry. They did not hear it again. Presently they heard feet moving about. Brinky took his gun from its shoulder holster and thrust it into his overcoat pocket. He kept his hand on it.

A door six feet away opened suddenly and a man came out, whistling to himself. He stopped short, his whistle faded. He was one of the so-called hoofers, hatless now, a small, dapper young man with a smoking cigarette in his hand.

"Who the hell—"

Brinky said: "We rang the bell, but got no answer. The door was open, so we walked in."

"Oh, you walked in."

Brinkhaus said with a pious face: "You hoof here?"

The dapper man took a couple of snatchy puffs at his cigarette.

"Nah," he said casually. "I live here."

Dan jerked a thumb, said: "See? He lives here?"

Another door opened and Weyland came out saying: "Who's—" He cut himself short, swallowed, looked with a dark sudden glance at the small dapper man. "What's this, Edgar?"

"They walked in."

"They—"Weyland stopped. "Oh, I see. Sergeant Brinkhaus! I didn't recognize you. Well, well!"

"Well," said Brinkhaus, moving forward, "it's like this. Let's go in that room you come out of."

"Okey. Come on," Weyland said cheerfully.

Dan was looking hard at Edgar.

"You was heading for that room, wasn't you?"

"Was I?"

Dan swelled his chest, tightened his lips. Edgar sauntered into the room behind Weyland. The other so-called hoofer was standing with a foot on a chair and leaning with his elbow on his knee. He was watching two men rolling dice. A faded, powdered blonde was pouring a glass of beer. She finished pouring and picked up the glass. She had a surly mouth, cloudy eyes. The two men did not stop rolling dice. The room was large, and there was a lot of furniture in it, but the furniture was shabby. The dice knocked on the table. The woman took a long swig of beer, went over to a corner, turned a chair around and sat down with her back to those in the room. She hooked her heels on a window sill. The man who had his foot on the chair yawned, took the foot down and, seeming oblivious to every one in the room, sauntered to a sideboard and poured himself a drink of whiskey. He turned then and leaned with one elbow on the sideboard, stared vacantly at the floor.

Brinkhaus said in a dull, placid way: "I come along to ask you again about that gal Florence Somers."

WEYLAND was expansive, grinning. "Why, of course! Park the tired body there, Sergeant. Have a drink?"

Brinky shook his head, said: "Did you see her last night?"

"Me? No, I haven't seen her in days."

"Not, say, after ten last night?"

"Not in days."

"You wasn't around her apartment at the Monterey?"

"Last night?" Weyland teetered on his heels, shook his head, smiled. "I'm afraid not. Why, if I had been, I guess I'd be able to help you out a bit."

"Oh," said Brinkhaus mournfully, "I guess you c'n help me out all right. Where's the gal, Weyland?"

"Where's—why, after all—"

"After all, you was in her apartment last night. You left her a note to git in touch with you."

Weyland put both hands to his chest. "Me?" he said mockingly. Then he laughed good-humoredly. "I'm afraid you're wrong there, Sergeant."

Brinky said: "Dan, go over and open that door over there. See where it goes."

"Right, Brinky."

Dan crossed the room, grabbed the knob, turned and pushed. The door was locked. He swiveled with the huge easiness of a bear, made a negligent gesture. "Open it, guy."

The dice lay on the table, inactive. The two players looked intently at the dice, but neither moved. The man leaning on the sideboard gazed intently down into his empty glass. Edgar was tossing and catching a coin. Weyland looked at the locked door, and the woman kept the glass of beer pressed to her lips and stared out of the window.

Dan lifted his chin high, moved it from side to side as his eyes cruised the room threateningly.

"You gonna open it or am I gonna take it down?"

Each man remained motionless, speechless.

Dan spun and drove at the door.

Edgar let the coin drop and his hand darted sidewise across his chest.

Brinky did not move his feet. He seemed not to move at all, yet he did; for his gun was in his hand. It thundered. Edgar looked shocked as his own gun, withdrawn as far as his lapel, dropped to the floor. Then he looked sick. The echoes petered off and Dan, who had pivoted, now held his own gun drawn. His lower lip was thrust far forward.

Brinky said morosely: "Weyland, open it."

Weyland nodded. "Okey."

He strode across the room swiftly, his jaw set, and as he reached the door he thrust his hand into his pocket. But the hand reappeared lightning fast—with a gun instead of a key. He fired as he drew—even as Dan struck down with his left hand and fired with his right. Dan got it in the left leg.

The guns' thunder interlocked. Weyland backed up, bending way over, holding his stomach. Dan's face was red with fury, his lip curled wolflike. He stepped back, balanced on his good leg and sent his two hundred pounds hurtling at the door. It crashed.

The woman stood up suddenly and as suddenly fired. The bullet hit Brinky's gun hand, traveled up the forearm and came out near the elbow. He dropped his gun. Dan spun, but he counted too much on his bad leg; it gave way and he spun to the floor, hitting hard.

The two men who had been rolling dice jumped up and lunged for the door. Edgar's companion tossed away his glass and lunged also. But he drew his gun too, looking at Dan. Brinky flung himself on the man, missed but made the man leap backward. The other two got the door open. Dan, on one leg, hopped mightily. Edgar's companion fired at Dan as Brinky lunged again and spoiled the aim. The man jumped back and swung his gun towards Brinkhaus.

There was a loud outcry and the two men who had started out of the room fell back inwards, got tangled up with each other and piled on the floor.

Joe Barnelli appeared magically in the doorway. His gun banged twice, and Edgar's companion hurtled backward, gagging and grabbing at his throat. He took a chair down with him. The woman dived for the door, but Dan, reaching out, caught her by the back of the neck, lifted her, dropped her to the floor.

Brinky got to his feet, holding his gun in his left hand, one leg of his trousers pulled up almost to his knees and exposing black woolen socks and a lavender garter.

Joe said quietly: "How're you, Brinky?"

"Just a bit winded, Joe. Where'd you come from?"

"Tailed you from Fessenden Street."

Dan leaned against the wall, said: "You mugs on the floor stay there."

Joe went across the room, through the shattered doorway. He reappeared a moment later carrying Florence Somers in his arms. She was bound, gagged. Joe's olive-skinned face was grim, set—but there might have been a tear in his eye.

Brinky said: "Where you going?"

"Get her out of here. You know where to find me."

He disappeared with the girl.

Weyland was groaning on the floor.

Brinkhaus went to the phone.

"Police Headquarters." He looked across at Dan. "How you feel, Dan?"

"Lousy."

Brinky ducked his mouth near the mouthpiece. "Hen?... This is Brinkhaus. Send the wagon down to 404 Flower Street. Send an ambulance. Send two."

CHIEF INSPECTOR Peter Larsen swiveled in his chair, took his briar from his mouth as Brinkhaus came in. The sergeant wore his bandaged right arm in a sling. He sat down, took his hat off and slapped it on the desk. He blew out a breath, wagged his boxlike head.

"Gosh, Peter, I figured that was the end o' me and Danny."

"Joe, huh?"

"Joe arrived in the nick o' time."

"Joe's quite a friend of yours."

"Yeah. But it was the gal he was interested in. You'd never ha' thunk it before. Quiet guy, Joe. I just come over from the horsepittle. Weyland 'll live. Tried to git him to talk, but he wouldn't. Wanted a lawyer."

Larsen puffed on his pipe, laid it aside. "We don't need him, Brinky. The woman talked. The blonde. Do you know"—he leaned forward, tapped Brinkhaus on the knee—"do you know, Brinky, that you and Dan turned up one of the worst skin games I ever heard of?"

"Huh?"

Larsen edged his chair closer.

"The blonde came clean. Weyland operated what ostensibly was a theatrical agency. He has branches in two other big cities. Most of the girls he took on knew what it was all about, but Flo Somers didn't. She didn't at first. Weyland apparently is a clever guy, a smooth actor. Flo Somers turned up at his agency one day three months ago looking for a job. She's pretty and she can dance. He took her on. She was broke. He advanced her money to buy an outfit and he wanted her to stay at a fine hotel. He said he wanted to build her up as a star, and he wanted her to have a swell background for the sake of publicity. It sounded like a business deal, and she agreed to the money advances, until he had advanced four thousand dollars.

"Then came the blow, according to the blonde. Weyland told Flo Somers what the game was. He'd been working it for several years and he'd amassed, according to the blonde, as much as two hundred thousand dollars. This is the game:

"Flo was, during her job as a dancer, to meet the son of a wealthy man. This was done through one of the other girls in the floor show. This girl made advances to the son first, but they were so obvious that he would naturally lose interest in her. Then she would introduce Flo, who is beautiful, I understand, and a fine type. Weyland had names and addresses, and he chose the night life sons. Flo balked at this, but Weyland reminded her that, besides her owing him four thousand dollars, he had the power to break her as a dancer. He wanted back his money. He threatened to sue her, and she was afraid. So she fell. He got the strangle hold on her.

"The idea is that after the girl meets the victim, she plays her cards so that the victim falls for her. Wallace Hessler fell hard. Then he wanted to marry her. That was what Weyland wanted and expected. And when that point had been reached, the old man was notified anonymously that his son had fallen for a dancer.

"Hessler went to Flo, offered her five thousand dollars to clear out. She had been instructed to accept no less than ten. Hessler got in a huff and slammed out. Weyland was waiting in the lobby below. When he saw Hessler go out, he phoned up to Flo. She said Hessler had refused and was on his way to see his lawyer.

"Weyland got panicky. Two of his men were waiting outside. He told them that Hessler must be stopped before he got to his attorney. Well—as you know—they stopped him.

"But that wasn't the end. Flo was horrified when she learned of the murder. When she met Wallace for tea that afternoon she told him she would not marry him, that it was all off. Then you scared her at The Wigwam.

"Later, at her apartment, she called up Weyland and was hysterical. She said she was going to the police and tell everything. She hung up, packed in a hurry, and went to another hotel, to duck Weyland. But Weyland saw her leave the Monterey, followed, waited until she was installed in another hotel and then went in and took her out. Is that a lulu?"

Brinky leaned forward, his voice clogged. "Listen, Peter. There won't be any trouble for Flo Somers, will there?"

"I hope not, Brinky."

"She's a nice gal, Peter. And besides—besides, I just stopped by Joe Barnelli's in time—in time—to—uh—"

"What? In time to what?"

Brinkhaus gulped. "Well, there was Joe, and there was Flo, and there was Father Bombino—"

"My God!" Larsen broke in. "She wasn't dying, was she?"

Brinky shook his head. "Gitting married. Her and Joe. And me—well, I hadda kinda be the best man sorta."